D1234791

MASTER
of the
CAULDRON

MASTER
of the
CAULDRON

DAVID DRAKE

A TOM DOHERTY ASSOCIATES BOOK
New York

MASTER OF THE CAULDRON

Copyright © 2004 by David Drake

Edited by David G. Hartwell

Map by Ed Gazsi

A Tor Book
Published by Tom Doherty Associates, LLC
175 Fifth Avenue
New York, NY 10010

www.tor.com

Tor® is a registered trademark of Tom Doherty Associates, LLC

Library of Congress Cataloging-in-Publication Data

Drake, David.
    Master of the cauldron / David Drake.—1st ed.
      p. cm.
    "A Tom Doherty Associates book."
    ISBN 0-312-87496-0 (acid-free paper)
    EAN 978-0312-87496-4
    I. Title.

  PS3554.R196M37 2004
  813'.54—dc22

                                                2004051690

First Edition: November 2004

Printed in the United States of America

0 9 8 7 6 5 4 3 2 1

For Dorothy Day

A friend, resource, and archive

Also a darned good cheering section

ACKNOWLEDGMENTS

Dorothy Day, Robyn Spady, and the Seattle Weavers Guild more generally were enthusiastically helpful on this one. They provided not only advice but many hanks of yarn dyed with berries, etc. (which draped my clothesline for weeks as I checked lightfastness), and also some remarkable swatches of double weave and other exotic fabrics. Believe me, what a skilled hand weaver can do really *is* magical.

Dan Breen was, as usual, my first reader. He pointed out not only where I dropped words but also where sentences I thought were clear did not appear so to an intelligent and educated person outside my head.

My Webmaster, Karen Zimmerman, and Dorothy Day both archived my text at stages in the process. One can never tell when one's computer will die.

Which brings me to the fact that No Computers Were Killed in the Writing of This Novel. However, a couple of them got very sick. My son Jonathan, with Mark L. Van Name and Allyn Vogel as his backup, kept me going.

I don't ordinarily mention secondary sources I've used in writing (and I use a lot of them), but Dr. Andrea Berlin is still alive to thank. Her "What's for Dinner?," in the November–December 1999 *Biblical Archaeology Review,* was not only informative but evocative. I got two separate settings from the article.

My British editor, Simon Spanton, provided me with some Lord Dunsany material that wasn't already on my shelves. Any reader of *Master* who's already familiar with Dunsany will realize how great my debt is to the *Tales of Wonder.* Those of you who aren't familiar with Dunsany really ought to give him a try (and Orion Books will accommodate you).

My wife, Jo, kept everything going at home while I was writing *Master,* which, given that the process of writing coincided with the repainting of the interior of the house, is pretty remarkable.

My thanks to all of you.

Dave Drake
david-drake.com

AUTHOR'S NOTE

Those of you who've read previous books in the Isles series will note some repetition in these notes, but I go to a good deal of effort to make each book accessible to people who've never read anything of mine before. Bear with me.

The religion of the Isles is based on that of Sumeria. The magic, however, is derived from that of the Mediterranean Basin during classical times (and probably originally Egyptian). The words of power are the *voces mysticae* of real spells, intended to get the attention of demiurges whom the wizard is asking for aid. I don't believe in magic myself; but a lot of other people, folks who're just as smart as I am, did and do. I'm not comfortable speaking the words of power aloud.

I use classical models for the literature of this series. For the most part this isn't important for *Master of the Cauldron,* but Celondre is modeled on Horace; the *Anglo-Saxon Chronicles* were the template for some of the documents; I used a snatch of the Homeric *Hymn to Aphrodite*; and there's a brief echo of the Ullman-Henry elementary Latin texts on which I learned to love Latin a very long time ago.

MASTER
of the
CAULDRON

Prologue

Water dripped somewhere within the cavern. It echoed among the stalactites into the sound of a distant stream, but the basalt on which Countess Balila of Sandrakkan stood with her companions was dry. Their two lanterns did little to illuminate the high dome, but the flames raised occasional iridescence from the pearly flow rock deposited there before the volcanic upheaval of a thousand years before.

The wizard Dipsas squatted before the eight-pointed figure she'd traced on the basalt in powdered sulfur. She tapped one angle with her athame as she called in a cracked voice, *"Phrougi panton!"*

To Balila, only a few feet away, the words of power were lost in the murmur of the cavern breathing and the earth's unfelt trembles. She hugged herself and trembled also, though the air in the chamber was warmer than that of the palace from which she and her companions had descended not long after sunset.

Balila had taken good care of her appearance. In the cave's dim light she could even now pass for the pink-cheeked, strawberry blonde of fifteen who'd married Earl Wildulf of Sandrakkan twenty years before. She was fearful and uncomfortable in this place, but she remained there because of the same determination that had preserved her looks through exercise and control of her appetite for sweets. Balila wasn't ambitious for herself, but there was *nothing* she wouldn't do to make her husband King of the Isles.

"Picale zamadon!" Dipsas intoned, tapping her athame, a knife of black horn cut out of a scale from the back of a huge reptile. Dipsas herself didn't understand some of the symbols carved into the blade. The athame had been found in the sarcophagus of a wizard of millennia past. As she dipped and raised the point in time to her words of power, quivers of vivid red and blue shone through its opacity.

"Alithe zamadon!" said Dipsas, her voice rising. Her wrinkled face had

the settled blankness of burgeoning fear. Her pronunciation of similar syllables had changed during the course of the incantation. The ancient words, the language of the demiurges who could adjust the powers on which the cosmos turned, were twisting themselves on her tongue.

The countess's pet and bodyguard was a flightless, hook-billed bird from the island of Shengy far to the southeast. It wore a silver collar with a staple to attach a chain, but she'd left it free to pace; its claws clicked on the basalt. The angry bird's head, as large as a horse's, darted from side to side like a grackle's. Occasionally it kicked viciously at something hinted in the shadows, but the blows never found a target.

Balila was of middling height for a woman. The bird was taller even when it stood relaxed; now the great bronze feathers of its crest were raised, glittering higher than the helmet of any human guardsman.

"*Alithe atithe hupristi!*" Dipsas said. She held an open scroll, but her left hand trembled too badly for her to read the vermilion writing. Nonetheless the words curled off her tongue: partly from memory, partly from the weight of their own power. "*Thestis!*"

The last of Balila's companions was a three-year-old boy. His hair spilled down his back like molten gold, and his only clothing was the harness that attached gilt wings to his shoulders.

The boy alone was unaffected by the psychic atmosphere. He ran prattling from the lamplight to the shadowed darkness, then back to clutch the countess's skirts and urge her to play with him. He had no more intelligence than a puppy, and like a puppy his disposition was sunny and laughing.

Dipsas' athame touched an angle of the figure again. A spark of red wizardlight snapped from the blade, igniting the sulfur. Tiny blue flames crawled in both directions from the point of contact. They provided almost no illumination, but smoke spread in a choking cloud just above the stone floor.

"*Darza!*" the wizard said.

"*Darza,*" the deeps rumbled. "*Badawa balaha!*"

The bird screamed in fury, spreading its stub wings as its tongue shrilled between the black shearing edges of its beak. The child bleated in wide-eyed surprise.

The countess stopped hugging herself; her face was set. She had a notebook of waxed boards in her left hand, a bronze stylus in her right. She was as literate as most women of her class. Though not enough of a scholar to write in the cursive Old Script, modern minuscules were sufficient to jot down the earth's responses phonetically.

Balila held her notebook so that light from the oil lamp in a niche beside her fell across the waxed surface as she began to write. When she'd filled one page, she flipped it out of the way on its leather hinges and went on to the next.

Dipsas coughed as she chanted, but her cracked voice and the thunderous antiphony from below continued for so long as the sulfur burned. Only when the blue flicker dimmed and finally died did the responses end.

The wizard slumped forward, her sleeve smearing the molten residue of the sulfur. If it burned her, she was too exhausted by the effort of her spell to react.

Balila tried to close her notebook. The thin maplewood boards clicked against one another; then the whole assemblage dropped to the floor. She bent to pick the notebook up, aware for the first time of the child bawling at her feet. She knelt, hugged him to silence, then put the notebook in the sleeve of her robe before walking over to the wizard.

"Dipsas?" she said. She shook the other woman's shoulder. Balila wasn't strong enough to carry the wizard back to the surface, and the child would probably need help as well. "Dipsas, get up. I have the responses. You can copy them off for the next time we come."

The wizard lifted herself with difficulty. For a moment her face was that of an ugly, frightened old woman; then she consciously re-formed her features into a mask of cunning and power. "Yes, yes," she said, her voice gaining strength as she spoke. "I'll be ready in a moment."

The bird screamed. Sensing departure, it stalked toward the fissure by which they'd entered the dome, calling its challenge ahead.

Balila suddenly began to tremble, but she caught herself at once. *Wildulf the First, King of the Isles . . .*

Chapter One

Ilna could see her reflection in the silvered backplate of the man who'd been her childhood friend Garric, the innkeeper's son—but who now was Prince Garric of Haft, the King of the Isles in all but name. He was speaking to his fiancée and secretary, Lady Liane bos-Benliman, as she jotted notes onto a thin board with a small gold pen.

As she watched, Ilna's fingers knotted and unknotted patterns from the lengths of cord that she kept in her left sleeve. The patterns were simple, as simple as so many knives; and like knives, they could be tools or weapons if the need arose.

Ilna's reflection was distorted, of course. She smiled—not bitterly, or at any rate without any more bitterness than her usual expression. Ilna prided herself on clear thinking, but there'd been a great deal of distortion in her view of her possible future a few years ago when she lived in the backwater of Barca's Hamlet on the east coast of Haft. For example, she'd imagined then that she'd make a suitable wife for her neighbor Garric.

"Easy!" bellowed the sailing master, leaning out from the pintle of the port steering oar. The *Shepherd of the Isles* was backing toward the beach on the reversed strokes of only one of its five banks of oars. "Easy! Easy!"

"Now you see why the men who aren't needed on the oars crowd into the bow, child," said Chalcus at Ilna's side. He held her ward, the nine-year-old Lady Merota, on his shoulder. "With their weight in the bow, we can back up onto the beach instead of crunching into it."

"Crowd more, you mean!" said Merota. "Will we have real rooms here, Chalcus?"

"Depending on the words our friend the prince has with the Earl of Sandrakkan," Chalcus said, laughing, "we'll have rooms or at least ground to pitch a tent on, I'm sure. The *Shepherd of the Isles* is as big as a warship gets, but I'll grant that with four hundred souls aboard you could find more room in a clothespress."

Chalcus dressed in as many different bright colors as a clown and had a clown's smile and cheerful laughter. As he spoke, he gestured with his free hand to point out this or that part of the business of landing that only an expert would see.

He was indeed an expert sailor. He'd learned his skill in the same hard school that taught him to use the slim, in-curved sword he carried stuck through his sash of vivid orange silk. As a youth he'd roamed southern waters with the Lataaene pirates, where the wrong choice meant death, and the right choice didn't guarantee survival.

Under his long-sleeved saffron tunic and his red-dyed leather breeches, Chalcus' body bore the scars of wounds that should have been fatal a dozen times over. That he'd survived said as much for his will as it did for the undoubted strength of his tautly muscular body.

Ilna smiled again. Lady Merota was her ward, as amazing as that seemed to an illiterate peasant girl. Chalcus was her friend and her lover and . . . well, not *her* man, because he wasn't the sort to be anybody's man save his own, but *a* man; and even at age nineteen Ilna was aware of how rare a thing real men were in this world.

Ilna's fingers wove, then opened the coarse fabrics to weave again. She'd always had a skill with cloth. She could run her hand over a bale of wool and hear it murmuring of meadows and clover, of the brook south of Barca's Hamlet and the insistent warmth of the lamb nuzzling your udder.

Then she'd made a mistake, a wrong turning that took her to Hell and brought her knowledge fit only for demons. She'd returned to the waking world without leaving Hell, becoming Evil's most skillful minion for a time. It hadn't been long by most reckonings, but Ilna knew that if she lived forever, she couldn't undo the harm she'd done while Evil rode her like a mettlesome horse.

"Here we go, child," Chalcus said in an eager voice. The *Shepherd* scrunched onto the sand, beginning to wobble as it ground to a halt.

The officers wore broad leather belts over their short tunics instead of sashes or simply breechclouts like the oarsmen who came from Shengy, Sirimat, and perhaps a few of the other southern islands. They shouted a confused medley of orders, but so far as Ilna could see the crew was already in motion.

Sailors from the lower oarbanks stepped to the outriggers, leaped into the sea, and splashed shoreward carrying ropes. Those from the top bank had already withdrawn their oars from the rowlocks on the outrigger; they thrust the blades down into the sand, bracing the vessel, which, for the moment, rested only on its narrow keel.

"Put your backs into it, Shepherds!" Chalcus shouted as though he was still a sailor instead of being one of Prince Garric's companions. His right arm pointed to the ship sliding onto the beach beside them, the five-banked flagship of Admiral Zettin, the fleet commander. "You're not going to let those scuts from the *City of Valles* berth ahead of us, are you?"

Ilna's brother, Cashel, stood across the narrow deck from her, one hand on his hickory quarterstaff and the other on the waist of his fiancée, Sharina—Princess Sharina of Haft and Garric's sister. She was lovely and blond-haired and tall; taller than most men in Barca's Hamlet, though a hand's breadth shorter than Cashel and with a willowy suppleness that made her seem tiny beside him.

Cashel was a massive oak of a man, his neck a pyramid of muscle rising from his massive shoulders. He looked anxious. Ilna knew his concern wasn't about what was happening, just that he wasn't part of it. For choice Cashel would be down in the surf, gripping a hawser and helping drag the *Shepherd* up the beach with the strength of any three other men.

He couldn't do that because he'd become Lord Cashel, a nobleman by virtue of being Garric's closest friend during the time they both were peasants growing up in Barca's Hamlet. If he jumped into the water and grabbed a rope, the officers would be embarrassed and the common sailors shocked and worried; so he didn't, because the last thing Cashel would willingly do was hurt or embarrass anybody unnecessarily.

Of course when he thought it *was* necessary, Cashel's ironbound hickory quarterstaff could do quite a lot of hurting.

Seated cross-legged on the deck between Cashel, Sharina, and the railing was Tenoctris, an old woman whose talents included being generally cheerful despite the things she'd seen in her long life. There she'd drawn a figure on the deck planking with a stick of red lead. She was muttering the words of a spell as she gestured with a thin split of bamboo.

Tenoctris was a wizard. A wizard of slight power, she repeatedly noted, even now that the forces on which the cosmos turned were reaching another thousand-year peak, but a person whose craftsmanship had gained her Ilna's respect.

Tenoctris' art never did anything that she didn't mean it to do. At a time when the hedge wizards of a decade ago could rip mountains apart—

generally by accident—Tenoctris' care and scholarship had a great deal to do with the kingdom's survival.

With the *Shepherd* firmly aground, the men from the lowest oarbank came up from the hold, sweating like plowmen. They stepped onto the outriggers. Many of them poised there a moment instead of dropping immediately to the sand into the knee-deep water nearer the stern.

They'd backed the great warship onto the beach by themselves, while the men of the other four oarbanks stood on deck to slant the stern into the air. Though the deck gratings had been removed before the vessel began these final maneuvers, there'd still been very little ventilation in the hollow of the hull.

The largest stern anchor was a stone doughnut attached to a section of cypress. The trunk was reeved through the central hole, and the three branches spreading just below the stone were trimmed to points to grip in the sea bottom. A pair of sailors lifted the anchor from where it'd been stowed, beneath the tiller of the starboard steering oar, and walked to the rail.

The sailing master leaned over the side, and shouted, "Ware below!" then nodded to the sailors. They half dropped, half threw the anchor onto the sand.

"Chalcus?" said Merota. She pointed toward the strait separating the little islet where they were landing from the mainland of Sandrakkan. "Why are those ships there still rowing? Isn't there room for them here?"

The child's high, clear voice cut through the scores of male shouts and snarls. For some reason, people always sounded angry at times like this. Maybe they *were* angry, frustrated by the complexity of what was going on.

For complex it was. Ilna couldn't count beyond the number of her fingers without beans or pebbles for a tally, but she knew that there was a ten of tens of ships in Garric's fleet, the royal fleet—and perhaps several tens of tens. Many were backing onto the beach to either side of the *Shepherd of the Isles,* others had anchored well out in the channel, sending the soldiers they carried to land in small boats.

In a few cases swimmers had dragged lines from vessels to the islet and tied them to the columns of ruined mansions lining the shore. Tunic-clad skirmishers armed with javelins and a hatchet or long knife clung to the lines with one hand as they splashed to land, safe even if they weren't able to swim any better than Ilna herself could.

"Sandrakkan hasn't any real fighting ships, dear one," Chalcus said, speaking to the child on his shoulder but pitching his voice so that Ilna could hear also if she wanted to. "Just some fifty-oared patrol boats to chase smugglers, you see. But somebody had the notion, Lord Attaper I shouldn't wonder, that even little ships might attack Prince Garric while he's all tangled up with landing."

Chalcus laughed. "Attaper is a fine man, to be sure," he went on, "but I think he worries lest a stone fall out of the clear sky and strike the prince down. Regardless, there's thirty triremes sloshing the sea between Garric and the mainland. It's good practice, I'm sure, and there's never a crew that wouldn't benefit from a little more practice."

Ilna allowed herself a slight smile at Chalcus' description of the commander of Garric's bodyguards, the Blood Eagles. Attaper was a fit, powerful man in his forties. At the moment he stood watchfully just behind the prince. Ilna was sure he was ready to react if Lady Liane tried to stab Garric with the nib of her pen.

Ilna's fingers knotted a tracery of cords, then undid them before their pattern was quite complete. Had she finished the design, a man who saw it clearly would hurl himself away, shrieking and trying to claw the horror out of his eye sockets. She didn't need such a thing here and now; but it was available, like the warships patrolling the strait and like the curved sword at Chalcus' side.

The equipment of all the Blood Eagles was blackened bronze, but Attaper's helmet and cuirass had been chased with gold so that they looked more like parade armor than anything meant for war. His sword hilt, though, had the yellow patina that ivory takes when a hand grips it daily at the practice butts if not to wield against living foes.

Ilna couldn't fathom the minds of men who made it their life's work to kill other men—and that was what soldiers did, when you boiled away all the nonsense about duty and courage and honor put on the business by the Old Kingdom poets that Garric so fancied. She couldn't understand, but she knew craftsmanship and honored it above all other things.

Craftsmanship meant doing a thing the single right way instead of any of the unnumbered wrong ways others might do it. The Blood Eagles were volunteers, veterans who'd proved themselves in other regiments before they were even permitted to join. By the standard of craft, the only standard that had ever mattered to Ilna os-Kenset, the Blood Eagles were worthy of her respect.

Lord Waldron, commander of the royal army, stood on the stern of another five-banked warship backed onto the beach a few places down from the *Shepherd of the Isles*. His aide raised a silver trumpet and blew a ringing note that was answered a moment later by the deeper, richer calls of several curved horns from the shore. The troops who'd already landed were milling like ants from a stirred-up hill, an image of hopeless chaos.

But it wasn't chaos, Ilna knew. Those scrambling troops were forming shoulder to shoulder with their fellows, under the standards of their proper units. Many were soaked to the waist and some had lost their shield or spear or helmet in the process of coming ashore, but even so they were an army rather than a mob.

Sailors were bracing the *Shepherd*'s hull upright with spars so that the crewmen who'd steadied her when she first grounded could ship their oars and jump down. Half a dozen men under a bosun's mate hauled the anchor and its trailing hawser farther inland to hold the ship even if an unexpected storm raced down the strait.

Ilna knotted her pattern, shaking her head in marvel at the scene around her. It was as if every thread in a loom had its own mind, but they *chose* to weave themselves into a complex tapestry instead of twisting off each in its own direction. It was a marvelous thing, but she didn't understand it, didn't understand how it could even be possible.

Chalcus and Merota laughed at some joke Ilna had missed in her reverie. She smiled also, though at a thought of her own.

Ilna understood very little about the world in which she found herself living. No doubt people like Garric and Sharina, whose father had educated them far beyond the standards of Barca's Hamlet, understood more than she did, but she was sure that even their grasp was slight compared with the world's enormous complexity.

Still Garric and Sharina and the others went on, guiding a kingdom through the darkness of their own ignorance; because if they didn't the kingdom—the *people*, the uncounted numbers of ordinary peasants and traders and fishermen—would surely be crushed into the mud by masterless chaos. Ilna didn't really believe in Good personified, but she had no doubt of the existence of Evil.

So she'd act to help Garric and Sharina, Tenoctris and Attaper and yes, Liane—the people who knew more than she did. She'd act without hope, without real certainty except in one thing: that whatever Ilna os-Kenset did, she would do with all the skill at her disposal.

Cashel looked over his shoulder. He gave Ilna the broad smile that was as much a part of him as cold stiffness was to Ilna's own lips.

Ilna's fingers made a last knot; she raised the completed pattern into the air. Everyone who caught sight of it laughed and pointed it out to their neighbors. It was only a rough, knotted fabric, but it brought a flash of joy and hope.

Even to the woman who'd knotted it.

Cashel, bursting with pride because his left hand rested on Sharina's waist, surveyed the island of Volita. From a distance the terrain looked rocky, but as the *Shepherd* approached the beach it became obvious that, except for the granite crag near the center of the island, the stones weren't natural outcrops. The shore was covered with the tumbled ruins of buildings that must've been palaces, even by the standards of what Cashel had seen in Valles on Ornifal, the capital of the Isles.

Cashel flexed his right hand on the shaft of his quarterstaff. The touch of the stout hickory, polished both by labor and by use, reminded him of who he *really* was: an orphan who'd grown up in a borough that the rest of the world had ignored for a thousand years.

His father, Kenset, had sold his share of their late father's grain mill to his brother Katchin and left Barca's Hamlet, seeking adventure and swearing he'd never return. When he did come back in seven years' time, he'd brought the infants Cashel and Ilna. People recalled that Kenset had left Barca's Hamlet with a song on his lips; but on his return he didn't sing, rarely spoke, and spent as many of his waking hours as he could drinking ale.

Before long Kenset died in a ditch—too drunk to find shelter and very likely seeking the end he found in the frosty night. He'd never explained where he'd been while he was gone, nor had he talked of the children's mother. His own mother had raised Ilna and Cashel; and after she died, they'd raised themselves.

A peasant village has neither the taste nor the resources for luxuries like charity, but the orphans had made do. They had half the mill to sleep in, for by their grandfather's will neither son could sell his portion of the building; and they earned enough for their bread in one fashion and another. Cashel had a man's strength early, and Ilna's talent with fabric was a marvel from the first time her fingers twisted raw wool into thread.

Cashel had never expected to leave Barca's Hamlet except perhaps to badger a herd of sheep across the island to Carcosa, the ancient capital of the Isles on the other coast. Instead he'd seen Laut on the far side of the Inner Sea, and he'd lived in the royal palace in Valles, a sprawling park with more separate buildings in it than there were in Barca's Hamlet and the borough around it altogether.

Cashel had gone to those places, and he'd gone to places that weren't in this world at all. He recalled how he'd felt scarcely a year ago when he'd first seen the crumbling walls of Carcosa. They'd been built during the Old Kingdom and used as a quarry by the city's remaining population for all the thousand years since the Old Kingdom fell. He'd been awestruck by the ruins that remained, almost unable to accept that so great a mass of stone had been created by men. Nothing in Cashel's previous life compared with those walls save for the sky overhead and the sea reaching eastward to the horizon from the shore of Barca's Hamlet.

But marvelous as Cashel'd found the places he'd gone and the folk he'd met there, none of them were as wonderful as the fact that Sharina loved him and had allowed him to love her. Her father, Reise, was the innkeeper, a wealthy man as the borough weighed such things and a learned one by any judgment. He'd come to Barca's Hamlet from Carcosa, where he'd been Countess Tera's chamberlain; and before that he'd served the king himself in Valles.

Reise had taught Garric and Sharina to read and to love the great writers of the Old Kingdom. They'd learned so well that Lady Liane had found the education she'd received at a school for the daughters of the wealthy made her no more than the equal of the innkeeper's children she met in Barca's Hamlet.

Reise's daughter was far too great a person to wed an orphan like Cashel, who couldn't write his name and who'd never handled a silver coin in his life . . . and besides that, Sharina was a long-legged beauty with blond hair as fine as spiderweb. Every year at the borough's Sheep Fair there'd been drovers and wealthy merchants who offered Sharina riches past a peasant girl's imagining if she'd come away with them.

A thundercloud of memory shadowed Cashel's face. Sharina had told them "no." The ones who didn't like the answer were told it again, by Sharina's muscular brother, Garric, and her even more muscular friend Cashel. If they had bodyguards—and they generally did—so much the worse for them. A swordsman in an open courtyard hasn't a chance against a strong man with seven feet of iron-shod hickory and the skill to use it.

Cashel's left hand rested lightly on Sharina's waist, not a claim but rather a badge of honor. He'd worshipped Sharina for as long as he could remember, but he'd never imagined that he'd be permitted to love her. Whatever else might happen in Cashel's life, it'd already been more wonderful than he'd dreamed.

He looked at the island. Volita didn't have much to see that Cashel cared about. Ruins were interesting to some folk, just as books were. Tenoctris could touch a carved stone and talk about where it came from, while Garric and Sharina nodded in understanding. But for Cashel, rocks were mostly important when they were where they'd grown, because then they gave him a notion about how good the grazing was likely to be.

Garric was sailing his fleet slowly up the western arc of the kingdom, halting at each of the major islands. He was making what his advisors called a Royal Progress. Cashel didn't need anybody to explain the sense of it: a shepherd who kept his eyes open saw the same thing happen every spring. Birds, squirrels—frogs, even—stared at each other and puffed themselves up, singing or screeching or croaking. All of them were trying to make their rivals back down.

With dogs you might get a fight, but that was dogs. It could be a fight between men too, but not if they were as smart as Garric.

Cashel was one of the people Garric talked to before he did things. Cashel hadn't understood why at first, he a shepherd who couldn't read or write sitting with nobles who were used to running things. He'd seen quickly that his knowing the things a peasant knows could be useful. With nobles, what they knew got mixed up with what they called honor. Honor to a noble generally meant acting like you didn't have any common sense.

About fighting, for instance. A fight meant the winner was hurt too, like as not, and maybe the losers from earlier fights would pile in and turn it into an all-against-one thing that no "one" could survive. It was a lot better in the long run to talk and posture and hop up and down—and not to have to fight—because you'd convinced your rival that he couldn't win but that you were going to let him not lose either.

So Garric arrived at each island with a fleet and army that the ruler knew he couldn't defeat; but instead of attacking, Garric told him how glad he was to have a loyal supporter of the kingdom like him in this place; and by the way, here was the new schedule of payments that his island would be sending to Valles to support the fleet and army.

That's what a Royal Progress was. That's why Garric and his huge fleet were there on an island just off the coast of Sandrakkan, whose previous ruler had claimed to be King of the Isles twenty-odd years ago, and who'd failed, but not by so much that his nephew mightn't have similar notions of his own.

Tenoctris had finished the spell she'd been working. Sharina bent down to talk with her, but Cashel remained where he was as a wall between the women and the bustle on the ship's narrow deck. No sailor would bump Sharina or Tenoctris deliberately, but they might not notice them. Most everybody noticed Cashel. If they didn't, well, they bounced off.

Cashel continued to scan Volita the way he would a new pasture. He'd seen a lot of places in the past five seasons. Many of them were cities, and the only parts of a city Cashel'd found he liked were the pictures city folk, wealthy ones anyhow, had painted on their walls. But there'd been countryside too, none of it really nicer than the borough in springtime but nice enough regardless.

A ewe with a black body and an all-white face stood between half-raised pillars on the horizon, staring at the ships and men on the shore. She chewed a grass blade with the same rotary motion as a woman mixing bread dough. The hooves of sheep had cut narrow paths that wound among the ruins wherever Cashel looked, following the least possible grade across the landscape. Sheep could find a slope where water'd give up and make a pool instead. . . .

Cashel smiled broadly and rested his hand gently on Sharina's shoulder, his eyes still on the shore. Volita might not be Barca's Hamlet, but it'd do. Any place in any world would do for Cashel or-Kenset, so long as he was there with Sharina.

Sharina saw the crimson spark vanish from above the symbol Tenoctris had drawn on the pine planking. She put her hand out to steady the old woman, but Tenoctris didn't sway with fatigue the way she often did after an incantation.

"I'm all right, dear," she said, though she raised her left hand for Sharina to hold and didn't look up for a moment. "I was determining the amount of power here, that's all. I'd never visited Sandrakkan before. In my former life, I mean."

Now she did turn to smile. Tenoctris appeared to be about seventy. Indeed she'd lived some seventy years, but she'd been born more than a millennium ago. She'd been ripped from her time by the wizardry that had drowned King Carus and brought the Old Kingdom down.

The Kingdom of the Isles today was only a shadow of the magnificence that had shattered a thousand years ago, the crudely rejoined fragments of the little that had survived the Collapse. Except for the help and direction Tenoctris had given Garric and the others who were trying to prevent it, a second, final Collapse would have destroyed what remained.

And that Collapse could still occur. The forces that wizards tapped with their art waxed every thousand years, and they were swiftly rising to their peak again. Wizards who in the past could only wither a tree with great effort were now able to blast whole forests—and might easily do so by accident, because an increase in power didn't bring with it greater learning and wisdom.

"I thought I must be mistaken about the skeins of force I felt here," Tenoctris continued, gesturing toward the ruin-speckled western slope of Volita. "I was right, though. Something really terrible must have happened, but—"

She grinned.

"—it was after I left my own age. Or I'd have been aware of it, even if there hadn't been time for human messengers to bring word."

The wizard shifted her feet in preparation to rise. Sharina stiffened to help, either by lifting or just to provide a fulcrum on which the old woman could lever herself upright.

After a moment's consideration, Tenoctris relaxed where she was. "Not quite yet," she murmured, mostly to herself.

When Sharina was a child who'd never met a wizard, she'd imagined that wizardry involved muttering a few words and having all manner of wonders appear from the thin air. Now she'd seen wizards of many different types and abilities. The one thing they all had in common was the bone-deep exhaustion that they felt at the conclusion of a spell.

A powerful wizard could do things that a lesser one couldn't even attempt, just as Cashel could lift a stone that wouldn't tremble if Sharina strained against it. That didn't mean lifting a heavy stone wasn't work for Cashel, though: just that it was work within his very considerable capacity.

Tenoctris was a little old woman with limited physical strength and similarly slight ability to influence through her art the forces she saw so clearly. Even minor spells were an effort for her. At need, she could function on sheer willpower for long *enough* in every case that Sharina'd had occasion to observe; but there was no need for Tenoctris to do anything just then except to sit on the deck as sailors completed berthing arrangements.

Volita lay in the Bay of Shelter. This western shore faced the mainland of Sandrakkan and the city of Erdin, the capital of the Earls of Sandrakkan from the founding of the Old Kingdom two millennia before. The surrounding water buffered the climate. Volita was close to one of the most vibrant cities of the realm, so during the Old Kingdom it'd become a summer resort for wealthy folk from the length and breadth of the Isles.

Today the remains of those homes lined the island's western shore and, as Sharina had seen as the fleet approached, the eastern side as well. Most'd had a slip for the owner's yacht, but the waves of a thousand stormy years had crumbled the pilings and stonework. They wouldn't have been large enough to berth warships two and three hundred feet long anyway.

But not all Volita's ruins were those of time and weather, though . . .

"Records of the Collapse aren't good," Sharina said. It seemed odd to be explaining what had happened a thousand years ago to a person who'd been alive then, but Sharina knew from her own experience that the person who lives an event often doesn't know more than a tiny shard of it. "Of course. But there's an account written in the monastery on Bridge Island, the Healing Brethren of Lady Erd. Nobody knows how accurate it is."

She cleared her throat and repeated, "Of course."

"Yes," said Tenoctris. "I understand. But there *is* an account?"

"Sandrakkan was attacked by pirates who came from the Inner Sea," Sharina said, not letting her tone carry any emotion. "There was much raiding then, after Carus and his fleet were overwhelmed. These pirates were led by a wizard."

She was surprised at how difficult it was to go on. When she'd found the codex with the story in a temple library in Carcosa, it'd been interesting enough to struggle through despite the copyist's awkwardly back-slanted hand—but it'd been merely an anecdote. Perhaps it was slightly more important than otherwise because it took place in Erdin, where the royal fleet would be going next; but only slightly.

What had seemed a scrap of history in an old book took on a disquieting immediacy here, staring at the ruins of Volita. All the more reason to go on, Sharina thought with a grin.

"The Earl of Sandrakkan had a wizard also," she continued. "The monk doesn't mention the wizard's name, but he was apparently more learned than he was powerful."

Sharina and Tenoctris exchanged broad smiles. Tenoctris was an exceptional scholar irrespective of the subject on which she focused. She could appreciate better than most a wizard of former time with greater learning than power.

"He summoned a third wizard from a distant place," Sharina said.

"Distant in time or space?" Tenoctris wondered aloud. "Though I don't suppose a monastic chronicler would know the difference."

"He didn't," Sharina agreed. " 'From a far country' was what he said. This third wizard met the pirates on Volita and raised great giants to battle them. At last the giants defeated the pirates and pent them under the earth. Erdin and the rest of Sandrakkan were saved, but everything on Volita was ruined. The island spat red and blue lightning for all the year following."

Tenoctris got to her feet with studied ease, barely touching a hand to the deck as she straightened. She smiled at Sharina, sharing with her younger friend a triumph over the insistences of age. She looked over the railing at Volita.

"Yes," she said, "I can imagine there *were* flashes of wizardlight that even those who aren't sensitive to the forces involved would notice. And I'm not surprised that the houses haven't been rebuilt even today."

She nodded toward the ruins marching up and down the beach. The location should've remained desirable for the same reasons it had been during the Old Kingdom, but the only present signs of human activity were wandering sheep and the beehive hut that a shepherd had built from fallen debris.

"It'll be uncomfortable staying on Volita," Tenoctris continued, "though it won't do us any harm. The soldiers will probably feel itchy, some of them more than others."

Sharina watched the troops and sailors scrambling over the shore of the island. Groups were moving up the slope, spreading the way spilled liquid does through a piece of cloth.

She turned back toward the wizard. "What about you, Tenoctris?" she asked sharply. "'Some more than others,' you said. The sensitive ones, don't you mean? Then you most of all."

Tenoctris chuckled. "Oh, child, I know what's happening," she said. "For me it's no worse than being out in the rain; and the land needs rain, you know. But what if you didn't know what rain was?"

With a sad expression she watched the busy men. Sharina pursed her lips, understanding now why this landing seemed a little different from those she'd experienced before. The shouts were harsher, angrier than they should have been at the end of a successful voyage. The crews and soldiers were already on edge; that would only get worse the longer they camped here.

"Perhaps I should've said something sooner," Tenoctris went on. "I didn't realize it would be quite like this."

"It wouldn't have changed Garric's plan," Sharina said, glancing sideways toward her brother among his aides and black-armored bodyguards. "He didn't want to land on Sandrakkan proper because there might be trouble between our soldiers and the Earl's. *Would* be trouble."

There always was trouble: between soldiers and civilians, even when the soldiers were in permanent barracks at home, and between soldiers of different regiments even in the same army. Dropping an army of twenty thousand, armed and full of themselves and secretly frightened, onto an island that had fought them during the lifetime of many on both sides, meant that the inevitable drunken insults and brawls over women were very likely to escalate into full-scale warfare.

Sharina knew that a bloody war between the royal army—which was still the Ornifal army in the minds of many—and the army of any of the major islands was likely to doom the kingdom no matter who won that particular battle. King Carus had fought a score of usurpers and secessionists, winning every time. Even if wizardry hadn't destroyed him and his army, there'd still have been a final battle that Carus lost if only because there were no longer enough able-bodied men to stand beside him.

The Old Kingdom had died with Carus. The New Kingdom would die just as surely with Garric if he started down the path of ruling by his sword arm.

Sharina looked at her brother in silence, feeling love and pride.

She also felt an embarrassing degree of relief. No matter how willing she was to help him for the kingdom's sake, the final responsibility was Garric's, not hers.

The Sandrakkan mainland was crowded with people, standing on the shore or already in the barges that would bring them across to Volita as soon as they'd gotten permission. Even a mile away they could see Prince Garric of Haft, Regent of the Kingdom, in his dazzling silvered breastplate and the silvered helmet, from which flared wings of gilded bronze.

Inside that splendid armor was Garric or-Reise, the peasant son of the innkeeper of Barca's Hamlet. There were many things Garric would rather've been doing than the job he had before him. They started with reading verse by the great Old Kingdom poet Celondre while he watched a flock of sheep on the hillside south of the hamlet, because *that* was a job he understood.

"You understand being ruler as well as any man does, lad," said King Carus, the ancestor who'd shared Garric's mind ever since his father gave him Carus' coronation medal to hang around his neck on a thong. *"Better than I ever did, as the Gods well know."*

Carus laughed, his presence unseen by others but to Garric as real as his own right hand. In life Carus had been a tall man with a ready smile and a swordsman's thick wrists. That was how he usually appeared to Garric as well, leaning on the rose-wound railing of a balcony in an indeterminate place. Carus' features and those of Garric, his descendant after a millennium, could have been those of the same man some decades apart in age.

We don't know what history'll say about me after I'm dead, Garric said in his mind.

"We know that if you don't continue to do better than I did," said Carus in what was for him an unusually crisp tone, *"there won't* be *any more history."*

"That's Marshal Renold's standard, a crow displayed," said Liane, slitting her eyes as she peered toward the waiting barge with a cloth-of-gold canopy shading the passengers amidships. "If he's present, he'll be in charge of the negotiations. The marshal traditionally commands the earl's professional troops, and he leads the left wing in a battle."

Garric followed the line of Liane's gaze. He could see the standard, a pole supporting a gilt bird with its wings spread. His eyes were as good as anybody in the borough's, but he couldn't have told it was a crow. Liane was probably guessing.

But possibly not. It was never a good idea to underestimate Liane.

Lady Liane bos-Benliman was dark-haired, gently curved, and as obviously aristocratic as she was beautiful. Her father Benlo had been a successful merchant, widely traveled in the Isles and perhaps beyond.

He'd been a wizard as well. Wizardry had cost him his honor, his life, and finally his soul.

Liane had gained a fine education before her father's disgrace. She retained that, along with a powerful intelligence and Benlo's network of contacts throughout the known world. She'd made herself Garric's confidential secretary and his spymaster, carrying out both sets of duties with a skill he couldn't imagine anyone else equaling. That Liane loved him was to Garric a greater wonder than the fact he shared his mind with his ancient ancestor.

"Is Renold a sensible man?" Garric asked. "Because if he is, he'll see immediately that my offer—the kingdom's offer—is reasonable given the balance of forces. If he does, then this can be a basically pleasant meeting."

"Reasonable or not," said Liane with a sniff, "your offer's the earl's only chance of survival. Unfortunately from what I can gather Renold is very similar to his master, and Earl Wildulf is barely intelligent enough to pull his breeches on before his boots!"

She cleared her throat, keeping her eyes toward the far shore, obviously embarrassed at her outburst. Liane shared a personality flaw with some other smart people Garric knew: she became genuinely angry when she had to deal with folks who refused to demonstrate common sense.

"She wouldn't do for a politician, lad," Carus commented from the back of Garric's mind. *"But then, neither did I. She's not in charge, as unfortunately I was."*

"I think we'll be able to work matters out with the earl in adequate fashion," Garric said, smiling toward Liane but speaking to his ancestor as well. "I don't doubt his pride, but he didn't rebel when we—"

And by "we," he meant the royal fleet and army.

"—had other things to occupy us during the past year. He and I will manage to agree."

Carus laughed cheerfully, seeing the mass of fears and indecision that roiled in Garric's mind while he calmly predicted success. Garric smiled also, at himself. He'd said the politic thing, after all. That it was more likely than not true was in a way beside the point; and that the uncertain future terrified him had nothing to do with the matter at all.

Ordinarily Garric expected to meet local dignitaries in their mansions or in public areas designed for the purpose. Negotiating among the ruins of Volita created some problems that Garric's staff had solved with impressive professionalism. A crew under the bosun of Admiral Zettin's flagship was raising a great marquee under which Garric and the Sandrakkan envoys could negotiate.

The fleet was equipped strictly as a fighting force; it didn't carry tents for the common soldiers, let alone the trappings of luxury that some nobles thought were required even while on campaign. The marquee'd been stitched together from the mainsails of several triremes and trimmed with signal flags for color. The sailors—soldiers weren't used to working with spans of fabric so great—used the concave ruin of a domed building for a back wall and had supported the front of the canvas with spars. The work of raising it was almost complete.

Garric turned to his aide, Lord Lerdain—a husky youth of fifteen— and said, "Lerdain, tell the signalers to summon the Sandrakkan delegation. By the time their barge gets here, we'll be ready to meet them."

"Right!" said Lerdain, resplendent in gilded armor even gaudier than Garric's own. He stepped onto the port outrigger, then jumped straight to the beach—a youthfully boastful thing to do. Lerdain's helmet fell off, probably after banging his head a good one. He thrust it back in place and scrambled toward the flagship, whose raised mainmast provided the fleet's signal station.

Lerdain was the eldest son of the Count of Blaise. He was there at Garric's side in part as a pledge of his father's continued good behavior, but he'd made an excellent aide nonetheless. He had the arrogance of youth and the occasional pigheadedness of his class, but pride made him keen, and he'd shown himself quite capable of thinking for himself.

There was another benefit to having a ruler's son as an aide. Garric'd found it useful to send a messenger who had no hesitation in passing on the prince's orders just as forcefully as the prince himself would've done, no matter how lofty the person receiving those orders might be.

Garric looked toward the shore of the mainland. Hundreds of barges lined it, ready to put out for Volita with provisions and recreation for the royal army as soon as Garric allowed them to. The royal army under Garric—as had been the case under Carus—carried silver to buy supplies locally so that it didn't have to proceed with a train of lumbering store ships.

The River Erd drained central Sandrakkan, bringing produce from the northern mountains and the plains alike to Erdin, where an extensive system of canals distributed it without the heavy wagons whose iron-shod wheels clashed deafeningly through most cities. Canal and riverboats weren't meant for the open sea, but in reasonable weather they were adequate for the narrow waters between Volita and Sandrakkan.

"I should've given the traders permission to go as well," Garric said, frowning at his oversight. There were too many things to keep track of. Many of those that weren't of life-or-death importance slipped through his mind, and he had the nagging fear that some that *were* critical were going to get past him also.

"I'll take the message, your highness!" said the next-senior in the cluster of noble youths detailed as aides to the prince. This boy was a cousin of Lord Royhas, the Chancellor and at present the head of government back in Valles. He was just as keen as Lerdain—and not a little jealous as well.

"*Stop* if you will, Lord Knorrer," Liane said. Her voice was emotionless but it was far too loud to ignore.

The youth, already poised to leap ten feet to the sand the way Lerdain had done, teetered wildly. Garric grabbed Knorrer's shoulder, steadying him until he could reach back to the railing.

"I believe your highness was correct to let the delegates arrive before you allow the traders to cross," Liane continued, smoothly and in a much quieter voice. "The traders will race one another for the best market, and it's very possible Marshal Renold and his companions would be overset in the turmoil. At the very least, they'd find the situation demeaning."

"Which would put them in a bad mood," Garric said, smiling at the polite way Liane had contradicted him in the language of agreement. "Or perhaps a worse one. Thank you, milady. The troops can wait for their bread and wine."

And women, of course. Some of the barges were laden with what looked from a mile's distance like a sampling of court society. Closer to hand the finery would be less impressive, but it'd serve well enough for the purpose. It would've dazzled folk in Barca's Hamlet, for that matter, except for Ilna, whose taste was as subtle as that of a great lady of Valles.

Garric glanced at those standing with him in the stern of the *Shepherd of the Isles*. He'd chosen to wait here till it was time to meet the Sandrakkan delegation, because the quinquereme's deck was a much better vantage point than the ground anywhere near the shore. The spine of Volita rose enough that not even the worst winter storms could send waves from the Inner Sea surging across the mansions on the western shore, but the only portion that could really be called high was the knob of basalt that stuck up like a raised thumb a quarter mile inland.

Sharina was talking to Tenoctris, but she met Garric's glance with a surprisingly warm smile. They'd always gotten on well, better than most siblings, but for a moment Sharina's expression suggested motherly concern.

Cashel stood just behind the two women; his face placid, his staff upright in his right hand. It was disconcerting to look from the granite knob in the middle distance to Cashel close at hand. The rock looked something like a hunched human being when you compared it to a man of equal solidity.

Ilna raised her hands, stretching the cords between her fingers into a sunlit web. Garric laughed aloud to see the pattern. There was just something about the way the cords crossed . . . it made him sure there was a way through all the tangles that were part of a prince's life no less than a peasant's.

Crewmen dropped a ladder over the quinquereme's stern. It was roped to the pintle of the steering oar at the top; a husky sailor braced the bottom rung with his foot so that it wouldn't shift in the sand. The barge from Sandrakkan was nearing the island.

"Time to go, I think, friends," Garric said. "Cashel, if you'll help Tenoctris . . . ?"

Without comment or hesitation, Cashel scooped up the wizard as easily as Chalcus held Ilna's ward. Close behind, Sharina carried the satchel holding Tenoctris' books and paraphernalia—liquids, powders, and a few crystals of greater weight.

Chalcus nodded to Garric. Then—still holding Merota—he followed after Ilna, who was tucking away her knotted pattern.

Still chuckling, Garric said, "Lord Knorrer, take Lady Liane's case if you will." He nodded to the traveling desk in which Liane kept the documents for which he had immediate use.

"I can—" she said.

Garric lifted her in the crook of his right arm and strode toward the ladder, laughing again. He was bragging, about his strength and also that this beautiful, brilliant woman loved him as he loved her; but he had a right to brag. Life was very good.

Earl Wildulf doesn't want a fight any more than I do, he thought, answering the grim speculation in the eyes of his ancient ancestor.

"Aye lad," Carus replied, but he wasn't agreeing. *"But fights can come even when neither side wants them to."*

Carus paused, then added reflectively, *"I've been in more battles than I could count, and mostly at the end the only thing I could say I was happy about was the fact I was still alive. The day came I couldn't even say that. I pray to whatever Gods may be that you never have to say that while the kingdom still has need of you!"*

Chapter Two

T he conference table had been improvised out of ventilator gratings from the *Shepherd* set on column barrels and covered with a sparklingly white sail from the same ship. Only the vessels carrying Garric, Zettin, and Waldron, the three leaders of the Progress, had sails of bleached cloth; the yellow-gray color of natural wool wouldn't have had the same effect.

Garric seated himself on a section of marble column. Troops had rolled it under the marquee, upended it, and created a throne by covering it with a fur-trimmed cloak of red velvet. He didn't have the slightest idea where the cloak came from.

"For all that, lad," said Carus, *"it's probably one of yours. No matter what I told my servants, they'd wind up packing what they thought was suitable clothing. Suitable for me!"*

Garric chuckled at the joke that nobody else had heard. So far as Carus was concerned, suitable clothing for a warrior—which he'd been, the greatest warrior of his age and perhaps ever in the history of the Isles—

was boots, breeches, a sturdy tunic, and a cloak of raw wool that'd double as bedding in the cold and wet.

Garric had similar tastes; indeed, he'd minded sheep on winter nights with less than that to wear. Palace functionaries, the servants and the officials who supervised them, had a very different notion of what a king should wear, though . . . and if a king was doing his job, he didn't have time to check his wardrobe to make sure it contained only the minimal kit he'd directed.

Liane cleared her throat in polite question. She was seated on a folding stool at the prince's right elbow, a respectful arm's length back from the conference table. Her traveling desk was on her lap; she'd laid out three wax notebooks and a small parchment scroll on its beechwood top.

"I was remembering," Garric explained in a low voice, "that when I was a boy I thought that princes gave orders and everybody obeyed. Either I was wrong, or I'm a very ineffectual prince."

"You're extremely effective," Liane murmured, her lips close to Garric's ear. "Not least because you see that's *not* how things happen."

Lord Waldron sat in the place of honor to Garric's right. Organizing a camp for twenty thousand men was an enormously complicated task, and Waldron was the final arbiter of arrangements. A middle-aged nobleman in cavalry boots knelt on his other side and spoke in urgent tones; several more officers bent close with the urgent expressions of little boys desperate to pee.

A horse on shipboard takes up the space of ten men. Besides that problem, horses are likely to kick a vessel to pieces in a storm, then tread over men swimming in the water. The army that embarked on Ornifal carried no horses. Waldron had dismounted two cavalry regiments, however, to use as heavy infantry.

That wasn't a choice Garric would've made, but he hadn't been willing to overrule his army commander. As Carus had pointed out, the cavalry regiments were recruited from the younger sons and retainers of Northern Ornifal landowners, the class to which Waldron himself belonged. If the commander felt more comfortable in battle because he had a thousand of his own kind with him, then so much the better for the army and the kingdom.

To Garric's left sat Lord Tadai, a wealthy financier from Valles who was as different from Waldron as either nobleman was from a Haft peasant like Garric. Tadai had general oversight of finance and the administrative adjustments—he and Garric both were careful never to use the word "reforms"—that had to be made to fully integrate the governments of the separate islands into that of the kingdom, for the first time in a thousand years. Tadai was fat and immaculately groomed—smiling, supercilious, and cold even in his passions.

Despite the differences in their tastes and attitudes, Waldron and Tadai were both intelligent enough to recognize the other's competence. They worked well together, though at a careful distance.

For these negotiations, Tadai and Garric would do most of the talking, but the presence of a straight-backed, grizzled warrior like Waldron might be crucial to their success. Waldron had stood beside Valence the Third at the Stone Wall when Ornifal broke Sandrakkan twenty-two years before. Even silent, he reminded the delegates across the table of what had happened before and could easily happen again.

Sharina sat behind the three principals, along with a score of military and civilian aides, people whose knowledge or expertise might be required. From beyond the marquee came the shouts of troops and sailors setting up camp, oblivious of the negotiations.

"Everybody has his own priorities," Carus mused with a smile.

A platoon of Blood Eagles ushered the Sandrakkan envoys up from the beach. Lord Attaper was at the head of his men; the guards must've spent the whole time since landing in polishing salt crust and verdigris from their armor. The guards separated as soon as they stepped under the marquee, lining up at either side and clashing their hobnails to a halt.

According to Liane's direction, the royal officials rose to their feet when the delegation arrived. Only Garric remained on his throne. After a count of three, he ordered, "You may all be seated!" in a parade-ground voice. His own subordinates sat down smoothly, while the Sandrakkan officials shuffled to find places across the table.

There were three men and a woman. "From the left," Liane muttered, "Lady Lelor, Chief Priestess of the Temple of the Shepherd Who Overwhelms; Marshal Renold, we've discussed him; Lord Morchan, he's a cousin of the earl, but he doesn't really have any power; and a palace official, I'll have his name in a few minutes."

"Marshal Renold, I'm glad to meet you and your colleagues," Garric said calmly, his hands loosely crossed on the table before him. "Let me say at the outset that Earl Wildulf's loyalty to the kingdom is not in doubt, nor is my goodwill toward the earl."

"So long as you understand that Sandrakkan is independent, under a man whose lineage is senior to that of any other nobleman in the Isles," Marshal Renold grated. "If you've got that, then you can take your goodwill back to Valles with you and not worry yourself about our affairs any further!"

"Well spoken, Renold!" Lord Morchan said, bobbing his wispy gray goatee. "That's it in a nutshell!"

Ignoring the envoys—they weren't going to be the problem—Garric turned his head to the right, and said, "Lord Waldron!" sharply enough to penetrate the sudden red rage that transfused the army commander. Quite apart from the deliberation of the insult, Waldron felt as an article of faith that *no* foreign noble was fit to be mentioned in the same breath as a Northern Ornifal gentleman.

Waldron had started to rise, his hand reaching for the long cavalry sword hanging at his left side from a baldric. He eased back down and put his hands firmly on the sailcloth table before him. He was looking straight ahead, between Renold and Morchan rather than at either one of them, and certainly not at Prince Garric, to whom he knew he owed an apology that he wasn't calm enough yet to provide.

Garric felt the image of Carus relax also. *Flinging that sort of insult at men who'd spent their lives training to kill—and using their training—was certainly a way to get the conversation moving. . . .*

Lord Tadai laughed like a benevolent uncle. "Very droll, Lord Morchan," he said. "Oddly enough, Lord Waldron and I were just discussing that splendid estate of yours twelve miles down the coast. Sea View, isn't it? More olives and grapes than a man could ride around in a whole day. But Waldron and I wondered how you'd defend Sea View if two thousand . . . pirates, let us say, landed at dawn and began cutting down the trees that've taken so long to grow. Perhaps you could answer that for us, Marshal Renold?"

Lord Morchan looked like he'd just sat nude in a nettle patch. His mouth dropped, and he stared at Renold.

The marshal banged his fist on the table—the grating on the Sandrakkan side tilted and would've fallen if the priestess hadn't caught it—and said, "Defend? Our cavalry would cut them all down, that's how we'd defend!"

"Really?" Tadai said. "Just how many cavalrymen are there in Earl Wildulf's household? I ask because my specialty is finance, and I well know how expensive horsemen are."

"That's none of your business," Renold said. His face had gone red, then white. "That's none of your *bloody* business!"

"He's got about five hundred troopers, Tadai," Lord Waldron said, leaning forward to look at the financier directly. He'd completely recovered his composure. "Lancers. And if he plans to send lancers against our skirmishers in an orchard—"

"Pirates, please, Waldron," Lord Tadai said with an oily grin. "We're talking about an attack by pirates."

"Right, pirates," Waldron agreed grimly. "Pirates with javelins, in an *orchard*. Well, all I can say is that I'd pay to watch it."

"Somebody would pay, I'm sure," Tadai said. "But not any of us who are loyal to Valence the Third and his regent Prince Garric, here."

"Thank you for that interesting digression, gentlemen," Garric said. "We need to get down to business, however. I propose that the first matter to be discussed is the confirmation of Lord Wildulf as Earl of Sandrakkan."

Morchan and Renold were too busy with their own conversation, conducted in snarling undertones, to really absorb Garric's statement. The third male envoy—

"Colchas or-Onail," Liane murmured, folding closed the limewood note that she'd just received from a nondescript man in the crowd. "Chief Clerk of the Office of the Privy Purse."

—said nothing, but his expression hinted at a smile whenever his eyes flicked toward his disgruntled colleagues. The fact that they were nobles while Colchas was a commoner might have been part of that smile.

The priestess, Lady Lelor, was probably the oldest member of the delegation, but she remained a strikingly handsome woman. Her black robe was well cut though severely plain, and her hair was piled high on subtly carven ivory combs.

"I'm not clear on what you mean about 'the confirmation of Lord Wildulf,'" Lelor said in a tone of pleasant inquiry. "Since he's already Earl of Sandrakkan by right of descent."

Garric smiled. At least two of the envoys weren't fools; or at any rate, hadn't yet proved themselves to be fools.

"Her temple's across Market Square from the palace," Liane whispered in his ear. That information was probably written in one of her notebooks, but since Liane had been schooled at an academy of young ladies in Erdin, she'd have known it already. "It's on a high platform with an altar in the middle of the steps."

"My thought, Lady Lelor," Garric said, "was that I'd crown Lord Wildulf on the platform of the Temple of the Shepherd Who Overwhelms, while you performed an Offering of Thanks. That permits the largest possible number of residents to watch this evidence of King Valence's approval of his lordship."

It would also explicitly demonstrate that the Earl of Sandrakkan wasn't independent of the government in Valles, let alone superior to it. A coronation made the point more politely than tearing a gap in the city walls and marching in at the head of the royal army, but even Lord Morchan—who seemed *almost* smart enough to come in out of the rain—could see that was a possible alternative.

Marshal Renold looked from Morchan to Garric, then blinked. "I'm not sure that would be possible," he said. He'd lost the belligerence with which he'd opened the discussions.

"I believe it would be," Lady Lelor said in a deliberate tone, her eyes on Renold. "I will certainly impress on Earl Wildulf my opinion that it would be a desirable way to display his authority."

"I'm not sure—" Renold repeated, then clamped his mouth closed over the rest of whatever he might have said. The muscles at the back of his jaw were bunched. There was clearly no love lost between the two envoys.

"*I had more trouble with priesthoods than I did with usurpers,*" Carus said, shaking his head at the recollection. "*I knew how to deal with a usurper, but I couldn't start looting the temple treasuries in loyal cities without having my own soldiers mutter that I was accursed of the Gods.*"

"Financial arrangements would remain unchanged following the coronation?" said Master Colchas. The clerk reminded Garric of a small dog: tense and ill-tempered, but well aware that if he snapped at the wrong person, he was likely to be kicked into the next borough. "Quite frankly, the earl's revenues don't fully cover expenses even now."

"In the main, that's correct," Lord Tadai said easily. In contrast to Liane, who made a point of having relevant documents at hand though she almost never referred to them, the desk or table before Tadai was always perfectly clear. A squadron of clerks stood behind him, however, each with an open file box just in case. "That is, the assessment of the Third Indiction of Valence the Second won't be increased in the near future. You and I will discuss at another time a schedule for the payment of the arrears accrued during the past seven years."

Colchas cringed. "I don't see . . . ," he began, then covered his mouth with his hand as if in an access of grief. "Oh, dear," he muttered through his fingers. "Oh, dear."

Garric permitted himself a smile. Valence the Third, his father by adoption, had lost control of everything outside of Ornifal—and indeed, almost everything outside of the walls of his palace—before a conspiracy of the most powerful men in the government forced him to accept Garric as regent and heir. The rulers of the western islands hadn't wanted to believe that anything was really different, but the arrival of the royal fleet and army was changing their minds.

"There's the matter of the upkeep of the three Sandrakkan regiments of the royal army as well, of course," Tadai continued. "That is—"

The sky darkened. It had been a brilliant morning before the conference started, but Garric had been under the marquee long enough that clouds might've blown in from the sea. It wasn't until he heard the shouts of fear and anger from everybody who could see the sky that he realized something was wrong.

He was up from his stone seat and running outside before he thought about what he was doing. That was partly a reflex of King Carus, but shepherds as well as warriors are faced with sudden crises. The reflex that drew the horseman's sword slung on his left side, *that* was from Carus alone.

"Sister take him!" Lord Attaper bellowed. It was an improper thing to say about his prince, but understandable under the circumstances. "Don't let anybody knife his highness in this crowd!"

There were men coming the other way, getting under cover of the marquee while they looked back over their shoulders. Garric shoved them aside. Before he reached the open air, there were Blood Eagles battering a path for him with their shields and breastplates.

The shape of a filthy black giant hung over Erdin. It was a sooty mass rather than the slate gray of even the darkest rain clouds, covering the sun and perhaps a third of the sky. The air all the way around it remained bright. It was monstrously unnatural.

As Garric stared up at the giant's eyes and gaping mouth, he understood why men had run beneath the marquee to avoid looking at the hideous thing. Logically a double layer of sailcloth wasn't much protection, and for all its unpleasantness, the thing seemed to be only a cloud. Logic didn't have much to the feelings the image aroused, though.

"Stand to!" Lord Waldron bellowed from the other end of the marquee. "Form on the standards, Ornifal! Cold steel's the remedy for all the kingdom's enemies, phantoms or not!"

Garric wasn't sure how much good swords would be against a cloud, but the image was already breaking into tatters that drifted eastward like smutty spiderwebs. He looked around him.

After the first frightened shouting, the troops had reacted pretty well. Squads were standing closely together, less formations than clumps but organized nonetheless. Most of the men wore only bits and pieces of armor, but they'd grabbed their shields and spears when the alarm came.

You couldn't train soldiers to deal with everything that might happen, but men whose response to panic was to find weapons and stand with their buddies were going to survive the shocks of war a lot better than other people did. Their commander was likely to survive longer too. . . .

The image in the sky had completely dissipated. *Had it blown in from the sea or just appeared in the clear sky like a meteor?*

Liane was beside him, holding her closed traveling desk against her chest. There were undoubtedly secret documents in it, but Garric suspected it was her equivalent of his bare sword: the desk was a tool familiar from other difficult situations, though inappropriate in this one.

He looked toward the mast of the *City of Valles*; no signal flags were flying. He hadn't expected an answer there, but it'd been worth checking. A trireme was beached beside Zettin's flagship, though, between it and the *Shepherd*. When had that happened?

"What Sister-cursed fool landed *there*?" snapped Admiral Zettin, who'd been with the support staff behind Garric during the negotiations. His sword was drawn, and at a quick glance he looked like any of the other officers looking into the sky or around at their fellows. Then in a different voice he added, "Say—isn't that the *Spiteful*?"

Zettin was the former Deputy Commander of the Blood Eagles. He'd known nothing about naval affairs when Garric put him in charge of the fleet, but he understood training, discipline, and the unit pride that'll often carry a nominally weaker force through a stronger opponent. All those things had been in short supply in the force that Valence the Third had allow to decay. That'd changed abruptly under Zettin.

"Is there a problem, milord?" Garric said, sliding his sword back into the scabbard. At times like this he always felt embarrassed to have drawn the blade, but the one time in a thousand he might *need* a sword was worth slight blushes the hundreds of times it hadn't been required.

"What's that?" the admiral snapped before he turned his head enough to realize who'd spoken to him. "Ah! Ah, I'm not sure, your highness. You see, I left the *Spiteful* with the squadron on guard in Valles. If it's here—"

"Sir?" said a junior officer with a sparkling helmet and gold-chased scabbard mountings. "The *Spiteful*'s brought a courier to Lord Waldron personally. They're talking now."

The young officer was one of the noblemen Zettin had brought into the fleet to lead, rather than one of the mariners who were responsible for ship-handling. It'd disturbed Garric, raised a peasant even if his lineage did go back to the Old Kingdom monarchs, to think that sailors might perform better under the command of lisping young snots of the nobility than they would for professionals of their own class—

But they did. About the only thing these young officers were able to do was to stand on the quarterdeck, a target in dazzling armor for any missile the enemy wanted to launch, and look coolly unperturbed. For the most part they did that superbly, giving their own oarsmen something to think about besides the crushing disaster they might be rowing toward as a flutist blew time for their strokes.

Garric followed the fellow's gesture. Lord Waldron stood with his head bent toward a younger man, who was speaking earnestly to him. Waldron's own aides ringed the pair with worried expressions, but at the distance of a full double pace—too far to hear what was being said.

"*It's a verbal message,*" King Carus mused, and the thought had a grim undertone. "*Something the sender wasn't willing to commit to writing, and he sent it to Waldron instead of you.*"

"It's another omen!" somebody called in a cracked voice.

Garric jerked his head around. Lord Morchan was speaking, his hands clenched against his cheekbones as he stared up at the empty sky. "The final days are surely here! The Gods have deserted Sandrakkan!"

"Morchan, you're a fool and a liar and a whining puppy!" Lady Lelor said, her face white with fury. "The Shepherd hasn't forsaken us and He won't, so long as we act like men!"

"You say!" said Morchan. "You say, priestess! But monsters keep swallowing the sun. Sandrakkan is doomed!"

"What's this all about?" Garric said. Morchan and Lelor were too caught up in their own argument to hear him. "Marshal Renold, what are they talking about? Has something like this happened before?"

The Sandrakkan commander was red-faced and looked uncomfortable. He'd been gripping his sword hilt for much the same reason every other armed man on the island had. Two Blood Eagles noticed and immediately stepped between him and Garric.

Garric grabbed the guards by the shoulders and pushed them to either side so that he could see Renold again. "Marshal Renold, *what* is going on?"

"That I can't say, sir," Renold said awkwardly. "There's been clouds like this over Erdin, that's true; three or four times in the past ten days. They cover the sun, then they go away. Nobody knows what it means, nobody who I've heard anyway. Some people—"

He looked at the priestess with a glumly speculative expression.

"—say that it doesn't mean *anything*, but I doubt even they believe themselves."

Garric thought for a moment. When he could, he'd discuss the business with Tenoctris. She'd been resting when he left her, guarded by a squad of Blood Eagles while Cashel wandered about Volita to loosen his legs, and Sharina observed the negotiations. Right then, however—

"Milady," Garric said to Lady Lelor in a voice loud enough to be noticed through her angry exchange with her fellow envoy. "Gentlemen! We're here to discuss the place of Sandrakkan in the kingdom. Let's return to the business at hand, if you will."

The three Sandrakkan envoys near Garric turned and followed him back under the marquee; the priestess gave him a shamefaced nod of apology. Master Colchas hadn't left his seat. Not, Garric suspected on looking at the man's face, because the finance official was abnormally calm, but rather because he'd suspected what was happening and didn't want to watch it again.

Tadai had walked to the edge of the marquee and looked up. He started back for his seat with a bland expression. The various aides and subordinates were returning to their places behind the negotiators. That left only Lord Waldron, who was still talking to the courier.

"Lord Waldron?" Garric called.

Waldron made a brusque gesture with his left hand, his eyes locked with those of the man who was speaking urgently to him again.

Garric pursed his lips. "Admiral Zettin," he said calmly, "please take the seat to my right for the time being, if you would."

Garric walked to the makeshift throne with an expression just as neutral as that of Lord Tadai. He'd disarranged the cloak when he jumped up, but a servant must've straightened it.

Garric had expected the Sandrakkan negotiations to be the most important thing he'd have to deal with for the next days or even longer. Judging by the furious disbelief on the face of his army commander, though, he'd be hearing about something much worse as soon as Waldron was ready to tell him.

Ilna held the wax tablet in both hands. She was as tense as if it was red-hot and burning her fingers. She took a deep breath.

"Wood is . . . ," she read. She grimaced. "Wood *comes* from the forest."

"That's right, Ilna!" Merota said. They sat together on a stone slab that'd fallen when one of the three columns supporting it slipped sideways sometime in the past thousand years. She held her hand out for the tablet. "Here, I'll write more."

Their moss-covered seat had words carved on it. Ilna could follow the letters well enough to draw them, though to anybody else the tiny green tendrils were as featureless as a polished tabletop.

But she couldn't *read* them, of course.

Ilna let the tablet dip forward slightly and breathed deeply several more times, almost panting. She'd run long distances though running wasn't natural to her; she'd fought, for her own life and for the lives of others; she'd woven patterns that twisted the cosmos itself, warped it into the form that Ilna os-Kenset chose it to have. She'd done all those things and *never* had she been as utterly drained as she was now, shaking and—

The realization struck her. She began to laugh, a reaction she displayed almost as rarely as she cried.

Merota jerked her hand back with a startled expression. Chalcus, juggling as he sat on the back wall of the ruined garden a double pace away, smiled pleasantly; only those who knew him well would've noticed that tension bunched the big muscles at the base of his jaw.

"It's all right," Ilna said, reducing her laughter to a wry smile. "Chalcus, it's all right. I just realized that I'm frightened, simply terrified, of reading. That's why it's so hard for me. Most things—most of the things I *do*—aren't.''

"I think you're doing very well, Ilna," Merota said. She was still too young to know her forced earnestness made her lie obvious. She took the tablet and firmly closed its two waxed boards. "But we've done enough today. I'm tired from being on the ship."

Chalcus chuckled. He'd been juggling three items while Merota gave Ilna her reading lesson. Now he let two of them, fist-sized chips of rock, mossy on one side, drop to the ground behind him; they landed within a finger's breadth of one another. Rising to his feet, he slid the third, his curved dagger, into the sheath stuck through the sash over his right hip.

"Merota, dear child," he said, "there's an hour's wait till supper. Why don't you rouse Mistress Kaline—"

Her governess and tutor, a severe woman with severe notions of propriety. To Ilna's mind, Mistress Kaline's only redeeming feature was the fact that in her way she loved Merota as much as Ilna herself did.

"—and resume your own lessons till Mistress Ilna calls you, eh?"

"Please, Chalcus!" the girl said, clutching the notebook before her. "Can I play in this garden while you talk to Ilna? You know Mistress Kaline's still going to be sick!"

Ilna smiled. Merota was a natural sailor; no matter how much the ship rolled—and a long, narrow warship could roll a great deal, even in moderate weather—the child would scamper around with no more discomfort than Chalcus himself displayed. Ilna, who was not infrequently queasy, envied Merota her stomach at those times.

But Ilna's problems were nothing compared to those of Mistress Kaline, who spent most of every voyage sprawled facedown on a grating, close to the gunwale so that she could stick her head over the side whenever another spasm struck her. She couldn't keep even water or nibbles of dry bread down more than a few minutes. She lay in the shade of a tarpaulin now as usual after a voyage, with a damp cloth on her forehead.

Chalcus looked at Ilna and raised an eyebrow in question. Ilna thought for a moment, then said, "Yes, all right. I'll watch the book. But don't go out of our sight!"

"I won't!" Merota said, trotting toward the ruins of a stone gazebo. Over her shoulder she added, "But what could happen with all these soldiers around?"

"Aye, indeed," said Chalcus in a very different tone as he seated himself where Merota had been. "And what *couldn't* happen, with things like that creature from the Sister's realm appearing in the sky?"

"Yes," said Ilna, looking about them. Her expression was more than a little grim, but that was from habit rather than any particular concern about their surroundings. "Though so long as it stays in the sky . . ."

They were in the extensive gardens of the mansion where Garric was meeting with the dignitaries from Sandrakkan. Buildings and gardens alike were in ruins: the walls shattered, colonnades thrown down, and briars choking the planters meant for exotic flowers. All around them soldiers were chopping brush, clearing places to sleep, and at the same time providing themselves with firewood.

Because the military surveyors hadn't had an opportunity to lay out the camp before the troops arrived, Ilna heard a number of heated arguments between officers of units competing for some desirable attribute: a stretch of level ground, a well that wasn't choked with rubble, or perhaps a large tree that offered both dignity and a vantage point to the troops who controlled it.

A ewe bleated irritably from nearby. It'd come around the blunt finger of granite and found its path was blocked by soldiers cutting a drainage ditch to guide water around their campsite in case of a storm.

Chalcus looked at the sheep and chuckled. "If she's not mutton stew by the morning," he said, "then our friend Garric will have good reason to congratulate himself on his army's discipline . . . and were I to bet, I'd say that she'll be wandering about being irritated at all these strange men till we take ourselves off."

"It was your suggestion that we land on this island, wasn't it, Chalcus?" Ilna said, looking about her. She didn't much care about her surroundings so long as they allowed her to weave—or at least knot patterns—but she was aware of them.

Sheep had grazed the slopes fairly clear, but the rock piles where buildings had been thrown down were overgrown with the wild descendents of ornamental shrubs. The few trees grew in places that were hard to get to. Woodcutters must visit the island regularly.

The soil was trampled bare there in the back part of the garden, which a shepherd had used for his byre. Wool clung to stones and in the brush growing around them. Most of the tufts were unweathered; the fellow must've penned his flock there before taking them on barges to the mainland just ahead of the royal fleet's arrival. The handful of ewes still wandering on Volita were the ones who'd been too skittish to gather up quickly before the shepherd fled.

"Aye, I did," the sailor replied, his tone guarded though not defensive. "When I heard the prince—" he nodded toward the curved wall beyond which the conference was taking place "—wanted a spot where an army could wait without causing too much bother with the local citizens, I mentioned that nobody's spent the night on Volita in the past thousand years save shepherds and sheep. And—"

Chalcus grinned engagingly, as though the next comment were of no great moment.

"—maybe a few pirates, doing business with folk in Erdin who preferred their neighbors not know the sort of men they went to for cargoes at a good price."

Ilna looked around again. She set the notebook on the moss and took the hank of cords from her left sleeve to give her fingers something to do. The lowering sun painted odd shadows on the face of granite spike behind them.

"The Demon, it's called," Chalcus remarked. "Though it was a quiet enough neighbor to the pirates, or so I believe."

"You never saw anything wrong here?" Ilna said. She knew she sounded sharp, but she always sounded sharp. Chalcus understood her well enough not to take offense at a question asked without the ribbons and lace that people in general tied their words up in.

"No, dear one, I did not," Chalcus said calmly. "Some of our folk heard sounds in the night, but that wasn't a marvel. They'd mostly done things that cause men troubles in the hours after the wine's worn off and before the sun rises. Eh?"

Ilna shrugged. "I never thought drink would make the things I've done not have happened," she said. "And if it caused me to lose control—"

She gave a tiny, metallic chuckle, then went on, "I was going to say, 'Who knows what I might do?' But in fact I know very well."

Merota was peering at the waist-high crosswall that the shepherd'd built to separate his byre from the front portion of the extensive garden. He'd laid the wall with pieces of the ruins themselves: facing blocks, masses of cemented rubble from the cores of walls, and broken statues. It'd probably been a one-man job, since the only really heavy stones were column barrels that an individual could've rolled into place.

Merota was staying in plain view as they'd told her to do. Ilna directed quick glances toward the girl, while Chalcus occasionally shifted to keep Merota in the corner of his eye. Though they were being careful, there wasn't any reason to expect more danger there than might have occurred back in the palace in Valles.

"I was wondering, dear one . . ." Chalcus said, his eyes wandering to avoid meeting Ilna's. "Have you given thought to the future?"

"Blaise is east of here, isn't it?" Ilna said, frowning to understand the sailor's point. "I suppose we'll go there, even though Count Lerdoc's friendly. And then we'll go back to Valles."

Ilna'd known more about far places when she was growing up than most people in Barca's Hamlet did. Her weavings were luxury stuff even before Hell taught her how to let or bind the cosmos itself. Ilna hadn't learned geography, however, but rather what the tastes of the folk in Erdin and Piscine and especially in Valles on Ornifal were, the people who bought clothing to demonstrate their wealth and taste.

"Prince Garric will likely visit the Count of Blaise, in the courteous fashion that the great and powerful of this world have with one another, that's true," Chalcus said with an edge to his voice. "But what I was wondering, dear one, was of our future, yours and mine together—for it will be together, you know that, for so long as you'll have me."

Ilna sniffed. "Which will be as long as I live and you live," she said sharply. "What would you have me say? That I'll weave when I have leisure to and do such other business as will help my friends—that's what *I* think of the future."

"And when you say help your friends . . . ," Chalcus said. He'd taken out his dagger again and was flipping it from hand to hand. His eyes watched Merota squirm through a wisteria whose stems were as thick as her waist. "You mean help Prince Garric for the kingdom's sake, where it may be that your skills count for more than a squadron of ships, not so?"

"Yes," said Ilna. "So. As I've done in the past. As we've done together in the past."

She paused, trying to read meaning in the profile that the sailor kept resolutely toward her.

"Is it wrong that I do that, do you think?" she went on. Her voice was growing harder, more clipped, despite her wish that it not. "For I'll tell you frankly, Master Chalcus, *I* don't think it's wrong!"

Chalcus laughed easily, sliding the dagger back into its sheath. "It's not wrong at all, dear heart," he said. "Whoever rules the kingdom will always have a use for such as you; and for me as well, it may be. But if the kingdom uses us at the kingdom's need, there'll come a day when the kingdom has used us up."

Ilna shrugged. She'd felt the tension drain away as soon as she learned that the questions weren't going in the direction she'd feared a moment previously.

"I don't care about kingdoms," she said. "I've never met one. But if Garric wants my help, or Sharina, or my brother . . ."

She smiled, suddenly warm in a fashion that she never could've imagined until the past year changed most of the things she'd learned in the previous eighteen. "Or if *you* want my help, Master Chalcus," she said, "then you'll have whatever I can give. If that means being used up, then I can't say I care. I did enough harm to other people at one time in my life that I won't complain about the cost to me of making amends."

"Well, dear heart," Chalcus said, grinning broadly again. "I'm an honest sailor with nothing on his conscience. But a man who looked a good deal like me sailed in past years with the Lataaene pirates . . . and I shouldn't wonder if that man did terrible things in his time."

"Chalcus?" Merota called. She was clinging to an ancient wisteria that grew where the rubble wall met the finished stones of the garden's original boundary, now half-tumbled. "Why's this statue black? It's basalt! Nobody carves statues out of basalt, do they?"

Chalcus squeezed Ilna's right hand with his left and rose to his feet. "I've never seen such, child," he said as he stepped toward the girl. "Basalt has too coarse a grain, I'd have said; though I suppose sculptors can be struck by freaks as surely as honest sailors who wake up with a girl's name tattooed over their heart and no idea who she might be."

"I scarcely think you can stay that drunk long enough to carve a statue," Ilna said tartly as she followed Chalcus, setting the cords back in her sleeve.

She didn't like stone, just as other people didn't like snakes or spiders; but there was a good deal of stone in the world, so she didn't cringe when she had to deal with it. Likewise there was a sufficient number of people in the world that Ilna didn't like, and she dealt with them too when that was required.

The wisteria flowed upward into a mushroom of green tendrils. The curve of the shrub's three thick stems looked almost natural, but where they bound the black stone figure at the heart of their knot—

"Merota, step back!" Ilna said. "Chalcus, you too. Let me look at this."

In this warm weather Merota was wearing only her inner tunic—normal for a peasant but not up to Mistress Kaline's standards of what was proper for a young noblewoman in public. If the governess managed to get up, she'd be very testy; though of course she was usually very testy.

The tunic was woven from a fine grade of wool, but it was sturdy enough that it didn't tear when Chalcus grabbed a handful and jerked Merota around behind him. His sword was a curved flicker in his right hand. Instead of looking at the wisteria as Ilna did, Chalcus kept his head turning to watch for dangers in all directions.

"It's all right!" Ilna snapped. All she wanted was to concentrate on the problem, but by asking people to get out of the way she'd managed to alarm them. "It's a puzzle, that's all. I just don't want you confusing it."

Faugh! That wasn't what she should've said either! But time to apologize later . . .

The statue had fallen facedown. The wisteria grew around both sides of the chest, with the third stem curving up between the basalt legs.

Ilna squatted, trying to make sense of the pattern. The size of the enveloping vine showed that the statue had been there long before the shepherd built his crosswall; indeed, he might have chosen the line simply to use the tree-sized shrub to anchor one end.

The wisteria was natural and had nothing to do with the reason the black statue was there. The way it grew, however, had been shaped by the same forces that bound the statue, the same spell that bound the statue. . . .

Ilna rose and turned. The soldiers at work just the other side of the garden wall weren't paying attention to the civilians.

"You there!" she said to the man just straightening from chopping roots that his fellows couldn't shovel through. "Lend me that hand axe, if you would!"

"This, mistress?" the soldier said, looking from Ilna to his hatchet with a puzzled expression.

"Yes, you ninny!" Ilna said. She regretted the word as it came out of her mouth, but he *was* a ninny. "The axe, please!"

Chalcus lifted away the tool with a graceful sweep of his left hand. He hadn't sheathed his sword, but he now held it unobtrusively down along his right leg.

"I can—" he said as he held the axe toward but not quite *to* Ilna.

"You may not!" Ilna said. She snatched the axe with a good deal less grace than Chalcus had displayed. "If this isn't done in *just* the right way, we'll crush it instead of freeing it. Just give me a little room!"

Tenoctris talked of seeing the forces with which wizards work. She'd explained that wizards focused the lines of force with words and symbols, and with objects that'd soaked those forces into their substance. The best focus of all was the lifeblood pumping from a severed throat, but only the strongest could even hope to control forces of the volume *that* created. From Ilna's observation, even the very strong were usually wrong when they thought they were that powerful.

Ilna couldn't see threads of force, but in this case she could follow the distortion they caused in the way the vine grew. It was like following the path of a cat through high grass by the waving seed heads.

She judged her spot, then chopped twice. The axe flicked out a thumb-deep wedge of bark and fibrous wood. She'd split kindling every day with a hatchet very similar to this one, and her loom's shuttle and beater board kept her wrists and forearms strong.

After the initial cut, Ilna edged around to get the angle she needed for the stem on the other side of the statue's torso. That meant climbing onto the knee-high remnant of the garden wall and bracing her left arm on the stem. She could go much deeper this time since by scoring the first stem she'd relieved the stresses that'd otherwise have been building opposite her strokes.

The stem began to wobble beneath her left hand. Wisteria this old tended to be more brittle than ordinary trees of the same thickness. Ilna paused, leaning back to take stock. Smiling, she stepped to the left side of the statue. The stem between its legs wasn't really part of the pattern; it was there for the same reason a blue thread and a yellow thread laid together made the person seeing them think of green.

Chalcus, holding Merota's hand, moved around to the side Ilna had just left. The child had a wide-eyed expression; if she'd been offended by the sailor's quick manhandling, there was no sign of it.

Ilna touched the notch her first strokes had made. The hatchet was iron and completely of this world. Its presence severed the unseen veins of the binding spell at the same time it cut through the woody stem.

"Now . . . ," she said, speaking to bring her concentration to the precise spot. She chopped into the center of the notch, twisted the hatchet free, and chopped again. Changing the angle, she made a third cut that spat out a chunk of wood the size of her fist.

The stem above the notch shook convulsively. Ilna bent it back with the flat of her left hand, then chopped a final time with all her strength. The stem broke, toppling sideways under the pull of its heavy foliage.

"There!" Ilna cried. She set the hand axe down.

The statue shifted. It twisted its face up, no longer basalt but a stocky man lying nude on the ground. "Get back!" he shouted. "You'll be caught when—"

Ilna plunged forward as the world around her blurred. She thought she heard Merota scream, but she couldn't be sure because the very fabric of the cosmos was shrilling about her.

The last thing Ilna saw in this world was the great granite spike glaring down at them. It looked almost human.

Cashel hadn't exactly been following the ewe, but he'd wandered around the granite spike alongside her, keeping two or three double paces away. Now and again you'd find a ewe that was jumpy about lambs she'd suckled, let alone human beings. This was one such. Some sheep were just like that, and some people too, of course.

The ewe had a stye in her left eyelid that ought to be drained, but it didn't seem her regular shepherd had managed to do it. Cashel figured he would, at any rate, if they stayed on this little island for a few days. It was a way to make it up to the shepherd who'd had to run when the fleet arrived; and anyway, the ewe would appreciate it.

A wren hung upside down on the trunk of a dogwood, singing with the loud determination of his kind. Other birds sing and maybe sing to you, but there was never any doubt that a wren was singing *at* the whole world. They were smart, talented little birds, pretty though without the flashy colors that got the attention; and they were also just as hard as the cracked boulder in which the dogwood tree had rooted.

Cashel smiled. Wrens reminded him of his sister Ilna.

He paused beside the boulder. The ewe stopped also. For a moment she stared at Cashel with one eye, then the other. At last she lowered her head and began to graze.

From there Cashel could look out over the island's east shore, the same view across the Inner Sea that he'd had from the pasture south of Barca's Hamlet. Ships were drawn up all along the beach below. Soldiers were setting up camp like ants scrambling to rebuild the hill an ox had trod on.

There was no end of ruins, houses fallen into rock piles and overgrown with brush. They'd been built with fancy stones, some of them, pinks and greens and yellows that showed through the alders and euonymus if you knew how to look. They were all knocked down, now. Sails for tarpaulins spread up and down the shore to shelter the soldiers and sailors from the forest of ships.

The ewe suddenly turned and bolted, her jaws still working with the sidewise rolling motion sheep and cows too used to grind up their food. Cashel heard the scrunch of boots to his right and leaned around the corner of the boulder to see.

A soldier was walking up the slope. There was no doubt what he was from the hobnailed boots, but he was using his spear, the only piece of equipment he carried, as a walking stick the way Cashel did his quarterstaff.

"Hello there," Cashel said, stepping into full sight so it wouldn't look like he was hiding behind the boulder. The soldier was a sturdy fellow, built like Cashel though on a smaller scale. His face and forearms were wind-burned, and there was a dent across his forehead where his helmet would rest.

"Hello yourself," the soldier said, looking startled. Cashel guessed the fellow was four or five years older than his own nineteen, though he'd noticed time in the army could do different things from ordinary life. "That your sheep?"

"No," said Cashel. "I'm a stranger here myself."

He heard the challenge in the other man's tone, but he wasn't going to let it put him out. Cashel felt cramped and uncomfortable on shipboard, and he knew that the common soldiers were packed in a good deal tighter than Garric and his friends were.

"Because if she is, she's got a stye on her left eye that oughta be taken care of," the soldier said.

"I noticed that," said Cashel patiently. "I figured the regular shepherd went to the mainland when the ships came, so I was going to drain it for him. I still will, when I get close to her again."

The fellow'd come up so they were both standing on the same stretch of level ground. He was a hand's breadth shorter than Cashel and probably that much narrower across the shoulders, but he was a husky man by most standards.

"Leggy devil, ain't she?" the soldier said, looking in the direction the ewe'd run off. "Putting horse legs on a sheep just wastes good feed that could go to wool and mutton."

"You'd be from Ornifal, then?" Cashel said. Ornifal sheep were short-legged butterballs, all right for flat meadows but nothing he'd have wanted to watch on the slopes of the borough. They went to market by water, he'd heard, because you couldn't drive them ten miles in a day.

"Aye, I am," the soldier said in surprise. "You know sheep, then, master?"

"Aye," Cashel said, not bragging exactly but letting his spreading smile tell the other fellow that he could've said a good deal more on the subject and not told a lie. "I'm from Haft, myself."

"Ah," said the soldier. "I've seen Haft sheep. They're three colors all on the same animal, ain't they?"

"That's so," Cashel agreed. "And a finer, softer fleece you couldn't hope to find."

The soldier hawked and spat. "Well, there's tastes and tastes," he said. "My name's Memet or-Meisha."

Memet leaned his spear against the boulder and thrust out his right forearm. Cashel took it, clamping his hand just below Memet's elbow.

"Cashel or-Kenset," he said. "Did they send you up here to find something, Master Memet?"

"No, I'm off duty," the soldier said. He turned his face away with a frown of embarrassment. "I ought to be sleeping, I guess, I'll have guard duty tonight, but . . ."

He let his eyes follow the ewe. She'd stopped a few double paces away and was grazing again. *The poor thing's scared*, Cashel thought. *She'd like to have that stye drained but she's too afraid to come to us.*

"I saw the sheep up here, you see," Memet said. "I was a shepherd back in County Hordin, but my mum died and Dad and me'd got to where nei-ther of us could say three civil words to the other. I figured I'd go for a soldier and be paid in silver. I'd come back with more money'n anybody else in the county 'cepting the Squire and marry who I pleased. That's what I figured."

"Ah," said Cashel without putting any weight on the word. He leaned against the sun-warmed boulder and used the stone to rub him where he couldn't reach, just the way a sheep would've done. "Most folks think money's a fine thing, or so it seems."

"So I hear," Memet said with a wry smile. "May the Sister strike me if I know where mine goes from one pay parade to the next, though."

He faced his palm out. "I'm not complaining, mind," he said. "I spend it myself, I know that. And if I've got help spending it, well, I pick the ones who help me."

He shook his head at the memory. "There's something about blondes," he said. "We never had blondes in County Hordin except the Squire's lady."

"I miss sheep too, since I've been traveling," Cashel admitted. "You know, if we just wait here a bit, I'll bet she'll come over to us. She must be really scared with the rest of the flock gone off and her left behind."

"Aye, that's so," Memet agreed. He glanced at the rock beside him, then said, "Say, take a look here. What do you figure this is that's carved here?"

Cashel moved around to the soldier's side of the boulder. It was carved, no doubt about that. It looked like the lines'd been touched with ochre, too, though most of the red had been washed away during rainy winters. But what it was—

A tall triangle, base down. A shorter triangle, base up below the tall one. A round ball, or as round as you can carve even in limestone with simple tools. The work'd probably been done with an iron knife a lot like the one Cashel and every other man in the borough hung from his belt. Lines from the open sides of each triangle, maybe meant for arms and legs.

"We had a stone up in the South Pasture where we offered bread and cheese to Duzi on feast days," Cashel said carefully. "Of course Duzi was just a little god who couldn't help me since I've left the borough. But you know, I still sometimes—"

"There's an oak where we'd hang offerings to Enver," Memet said in the same tone of quiet embarrassment. "I thought of that too."

"You're correct in your assumptions," said a female voice from behind them. Cashel turned *fast* and took a step back. That was a mistake because it put him onto the slope. He jabbed his quarterstaff down, digging one ferrule into the soil to keep from falling.

"Shepherds worship the nymph Serkit here," said a woman with tightly braided black hair and a face like polished ivory. The nails of her right hand were enameled sapphire blue, while those of her left were ruby. "She wards off lightning and protects the flock from scrapie."

Cashel stepped up onto flat ground again, though he kept to the side so he wasn't crowding the lady. She wore the usual two tunics cinched with a sash. They were as lustrous as silk, but Cashel was sure that the fabric was something different. You didn't grow up with Ilna and not learn about cloth.

"Lady?" said Memet. He was thinking as Cashel did: whoever the woman was and wherever she came from, she wasn't a peasant girl. "Aren't you afraid to be here with so many soldiers?"

"Afraid?" she said. She sniffed. "Afraid of *you*?"

"Not me," the soldier said, blushing. "But all these other people. Men."

"No," the woman said, "I'm not."

Cashel stood eyeing her closely, his staff planted upright at his side. She turned her attention to him, but before she could speak, he said, "Lady, who are you?"

From any distance he'd have guessed the woman was thirty years old. Something at the back of her eyes was much older than that, for all that her complexion was as perfect as a baby's.

"You can call me Mab," she said, "but that doesn't matter. What matters, Cashel or-Kenset, is that your mother is in great danger. Unless you help her, she'll have no help and no hope. Will you come with me?"

"*My* mother?" Cashel said. He turned his head and looked down. The shore below was the same jumble of ships and bustling men that it'd been a moment ago. He wasn't dreaming, then. "Lady, I don't have—"

He broke off before he finished what would've been as silly a thing as he'd ever said in his life. Everybody had a mother, whether or not they'd met her.

"Lady," Cashel said. He swallowed. "I don't understand."

Memet was looking from Cashel to the woman, his mouth slightly open. He rubbed his eyes with the back of his hand, so he must've been wondering about being awake or dreaming too.

"There's very little to understand," Mab said in a thin tone. "You'll come with me now, before the portal closes, or you'll leave your mother to her fate. If you choose the latter, you won't be man enough to help her in this crisis anyway."

Cashel laughed. "I said I didn't understand, not that I was afraid," he said gently. "I still don't understand, but I'm used to that. When will we leave?"

"We'll leave immediately, from this place," Mab said. "The shrine will make it easier. Are you ready?"

"Yes," said Cashel. He smiled at the soldier, and said, "I guess you'll have to take care of the ewe yourself, Memet. But before you do, please tell Sharina that I've gone—"

He wasn't sure what to say next. "Well, tell her what you heard here," he said, "because that's as much as I know. That's Princess Sharina of Haft I mean."

"Come now, or you won't be able to come," the woman said crisply. She stepped around to the side of the boulder where the carving was. Her bright nails traced a pattern in the air. "Here, stand facing the shrine."

Cashel grimaced and obeyed. He'd rather a lot of things, but he knew there were times you had to act without worrying about the details. Mab didn't seem any more the sort to exaggerate than Ilna was, or Cashel himself.

She was standing behind him, murmuring words of power. Her hands moved above Cashel's head, then to both sides of him. He felt the tingle of energies building.

The air danced in a cocoon of red and blue wizardlight. The solid rock gaped into a doorway.

"Tell Sharina I love her!" Cashel said. He strode into the opening with his quarterstaff before him.

Sharina sat as primly as she could with the other specialists ready to advise Prince Garric. The servants had fixed her a throne of sorts: a wide-mouthed storage jar, upended and covered with a swatch of aquamarine silk brocade. Though backless, the result was attractive enough to pass muster in a real palace.

Unfortunately, the potter'd left a central lump when he cut his work off the wheel. Normally that'd just mean the jar rocked if it were set on a hard surface instead of being part-buried in sand. It was a real problem during the jar's present use, however. Sharina had quickly learned to check with her hand the next time before sitting down to listen to hours of negotiation.

One of Lord Waldron's aides was speaking to Liane. She'd turned her head sideways but continued to take notes in the tablet in front of her. Liane's expression showed mild interest, but her stylus scored quick, brutal marks in the wax.

Lord Waldron was still missing. He'd gone off with the courier, his head bobbing in angry argument. He'd given no explanation, just snarled over his shoulder that his staff should remain under the marquee. Sharina'd seen Waldron in circumstances where he reasonably expected to die in a short time, but his expression had never before been so bleakly miserable.

"I'm sorry, Marshal Renold," Garric said in the same calmly reasonable voice he'd have used on a merchant who was sure he could get a private room during the Sheep Fair if only he kept saying so long enough. "Three regiments is the minimum that Sandrakkan must supply to the royal army and provide the upkeep for."

Lord Tadai leaned forward with a stern expression, and added, "I'll tell you frankly that according to my estimate of Earl Wildulf's potential revenue and manpower, Sandrakkan should be providing four regiments. It's only King Valence's unwillingness to insult the Count of Blaise, who's supplying three regiments, that decided him to reduce the Sandrakkan levy."

In her fatigued discomfort, Sharina took a moment to parse exactly what Tadai had just said. Because of that delay, she managed not to chortle in amusement. *You couldn't even call Tadai's words a lie because nobody was expected to believe them. He'd been polite, but he'd made it perfectly clear to the Sandrakkan delegation the direction in which the royal position would move if they kept belaboring the point.*

Lord Morchan thumped his fist on the table, making the Sandrakkan side bounce wildly. "Curse it, we shouldn't be here!" he blurted. "Everybody knows Volita's cursed. That's why none of this makes any sense!"

It seemed to Sharina that the negotiations, though tedious, had been very productive. They'd involved the Sandrakkan envoys giving way on one point after another, of course, but that was primarily because Garric's position—the royal position—had been reasonable to begin with.

Admiral Zettin drew himself up straight and said in the drawl affected by the Valles nobility, "Quite the contrary, my good man. We've made great headway, and we'll make more. That's surely better than sweeping all

Sandrakkan commerce from the Inner Sea and burning the estates within five miles of the shore. Not so?"

"Look, I'm just saying that we ought to get off Volita," Morchan insisted truculently. "It's an uncanny place, that's all. Everybody knows that if you go up to the top of the Demon—"

He bobbed his head, presumably indicating the granite spike that wasn't visible from under the marquee.

"—you'll see a wonder—but you may never come down again!"

"Morchan," said Lady Lelor in a poisonously calm voice, "if you'd give us just a little help, we'd all pretend to ignore the fact you're a superstitious ninny. Do you know a soul who's climbed—"

"Everybody knows what I say is the truth, milady!" Morchan snapped. Marshal Renold, seated between them, leaned back from the table with a sour look and his eyes unfocused.

"Everybody isn't such a fool!" the priestess said. "Do you know even a *sheep* who's climbed the Demon, Lord Morchan?"

Morchan stood up, his face white. His mouth opened and closed silently. He repeated the process, then sat—collapsed into his seat like a pricked bladder—again, blushing furiously.

Sharina looked at the embarrassed nobleman with a rush of sympathy that surprised her. Morchan was superstitious, and he was a ninny—which he'd proved amply in the course of the negotiations. But he was also more right than wrong in what he'd said about Volita.

Sharina would've known that even without Tenoctris' warning as the fleet landed. Volita was a center of power. Sitting there was like being in a wind blowing sand too fine to see but which prickled through your tunics. Her eyes felt scratchy no matter how often she blinked.

Tenoctris had said that some people were more affected than others. Sharina supposed that she herself might be one of the sensitive ones, if only because of the things she'd been a part of in the year since she left Barca's Hamlet. Everyone on the island must feel it to a degree, but . . .

Sharina smiled. She'd learned a great deal about politics in the past year. Her brother was uncomfortable also, but by smiling and holding his position with bland insistence, he had an advantage over the less-disciplined Sandrakkan envoys. Their present loud squabble was an example of that, and their irritable fidgeting throughout had been made worse by an atmosphere charged with wizardry.

"Lady Lelor," Garric said in a voice raised enough to end the bickering across the table.

When everybody looked at him he went on, "Milords. We've decided the general form of Sandrakkan's future place in the kingdom. The details can be worked out over the next days or if necessary months. The only outstanding point is the fashion in which I enter Erdin."

"What—" Marshal Renold said, then stopped.

"My preferred option is to cross the strait tomorrow"—he nodded toward the beach and the mainland visible beyond it—"with my bodyguard regiment, the Blood Eagles, and a single line regiment, one of Blaise infantry under their own officers. The remainder of the army will camp here on Volita until after—"

"Your highness, that's not safe!" Lord Attaper said, standing at the right of the table. Till he spoke, he'd been only another of the guards. "You need—"

Garric turned without rising from his seat. "Lord Attaper!" he said. *"Be silent!"*

One of the Blood Eagles dropped his spear with a clatter. He grabbed for it, fumbled, and finally picked it up in both hands.

"Right," said Garric in a quiet, shaky voice. *The atmosphere worked on everybody, whether or not they were generally able to control their reactions.* "That's my preferred option, as I say. The other choice, milady and lordships, is for me to march in at the head of the entire royal army."

He licked his lips, forced a smile that Sharina could just see from where she sat, and continued, "In the first case I'll crown Earl Wildulf on the steps of the temple in two days' time."

"Your highness . . . ," said Lady Lelor carefully. "Earl Wildulf will be persuaded of the reasonableness of your arguments, I'm sure. But it may take some time—"

Garric rose to his feet. "I hope Earl Wildulf will be able to send me an answer before the second hour tomorrow, milady," he said, "because that's when I'll begin making preparations for the next stage of the proceedings. There must be extensive planning, as you can imagine. Whichever choice the earl makes."

Liane got to her feet. "All rise!" she said, putting a close to the negotiations on Garric's behalf. Sharina stood gratefully in the coughs and shuffling of all the others under the marquee.

The Sandrakkan envoys rose and started toward their waiting barge. The priestess paused, leaning over the conference table. "Your highness," she said, "there was a foolish rumor that you weren't really a member of the royal house. I can't imagine who started it, but I'll assure you that nobody who's met you in person will credit it."

Garric watched the delegates leave. His back was straight, but Sharina could see tension in the way the muscles of her brother's neck and shoulders bunched.

Admiral Zettin was talking at Garric about plans and options. His tone was professional, but he was obviously exulting at the fact he'd been chosen to fill the seat that Lord Waldron vacated.

Triumph had blinded Zettin, ordinarily a very intelligent man, to the obvious: Prince Garric was lost in his own thoughts. He wasn't listening to a word of his admiral's self-satisfied babble.

Liane hovered at Garric's left side, afraid to touch him or even speak. Sharina stepped up to the table, brushing her brother with one shoulder and forcing Admiral Zettin back with the other. Garric's fists were clenched against the front of his thighs. She covered his right fist with her left hand.

"Do they know how many people will die if Wildulf doesn't listen to reason?" Garric said in a shaky voice. "Do *you* know, Sharina?"

"I know that not as many will die as would if the kingdom fell apart again," she said calmly, turning toward her brother. "We'd start with the islands fighting one another. Then there'd be something else that'd sweep us all away, sweep away everything human. You know there would, Garric!"

Liane touched Garric's left fist. Many members of Garric's entourage wanted to speak with him, but they were giving space to the two women. "This is the millennium," Liane said. "It requires the united strength of the Isles to prevent the powers from tearing everything apart when they reach their peak, as they did a thousand years ago."

Garric shook himself like a dog come in from the rain. He put his arms around Sharina's and Liane's shoulders and gave them a firm squeeze. "Now . . . ," he said, turning to face those who'd waited under the marquee to advise or simply observe, "We've got our own planning to do. Who's Waldron's deputy? I need to know—"

"I'm here, your highness," said Lord Waldron, pushing through the crowd of common soldiers who'd been watching the conference from outside. There was no sign of the courier who'd led him off. "I'm here, but I'm bringing worse news than I ever imagined I'd have to bear."

"All right," said Garric. He sounded calm. The tremble was gone from his voice, and his muscles had relaxed into their usual supple readiness. He gestured to the seat across from where he stood, the one Marshal Renold had vacated. "Sit if you like, but *speak*."

"I'll stand, thank you," Waldron said with harshly minimal courtesy. He looked around at the crowd—gaping, murmuring, gesturing to friends to come close and hear the revelations—and for a moment flushed with the fury that was so much part of him normally.

The anger vanished like a snuffed candleflame, replaced by an unfamiliar gray misery. "A man who calls himself Valgard, son of Valence Strong-hand, has raised a rebellion on Ornifal against what he chooses to call his senile brother Valence the Third and the Haft peasant Garric."

Waldron shrugged in stiff-faced embarrassment. He was standing as stiffly as if he'd been tied to a stake to be burned.

"Go on, Lord Waldron," Garric said in the same pleasant tone as before. Sharina, knowing her brother, understood why he was so calm. The Earl of Sandrakkan could choose either war or peace. If he chose war, then thousands would die, and the kingdom might tilt toward collapse, and Garric would never doubt that the fault was his for not handling the negotiations properly.

That responsibility was terrifying. A usurper in open revolt was a merely a tactical problem, not one in which a mistake would turn peace into war.

"This Valgard—and he has a wizard named Hani with him, *behind* him I shouldn't wonder . . . ," Waldron continued. "He's gathered a band of fools to support him. I'm very sorry to admit that my cousin Bolor bor-Warriman is one of those fools."

Waldron took a shuddering breath. There were tears at the corners of his eyes. "My lord prince, I beg you accept my resignation as commander of the royal army. I need to return to Ornifal to deal with a family problem!"

"Request denied, Lord Waldron," Garric said easily. "At least until you've helped the kingdom deal with a problem that isn't limited to the bor-Warrimans. Now—"

"I'll capture the *Spiteful* and the traitors aboard her, your highness!" Attaper said. "Okkan, sound Assemble on the Standards!"

"No!" said Lord Waldron. "My word is—"

"Okkan, put down that trumpet!" Garric thundered, pointing his whole left arm at the Blood Eagle signaler. Okkan froze, his silver-mounted instrument to his lips. His eyes sought Attaper's.

"Your highness!" said Attaper, "this is the kingdom's business, not—"

"Yes!" said Garric, his voice riding down that of his guard commander. "And if the courier who brought us first news of a rebellion wasn't on the kingdom's business, who is?"

He turned to Waldron. "Now, milord," he continued mildly, even cheerfully. "Just how dangerous do you judge this affair to be?"

This isn't my brother, Sharina thought. But that was only partly true, because this self-composed prince was the person her brother could have grown into on his own.

The spirit of King Carus provided Garric with political experience that no nineteen-year-old peasant could have amassed; but much of that experience was of how *not* to do things, as Carus himself would be the first to say. It was Garric's own quick, disciplined intelligence that had just avoided a crisis by refusing to arrest a rebel under circumstances that would have dishonored his army commander in the eyes of his family, his class, and himself.

"It'd be serious if we let it grow," Waldron said, "but of course we won't. Bolor thinks the levies he can draw from the northern districts can sweep away the regiments you left in Valles. He might be right."

Waldron cleared his throat and looked down; the toe of his right boot gouged the ground. He straightened again and glared at Garric, a fierce old man who couldn't understand the concept that honor might *not* be dearer than life.

"Look," he went on, "I don't want you to misunderstand what just happened. Bolor was giving me warning so that I could run before you learned about the rebellion and had me executed. He was a fool to think that I'd run, but he wasn't so great a fool as to imagine that I'd harm the prince to whom I pledged my loyalty."

The trireme that'd brought the courier was getting under way. The oarsmen were probably upset not to be given a chance to rest now that they'd reached Volita.

Sharina smiled. It could've been a *lot* worse for everybody aboard the ship if Garric weren't in charge.

"Of course, your cousin knew he was dealing with a bor-Warriman," Garric said. "As do I."

Garric sighed and bent deeply forward, stretching his locked hands backward and up to loosen muscles cramped by the previous hours of negotiation. He straightened.

"Lord Attaper," he said, "have your men move people two double paces away from this marquee. I'm going to meet here with my inner cabinet, and the discussions may require privacy."

Garric quirked a smile. "And does anybody know where Lady Tenoctris is?" he added. "Because if there's a wizard involved with this business, I want to know what she thinks about it."

"I'll get Tenoctris," said Sharina, squeezing her brother's shoulder as she turned to trot off to where she knew the old wizard lay in her shelter. "And I couldn't agree with you more!"

Chapter Three

Garric sat at the makeshift conference table and for a moment rested his face on his hands, rubbing his brows and cheekbones hard. *There's too much for one man to do*, he thought in a sudden rush of despair.

"No, there's not," said the image of King Carus, grinning at Garric with cheerful understanding. *"Not if he's the right man, as you are, lad. Not if you do the part that has to be done."*

And that, of course, was the key: first things first. In a swirling battle, the spirit of Garric's warrior ancestor generally took charge. Afterward Garric was always surprised at how little he remembered—how little he'd actually *seen* while the fight was going on. Carus focused only on essentials: the shimmer of movement to the side that was the edge of an axe; the bare wrist between an opponent's mail shirt and his gauntlet; the slight lift of a creature's upper lip that meant its lionlike jaws were about to gape wide enough for the point of a thrusting sword.

The same was true in any complicated situation, and the politics of a kingdom could be more complicated than any mere battle. You had to deal with the crucial items while the rest waited, no matter how important those lesser things might've appeared by themselves.

"And doing that was harder for me by a long sight that deciding who to put my sword through next ever was, lad," Carus said with a wistful smile. *"I marvel to watch you, I swear I do."*

Garric lowered his hands and smiled at the women and men around him: Liane, Sharina, and Tenoctris; Tadai, Waldron, Attaper, and Zettin. They were his close companions, many of them friends and even those who weren't friends—Lord Waldron certainly wasn't a friend—were people whom he respected and who respected him.

Cashel and Ilna weren't here. Garric wasn't surprised that they hadn't been located in time for an emergency meeting, but he regretted their absence. Cashel and Ilna weren't sophisticated, but they shared a clarity of vision that cut to the heart of problems where others tangled in the nonessential fringes.

Peasant wisdom—the part that wasn't superstition and platitudes, at least—was merely common sense. That was as valuable in high governmental circles as it was most other places.

Waldron still stood, glowering at the world at large. Garric pointed to the stool at his right, which Admiral Zettin had properly vacated for the army commander. "Sit down, milord," he said a trifle peevishly. "I'm not going to make Lady Tenoctris stand, nor do I care to look up at you while we're trying to solve the present problem."

Waldron glared for an instant. Before Garric had to repeat what was, after all, a royal command, he sat down. "I still say it's a family problem," he muttered, but he wasn't really arguing.

"If your cousin were intriguing over the title to your estate, Waldron," Garric said, "I'd agree with you. As it is—well, more than half the army comes from Ornifal."

"And three-quarters of my officers," added Zettin, who'd placed an upended bucket at one end of the table for his seat. "The common sailors could be from anywhere, but an officer whose home and family are under a usurper's control, well . . ."

Lord Attaper shrugged. "When Sandrakkan rebelled twenty years ago," he said, "King Valence took the army to Sandrakkan and put down the rebellion. If the rebels're on Ornifal, I still think it's work for the army."

He looked up from his hands on the table before him, to Garric, then to Waldron. Both soldiers were nobles from Northern Ornifal, but Attaper was from a minor house with less land and money than some prosperous yeomen in the west of the island. He'd joined the army from necessity and risen through skill, intelligence, and unswerving loyalty first to Valence the Third, then to Garric when Valence abdicated in all but name.

Waldron was a warrior beyond question, but he commanded because he was head of the richest and most powerful of the northern families, who traditionally provided officers and cavalry regiments for the royal army. He considered Attaper an upstart who needed to remember his place, while Attaper viewed Waldron as arrogant and narrow to the point of being a fool.

"Rivalry isn't an altogether bad thing, though," Carus said, musing on the problem. *"Since they're both honorable men—and bloody good soldiers too, in their ways."*

"Ornifal isn't rebelling!" Waldron snapped. "Not yet, at any rate, but that'll change in a heartbeat if this boy from Haft sails back at the head of an army."

He turned from Attaper, across the table, to Garric beside him with an apologetic grimace. "Sorry, your highness, but that's what they'll say, you know."

"Understood," Garric said calmly. He wished he could feel like a boy again; though he'd thought he'd had problems when he lived in his father's inn. It was all a matter of your viewpoint, he supposed.

Admiral Zettin pursed his lips. He was in his mid-thirties, a decade younger than Attaper and only half Waldron's age. The royal fleet had had low status during most of the past millennium, but Zettin had accepted the appointment with enthusiasm. He was working to bring his command up to the standards of the Blood Eagles, where he'd served as Attaper's deputy.

"Is it possible," he said, "that this Valgard really is the son of Valence Stronghand? I realize it's still a rebellion, but—"

"There's *no* possibility!" Waldron said. "Bolor says the fellow claims to have been born to a princess of the People whom Stronghand captured in the Battle of the Tides. Supposedly Stronghand sent him back with the mother to be fostered in her country. There weren't any women with the People! I'll swear to that, and so will anybody else who was there!"

Garric frowned. "The People?" he repeated. "Who are they? I don't . . ."

"Ornifal was invaded from the east in the fourth year of King Valence the Second," Liane said.

"That's Stronghand," Waldron said, looking glumly at his hands again. "Everybody called him Stronghand after the Battle of the Tides, but to tell the truth, he never was that again. He took a spear in the hip joint and fought another hour with it sticking out of him, the point stuck in bone. But it ruined him, it used him up."

Liane had opened her traveling desk. She reached among the books filed in pigeonholes within, then stopped with a stricken look on her face.

"I didn't bring it," she said in barely a whisper. "I didn't think I'd need—"

She broke off, clacked the desk shut, and resumed in a crisply businesslike tone, "That was forty-nine years ago, I believe."

She grimaced, and returned to the snarling whisper to add, "I should have brought the *Eastern Chronicles* with me!"

Reise'd given his children an education in the classic literature of the Old Kingdom. He hadn't taught them modern history, though, the history of the age in which they lived—because he wasn't interested in the subject.

Garric didn't know who'd preceded his real mother, Countess Tera, on the throne of Haft, let alone what had been happening across the Inner Sea on Ornifal generations ago. This was one of the rare times that he felt the lack of that knowledge.

"Forty-nine years, right," said Lord Waldron, looking up at a corner of the marquee while his mind stepped briefly into the past. "I was there, in Lord Elphic's squadron, my foster father. . . ."

"Yes," said Garric, hoping to cut off a digression into history that—however interesting in the abstract—had no bearing on the present problem. "We can be sure that this Valgard is an imposter, but since he's been accepted by Lord Bolor—and I assume others—already, that doesn't help us."

"It could," Waldron said, returning to the present with the crashing abruptness of a cavalry charge. "It *will* if I'm there to talk to Bolor and the others like him. The claim's preposterous, and they'll believe me when I tell them that to their faces."

"Granting what you say for the sake of argument," Lord Tadai said, touching his fingertips together in a precise pattern. "There'll be others in the conspiracy purely for the hope of gaining wealth, and very likely there are supporters of the former queen who've been hiding since we overthrew her. They know they won't be safe until we, that is Prince Garric, are put down in turn."

"There'll be rabble," Waldron snapped. He knew Tadai well enough to respect him, but he and the Valles merchant had so little in common that they consistently spoke past one another while trying to hold discussions. "There's always rabble. But it's the northern squadrons who're a danger to the kingdom, not bullies and footpads!"

"That may be," Tadai said in a pointedly patient tone. "And you may be right to discount the presence of a wizard with the conspirators as well. But it appears to me that this rabble has a vested interest in not allowing you to have a manly, honorable chat with your cousin and neighbors as you seem to intend. I'm not usually an advocate of military force, but I'm afraid in this instance it seems necessary. If you go to Ornifal without the army, you'll be assassinated."

"And while I understand your concern about my presence inflaming the situation," Garric said, nodding to Waldron, "I don't want to give the false impression that Ornifal is less important to me than Sandrakkan. I think I need to deal with Valgard myself."

"*Not* without the army!" said Attaper. With a pained expression he raised both hands before him to forestall the reaction his outburst merited. Apologetically he offered an edited version: "That is, I hope you won't go without the army, your highness."

"No, I won't," Garric said, smiling faintly. King Carus in his mind wore a rueful expression. If one of *his* officers had flared at him that way, Carus would've had his sword clear of its sheath before the statement was complete. They both knew that would've been a bad response. "While I think, I *hope*, that the presence of the army will convince Valgard's supporters to put down their arms, in the end I'm afraid Lord Attaper is correct. Rebels are rebels, wherever they are."

"Your highness," Waldron said, clasping his heavy belt in both hands to keep them away from the hilt of his sword. He looked down at the table for a moment before he was able to raise his eyes to meet Garric's. "Your highness, send me and one of the Ornifal regiments. Let me try. Please. For the sake of—"

He paused, then burst out, "For the sake of the kingdom!"

"Garric?" Sharina said. She was sitting across the table from him in the seat Lady Lelor had filled during the negotiations. "If Lord Waldron goes back with enough soldiers for safety—"

She quirked a smile that perfectly mirrored the one Garric felt bending his own lips. They both knew that no number of soldiers could guarantee safety.

"Anyway . . . ," Sharina continued. "If Waldron goes back, and I go with him—then you're neither slighting Ornifal nor antagonizing those who don't like the thought of being ruled by—"

She grinned very broadly, at Garric, then at Waldron beside him.

"—a warrior king from Haft, let's say," she concluded.

"That would also permit your highness to conclude the present negotiations with Earl Wildulf without appearing to be under pressure," Liane said, holding a document that seemed to have been written on a sheet of lead foil, like a curse to be buried in a graveyard. "While I don't want to seem alarmist, it's public knowledge that there's hostility toward the kingdom at all levels of Sandrakkan society, and other indications—"

Her spies, she meant. Liane appeared to have agents on every island, though for the most part she kept their operations secret even from Garric.

"—suggest that there would be a very real danger of revolt if your highness were to suddenly withdraw with the royal army at this stage."

Garric took a deep breath. He smiled, but the expression didn't go deeper than his lips. "Doesn't anybody think I ought to go to Valles?" he asked.

The truth was, *he* didn't want to return to Ornifal, not under these circumstances. He'd never felt comfortable in the society of the Valles court. Half of Ornifal's nobles viewed him as the next thing to a usurper, and all of them to some degree resented him for being from Haft. Whatever they might say in public, they knew in their hearts that Garric's ancestors had raised the kingdom to heights it had never regained under the Dukes of Ornifal.

"Prince Garric" had been accepted because he brought the stability that'd vanished under Valence the Third; but if a strong leader from Ornifal appeared, one who claimed to be the son of the warrior king of the past generation, there'd be many who'd be glad to support him. Courtiers, bureaucrats . . . soldiers. Even some Blood Eagles, perhaps. It was one thing to face enemies. It was another to turn your back on a seeming friend in the knowledge that he might be waiting for just that chance with a dagger in his sleeve. . . .

"We don't want you to go if there's another alternative," said Tadai, glancing around the table to a series of nods that proved he was speaking for all. "And Princess Sharina just showed that there is."

Garric nodded. "All right," he said. "But there's something none of us are talking about. Even you, Tenoctris."

The old wizard sat beside Sharina, her satchel of paraphernalia placed discreetly on the ground under the table, where others wouldn't have to look at it. She gave Garric a quick grin.

"That's Hani, the wizard who's with Valgard," Garric continued. "If Valgard came from nowhere, then it seems as likely to me that he's Hani's pawn rather than the other way around. And much as I respect your abilities, Lord Waldron, they don't include wizardry."

"And may the Lady grant that they never do!" Waldron said in gruff honesty. "I figure a wizard's throat cuts as easily as a decent man's, though, and I've got the sword to do it!"

"Very possibly," Garric said. "But Tenoctris? I'd very much appreciate it if you would accompany Lord Waldron and Sharina. It's not that I don't want you here—and I may very well want your help, I know that. But I'll have the whole royal army, while on Ornifal—"

He didn't try to finish the thought, just shrugged. He didn't know what words he could've used. Images of numberless disasters kept whirling through his mind like the flakes of a snowstorm.

Tenoctris nodded agreement. "Yes," she said. "I can be only one place at a time, of course. I just wish—"

She stopping, beaming with the familiar, transfiguring smile that took decades off her apparent age.

"I wish I had greater powers," Tenoctris said, "but I'll use what I have for the sake of the kingdom, and for Good—which must be real, since Evil so obviously is. And we'll hope that's enough."

Garric rose to his feet. "Well, friends and fellow soldiers," he said. "Nobody can ask for more than the best we can give. Lord Waldron, you have matters to attend, I'm sure. Sharina and Tenoctris will inform you of their baggage requirements when you consider transportation. Lord Zettin, provide whatever Lord Waldron requests. Inform me after the fact, if you will, but you have my approval already."

"Of course, your highness," Zettin said, glancing toward the aides waiting outside the ring of Blood Eagles who were ensuring privacy.

"As for the rest of us," Garric concluded, "I see the barge coming back from Erdin already. I doubt Earl Wildulf would be quite so prompt if he'd decided on war, so we'd best consider the procedure for crowning a loyal vassal. It's something I got very little practice at"—he grinned broadly, light-headed to have resolved the question of how to deal with events on Ornifal—"when I was living in Barca's Hamlet."

Everybody laughed—even Lord Waldron, who burst out with a gust of laughter after he finally understood he'd really heard what he thought he had.

Garric watched Tenoctris leaving, helped by his sister. They'd have Cashel with them, of course. That was the next best thing to having a whole army. . . .

Cashel stepped from the sunlit hillside onto the parapet of a huge palace in the minutes before sunrise. The haze of light that precedes the sun had already turned the eastern sky into liquid crystal bright enough to hide the stars. The hard, smooth surface beneath Cashel's feet was just as translucently pure as the air above.

"Oh!" he said, as much in delight as wonder. He'd poised his quarter-staff at a slant before him as he stepped through the portal, ready for whatever danger might be waiting. He shifted it to his side but held the ferrule a trifle above the ground. He didn't suppose the iron would mark the gleaming surface, but it still seemed wrong to be rough with something so beautiful.

Mab was beside him. He hadn't heard or felt her appear. She'd been with him on Volita and she was with him still; it didn't seem to matter that they weren't in the same place as before.

"This is Ronn," she said, looking around with the gentle smile of a person seeing familiar wonders through the enthusiastic eyes of a stranger to them. "You can think of it as a city, if you like, or as a palace; but all the thousands of citizens live in the same splendor as their ruler."

Cashel looked at her again. She *was* Mab, he was sure of that, but—

"Lady, your hair is dark now," he said. "And you're younger, and you're, well, fuller."

The woman shrugged dismissively. "Yes," she said, "and very likely I'll change my tunics and sandals at some point as well. Does this concern you?"

Cashel blushed in embarrassment. "I'm sorry, lady," he said. In truth, her clothes and the jewel-bright paint on her nails were the only parts of Mab's appearance that weren't subtly different from the woman he'd met on Volita. "I don't normally poke into other people's business. I won't do it again."

Mab smiled. Cashel turned his attention back to his surroundings, where he wasn't so apt to make a fool of himself. He hadn't been prying, just surprised; but when you asked folks about how they looked, you *were* being personal whether you thought about it that way or not.

There was any number of people around, more than he'd guessed at first because he could see for such a long distance. He was standing near the southeast corner of a broad, curving terrace. It stretched for farther than Cashel could be sure of. To the west, across the ship-filled harbor far below, lights twinkled on the other end of the crescent.

Because the plaza was so broad, the people got lost in it until you really thought about how many there were. Cashel didn't suppose he'd seen so many folks in one place except when Garric was mustering his army. There were too many to see them all, really, even if the sun'd been fully up.

"It's like being up on a mountain, mistress," he said. "And it's very beautiful."

"Ronn was built to be beautiful," Mab said, with a nod of agreement. "And it was a mountain, before the city was built. The foundations are carved into the rock to support these crystal levels reaching into the sky."

Cashel glanced at those standing close by, showing polite interest but being careful not to stare. People stood in pairs and small groups; occasionally one would be alone. They were waiting for something, though they didn't seem to be tense.

They were an army in numbers, but nothing could be more peaceful than the folk themselves. Almost all wore a loose, flowing robe, thin as the finest silk, over an opaque, richly embroidered garment that covered them from feet to neckline as tight as a stocking. The women's fingernails were painted like Mab's, blue on one hand and red on the other, though nobody else's seemed to have the same inner shine as hers.

The people who weren't dressed in that fashion were probably foreigners like Cashel, though he guessed they'd come from the ships in the harbor instead of stepping out of the air. There were more different kinds than he could've counted on both hands, ranging from small, dark men in wrappers of patterned cotton to a pair of hulking, red-haired fellows who wore furs. Those two were taller than Cashel—taller than Garric, even. They gave him the same kind of appraising looks that he offered them.

"Ah, did wizards build the city, mistress?" Cashel asked, rubbing the pavement with his bare toe to see if he could feel any sort of join between blocks. It was as slick as polished metal, all one piece and not even roughened by the feet that'd walked it over who knew how many years.

"One wizard did," Mab said, turning toward Cashel. Her voice was calm, but there was something more in her eyes. "He built Ronn, and he ruled as the king for a thousand years."

She gestured with her left arm and continued, "The plain from Ronn to the northern hills—"

Cashel could see the hills she meant in the far distance, an irregular darkness rising on the horizon. From where he stood on the southern edge of the broad terrace, the lowlands between city and hills were out of sight.

"—was planted in crops to feed the city's population and worked by the Made Men whom he'd created as he created Ronn. For a thousand years, till a thousand years ago."

Cashel nodded to give himself time to decide just how to respond. He wouldn't want not to work himself, but he knew a lot of people didn't feel that way. After fitting the pieces together in his mind, he said, "That sounds, well, pretty good, mistress. Did something go wrong back a thousand years ago, then?"

Looking at the comfortable people, well fed and well dressed, it didn't seem like very much could've gone wrong. There had to be something he was missing, or Mab wouldn't have brought it up.

"Something went right," Mab said. "The Made Men looked like real men except that they couldn't bear the light. They worked in darkness. At first they had windowless huts in the fields. Each dawn they went into their huts and hid from the sun. Little by little they began moving into Ronn, first in the lowest vaults but moving higher as time passed. They blocked the crystals that brought the sun and moon down from the sky to every level. And then a thousand years ago the people rose up behind a queen, and they drove the king and his creatures into the hills."

Cashel looked at the other people waiting on the terrace. It was hard to imagine these folks driving anybody anywhere. All but the foreigners looked as smoothly plump as so many palace servants back in Valles. It made him remember what Mab had said before, about Ronn being a palace where everybody lived like the ruler.

"Well, it seems like things are fine now," he said aloud. He smiled at Mab. "People aren't starving, I can see that."

Food was on his mind, he guessed. He'd brought bread and cheese in his wallet, figuring that there must be water on Volita since it pastured sheep. It was past time that he'd have eaten if he'd stayed on the island, but he guessed he'd wait a while longer since it was just dawn here.

"The queen was a wizard too," Mab said. "She caused crops to grow inside Ronn, where the residents themselves could tend them without fear of the Made Men attacking during the night."

The spectators—despite their total numbers, they were too spread out to call them a crowd—gave a spreading sigh like the murmur of doves in their cote. A group of men and women wearing high golden headdresses walked toward the eastern edge of the terrace. There were seven of them, a handful and two fingers of the other hand.

"That's the Council of the Wise," Mab said in a quiet voice. The newcomers passed almost close enough for Cashel to have touched them with his quarterstaff. "They aid the queen with certain tasks, including this one."

The Councillors reached the parapet and lined up along it. Together they turned westward, stretching both arms out as they began to chant.

"They're wizards?" Cashel asked, his eyes narrowing slightly. "Or just priests?"

"Wizards of a sort," Mab said. "Useful in their way, but only candles in the sun compared to the king."

She sniffed, and added, "Though 'sun' is the wrong word to describe what the king's become in a thousand years of rule and a thousand more of exile."

The Councillors murmured a final word, their voices slurring together so that even though they spoke louder Cashel couldn't have repeated it. Not that it would've meant anything except to another wizard, of course.

A man who must be at least a mile high appeared in the middle of the terrace, facing the eastern horizon. His whole figure shone slickly. Only the feathered cap on his head should have been catching sunlight, the way tall trees do while the ground beneath them remains in darkness, but his boots had the same gleam. He raised a golden trumpet to his lips and blew a long call.

As the sweet, rolling note died out, the sun rose above the horizon and threw the dawn's first real shadows. The trumpeter melted back into the air.

The spectators resumed their conversations in quicker, brighter tones. The foreigners were jabbering among themselves in wonderment; one of the tall, fur-clad men had half drawn a long sword before the spectral giant vanished.

"You're not afraid, Cashel?" Mab asked with a knowing smile.

"No, ma'am," he said. "But it was a pretty thing."

The Councillors were silent. They'd drawn together like sheep in a thunderstorm; a couple of them were so tired that others had to steady them. It'd been an impressive illusion, but for seven wizards working together, well, Cashel saw what Mab meant about them not being powerful.

"Yes, very pretty," Mab said as she looked out toward the barren hills. The sunlight falling on them somehow made them seem all the darker. "There are many pretty things here in Ronn, but only the queen could withstand the king when he led his Made Men back from the hills."

"The queen's a wizard too, Mab?" Cashel asked. People were dispersing, either going down broad staircases built onto the city's gleaming flanks or simply promenading along the terrace.

"The queen is a great wizard, Cashel," Mab said, still looking northward. "For a thousand years she kept back the king, and her Heroes led the people of Ronn against the Made Men. But—"

She turned to face Cashel. For a moment he thought her eyes blazed with the same perfect blue as the nails of her right hand.

"—the Heroes all sleep in a cavern beneath Ronn . . . and yesterday, the queen vanished."

Ilna felt momentarily as though her skin had been turned inside out and bathed in ice water. A flash of crimson light left her sitting on pebbly soil at the base of an escarpment. It was night, and blinking afterimages of the wizardlight filled her eyes.

There was another flash, silent but so vivid that Ilna's ears rang with the expectation of a thunderclap. Light rippled up a section of the rock face nearby.

"Don't move!" shouted a voice, unfamiliar but the same one that had warned them to get away in the ruined garden. Too late, of course, but Ilna couldn't complain since the person speaking was the one who'd been transformed from a statue when she severed the spell binding him. "The troll can't hear, but it sees well even in the dark."

What does he mean by "troll"?

A second flash outlined a section of the escarpment. It scaled off of the surrounding rock, crackling and popping like a much louder version of the sounds a tree limb makes when the weight of ice breaks it.

Landslide! Ilna thought, but she was wrong. It was a stone *figure,* walking away out of the wall it'd broken free from. Her eyesight was returning, but from what she could see in the moonlight the creature was featureless— a lump of head on a squat torso with arms and legs as crude as a child's clay figure. It was easily four times her height, however.

"We're all right unless it happens to walk toward one of us," the voice said. "If it does, run—and pray if you're of that persuasion. Generally a troll will wander into the desert, though, so we ought to be all right."

"Ilna, my heart?" Chalcus called from Ilna's right, the other side from where the stranger was speaking. "Are you in this place as well?"

The figure—the troll—was between them, but as the stranger said, it was shambling away from the cliff without taking notice of the humans nearby. Its limbs bent where the knees and elbows would've been on a human being, but the joints made a squealing hiss. Its weight shook the ground.

"Yes," Ilna said. "Merota, are you here?"

No one answered, just the wind and the wheeze of the troll walking away from them. The girl had been standing just a little behind Chalcus on the other side of the wisteria when Ilna made the final cut. Was there a range beyond which the broken spell had no effect? There must be, or all Volita would be here in this stony wasteland!

"Merota, child?" Chalcus called. She still couldn't see him or the stranger on the irregular ground, though they must be close. "Can you hear my voice, dear one?"

Still no reply. Perhaps the child was safe, then.

A pine tree grew within a furlong of the escarpment, silhouetted against the brighter sky. Dead limbs thrust straight out from the sides all the way up the trunk, but at the top, sprays of needles formed a flat brush. The troll stumbled into the tree—literally, it seemed to Ilna. The creature walked with the rolling gait of a sailor on land, and the ground's slight slope nudged it toward the tree in a slow curve.

The troll's right arm lashed horizontally at the thick trunk. Splintered wood sprayed outward. The stone hand smashed through the tree so swiftly that the top portion hung for a moment, then fell straight down onto the stump instead of being flung outward by the blow.

The troll staggered on. It'd destroyed the pine tree in no more than the time it'd take to sneeze. The severed bole wobbled, then toppled sideways onto the creature's head.

Wood splintered on stone. The tree rolled off and crackled into the ground, shedding branches. The troll didn't seem to have noticed the impact. Ilna could hear the wheeze of rock bending and the *thud* of heavy footfalls long after the creature was out of sight in the darkness.

"There's no danger now," the stranger said, rising into sight beyond a patch of wormwood whose white-dusted leaves glowed in the light of the quarter moon. He was nude; as the statue had been, of course, but it was still a surprise to see what had been a crude carving re-formed in tightly muscled flesh. "Not for us, at least. If it stumbles across a village in the night, it'll treat the huts and the people in them just as it did the tree."

Ilna got to her feet, patting the grit off her tunic. Chalcus rose also. His sword drew a figure in the moonlight, then slipped back into its sheath as quickly as it'd appeared. He stepped over to Ilna and hugged her fiercely— but only with his left arm, as his eyes continued to dart about the landscape.

He stepped away from her. "My name is Chalcus, friend," he said to the stranger, "and the lady is Mistress Ilna."

His tone was friendly, but the quick dance his blade had made a moment before was as much threat as anyone with eyes needed. "Who would you be, then? If you don't mind my asking."

"I'm Davus," the man replied. "And since you must be the ones who freed me, then you have my thanks and my sincere regrets that the backlash brought you to this place also when it snatched me home."

Davus picked up a pebble, caressing it with the thumb of his other hand. Chalcus was poised to move with what Ilna knew was lethal speed, but Davus dropped the stone by his side instead of throwing it. He seemed to have wanted nothing more than contact with the pitted surface.

"When we saw you," Ilna said carefully, "you were a statue. Were you alive, then?"

Davus laughed. "That I can't say, milady," he said. "I wasn't aware, that I can tell you with certainty. I was in a garden, a lovely green place. A wizard had brought me there, *pulled* me there, I think. And then the garden was a ruin. I saw you bending over me, and I was slipping back here. I didn't know anything in between."

He chuckled. "Time will have passed, I'm sure. Likely a good deal of time."

"Tenoctris said the buildings on Volita were destroyed a thousand years ago," Ilna said. She tried to imagine a thousand years. She couldn't. All it meant was a time long enough to throw down the walls of Carcosa, which were still a mountain range in their ruin.

"Then a thousand years," Davus said, shrugging. "It doesn't seem to matter when you're stone. Though I wouldn't mind having clothing again, for the nights here near the rim can be chilly, and the sand the wind blows stings me."

"Here," said Ilna, loosing the redoubled silken noose she wore in place of a sash. She lifted off her outer tunic and tossed it to him. "This may be a little short for you, and you may feel that the pattern doesn't suit, but perhaps it will serve for the time being."

Davus held the tunic to the moonlight and let his thumb trace the swirls woven into the hem of the garment's sleeve. Ilna'd used gray fleece from three ewes. The shades were so subtly different that she hadn't thought anybody else would notice the distinctions. She'd been wrong about that.

"I'm honored, Mistress Ilna," Davus said. "This is your workmanship?"

"Yes," said Ilna, letting the syllable stand for itself.

"Honored indeed," Davus said, and shrugged the garment over his head. It was a little tight at the shoulders until he loosened the neck laces; otherwise, there was nothing to complain about in the fit.

Ilna started to tie the rope around her waist, then thought again about it. In daylight she usually depended on her knotted patterns for defense. Now, with only the doubtful light of the moon to display her work to an enemy, she supposed the running noose in the silken cord was the better weapon. She held the coil in both hands, ready to cast if necessary.

Animals too small to see clearly scurried in the shadows, movements rather than shapes. Quail called, and once she heard the *whit-whit-whit* of an owl. The landscape wasn't familiar, but it seemed normal enough.

Apart from the fact that pieces walked away from cliffs.

Chalcus stretched his arms up, then back, without ever ceasing to scan his surroundings. "So, Master Davus," he said, "are these trolls a common thing we'll meet here?"

"That was a small one," Davus said easily. "I once saw one hundreds of feet tall."

He scooped up pebbles, a handful of them this time, and began to juggle with the same unthinking skill as Chalcus sometimes spun his dagger while his mind was working. "There's a good deal of power in this place," he went on. "The sort of power wizards use, I mean. But you'll have known that, I suppose, since the way you freed me shows that you're"—he nodded first to Chalcus, then to Ilna—"wizards yourselves."

Chalcus said nothing. There was enough light for them to see one another's features but not enough to read them.

"I see patterns," Ilna said harshly. "I broke the pattern I saw in the vines that were holding you, Master Davus. I'm *not* a wizard."

"No offense meant, mistress," Davus said contritely. He gave her a small bow. "But there's power in this land, as I say; in the earth more than in the air or the water. When it builds, or a spell like the one you broke pours itself over the landscape, the rocks can come alive. As you saw."

Ilna stared in the direction the troll had taken. She couldn't hear it anymore, though she thought she felt its tread through the soles of her bare feet.

"I hate rocks," she said, musing aloud rather than intentionally talking to her companions. "They're bad enough when they lie still like they're supposed to, but walking around like this . . ."

Davus laughed, tossing his pebbles one at a time over his shoulder. They fell to the ground in a tight group. "There's good rocks and bad rocks, mistress," he said. "Like everything else."

He walked a little way out on the plain and turned to view the escarpment. It curved for as far as Ilna could see in either direction.

"The king who ruled in my day," Davus said, "was a great wizard. He ordered trolls back into the cliffs here, then turned them again to rock. But that hasn't happened for a long time."

He gestured. "See the niches in the cliffs? And at the bottom of each there's the chips that fell where the overhang weathered out after the troll walked away."

Ilna dutifully turned and looked. Chalcus gave only a quick glance before he resumed scanning the brush and sparse trees of the plain into which the troll had gone. The sloping cliffs were notched, right enough, and there were spills of pebbles and larger rocks at the base of them. That was nothing that would've seemed unusual if Davus hadn't called her attention to it. He seemed to be an expert, though.

"Who rules now," Ilna said, "if your wizard-king doesn't?"

"I don't know," said Davus with a smile. "I know only that the Old King wouldn't have allowed this to happen. Therefore"—he turned his palm up as if holding the proof in it—"he no longer rules."

In a more sober tone, he went on, "He wasn't perfect, the Old King. It's not good for any man to hold the power he did. He kept a loose rein on this land in the main, but he wouldn't abide kings or armies. When folk made enough problems that he took notice, he changed them into stone. Like enough he made mistakes; he was human, after all. But he took his duties seriously."

"If they say no worse of me when I die . . ." Ilna said. It was only when she heard the words that she realized that her thoughts had reached her lips. "Then I'll have no right to complain."

She cleared her throat and looked sharply at Davus, bringing her mind back to the present. She'd been lost in memories of the things she'd done in the past. "Was it your wizard-king who made you into a statue, then, Master Davus?"

Davus chuckled. "Not that I recall," he said, "and not that I believe, either. A wizard of your world drew me to him, for purposes that were none of mine. But who turned me to stone . . . I don't know."

"There's a thing I see in the distance there," Chalcus said. He pointed his whole left arm to indicate a glitter where the dark gray sky met the black horizon to the north. "That looks like the face of a glacier, which is nothing I'd expect to see in these warm latitudes. Can you tell me what it is, friend?"

"I could say that it's new to me as well . . . ," Davus said, following the line of Chalcus' arm with a grim expression. "For it's been built since I was snatched away. In my time the Citadel was in that place, the King's dwelling, on a tall spire of rock standing out from the plain."

Chalcus nodded. "That's the palace, then," he said, seeming to settle inside now that he had a name to give what had been unknown and therefore threatening.

"You can call it that if you like," Davus said, his tone cool but leaving no doubt of his disagreement. "They say the king lived as simply as any peasant, though; the king that was, I mean. And those crystal spires that're so high we can see them even from here on the rim, well, they're nothing that king built in the thousands of years he ruled this land."

He grinned with a sort of humor that made Ilna realize that Davus, whoever he was, wasn't out of place in company that included folk as hard as Chalcus and herself.

"So there's a new king in the land," he said, sweeping up more pebbles. "And he's a wizard too, a great one to have built such a splendid thing as we see. But he's not so good for the people of this land as the man he replaced, I fear; and maybe he's not a man at all."

He turned slightly. Instead of resuming his juggling he drew back his right arm, then snapped a pebble toward the base of a stand of thorn scrub several double paces distant. Ilna heard the *thwock!* of the stone hitting flesh. A quail shot straight into the air, thrashing wildly but silent. It flopped back onto the dry ground, still twitching. It'd been dead from the instant the stone took its head off.

"Well thrown, friend," Chalcus said, his voice neutral but leaving no doubt at all the praise was sincere.

"It won't make much of a dinner for three," Davus said. "Still, it's something to sleep on, and at dawn perhaps we can do better."

Ilna grinned as she walked over to clean and pluck the bird. Davus was obviously proud of his skill, but the quiet fashion in which he displayed it was one she found familiar from her own life.

Chalcus began shaving twigs to make tinder into which he'd strike a spark from the back of his dagger. Davus cleared his throat, looking at neither of them. "Mistress," he said uncomfortably, "I saw three persons around me in the moment you broke the spell. The third would be the child Merota you were calling?"

"Yes," said Ilna. Then, with emphasis, "*Yes.* But she wasn't caught in this . . . trap the way Chalcus and I were. That's right, isn't it?"

"From where Mistress Merota was standing," said Davus, his eyes on the far-off crystal glint, "I'm afraid she must have been caught as well. If she's not here on the rim of the land, close by the rest of us—"

"She'd have answered if she was," Chalcus snapped. "Unless she was hurt?"

"The transition would no more have hurt her than walking through a doorway would," Davus said, dipping his chin in negation. "But if she's not here at the edge, then she's at the center. She's at the Citadel."

Ilna eyed the jagged glitter on the horizon. Normally moonlight softened the lines of what it fell on. It wasn't softening that thing; or if it was—

She chuckled, a brittle sound in keeping with her present mood. She began to pluck the quail, anger and her strong fingers making up for the fact she hadn't been able to scald the feathers first to loosen them.

"If that's a mast of rock, then it's a very long way from here," Chalcus said as he laid his fireset methodically. He looked up at Davus. "Not so, sir?"

"Very much so," Davus agreed. "Since we've only our legs for transport, it'll take us many days to get there."

"Us," repeated Ilna without expression. "You plan to come with Chalcus and me, Master Davus?"

"I'm the reason you and the child are here, mistress," Davus agreed. "It's only justice that I should help you as much as I can. Don't you think so?"

"Yes," said Ilna, thrusting the point of her bone-cased paring knife under the quail's breastbone and slicing its belly open. "I do. And the fact you do as well, Master Davus"—she looked up at him with what was for her a warm smile—"is the best news I've heard in this place!"

"One advantage of having been poor all of my life . . ." Tenoctris said, eyeing her sturdy leather satchel. It held the tools of her art and was the only luggage she was taking to Valles, ". . . is that I don't find it difficult to pack all I need."

Sharina laughed. Tenoctris was a friend and colleague, but she'd been born into a noble family. An impoverished noble family, to be sure: but that meant there were only half a dozen servants in Tenoctris' household. Sharina'd served tables herself for the customers in her father's inn.

"I never thought of myself as poor," Sharina said. "We *weren't* poor for Barca's Hamlet, of course; but nobody in Barca's Hamlet had very much. I didn't have trouble packing either."

"People don't need very much," she added, watching the bustle as Lord Waldron's squadron loaded for the voyage east. By then she'd seen enough similar scenes to appreciate what was really going on instead of viewing it as a wildly chaotic swirl.

For all the great weight of gear going into the five ships of the squadron, the individual soldiers had almost nothing of their own. Besides arms and a spare tunic, they might carry some little talisman of home or souvenir of a place they'd been and liked. A religious icon, a flute or ocarina; perhaps a letter or a girl's face painted on the inside of a folded wooden notebook.

"A little peace wouldn't come amiss," Tenoctris said, a trifle wistfully. "I had that when I was poor, too."

She laughed, back to her normal sprightly self. "Until the world ended, literally for tens of thousands of people and very nearly for humanity," she added. "In part because I was living peaceably with my books instead of helping whoever was trying to prevent the disaster."

"King Carus was," Sharina said, looking down the beach to where her brother met with the second delegation from Earl Wildulf. She couldn't see Garric. He was encircled by Blood Eagles, and around them a thicker ring of people who wanted to talk with the prince or be close to the prince or just *see* the prince. It was hard to imagine that . . .

"Carus was trying," Sharina repeated, "but wouldn't have welcomed your help or any wizard's help. He was determined to hold the Isles together with his sword and army alone, and so he became part of the problem."

As Carus himself would say—and had said, using the tongue of his distant descendent Garric or-Reise to shape the words.

Tenoctris looked back into the distant past, her face turned in the direction of the granite knob. She focused on Sharina again with a smile of apology for her brief absence. "Yes," she said, "I suspect you're right. But that doesn't matter, dear. I should've tried, and I didn't."

"Well, you're trying now," Sharina said, getting up from a block of the fallen porch that also supplied the older woman's seat. She hugged Tenoctris. "We all are, and so far we're succeeding."

She looked back the way Tenoctris had been facing, feeling an edge of disquiet. She'd expected Cashel to be back by now. The messengers she'd sent should've brought him if he hadn't simply returned on his own after stretching his legs from the confinement of being on shipboard.

Barely aloud, she said, "Of course Cashel has even less to pack than you and I do."

Still, she wished she saw his big, comfortable figure ambling through the ruins with his quarterstaff over his shoulder. Cashel rarely moved quickly, but he never failed to get where he was going—no matter what was in the way.

Instead of Cashel she saw a pair of soldiers from one of the line regiments approaching: a common soldier with a puzzled expression and a half-angry, half-worried company commander whose horsehair crest was across his helmet instead of running front to back like the soldier's. They stepped purposefully through the stones and shrubbery, ignoring other soldiers except as obstacles to go around.

Tenoctris watched the men also, her lips pursed. Soldiers who weren't on guard duty didn't usually wear their helmets in camp, let alone mount the detachable crests. The most likely reason for these two to be formally dressed was that they were coming to see Princess Sharina . . .

The six Blood Eagles loosely guarding Sharina and Tenoctris stiffened noticeably when they saw the men approaching. Lord Attaper had probably placed the guards by his own decision. Sharina hadn't protested, though she found their presence uncomfortable and probably pointless. She knew that she or Tenoctris, either one, *could* be attacked, even there in the midst of the royal army. She didn't believe there'd be an attack of a sort that soldiers could prevent, however.

"I'm Lieutenant Branco, Third Company of Lord Quire's regiment," the officer said. He spoke to the undercaptain commanding the guards but in a deliberately loud voice so that Sharina and Tenoctris couldn't help but overhear. Branco was at least forty, a commoner promoted to company command after long service instead of a noble on the first step of his military career. "Trooper Memet here says he's got a message for Princess Sharina from Lord Cashel."

Memet had been looking straight ahead, uncomfortably waiting for his commander to sort things out while he pretended he was a piece of furniture. Now his eyes flew open. "*Lord* Cashel?" he blurted. "Enver bless me, I thought he was a shepherd like me!"

"Memet," snarled the officer, "if you made this up, you're going to wish you *were* a shepherd. You're going to wish you were a *sheep!*"

Branco looked at Sharina and, without even pretending he wasn't addressing Sharina directly, said, "Your highness, Trooper Memet here hasn't ever lied that I know. There's some who'd say he doesn't have brains enough to lie. His story don't make sense, but I brought him to you anyhow."

Four Blood Eagles were lined up between the women and the two soldiers like thick bars across a window. The other two were behind them, watching the other way in case Memet and Branco were a diversion from the real attack. Sharina didn't imagine the guards really thought there was any risk—she herself certainly didn't—but they viewed their duties as putting themselves between the women and any possible danger. Branco and Memet were the closest thing there was to a threat, so they were making the most of it.

The Blood Eagles didn't keep Branco from talking to Sharina, though. Unless she told them different, that *wasn't* any of their business.

"Let the trooper talk for himself, Lieutenant," Sharina said, hoping the words weren't as harsh as they sounded in her ears. She was afraid for Cashel and afraid for the kingdom, because anything that could harm Cashel was a danger to far more besides.

"Right," Memet said, standing at attention with his eyes on the far horizon. "Ma'am, this big guy, he said he was Cashel or-Kenset, not any kind of lord?"

"She's a princess, you bonehead!" Branco whispered savagely. "Call her 'your highness!'"

"That's all right, Memet," Sharina said. "Go on."

Tenoctris had seated herself on the ground, tracing a figure in the dirt with a bamboo splinter. Bits of stone that'd crumbled off the ruins made the task difficult.

"We were talking about sheep," Memet said. His eyes edged toward where Sharina stood before him, then jerked to the side as though sight of her had burned him. "I'd been a shepherd on Ornifal, though I stuck with the army even after my dad died. A lady came and talked to us. I didn't see her come up, but she must've done. She said her name was Mab and Cashel had to come right away or his mother was in trouble."

"His mother?" Sharina repeated, shocked into speaking when she'd intended to let the soldier get his story out in the way he found easiest. Cashel didn't have a—

But of course he did.

"Right, his mother," Memet said. He wasn't relaxing, but he seemed to have sunk deeply enough into telling the story that he could forget to whom he was telling it. "So he said he'd go, Cashel did, and he told me to tell Princess Sharina what he was doing. And then . . ."

He suddenly met Sharina's eyes squarely. "Ma'am? Princess, I mean?" he said. "Then they walked into the rock. It was just a rock, I swear, till she said words, and they walked into it. And it was a rock again."

The soldier scratched his scalp under the brow of his helmet. This unique experience had driven years of training out of his head. He was a puzzled shepherd again who didn't remember he was talking to a noble because his sort *never* talked to nobles.

Sharina's stomach knotted. She looked at Tenoctris, still sitting on the ground though she'd given up on the figure she'd started to draw. "Tenoctris," she said, "nobody who knows Cashel would expect him to do anything but go. Do you think it was a trap?"

"Cashel always seems to make the right decision in a crisis," Tenoctris said. "His simplicity cuts to the core of matters that less . . . simple people get confused by. Myself, for example."

She put one hand on the ground. Sharina knelt immediately and helped the old woman up. Leaning forward to see past the backs of the Blood Eagles, Tenoctris said, "Can you take me to where this happened, Memet?"

"Sure, ma'am," the soldier said. He looked sideways at Branco. "I mean, if the lieutenant says it's all right?"

"It's all right with Lieutenant Branco," Sharina said absently, taking a wax tablet and stylus out of her sleeve. "One moment, Tenoctris. I'll need to write a note to Garric, telling him what's happened. He'll want to know. And to Ilna. Then we'll both go with Memet."

The undercaptain of the guard detachment looked at her. "Then we'll *all* go, your highness," he said, "if that's what you're bound to do. And if anybody gets the notion that you and Lady Tenoctris ought to step into rocks too, well, they'll discuss it with us first."

Chapter Four

P ardon me, milords," Garric said to Lord Tadai and the troupe of officials accompanying him to Erdin. "I'd like a word with the commander of our escort."

"*It's Lord Rosen,*" said King Carus approvingly as he saw the commander of the Blaise regiment that'd be crossing the strait. The sun was just risen high enough for even Garric's excellent eyes to distinguish one man in armor from another at a distance of thirty feet. *"He was in charge when we had trouble at that temple in Carcosa."*

I recall, Garric thought, a little irritated to be reminded of somebody he remembered quite well. On the other hand, Carus was reputed to have known every one of the forty thousand men in his army by name—

"Not so, lad," the king's spirit said with a smile. *"But maybe everybody above file closer in rank, maybe that."*

—and it was a *very* valuable trick for a commander who wanted troops to follow him into hard places.

"Lord Rosen!" Garric said, stepping forward to clasp right arms with the Blaise officer. "I left to Waldron the choice of the regiment that'd accompany me, but I couldn't be more happy than to be working with you again!"

That was all true. Rosen had proved to have a quick mind. Even more important, Rosen had enough of a grip on his temper that he hadn't taken offense when Garric snapped orders curtly. That wasn't a given among noblemen, especially those who'd chosen the army for a career.

But it was also true that he was greeting Rosen with this warmth for political reasons. Garric wanted an officer who'd do what he was told promptly and without argument. If that officer was convinced the prince really liked and cared about him, he was likely to behave the way Garric needed him to.

In a way, this was no different from the way a successful innkeeper behaved to his guests. It wasn't exactly lying. By demonstrating enthusiasm that maybe you don't feel just at the moment with a lot of other things on your mind, you made the guest feel comfortable. Garric was actually better at that part of business than his father had been.

"And better than I was, lad," Carus agreed, *"for all I knew what I should do."*

"Pleased as well, your highness!" said Rosen, a plumpish fellow of average height with the flaring moustaches that Blaise aristocrats favored. "Honored, if I may say. The lads and I are rather looking forward to a chance to sort out these Sandrakkan weasels."

"While I'm sure your men are capable of doing just that, milord,"

Garric said, smiling to emphasize that this was a friendly comment rather than a rebuke, "it'll be a disaster if that happens. I'm going over with your troops rather than an Ornifal regiment so as not to inflame the Erdin mob, but I'm sure there'll be provocations nonetheless. I trust your discipline not to respond to anything less than an outright armed attack."

I pray to the Shepherd your discipline is that good, Garric thought, but he knew sometimes you simply had to face problems. There couldn't be parts of the kingdom into which royal officials couldn't go, not and it really be a *kingdom*; and if there was going to be trouble, then best it happen when the entire army was on hand to finish whatever the Sandrakkan mob might start.

"You can count on us, your highness!" Lord Rosen said, stepping back. He raised his right arm straight up in a Blaise salute, then returned to where his regiment waited. It was on the shoreline, broken into companies alongside the triremes that'd ferry it across the strait.

I have to count on them, Garric thought, continuing to smile while he felt a surge of bleak despair. *Every*thing had to work, every*one* had to do his or her job without getting lazy or angry. Otherwise, the Isles would shatter into a hundred little principalities that squabbled among themselves till some great, united evil swept them all into oblivion. As it surely would.

"You have to count on them, and they have to count on you," Carus agreed quietly. *"And thus far, neither of you has disappointed the other."*

Garric glanced at the Sandrakkan delegation, the same four officials as before, who waited to return to Erdin with Garric and his escort. The priestess and the courtier talked to one another with stony expressions. The commoner kept to himself in the background, and Marshal Renold was watching the phalanx go through evolutions on the rubble-strewn foreshore.

The demonstration—because that's what it was—was worth watching. The phalanx was formed sixteen ranks deep and armed with twenty-foot pikes. These were heavy, awkward weapons, difficult to handle even on a level field. That the phalanx kept good order as it advanced and counter-marched across broken ground would impress any military man—and would seriously worry an enemy who realized there'd be at least five pike points aimed at the face of every soldier in his own front rank.

"By the Shepherd!" Carus said, watching through Garric's eyes. *"Yours*

are as good as mine were, lad. Ours *are as good as mine were a thousand years ago!"*

Liane stepped close to Garric's right elbow. In the formal tone that she always used to him in public, she said, "Your highness, I've just received some information that I'd like to go over with you in that tent—

She nodded toward an ordinary canvas tent meant to hold an eight-man squad. The sides were lowered, which was unusual for the temperate weather even in the early morning. The person waiting inside—the spy waiting inside—wanted to conceal his features as much as possible from the Sandrakkan traders mingling with the royal army.

"—as soon as possible."

"Yes, of course," Garric said. Liane didn't say 'as soon as possible' idly.

He glanced again at the Sandrakkan envoys. Their vessel was an ordinary river barge, draped for the occasion with tapestries over both sides. Seawater sloshing during the short voyage had soaked the fine fabrics.

"Ilna won't like that," Garric said, grinning at a homely memory, and sobering at once. He didn't realize how despairing he must have looked until Liane touched his hand, a rare public display of affection. Well, he *was* better for being reminded just then that he had friends.

His mind went back to the news he'd gotten the previous afternoon. "What particularly bothers me is that both Cashel and Ilna disappeared," he said to Liane quietly. "As if it was coordinated."

A senior clerk stepped into Garric's path with his mouth open for a question. Lord Tadai said, "Morschem, come here. *Now.*"

The clerk's mouth clamped shut. He hopped sideways to Tadai in a motion more like a crab swimming in clear water than anything Garric had seen on land before. Tadai, who was in his way every bit as ruthless as King Carus, had no intention of letting somebody in his department disturb Garric at that moment.

"Cashel wasn't attacked," Liane said, mincing along so that there'd be time for her and Garric to talk before they met the spy. "And Ilna and her friends may not have been attacked either, since the soldiers nearby are sure they heard someone shout a warning."

She cleared her throat, then added carefully so she wouldn't sound as though she was being falsely optimistic, "Tenoctris says that there's a great deal of power focused here on Volita. That might explain what's happened without positing hostile action."

"True," Garric said, because it *was* true. He grinned, feeling much better for an honest discussion of what'd happened. "And while that doesn't mean they aren't in danger, anybody who dares to threaten them is in a good deal more danger. So we'll take care of our end and trust them to take care of theirs as they've done in the past."

Two tough-looking men in civilian clothes stood by the tent, one at either end. They were Liane's retainers, guarding her unobtrusively but probably as effectively as Blood Eagles. Attaper must have believed the same thing, because Garric's own guards kept discreetly to the side instead of thrusting themselves into the tent ahead of him to see that no assassin lurked there.

The fellow who waited in the dimness wore a long, hooded cloak over his clothing. He bowed slightly to Liane, and said, "Mistress. I've brought a full report."

He handed her a tight parchment scroll the diameter of a man's thumb. Garric didn't recognize his accent. The fellow failed to add, "Your highness," to his salutation the way a citizen of the kingdom should have done.

"We'll go over this when we have leisure," Liane said in the coolly businesslike tone of a master speaking to a servant. "Give us a quick overview of the situation."

The spy shrugged under his cloak. "Earl Wildulf doesn't rank with the Seven Sages," he said, "but he's got a shrewd grasp of the possible. He'll bargain for as much autonomy as he can get, but he won't rebel unless something happens to the royal army first."

"Will he be able to work within the kingdom?" Garric asked. "I've heard that a lot of people on Sandrakkan hate Ornifal because of the way the royal army crushed the rebellion last generation at the Stone Wall."

Instead of replying, the spy turned his shadowed face toward Liane. "Answer him, Kaskal!" Liane said sharply.

The spy's head jerked back; Liane had used his name openly in an implicit rebuke of his posturing. He coughed, and said, "As best I can judge, Wildulf doesn't have any real hostility toward Ornifal. He's aware that if his uncle and cousin hadn't died at the Stone Wall, he'd be managing the family's vineyards in the west of the island. He'd never say that, of course."

Outside a trumpet called to end the phalanx exercises. The troops gave a loud cheer in unison. They'd be raising their pikes straight in the air and carrying them to covered storage to protect the slim shafts from the elements. Every aspect of the phalanx required forethought and extreme care; but when all the pieces worked together, the pikemen could cut the heart out of any other army in the Isles.

Kaskal had jumped when four thousand soldiers bellowed. With a self-directed scowl, he resumed, "There are plenty of people, especially among the nobles, who hate anything to do with Ornifal or the kingdom worse than a viper. Lord Tawnser's one of them. He has support in the court and outside it. If he stirs up trouble, it'll be against Wildulf's orders—but he's stupid enough that he might stir up trouble anyway."

"If there's a riot . . . ," Garric said. His mind was full of images from King Carus' memories: men in armor breaking down doors while people on the roof hurl down tiles; buildings alight and the flames spreading across whole districts, trapping fighters and the innocent alike. "Will the earl's troops put it down, or will we have to do that ourselves?"

"I don't know," the spy said. "It depends on just what the event is, who's in command of the troops on duty at the time, that sort of thing. I think Wildulf'd order his men to stop the riot, but how fast they'd obey— or how soon he'd be told what's going on—that I wouldn't bet on."

He pressed his fingertips together and frowned at them, deciding whether or not he was going to say more. Garric bit off a snarl, permitting Kaskal to decide to speak on his own. If the fellow thought he was going to get out of this tent *without* saying the rest of what was on his mind, though, he was badly mistaken.

"There's Countess Balila," Kaskal said at last. "I don't know about her. She's devoted to her husband, that I'm sure of. He seems to love her too, but Balila's . . . more than that. She worships Wildulf the way people are supposed to worship the gods."

"Do you see the countess's attitude as a danger?" Liane said. She held a wax tablet in one hand and a stylus in the other, but she wasn't taking notes; it was just a way of occupying her fingers while her mind was on the spy's words.

"Not unless she thinks the prince is a danger to her husband," Kaskal said. "I can't estimate how likely that is because I don't understand how her mind works. Balila doesn't have any real power, but she could probably find servants to poison a cup if she wanted to. And for the past year she's been thick as thieves with a wizard, an old woman who calls herself Lady Dipsas. I can't find out anything about where Dipsas is from, but if she's really a lady, so's my uncle's sow."

"Her birth doesn't matter," Garric said, feeling the spirit of Carus draw itself up in disgust. "How serious a wizard is she?"

He was well aware that he'd sent Tenoctris off with Sharina and Lord Waldron. Their squadron hadn't sailed from Volita yet—at the current rate of preparations, they'd leave a few hours after Garric and his escort crossed to Erdin—but he wasn't willing to renege on an offer he'd made his sister. Apart from personal reasons, it'd make him look vacillating. That was more of a danger to his leadership than the possibility that his initial decision had been a bad one.

"I don't know," Kaskal said. Then, angrily, "I don't know anything about that sort of business. I've seen her do tricks. If she does more than that, I don't know about it!"

The spy had the same attitude that King Carus and quite a lot of other people did: wizardry was evil, dangerous, and deeply disgusting. In the main, Garric, who'd had a good deal of experience with wizards in the past two years, agreed with them. But though the bloody dismemberment of thousands of men in battle was also evil, dangerous, and deeply disgusting, sometimes battle was necessary if the kingdom and mankind itself were to survive.

A trumpet and a long, curved horn blew together, signaling that the ships were ready to carry the prince and his escort to Erdin. Garric sighed. He didn't want to go, but it was his duty—and one he'd taken upon himself willingly.

He rose to his feet and shrugged. "I suppose we'll learn for ourselves in good time," he said mildly. "We'll hope that the countess realizes we won't harm her husband unless he initiates hostilities, and we'll hope that the countess's wizard shows similar good judgment. If they don't, then we'll deal with the situation as it arises."

Through Garric's mind cascaded more of Carus' memories, the faces of wizards who'd learned that the spells they were babbling weren't sufficient to fend off either the king's long sword or the death that came on its edge and point. It was a comforting reminder just then.

Ilna rose, feeling the chill and the emptiness of her belly as well. She'd always treated food as a necessity, not a pleasure in itself. Though an orphan thrown on her and her brother's resources at age nine learns what it means to go hungry, Ilna hadn't missed meals in a long time. When the orphans are as able as Ilna and Cashel, they earn enough to feed themselves in short order.

Well, she wouldn't starve for a good long while. Water was more of a concern, but not yet a serious one.

"I heard rabbits running about all night," said Chalcus ruefully, looking across the brush and straggling trees around them. "I've fished for everything from whales to fingerlings for bait. If I'd spent a little of that time learning to lay snares, we might have breakfast waiting for us."

He and Ilna had slept on pine boughs, a good enough mattress if they'd had a ground sheet to lay over it. As well wish for a down comforter, which would've been more use yet. The night air there was beyond cool.

Davus had made do with a scrape for his hip in the coarse soil and a smooth rock for a pillow. He seemed no worse for the experience than they were, and all three of them were fit to meet the day and whatever it brought.

Davus laid out a selection of pebbles, each about the size of a walnut, then picked three from the lot and left the remainder on the ground. "We should have lunch, at any rate," he said, tossing the stones from hand to hand in a pattern that was remarkably complex for only three stones. One was white quartz and served as a marker for Ilna's inexpert eyes.

Davus gathered the stones into his left hand. "How do you choose to proceed, sir and madam?" he asked with polite formality.

Chalcus raised an eyebrow toward Ilna. He could've spoken as easily as she—there was only one possible answer, after all—but since he put it to her, Ilna said, "If Merota is at the Citadel, we'll go to the Citadel."

"We won't lose our direction, whatever else we may lose," Davus said, his tone making the words approving rather than a criticism. He stepped forward, taking the lead without pointless dithering. Ilna could've had worse companions in a situation like this, whatever *this* really was.

"What are the people like here, Davus?" Chalcus asked from a double pace behind Ilna, the same distance at which she followed Davus. There was no obvious reason why they shouldn't have walked in a close group like three acquaintances on the only street of Barca's Hamlet's, but it felt more comfortable to spread out slightly so that everybody had an unobstructed view.

"In my day, all sorts," Davus said with a chuckle. "On the grasslands, nomads and hunters. That's northeast of the Citadel, though, and we're on the southern rim, so it's nowhere we'll be going"—he glanced over his shoulder and grinned—"for a time, at least."

A bird sailed through the high sky, a black cross against the pale blue. Though Ilna couldn't see any details at that height, the bird's wings were steady like those of a hawk instead of tipping on air currents the way a vulture would.

A ground squirrel whistled from an outcrop ten double paces distant. Davus flung a rock sidearm with no more hesitation than a trout taking a mayfly. The squirrel sprang into the air, as instantly dead as the quail of the night before.

Ilna walked over to the dead rodent. She tucked it under her sash to clean when they next stopped. It wasn't a species she'd encountered previously, but she wasn't in a mood to be fussy. An animal that turned grass into meat was likely to be good eating, even if it didn't look much like a sheep.

Davus rubbed the ball and big toe of his right foot into the soil. The action puzzled Ilna until he reached down and came up with a pebble he juggled briefly along with the two remaining from his original trio. He caught Chalcus' eye, and said, "It'll do till something better comes along, I think."

"In your hands," the sailor agreed, "I daresay it will."

"Here in the south," Davus said as they continued, "there are villages but not so many. Near the cliffs"—he crooked a finger back toward the rocky slopes behind them—"there's a great deal of power and things happen, as the three of us know better than most. The folk we're apt to find here are mostly solitaries for one reason or another, those who don't fear wizardry or who fear other things more. In my day, the king didn't chase down outlaws who took themselves here to the Rim, so long as they didn't return to trouble others."

"And the wizards who lurk here?" Chalcus said with a hint of challenge. "What of them?"

"The same," Davus replied. "Those who kept to themselves were allowed to keep to themselves. Those who thought otherwise found themselves stone statues, as"—he turned his head, his lips but not his eyes smiling as he looked at first Chalcus, then Ilna—"I was when you freed me, mistress. But in my case not, I think, because the Old King found me troublesome to my neighbors. Which you can believe or not believe as you choose."

"What I believe, Master Davus," said Ilna, meeting the fellow's eyes and speaking with her usual lack of emphasis, "is that I'm glad to have your company. If others at another time felt otherwise, then I suspect they're not people I'd warm to myself."

She laughed and added a further truth in a tone that made it a joke. "Of course it's easy to find people I don't warm to. No doubt most of them feel the same way about me."

A brightly colored lizard the length of a man's forearm raised its head toward them from the trunk of a dwarf almond tree. "Do we eat lizards?" Davus asked.

"We do not," Ilna said. "At least as yet."

"I ate steaks from the tail of a seawolf, once," Chalcus said.

"Seawolf?" asked Davus. If he came from this dry upland, he wouldn't have seen the long-jawed sea reptiles who'd occasionally come ashore near Barca's Hamlet to snatch a ewe or even a shepherd if he wasn't paying proper attention.

"A lizard twice as long as I'm tall," Chalcus explained. "It weighed as much as a grown bull, I'd judge, and seemed hungry enough to eat one. It had similar thoughts about me, but as it chanced, I learned that it tasted fishy instead of it complaining to its scaly kin that I was stringy. So I'll willingly forgo lizard today as well."

Davus stooped and came up with another chip of rock, this one pinkish and jagged. He juggled as he walked along, all four stones for a moment; then one flew onto a patch of bare earth and the other three vanished into his left palm again.

"There's good enough," he said, "and there's better. And sometimes there's better for a particular thing."

"Even among rocks," Ilna said, in so flat a tone that she thought only Chalcus would catch her self-mockery.

"Oh, especially among rocks, mistress!" Davus said, chuckling in full understanding. "Why, by the time we've rescued your friend Merota, I'll have taught you to appreciate the subtle delicacy of a bit of gneiss against the boldness one expects from an agate, eh?"

The three of them laughed together. In a quieter, sober voice, Davus went on, "I don't think the pattern of life here will have changed much since my time. The Old King didn't let men rule other men because he thought it was wrong that they should. The king who replaced him cares little for men, as we see from the fact he allows the trolls to walk, but he must care a great deal for his own safety. He won't allow a power to rise that might threaten him. There'll be farmsteads and villages, nothing greater than that; and no king but the king, as he now is."

A trio of small doves flew from a clump of laburnum, their flight feathers clattering together louder than the soft coos they uttered. Davus poised, then slipped the readied stone back into his other hand.

"There's a patch of bright green on the horizon," he said. "Maybe a spring where we'll find food, maybe a settlement. Those doves are pretty things, and if we don't need them to eat, then I'll let them go on being pretty till a hawk takes them or a fox takes them or perhaps they break their fool necks flying into a slab of mica that reflects the sky."

They laughed again, all in agreement; but Ilna noticed that Chalcus slipped his sword and dagger loose in their sheaths. She began to plait cords from her sleeve into a pattern that would be of use if what waited in the green wasn't a friend to them. She and Chalcus were willing to live and let live if other parties were of a similar mind; but if the others weren't, well, she and Chalcus were ready for that as well.

"Why are we here, ma'am?" Cashel asked, looking about the vast, domed hall with the interest its magnificence deserved. The roof was clear crystal. You could see fluffy clouds through it, but though the just-risen sun filled the room with light, it didn't heat things up the way Cashel was used to from working outdoors.

Because the room was so big, the number of people inside didn't fill it any more than the terrace up above was crowded by a similar assembly. A dais rose in two steps at one edge. The first level was just above the heads of the spectators. On it sat the seven wizards Cashel'd seen at the dawn ceremony, still wearing their golden headdresses and gold-embroidered robes.

The step above was the same amount higher. On it was an empty throne of interwoven ruby and sapphire threads.

"Every visitor to Ronn should see the Morning Levee," Mab said with a faint smile. "I'd be remiss in my duties as hostess if I didn't bring you."

She paused, then added, "I expect to introduce you to a man here after the levee. But it really is an attractive pageant, even to me who's seen it often. I thought you'd enjoy it."

"Yes, ma'am," Cashel said. "It's pretty, all right."

"Ronn has many attractive pageants," Mab said, but she seemed to be talking to herself.

They'd crossed to the north side of the terrace and gone down an outside staircase, then walked through any number of branching halls to get to this high room. Cashel found it like hiking through canyons, though, not a series of caves like it was in most big buildings. It wasn't just that the halls were wide and had high ceilings: the walls and everything seemed full of the same light as up on the terrace.

Instead of being covered with paintings on plaster, the translucent walls of Ronn were molded inside with curves and sweeps and dadoes. Some panels were knots of leaves and flowers, but Cashel didn't see any birds or animals in the designs as he went along.

Ronn was a pretty place to be, at least for a visit. The folks passing in the halls seemed happy too.

That was pretty much true here under the crystal dome also, where he saw an even wider assortment of foreigners than on the terrace. As Mab and Cashel entered, ushers were guiding an animal toward the front. It was as big as an elephant, but shaped very different. Instead of a trunk and tusks, its head was curved in to make a saddle with a pair of broad, flat horns over the nose. A tasseled scarlet drapery covered the creature's back, and on that was a gilded palanquin in which rode two women.

"They're ambassadors from Tiree, far to the west," Mab said. "They came overland along the coast road."

Behind the ambassadors were more attendants than Cashel could count on both hands, wearing puffed white shirts and pantaloons. Two carried brooms and buckets. The creature must be well trained to be trusted to walk through so large a crowd, but there were some things that a big plant-eater *had* to do, training or no. Their stomachs just worked that way.

Cashel got a good look at all the traffic because Mab had placed them at the middle of the room instead of near the dais where the crowd was thicker. They were far enough from the walls that Cashel wasn't sure he could make himself heard to people just entering, even though he'd learned to throw his voice while calling to other shepherds across the hills of the borough.

"The delegations from the eastern cities of Hyse, Ernle, and Renfell are coming in to your left," Mab said, nodding minusculely rather than point past Cashel toward another of the many, many doors into the chamber. "They came along the coast as well."

Cashel's hands tightened a trifle on his quarterstaff. Each of the three eastern ambassadors rode on a sedan chair carried by two metal giants half again as tall as Cashel. The first pair were covered in copper and had agate eyes; the second silver and glinting sapphire eyes; and the third were shining gold whose eyes were diamonds cut to sparkle like a bee's.

The giants stumped forward slowly without looking to either side. The third pair didn't march with quite the same pace, so the chair rocked side to side. The fat, smooth-faced man riding on it kept his expression as fixed as that of his metal bearers. He had to reach up quickly to keep his bulging turban from toppling off his head.

"They're automatons, clockwork pieces," Mab said dismissively. "Clever toys, but merely toys. Of course the phantasms that the Councillors control are toys also, though of a different kind."

As the ambassadors from the east clumped to places of honor near the dais, curtains fell from galleries to either side, just below the dome. Whole squads of trumpeters there began to call. Their gold-gleaming instruments were of different lengths, and the music sounding from them was just as liquidly complicated as the tunes Garric played on his pipes in the days when he and Cashel watched the borough's sheep together.

The eldest Councillor rose from his ivory chair. "The Assembly of the City of Ronn is open," he said. His voice was thready, the way old men's voices often are, but to Cashel's amazement every word was clear as Mab's had been. "The Assembly will now receive the greetings of our brother cities."

He sat down unsteadily, and the female Councillor on his left got up in his place. There was a brief hush; then a male voice, just as easy to hear as the Councillor's, said, "The Primates and People of the Nagaro greet the Assembly of Ronn and wish it eternal splendor."

Cashel couldn't see who was speaking. The voice seemed to come from everywhere. Mab gestured with an index finger, saying, "There's too many people in the way to see them from here, but the delegates are in the center closest to the throne. The Nagaro's a river draining into the Great Sea on the opposite side of the continent."

"The Assembly of the City of Ronn accepts the good wishes of the Primates of Nagaro," said the standing Councillor.

"The ambassadors from the Nagaro came by sea," Mab said, speaking softly, her lips close to Cashel's right shoulder. "All the delegations from the north came by sea, just as those of the southern islands did. No one crosses the mountains to reach Ronn anymore. Nobody's crossed them in a decade."

More delegates, about a double handful though Cashel wasn't interested enough to actually count them off on his fingers, spoke and were recognized the same as the first one. Apart from the ambassadors from the cities of the south coast, lifted high by the mounts that'd carried them in, he couldn't see the speakers themselves. He mostly looked around at the hall and the spectators nearby.

Cashel tried to guess how high the dome was, but he couldn't come any closer than being sure there weren't any trees in the borough that wouldn't have fitted inside without trouble. Since he left Barca's Hamlet he'd seen temples with domes, but they'd had a hole right in the top for lighting. Here it was solid, though in the center of the crystal swirled a pattern that had at least three strands and might be three threes.

Mab made little comments about the ambassadors and the places they came from, but she didn't seem to be too interested in all this either. It was pretty, but pretty the way a painting is instead of being like Cashel's smooth, perfectly balanced quarterstaff.

The whole business reminded him of the Tithe Procession, when priests from Carcosa dragged big statues of the Lady and the Shepherd through the borough on carts. They wore fancy costumes and talked fancy words, but none of it came to anything.

Unlike his sister Ilna, Cashel believed in the Great Gods. Whatever the Gods were, though, he didn't figure They had much to do with a bunch of tired, red-faced city folk chanting words that meant as little to them as the color of the dust in the street.

"The Assembly of the City of Ronn will now hear petitions from her citizens," the Councillor said. The woman who'd taken over from the old man was still doing the talking, not that there was much to it.

"Normally there'd only be one or two Councillors at the Morning Levee," Mab said. As usual her voice was calm and sounded slightly amused, but that was a gloss over something else that Cashel wasn't sure of. "Because the queen's absent, they decided they should all appear."

"Has the queen's reign ended as the legend says?" a man called. His voice filled the air just as those of speakers near the dais had, but he was actually standing close enough to touch with the quarterstaff if Cashel'd needed to. He was a sturdy young fellow of about Cashel's age. "Will the king now return to rule Ronn for a thousand years?"

Spectators turned to one another and whispered excitedly; the motion reminded Cashel of a breeze dancing over a meadow of brightly colored flowers. The vast crystal room swallowed the sounds as completely as the sea drinks in raindrops.

The standing Councillor stepped back, turning to her seated senior. The old man struggled to rise.

Without waiting further for him, the female faced the audience again. "The legend is just that," she said. "Legend, myth! There's no truth to it. The queen is tending to the welfare of the citizens of Ronn, as she's done for a thousand years and as she will continue to do forever!"

The eldest Councillor got to his feet, supporting himself by gripping the back of his chair with one hand. "The Assembly is closed!" he croaked. "Go to your homes and praise the queen for her kindness and foresight!"

"Forever," Mab repeated in disgust. "They wouldn't say that if they had any more conception of what 'forever' means than they do of what's really happened to the queen."

People were going out of the big room quicker than they'd drifted in to begin with. The question the fellow asked had bothered folks, that was for sure. Some of those who'd been close enough to see who was speaking glanced at him, but they dropped their eyes and moved toward a door when he glared in their direction.

"They *don't* know where the queen is?" Cashel said, making sure that he'd understood the part that Mab hadn't said directly.

The speaker saw Cashel looking and scowled back at him. He was solid-looking, but he'd have had to be a good deal bigger and solider before he ought to go picking a fight with Cashel or-Kenset.

Not that Cashel was going to let anything like that happen. He gave the fellow a friendly smile and a nod, standing with his feet spread a little and his staff planted straight up from the floor in his left hand.

"All they know is that the queen vanished," Mab said. "I shouldn't wonder if they don't believe the legend themselves."

"Do you believe the legend, ma'am?" Cashel said. Just so he knew . . .

"No," said Mab flatly. "But this is a crisis for Ronn and her citizens, and the king's return isn't the worst of what could happen in the near future."

She grinned at Cashel. "Almost the worst, though," she added, placing her left hand on his biceps. Her fingers were white, and the nails stood out like dazzling jewels against his dark skin. "Come, it's time that I introduce you and Herron to one another. He's the one who spoke."

The angry young man must've heard his name; his mouth opened in surprise as Mab led Cashel up to him. "Master Herron," she said, "this is Cashel, a stranger to Ronn but a good man for you and your fellows to know."

"Who are *you?*" Herron said, staring at the woman in amazement. Cashel knew how he felt.

"Cashel," Mab continued, ignoring the question, "Herron is the leader of the Sons of the Heroes. The six of them are the only citizens of Ronn who're taking action to deal with the threat."

"How did you *know* that?" Herron said. "Nobody knows that! Who *are* you?"

"Does it matter?" the woman said, brushing the question away with a sweep of her hand. "There's nothing improper in what you're doing, is there?"

"Well, no," said Herron. "But we don't talk about it except, you know, among ourselves."

"Her name's Mab," Cashel said. Mab stepped to the side, allowing him to offer his right arm for Herron to clasp if he was of a mind to. "I'm pleased to meet you, Master Herron."

It amused Cashel to hear somebody wrapped up in knots when he asks questions that weren't going to be answered. He'd generally found that by keeping his mouth shut and listening, he'd learn as much as the other person was willing to tell—and sometimes more. That's why he hadn't asked Mab about his mother.

"Yes, I'm Mab," she agreed with a faint smile. "Master Herron, I suggest you call a meeting of your brotherhood immediately to meet Master Cashel and discuss how to deal with the crisis."

"But . . . ," Herron said. He clasped arms absently, then stepped away to look from her to Cashel and back again. Herron was probably used to being bigger than most of the men he met. He seemed uncomfortable to see that wasn't the case now. "Mistress, I don't see—"

"Do you doubt that this *is* a crisis?" Mab said harshly. "With the queen missing, how long do you think it can be before the king and his

Made Men try to return? We'll meet you and your fellows on the exercise ground you train on. In an hour's time, shall we say?"

Herron blinked, then swallowed. "Yes, ma'am!" he said, and turned off toward one of the many exits. He started out walking fast, but he was jogging through the dispersing spectators by the time he reached the high archway.

"Only six of them," Mab said, though she didn't sound too concerned about it. "It's not very much to work with, is it?"

Cashel shrugged. "It depends on who they are," he said. "And who the other fellows are too."

He raised his arms overhead, holding the quarterstaff between them, just stretching a little. He wouldn't do real exercises with the staff till he was outside somewhere, though there was probably plenty of room right there the way the hall was emptying.

"Anyway," he added, "I guess it's seven of us now."

"Lady, fold me under the cloak of Your protection," Sharina said. She was kneeling before what had probably been intended as an ornamental yew; now it was nearly thirty feet high and spread roots across the rubble of the wall it'd been planted to screen. "Protect my soul and body from danger, and help me protect those who depend on me."

She'd scraped off a patch of bark near the tree's base, then used the point of her Pewle knife to scratch a figure on the bare yellowish wood. She wasn't an artist; a more delicate tool wouldn't have improved the result she'd gotten with the big knife. Only Sharina herself could tell that the crude strokes were meant to represent the Lady.

On the foreshore behind her, Lord Waldron and his aides were preparing to board the five ships that would carry them and Sharina to Valles. Farther downbeach, Garric and his entourage were also about to get under way; trumpets and curved horns called together in a fanfare.

"Lady," Sharina whispered, "if I must take the lives of others to save my friends and myself, gather the souls of my victims to Your bosom as I pray You will gather mine when I die."

Half the royal army stood in formation, fully armed, along the stretch of beach from which Garric was setting off. When the signallers blew a second fanfare, the thousands of troops bellowed together, "Garric and the Isles!"

Well, something close to together: that many people couldn't possibly act in perfect unison. The result from even Sharina's slight distance was a bestial growl. To those listening on the Sandrakkan side of the strait, it'd be a threatening rumble like that of a restive volcano.

Sharina touched the hem of the stick figure she'd carved, then got to her feet. A pair of Blood Eagles guarded her from a discreet distance. Tenoctris sat cross-legged nearby.

The old wizard had drawn a six-sided figure on the ground with white powder, very likely flour. She must've completed whatever incantation she'd been performing because the bamboo splinter she used as a wand lay in the center of the hexagon. She'd broken it so that she wouldn't accidentally use it again.

Many wizards performed their spells with athames, knives decorated with words and symbols of power and often made of exotic materials. Such tools gathered power with every use, increasing the effects the user could achieve with them.

But with the greater power came an equal loss of control. Even now as the millennial cycle built to its peak, Tenoctris couldn't work the great feats of wizardry that others did—but her spells achieved precisely what she intended, never more. A thousand years ago the end of the Old Kingdom had come when a mighty wizard had overwhelmed King Carus and his whole fleet—but in the backlash of that same spell, the wizard had sunk himself and the usurper for whom he acted into the depths.

Tenoctris had a book—a codex of bound parchment leaves rather than a scroll—open on her lap, but she didn't seem to be reading it. She acknowledged Sharina's glance with a weary smile. Wizardry was hard work.

Sharina started over to the older woman, but she paused for a moment to watch Garric set off for the mainland. His ships had their masts and yards raised though their sails remained on Volita. Signal flags flew from the spars and rigging in colorful but meaningless profusion, the visual equivalent of the horns calling across the water.

Under the brassy cacophony, Sharina heard the faint, rhythmic music of a double flute being played in the stern of each vessel, marking time for the rowers. Garric transported his army in warships, triremes with oarsmen in only the lowest level and ordinary soldiers filling the other two. It was horribly uncomfortable, but a sailing ship packed with troops wasn't a palace suite either—and a sailing ship might find itself becalmed for days and weeks. That was a minor frustration for the crew of a cargo vessel, but it could be lethal when hundreds of passengers had water for only a day, and that if rationed sparingly.

In addition, oared vessels travelled at known speeds, arriving when they were expected regardless of any weather except severe storms. If the wind was favorable, so much the better; but man, not the elements, determined the voyage. No captain of a sailing ship would make that claim, even in drunken exhilaration.

"May the Shepherd stand at your side, brother," Sharina said, though she wasn't sure the words made it all the way from her mind to her tongue. "May the Lady shine Her light through the darkness to guide you."

She stepped to Tenoctris' side. When the old wizard smiled greeting and raised her right hand, Sharina braced her own arms to allow Tenoctris to pull herself up from the ground.

"I wasn't religious until Nonnus died to save me," Sharina said in a quiet voice. Tenoctris had known the hermit, though only for a few days. Nonnus had settled in the woods near Barca's Hamlet at about the time Sharina was born. He'd provided the community with the sort of practical medicine he'd learned as soldier. "I'm not sure I'm really religious now, but . . . I think he'd be pleased that I worship the Lady."

"Yes," said Tenoctris, understanding a great deal more than Sharina had said. Understanding, perhaps, that Nonnus might not really have believed in the Great Gods either, but he'd hoped, prayed, that They might be real. If They were, there was someone to forgive him for the *other* things he'd learned and done as a soldier. "I think he would too."

Six Blood Eagles in full armor strode up to Sharina and Tenoctris. Their officer, an undercaptain—what in a line regiment would be a lieutenant—shouted, "Halt!"

The squad clashed to a halt, raising their knees high to bang their hobnails on the stony soil and making the studs of their leather skirts jingle against one another. Besides their arms, each man carried his traveling cloak rolled over a few personal possessions and slung over his right shoulder.

"We'll take over from here," the undercaptain said, handing the senior of the present guards a chit written on a piece of potsherd. Sharina remembered the officer and some of his men, though she couldn't put names to them. So many soldiers had guarded her since she became a princess . . .

One of the soldiers lifted his chin a trifle in greeting. Sharina recognized the men now: they were the squad that'd escorted her to the Temple of Our Lady of the Sunset in Carcosa, where the priests had thought they'd turn Sharina into a cynical politician like they were.

"Trooper Lires!" Sharina said in pleasure. "And you're Undercaptain—"

"Ascor, your highness," the officer said, obviously pleased that she remembered him. "We were honored that his highness Prince Garric detailed us to accompany you and Lady Tenoctris."

Ascor was neither a nobleman nor a grizzled veteran who'd been promoted from the ranks after decades of hard fighting. From his accent, Sharina guessed he was a younger son of a middle-class merchant family in Valles: an educated man though not particularly wealthy, supported by the influence of some civilian like Lord Tadai rather than a military officer.

"Accompany?" Sharina said. "To Valles, you mean?"

"Yes, your highness," Ascor said. "And it looks—"

He nodded past Sharina. She glanced over her shoulder. A young officer with the ivory baton of a courier trotted toward them from the group around Lord Waldron.

"—like it's time to board."

Tenoctris closed her satchel; Sharina picked it up without being asked. "Let's go, then," Sharina said. "I must say"—she looked around Volita, the tumbled ruins everywhere and the black granite outcrop lowering over the shore—"that there are places I've more regretted leaving."

"I can carry that bag, your highness," Trooper Lires said as they started forward.

Sharina smiled at the heavily laden soldier. "I'm sure you could," she said. "But not nearly as easily as I can."

The courier reached them. "Lord Waldron presents his compliments," he blurted, "and hopes your highness will follow me to the flagship at your earliest convenience!"

"If you weren't standing in our way, kiddie," one of the Blood Eagles said, "we'd likely be there already. Move it, why don't you?"

The courier glowered, then realized that even though a common trooper shouldn't be talking to an officer that way, the statement was more or less true. "Right!" he said, and turned back the way he'd come.

"I'm fine," Tenoctris said, catching the glance Sharina threw her as they followed the courier. "I've been trying again to learn what's happened to Cashel and Ilna."

"Did you succeed?" Sharina said. The slope was gentle, but the footing there could be awkward because stone blocks were scattered in the high grass.

"Not really," the wizard admitted. "Though I'm sure that Ilna's disappearance had something to do with the Demon, but Cashel's didn't. That's only useful in the sense that it means they weren't victims of a concerted attack. It doesn't help us bring them back."

"We will, though," Sharina said. Her stomach tightened at the thought, but she kept her tone bright. "Or they'll bring themselves back. They have in the past."

"Yes, that's so," Tenoctris said, cheerfully agreeable. Sharina wondered whether the older woman was just concealing her fears; and if she was, whether she could teach Sharina to conceal her own equally well.

The courier took them to where the army commander stood, but there he halted in indecision. Lord Waldron was facing away, saying in a rising voice, "Look, Master Bedrin, I may need a full hour to get all the men aboard. I'm not asking you, I'm telling you!"

"Looks to me like he'll need longer than that," Trooper Lires snickered, to his fellows and to Sharina both. "He's taking Podwils' regiment. They was cavalry till Prince Garric wouldn't bring their horses along when they left Ornifal. It'd have been easier to get the horses aboard than them splay-legged jockeys!"

The comment wasn't completely fair—there was a great deal of rivalry between infantry and the higher-paid cavalrymen, and the fact that these infantry were the royal bodyguard didn't change the ill feeling for the better. On the other hand, it wasn't completely unfair either. The men climbing the gangplanks onto the ships were hampered by long cavalry swords, and many of them were in high horseman's boots as well. From what Sharina could see, most had more than the bare minimum of possessions with them also, which would further complicate the process of loading.

"Well, I'm sorry, milord," said the man facing him, presumably Master Bedrin. He didn't sound in the least sorry. From his attitude it was obvious that Bedrin was a fleet officer and, therefore, not under the army commander's direct control. "If we can't set out within the hour, we'll have to wait till dawn tomorrow. Otherwise, we're likely to be benighted in a stretch of shoals, which I'm unwilling to risk."

It seemed to Sharina that Bedrin would've been wiser to keep the cheerful insouciance out of his voice. The chain of command was one thing, but the way Lord Waldron's hand rested on his sword pommel was quite another. The old warrior wasn't a man you wanted to goad into a rage.

"*You're* not willing?" Waldron said. "Well, you'd—"

"Milord," Sharina said, close enough to Waldron's left ear to make him jump. "If Master Bedrin allows you to be drowned, the conspiracy on Ornifal will go unchecked with the Gods-know-what result for the kingdom. Please, humor him for Prince Garric's sake."

"Ah!" said Waldron, turning to face Sharina and her companions. A series of emotions cascaded over his face. In a much milder tone, he said, "Ah," again.

"And not to sound selfish . . . ," Sharina continued, smiling broadly. "But *I'd* rather not drown either."

She respected and even liked Lord Waldron, because he was the best man he knew how to be under all circumstances. Waldron was narrow, choleric, and not infrequently stubborn to the point of being pigheaded—but he was always true to what he saw as his duty.

"Ah," Waldron repeated. "But the thing is, your highness—time's short. Maybe too short already. If we get to Ornifal after this usurper's captured Valles, then there's no choice for anything but the whole army and full-scale war."

"Milord, I can't keep the sun from setting," Master Bedrin said peevishly. "It—"

Sharina pointed her left index finger at the naval officer's face. She'd dealt with angry, argumentative men on a regular basis at her father's inn. At least neither of this pair was drunk.

"Master Bedrin, your men can hold a stroke and a half rate for four hours, can't they?" she said. She'd learned a great deal about ships and sailors since she'd left Barca's Hamlet, not least by listening to the stories Chalcus told in the evenings Garric and his friends spent together on islets while crossing and recrossing the Inner Sea. "They've rested since we landed on Volita, and the run north from Carcosa wasn't a hard one either. Not so?"

"Well, yes, four hours—but not tomorrow and the next day and the next besides!" Bedrin said with an expression somewhere between surprise and anger. He was unusually tall, red-haired, and from his accent a native of Cordin.

"Nor will they have to," Sharina said. "*And* they'll be paid a third silver wheatsheaf for the run instead of the usual two per day. Lord Waldron, that gives you two hours to get your men aboard. Will that be sufficient?"

"It will or I'll have broken some troop leaders down to the ranks!" Waldron growled, nodding approval. He noticed the Blood Eagles and scowled again. "Who're these?"

"Undercaptain Ascor," the squad commander said, striking a brace. He couldn't salute properly because he was loaded in marching array. "Prince Garric ordered us to accompany her highness the princess."

Waldron grimaced. "Six more bodies to fit where there's not room for what we've got already," he grumbled. "All right, Ascor. Three of you go aboard the *Star of Valles,* the other three on the *Victory of Ornifal.* They're at the end of the row."

He nodded toward the readying vessels farthest up the beach.

"I'm sorry, milord," Ascor said, "but Prince Garric ordered we stay with her highness. I'm afraid that means we travel on the same ship as she does, whichever one that is."

"Do you think that black lobster suit means you can order me around?" Lord Waldron shouted, tapping the knuckles of his right fist on Ascor's breastplate of blackened bronze. "Well, you can—"

He stopped and guffawed. "No, you don't think that," he resumed in a wholly reasonable tone. "But Prince Garric thinks he can. And since there's one traitor in the bor-Warriman family already, there's no need for me to become one myself."

Waldron bowed to Sharina. "Come aboard the *Star of Valles* with me, your highness," he said. "And we'll try to find room that we can all stand without becoming better friends than propriety would allow!"

Chapter Five

This is my second visit to Erdin," Garric said to Liane, in the stern of the *Shepherd of the Isles* as the big vessel stroked slowly across the strait. "The first time I was a peasant who'd never seen a gold coin."

Unlike merchant vessels, warships couldn't remain tied up to quays while in harbor: their light hulls would become waterlogged. Erdin had no open beaches nor a dry dock large enough to haul a five-banked monster like the *Shepherd* out of the water, so she'd return to Volita after delivering Garric with the pomp appropriate to a ruling prince.

Garric grinned. "The city looks different now."

The *Shepherd*'s fighting towers of canvas-covered wicker were raised in the bow and stern. The balistas mounted on them had bolts in their troughs, and the only reason the weapons weren't cocked was that Garric had absolutely refused to chance one of them letting loose by accident.

Attaper had thought the extra protection from having the artillery ready to shoot was worth the risk; Garric's other military officers simply weren't bothered at the possibility of a dozen or so Sandrakkan spectators being killed if a bronze-headed bolt ripped through the crowd. Garric *did* care.

"You're right to worry about civilians, lad," King Carus noted with a broad grin. *"But it's only because I saw where the other way of thinking led that I didn't argue with you myself."*

The triremes transporting the Blaise regiment were in line abreast to the *Shepherd*'s starboard. They bucked the current between Volita and the mainland with more difficulty than the larger ship because they had only one bank of oars manned. Even so they kept station well. It was a short voyage, and Admiral Zettin had made sure the transports had picked crews.

The admiral himself was aboard one of the ten fully crewed triremes maneuvering in the strait. Sections of five ships combed through one another, then reversed direction and did the same thing again. It was an impressive ship-handling demonstration, but it was also a warning to anybody who'd thought of putting out from the mainland with hostile intentions.

Garric hadn't ordered him to put on that show of force, but Zettin didn't need orders to get him to act. If anything he was *too* zealous.

"He's very able," Liane said, following the line of Garric's gaze and noting the slight frown. Her tone held the same doubt that he was feeling. "And intelligent, for that matter. But he doesn't always see that his duties are part of running the kingdom, instead of being the kingdom existing to support a fleet."

"He probably wouldn't be as good a fleet commander if he weren't focused on that alone," Garric said. "But I have to watch him a little more carefully than I sometimes have time to do."

"*Right,*" said the image of Carus, nodding grim-faced agreement. "*Just in case he decides to take a squadron into a fishing village by night and carry off all the able-bodied men to fill empty oar benches. And don't say it couldn't happen, because it did. And it was me who did it, I'm sorry to say.*"

Garric chuckled, causing Liane to smile at his pleasure. He could imagine the effect kidnapping crews had on the kingdom in the longer run, though. The same was true of extortionate taxation, of course, but both Lord Tadai and—back in Valles—Chancellor Royhas showed more awareness of long-term considerations than Zettin did.

Zettin's job was at its simplest level killing other people. It didn't encourage viewing things in the long term, and realities of the work led to the early deaths of soldiers who forgot the basics.

The trireme manned by Blood Eagles under Lord Attaper's personal command slid up to the quay where soldiers in bright armor, courtiers, and, in the center, Earl Wildulf himself waited. The guards disembarked swiftly, setting helmets in place and hooking shield straps to the staples on their backplates to transfer some of the weight off their left arms.

"How do they row wearing breastplates?" Liane asked wonderingly.

"It can't be easy, even for the distance from here to Volita," Garric agreed. "I think Attaper's being excessive in demanding that his men be trained to row at all. But I suppose he'd say that it was his job to be excessive, and since the men themselves don't complain—"

"They do complain!" Liane protested. "I've heard them."

Garric grinned wider. "Love, they're soldiers," he said. "They breathe and they eat and they complain. But they're not real complaints, the kind that meant Attaper would need to worry more about his own men than the enemy in a melee."

That was the sort of truth that a natural warrior like Carus probably knew before he was able to crawl. By then Garric had enough experience with armies to have learned it also.

The *Shepherd's* officers, both those on deck and the others unseen among the oarsmen in the hold, shouted orders. The oars in the topmost three banks rose horizontal, dribbling strings of water like sunlit jewels back into the sea. The rowers of the lower banks backed their oars, though inertia kept the quinquereme sliding forward without seeming to slow.

The Blood Eagles formed eight ranks deep in front of the earl and his entourage. For most public functions the bodyguards stuck wooden balls onto their javelins, turning the weapons into batons suitable for pushing back spectators without injuring anybody. Garric noticed that this time the steel points were bare.

He grimaced, but he wouldn't complain to Lord Attaper for making that choice. Attaper was already so uncomfortable about what Garric was doing that nothing short of dismissing him from his command would have any effect on his orders.

"Besides which," Carus noted with approval, *"his replacement'd do the same thing. At least he would if he was any good. Pretending this is a victory parade in Valles is likely to get you killed, lad."*

The six ships carrying Lord Rosen's regiment made for the quays to either side of the one where Garric would land. The Blood Eagle trireme rocked in the turbulence as the other ships backed water. From what Garric could see, there wasn't a soul aboard her. The vessel could scrape its sides off against the stone quay so far as Attaper was concerned. All *he* cared about was putting as many of his men as he could between Garric and people who generally wished Garric was dead.

Erdin would've been an open roadstead, very dangerous in a storm, if Volita hadn't provided a windbreak. Six major canals and a network of lesser ones crossed the city, opening the River Erd to the Inner Sea some miles west of its natural mouth. All but the largest vessels could be towed into the river and docks, which were even more sheltered, so the facilities on the seafront were less extensive than Erdin's size and commerce normally would merit.

The *Shepherd* nosed into the slip; the captain and sailing master had judged matters well, particularly since warships almost never pulled up to a dock. The group of aides and officials were waiting near Garric in the stern—very near him, since with the fighting towers erected the quinquereme had even less than a warship's usual slight amount of deck space. They straightened, and Lord Lerdain—with a youth's impatience and the arrogance of a count's heir apparent—stared meaningfully at Garric.

"Time we go forward," Garric said, smiling more at himself than at Lerdain. Had he ever been that young? And of course he had, only a few years ago.

As they started up the narrow catwalk between the ventilator gratings, sailors in the bow began shouting angrily at the Blood Eagles. Soldiers in the rear rank looked around in puzzlement, then called for their own officers. The *Shepherd* was drifting outward, toward the quay on its port side.

"Sorry, your highness, sorry!" said an officer—probably the sailing master—who turned from the sudden crowd on the foredeck. "Those bloody fool landsmen cleared all the dockers away, so there's nobody to grab a line to tie us up! Sorry, but we're getting it sorted."

A sailor leaped to the quay, fifteen feet away and a very good jump even from the height of the *Shepherd*'s deck. He grabbed a flung line and snubbed it to a bollard just as two Blood Eagles trotted back. The ship eased to starboard again as sailors in the bow hauled on their end of the line. The gangplank—a long grating covered with blue wool—thumped onto the dock even before the stern lines were set.

Garric started forward, with Liane a step behind. Over his shoulder, in a voice just loud enough for her to hear over the sailors' continued chatter, he said, "If we could foresee everything that was going to happen, then we'd be gods and not men. I'm not sure I'd want that; and anyway, it isn't going to happen."

"No," said Liane, sounding surprisingly cheerful. It'd done both of them good to get away from the oddly tense atmosphere of Volita. "But the things that happen are getting fixed. That's what men do. The best kind of men."

The signallers on the royal vessels blew another fanfare, and the Blood Eagles clashed to attention. Spectators filled the waterfront and the balconies of buildings facing it. Their mood was sullen, with little of the carnival atmosphere generated by every other parade Garric had seen since his first Tithe Procession in Barca's Hamlet.

Attaper shouted an order from the front of the formation. The solid mass of Blood Eagles shifted like sand running into a mold, forming an aisle between black-armored spearmen. It was just wide enough for two people to pass down it abreast.

The three Sandrakkan negotiators and half a dozen other courtiers stood with Wildulf. The earl wore armor, a molded cuirass, and a helmet crested with plumes that were violet or bronze depending on how the light struck them. The full-bodied natural blonde at his side must be the countess. She wore a tiara of blue stones.

"Lord Tawnser isn't here," Liane murmured. "I've never met him, but he lost an eye at the Stone Wall, so he'd be conspicuous."

"Right," said Garric. If the leader of the anti-Ornifal faction chose to absent himself from court while the royal delegation was present, so much the better. He started forward.

"Wait!" said Liane. "Attaper and I discussed this."

"Your lordship," Attaper called to Wildulf. "His highness Prince Garric will receive you now."

Marshal Renold spoke something into Wildulf's ear. The earl grunted a reply, then gave his arm to Countess Balila and strode down the aisle. The countess avoided looking to either side, keeping her gaze regally fixed on Garric. Her eyes were blue, matching the tiara, and they blazed with anger.

"Your highness," Wildulf said. He was a big man, not fat but certainly going to be fat by the time he was fifty in another few years. His tone wasn't overtly belligerent, but Garric noticed he hadn't said, "Welcome," or offered his arm to clasp as one man greeting another.

"Lord Wildulf," Garric replied with smiling reserve. "I'm pleased to have the opportunity to visit you in this fashion. I believe my associates have discussed matters of accommodation with you?"

"There are rooms ready for you in the palace," said Wildulf. He eyed Liane, and added, "We brought horses, though maybe the lady would like a sedan chair?"

"Thank you," said Liane, speaking in the coolly aristocratic tone she used on those rare occasions when she wanted to emphasize that she was *Lady* Liane. "For the occasion I prefer to ride with the countess and your advisors, Lord Wildulf, ahead of you and Prince Garric. The order of march which his highness has decided—"

Carus guffawed in Garric's mind. This was obviously something else that Liane and Attaper must've decided without Garric's involvement. That was probably out of fear that he'd have a different opinion. . . .

"—is for your cavalry to lead, followed by the members of your court and the prince's advisors, along with the countess and myself."

The regiment of horsemen drawn up on the boulevard joining the waterfront from the north were working soldiers, not parade troops in gaudy trappings. Carus murmured, *"They're not as pretty as some I've seen, but I shouldn't wonder if they wouldn't be more useful than an equal number of Waldron's kinsmen just for being better disciplined. Though Waldron'd have apoplexy if he heard you say so."*

"A section of Lord Attaper's troops will follow us"—she hadn't said, "the bodyguards" or "the Blood Eagles," but Lord Attaper's bleak-faced nod made that explicit—"with the remainder of that unit following the prince and yourself. Lord Rosen's regiment will bring up the rear. They'll be billeted in buildings adjacent to the palace, I understand."

Lord Rosen himself appeared, accompanied by a senior noncom whom Garric had met before. He waited to the side while Garric was meeting with the earl. His men were drawn up across the narrow slips to either side of this one.

"We figured that—" Earl Wildulf began, scowling like a thundercloud.

"Ornifal nancy boys!" somebody shouted from the crowd. The breeze carried the words clearly over the royal contingent.

The noncom with Rosen—Serjeant Bastin, that was the man's name!—raised his shield up beside his face to form a sounding board. "I'm a Blaise armsman!" he bellowed back at the crowd. "And I'd rather prong one of my daddy's pigs than what passes for men in Erdin! Or women too!"

Garric gasped to keep from laughing out loud. That would've been partly hysteria, he supposed, but the sudden relief of tension was a wonder and a delight.

"Lord Wildulf," he said, ignoring what were probably going to be arguments, over the order of march, "all that needs to be said here has been said. Let's get to your palace, and we can continue matters there."

He reached forward, offering Wildulf his arm. Wildulf, by reflex or perhaps out of equal relief, clasped it.

"Right," he said. "The horses are back with my guards, your highness."

It wouldn't have been quite right to say that seeing the boxwoods up close took Ilna's breath away, but the mass of dark green let her know how much she'd been worn by a day of hiking on gritty soil through sere vegetation. She'd taken grass and trees for granted in Barca's Hamlet.

She smiled, wryly but without the bitterness she might have felt in the recent past. If her life had followed the course she'd expected, she'd never have known how many places there were that she liked less than she did Barca's Hamlet.

This country seemed to have a general slope from the southern cliffs northward, but no terrain is perfectly flat—not even the surface of the sea. The vegetation they'd seen at dawn had been out of sight for most of the past several hours. Now it appeared directly before them, an interwoven wall of branches reaching from the ground to several times a man's height.

"It's been planted!" said Chalcus. "There's never a chance that those trees grew together naturally."

"It's a maze," said Ilna. The entrance wasn't on the near side, but she knew it existed as surely as she knew which warp threads to raise when she ran her shuttle through. "It's a maze of more than bushes."

"This is a barrier too," Davus said, indicating a fist-sized chunk of porphyry with the big toe of his right foot. It was lying on the crest of the rise they'd just walked up. "Of sorts. See there—"

He pointed, still using his foot. "And there?"

Now that he'd pointed them out, Ilna saw other rocks, some basalt and some porphyry, scattered in a wide arc to either side of the first. There was a distance of several paces between rocks, and they were of course—Ilna smiled as the words formed in her mind—just rocks.

"They circle the grove," Davus said. "They're to keep trolls out."

Chalcus stepped forward and paused, frowning angrily. He touched his sword hilt.

"Just a moment," said Davus, bending to lift away the stone he'd first indicated. "Now go through."

Chalcus stepped past him and nodded thankfully. Ilna followed, standing to the side as Davus backed after them and set the stone precisely where it'd been before.

"It was like stepping into warm blood," Chalcus said quietly. "A pool of warm blood. I could've gone on, but—I thank you, Master Davus."

"This way, I think," Ilna said, taking the lead without thinking about it. Seeing patterns was her work, her *life*; that was the skill they needed at present. She crunched over the ground, keeping just beyond arm's length of the hedge so that she didn't brush the boxwoods by accident. It probably wouldn't matter, but she didn't care to take the chance.

The weather appeared to follow the ridge they'd just crossed. The country Ilna saw to the north must be better watered, as it was grassy instead of being sparsely sprinkled with vegetation.

"Dear one?" said Chalcus, a few steps behind her with Davus. "What would happen if we were to cut a path through the branches here?"

"Nothing good," said Ilna. She usually plaited patterns in yarn as she walked along, a way to occupy her hands while her mind was elsewhere. Now she put the hank of yarn away because she needed that part of her to deal with the maze. "It isn't only brush, as I say. In fact, I suspect the trees were planted to conceal the real barrier."

The entrance was on the east side of the circle. It was a simple gap, wide enough that two could walk down it abreast if they didn't mind their shoulders touching the dense green branches.

Without looking at the men behind her Ilna said, "Follow me in line. Don't touch the branches, and on your *lives* don't go down any path except the one I lead you on."

She didn't bother to add, "Do you understand?" because they did understand. And if they'd been the sort of people who didn't, a few more words from her weren't going to prevent them from killing themselves.

Ilna stepped into the maze. The air was noticeably more humid, and she no longer felt the wind that'd been so constant since they'd arrived. The path was shaded even more than the tall boxwoods explained, and the light had a bluish cast. The changes from the arid waste outside weren't unpleasant in themselves, but they made Ilna think of bait in a trap.

She smiled. If the person who'd built the maze trapped her, then she deserved to die. It was a perfectly fair wager so far as she was concerned. She'd regret what happened to her companions, of course; if she had any time for regrets.

At the first turning Ilna took the left branch, but as she stepped past the fork she felt a surge of hopeful warmth, of longing even, to turn the other way. She looked down the narrow corridor. When she held her head just *so*, the green walls to either side vanished and she was instead peering into a deep well. At the bottom something waited, holding its raised tentacles close against the stone walls, where they were ready to enwrap anyone who fell into its lair. Waiting, *wanting* more desperately than any young lover. . . .

Ilna walked on, grimacing. She wanted to go faster, but though she trusted her instincts, she was too careful a craftsman to increase the risks even marginally. There was always the chance that one of her companions, hurrying to follow, would make a mistake that *his* instincts wouldn't warn him against.

She turned left again at the next fork. If space within the maze were the same as that outside it, she and her companions would've been back on the windswept waste . . . but it wasn't, of course, and they continued down another boxwood aisle.

There was nothing down the other fork: gray, palpable nothing, stretching on forever; a Hell of emptiness, without hope or end.

Ilna's face was set. She wouldn't show fear, even to herself; but she knew that someday she would die, and she wondered/suspected/*feared* that the same endless gray waited for her when she did.

She couldn't control that, nor was it her present concern. Her task, her duty, was to bring her companions through the maze to where they could expect to find food and water better than the brackish trickle they'd sucked from the underside of a limestone outcrop not long after noon.

The next branching puzzled her: neither path was the right one. Then something *shifted* and she stepped through on the right, calling over her shoulder, "Quickly, now. It'll change back shortly."

She didn't take the time to glance down the left-hand branching, but there were scattered bones along the portion of the path she was walking. Some were human, but another cleaned skull lying against the boxwoods showed horn cores over the eye sockets.

When Ilna reached the next branching, she looked back. The men were with her, Chalcus leading Davus, both of them still-faced and precisely in the center of the path. Chalcus threw her a smile, real enough she supposed, but the fact his right hand hovered over the hilt of his incurved sword showed that he was more tense than when she'd seen him in bloody combat.

But of course in combat, Chalcus had a task that he knew perfectly how to accomplish. Here his duty was to follow and keep out of the way. He'd do that as he'd do whatever his duty was, but for some people it's harder to watch than to act.

Ilna grinned. As she herself knew well.

"We're getting close," she said as she continued on. Her companions had remained silent ever since they entered the maze, but they must be wondering even though they had the wit and courage not to chance distracting her with questions.

Ilna was judging their location by the pattern instead of any fancied judgment of how far they must have come along the path's windings. Distance had its own laws among these boxwoods, different from those it followed in the world outside; but patterns were fixed in the fabric of the cosmos.

The path kinked to the right. Instead of following it, Ilna paused, frowning because she knew that couldn't be correct; and as she hesitated, she saw the gap between boxwoods straight ahead where she'd have sworn their branches interwove.

She stepped forward but looked to the right, toward the path she hadn't taken. That was a mistake, almost a fatal one: she shouted and stumbled to her knees.

"Dear heart?" Chalcus said, his left arm about her shoulders and his right flicking his swordpoint in tight arcs before her.

"Don't look to the side!" Ilna said. Her eyes were closed. She set her knuckles against the ground, grinding them hard enough that pain blurred the memory of what she'd seen. After some moments, she opened her eyes again and rose. Chalcus hovered behind her like a protective spirit.

Neither of the men spoke. Looking ahead rather than back at them, Ilna said, "There's what I suppose is a mirror down that aisle. It shows you the mistakes you've made in life, all of them; and it shows you what might have been if you hadn't made the mistakes. I think it would disturb a saint, and I haven't lived a saint's life."

She took a deep breath, and added, "I've woven patterns to do that same thing. The people I've shown them to haven't recovered. I must not have gotten a clear look, or . . ."

"Are you able to go on, dear one?" Chalcus said softly.

Ilna gave a harsh laugh. "Of course," she said. "Until I die."

She strode forward. *A very clever man, Chalcus; and a very understanding one. He knew that the last thing she needed was to stand, thinking about what might have been.*

There were no more branchings. Ilna walked between the boxwoods, feeling the path spring comfortably beneath her feet. The aisles were too shaded to support grass, but moss carpeted the moist soil.

The path ended in a small clearing. In it stood a low stone house with a slate roof and a walled garden in back. In front was a door of reddish wood framed by casement windows with panes of frosty isinglass. At the left side, a thin trail of smoke rose from the chimney of flint nodules set in brilliantly white lime mortar.

Chalcus stepped in front of Ilna. "My turn to lead," he said, walking forward with an easy roll to his step. He slanted his sword across his chest, where it was instantly ready to slash or parry but less obviously threatening than if he'd pointed it out in front of him.

Ilna glanced back at Davus; he smiled tightly and nodded her on ahead of him. He held a rock in either hand. These were larger chunks, each the size of a clenched fist, rather than the pebbles he'd used to bring down small game.

Ilna nodded back and followed Chalcus at a safe distance, just farther than his arm and curved sword would reach in a wide sweep. Her fingers were plaiting a pattern, keeping it doubled over between her palms so there was no danger if Chalcus looked over his shoulder at her.

She couldn't see movement through the windowpanes, and the only sound was the whisper of her feet and the sailor's against flagstones; Davus didn't make even that much noise. The latch chain of bronze links hanging from the notch at the top of the door was verdigrised except for the flat plate on the end, where use had worn the metal to a natural golden sheen.

Chalcus gripped the chain in his left hand, then glanced back to be sure his companions were ready. Davus gripped the vertical pull, also bronze, with two fingers of his left hand. He still held a stone with his thumb and the other two fingers. He and Chalcus moved in perfect sequence, one lifting the latch and the other hauling the massive door open.

Chalcus was inside as soon as the door swung enough to pass his body by a finger's breadth. Ilna followed, the pattern cupped in her hands against need.

The interior of the house was a single room, lighted by windows on three sides. Several layers of carpets covered the floor, their patterns subtly pleasing through the soles of Ilna's feet. A small cauldron hissed on a hearth crane over a charcoal fire.

A man with a goatee sat on a chalcedony throne in the center of the room, facing the front door. Curving designs were worked in silver thread on his purple velvet robe. Ilna sniffed to note that the embroiderer had been much more skillful than whoever'd woven the fabric to begin with. In the back wall was another door, less ornate, to serve the back garden.

The man's right hand rested on the arm of the throne, holding a gold-mounted goblet of etched glass. It was empty except for russet dregs. His eyes were unfocused, and his mouth lay slackly open.

Davus stepped in behind Ilna and pulled the door closed to cover their backs. When the heavy panel thudded against the jamb the man woke up, staring in fury at the three of them.

"Your pardon, good sir—" Chalcus began.

The man dropped his goblet and jumped to his feet. Standing, he was no taller than Ilna and noticeably pudgy despite his loose robe. He drew an athame of dense black rootwood from beneath his sash. He probably meant to point it at the intruders, but Chalcus moved more quickly and flicked the athame out of the wizard's hand with the back of his sword.

The blade wavered back like a curving beam of light. Its point paused a hand's breadth from the wizard's nose. He made a strangled sound and jerked away, only to trip over the goblet and fall beside the throne.

"As I was saying, good sir," Chalcus said. This time his voice was the deep, rasping purr of a big cat. "We're visitors in need of food and shelter, and though we beg your pardon—you *will* provide what we need."

He smiled down the length of his extended arm. The swordpoint was still centered on the wizard's nose.

Ronn sloped to the east in steps like those of a giant staircase. The exercise field was on the lowest level. Cashel looked over the parapet. The nearest ground was forest, covered with trees tall enough to overhang the edge of the field.

Cashel hadn't ever looked at the top of trees so big—or the tops of any trees, really, except after he'd cut them down. Seeing them this way was a pretty sight, no mistake.

Kinked and knotted vines grew everywhere, between the trees and from the crowns to the dirt. The branches were narrow meadows covered with mosses, plants that looked like cups or whose leaves were turned up to catch the rain, and bright, dangling flowers. Birds of even more colors than the flowers hopped and fluttered among the foliage, and equally gorgeous butterflies caught the sun like drifting jewels.

"We're on good terms with the jungle here in Ronn," Mab said. She smiled at him, but not in the coolly amused fashion he'd seen most often on her face. This was a warmer expression, like a mother gives a sleeping baby. "It creeps into the palace here on the east side. Some of the lianas stretch a hundred feet down the corridors, and when they bloom their flowers perfume the rooms even farther in."

She turned, drawing Cashel's eyes with her, and added, "But I see the Sons have arrived. Come, I'll introduce you."

The exercise field was an enormous thing; everything in Ronn was on a grand scale. There was an oval track around the whole terrace, and inside it straight tracks of a furlong and two furlongs. Ball courts stood at one end, and arrangements of poles for climbing and swinging were at the other. Down the middle ran long rows of dressing rooms, which men and women both came in and out of with the irregular busyness you see at the mouth of a beehive.

Ronn towered to the west, but because of the way it was stepped back, it didn't feel oppressive the way a wall straight up and down would've done. Cashel had seen mountains since he'd left the borough, real ones that hadn't been hollowed out into cities, and he'd learned that they never looked as big as they really were except when you were at a distance from them. Close up, the nearby bits got in the way of your feeling the size of the whole thing.

Six young men wearing helmets and breastplates walked from the dressing rooms toward the stretch of sod in a corner where Mab and Cashel waited. They carried shields with designs on the facings but no spears. Instead of real swords they held awkward-looking wooden affairs. Herron was in the middle.

They looked uncomfortable. Cashel gave them a friendly smile. Duzi knew he'd spent much of his life feeling uncomfortable around other people.

"Mistress?" Herron said to Mab. "You told us to meet you here?"

"Yes, to give Cashel a demonstration of your abilities," Mab said briskly. "And to introduce him to the rest of you."

She gestured toward the youths with her palm turned upward and continued, "Cashel, these are the Sons of the Heroes. They take the name of their group from the six Heroes who in past centuries defended Ronn from the Made Men. The real Heroes now live in the Shrine of the Heroes, a cave beneath the city's foundations. Only their semblances walk the walls of Ronn at night."

"That's all a myth," said a dark, studious-looking youth, dropping his eyes as he spoke. "Nobody lives for centuries in a cave. The Heroes died and maybe their bones are buried there, that's all."

"That's Master Orly, Cashel," Mab said coolly. "Herron you've met, and their four companions are Manza, Athan, Enfero, and—"

"I'm Stasslin, Master Cashel," said the sixth man, red-haired and the shortest of the group but built very solidly. He transferred his wooden sword to the hand gripping his shield, a little buckler with a wolf's head device, and stepped forward to clasp arms with Cashel.

Stasslin squeezed a trifle harder than he needed to. Cashel didn't squeeze back, but he tensed his biceps to convince the shorter man that he was all muscle under the tanned skin. Stasslin backed away, pursing his lips.

"Glad to meet you," Cashel said. "Ah, all of you, masters."

"And as for you, Orly," Mab said in a voice that cut like the winter wind. "You've been down to the Shrine of the Heroes, have you?"

The dark young man flushed. "I haven't been there, of course not," he said. "I'm just not a fool. I've read books, I've studied *all* the legends."

"And the people who wrote the books?" Mab continued in the same tone. "Had they been to the shrine?"

"Mistress," said Herron, edging forward a little to partly shield his embarrassed friend from the woman's glare. "Nobody's been to the shrine in, well, a hundred years. It's not safe, not now with the way things are, with the king threatening."

"So, Master Orly . . . ," Mab said. "You believe things you've never seen because you've been told them by other people who've never seen them. Isn't that how you'd define 'superstition,' Master Orly? Or would you prefer to call it childish prattling?"

Cashel wouldn't have treated a beaten enemy that way—and Orly surely was beaten, for all he was too young to admit it out loud—but he knew Ilna would do just the same to the boy as Mab was doing. He'd seen Ilna flay people with her tongue more than once, but only once per victim.

"All right!" Orly blazed. He tried to meet her eyes but blushed and ducked away again. "Have you been into the shrine yourself, then?"

"Would you believe me if I told you I had?" Mab said. "Well?"

Orly didn't speak. Herron said, "Mistress, we're sorry if we offended you. But this isn't why you wanted us here, is it?"

"Of course," agreed Mab mildly. "Let's draw a curtain over it, shall we?"

She slashed her right hand through the air, her fingernails trailing a cloud of sapphire glitter that drifted toward the ground and vanished. The Sons gaped at her. She smiled.

"A trick," she said. "A trivial illusion. Now, Master Herron—I wanted Cashel to watch you at your practice. That's what you'd usually be doing at this hour of the afternoon, wouldn't you?"

Several of the Sons looked at one another. They were Cashel's age or maybe a little older, but they all seemed *boys*. Herron not as much as the others, but . . .

Cashel had seen Garric at age sixteen quiet a pair of drunk bodyguards in the taproom during the Sheep Fair. He hadn't hit them or called for help, though he'd have had help if he'd needed it; he'd just grabbed both men by a shoulder and shouted for them to belt up as he hustled them to the door.

None of the Sons had Garric's presence. All of them together couldn't have done what Garric had that night.

"Well, yeah," Herron said. "When the sun's hot, there's not so many people here to, you know, watch us."

He looked over his shoulder. Given the size of the field, it wasn't anything like crowded by the number of people present. A double handful were kicking balls against a wall in some kind of competition, and maybe twice that many were running around the track. There was only a scatter of people swinging on the bars, throwing weights, or jumping for distance.

"Does it bother you to be laughed at?" Mab said. She wasn't asking from curiosity: she was really prodding the youth, though in a teaching way instead of just trying to hurt him. "You think you're right, don't you?"

"Mistress," said Orly fiercely, "we *know* the king is threatening Ronn again. At night the Made Men are all around us on the plain, and the lower levels keep getting darker. I've gone far enough down to see that. Somebody has to be ready to defend the city!"

"Yes," said Mab. "I quite agree. Now, why don't you show Cashel your exercises."

The words were a question but the tone was an order. The Sons looked at each other again. "All right," said Herron. "Usual opponents. Let's go."

The Sons spread out into three pairs. Cashel backed away, but Mab tugged him farther yet, till they were standing with their backs against the parapet. "Be ready to move toward the corner," she murmured.

Cashel thought she was worrying too much. He'd given the nearest pair, Herron and Stasslin, as much space as he'd have done for a quarterstaff bout. The Sons' sword-shaped clubs weren't but a third the length of his staff. Mab was a woman, so she probably didn't understand how these things were done.

Some of the people who'd been exercising drifted closer, while others stopped what they were doing and turned to watch. A man—he was with one of the few women, which probably had something to do with him showing off—called, "Hey, boys! You're a hundred years late for that stuff, you know?"

"Just ignore them," Herron growled. "Get set."

The Sons hunched over and faced each other. About a double pace separated each pair. "Now!" Herron said.

Cashel expected the Sons to start by taking each other's measure, though maybe since it seemed they did the same thing each day, they wouldn't need to do that. In a group this big there'd always be one who rushed straight in, trying to overwhelm his opponent with a sleet of blows. Because they'd trained themselves, maybe they'd all do that—

Except they didn't. Each pair circled widdershins around its center without getting closer. They were too far back to hit. They were barely close enough that the tips of the wooden swords could touch each other if they both waggled them toward the other at the same time. Every once in a while a Son stamped his foot and leaned forward like he was about to lunge, but it was always a feint.

"Are you impressed, Cashel?" Mab asked in a tone of amusement. She spoke in a normal voice, one that the Sons could maybe hear over their own hoarse panting.

"No, ma'am," Cashel admitted. "Not, you know, in a good way."

Herron must've heard the exchange, because he jumped toward Stasslin with a wild, overhead swing like he was splitting a log with an axe. Stasslin threw his shield and sword both up above his head. Herron's sword banged hard on the buckler—it was a powerful blow, no mistake—but then instead of kicking Stasslin in the crotch, he backpedaled wildly.

Cashel saw why Mab had moved them so far away. Instead of jumping clear as Herron rushed backward toward them, he raised his staff crossways in both hands to cover him and the woman both. In the event, Herron stopped just before he ran into the thick hickory instead of just after he did.

"I believe that's enough of a demonstration," Mab called in a clear voice. "Come back over here, if you will."

The Sons lowered their arms and walked to where Mab and Cashel stood. They were red-faced and panting: what they'd been doing was certainly exercise. It just wasn't fighting.

The wooden swords didn't have sheaths. Herron laid his on the ground and set his buckler on top of it, then lifted off his helmet. Sweat plastered his hair to his scalp, turning it two shades darker. He looked at Mab, then looked away in embarrassment.

"This is the army that plans to defend Ronn, Master Cashel," Mab said. "What do you think of it?"

"Ma'am, I'm not a soldier," Cashel said. That was true, but it wasn't the real truth. He went on, speaking directly to Herron instead of talking about him as if he wasn't there, "You fellows aren't soldiers either. You're . . ."

He didn't know how to put it. He frowned and lifted his hand toward the mass of the city rising to the side. "Ronn's a wonderful place, I can see that," he said. "It's like Mab told me, a palace with everybody living like kings. You're not used to getting hurt—and that's good, I'm not saying it shouldn't be that way for everybody. But back where I come from, people are used to getting hurt, and we're used to fighting. And when you fight, you're likely going to get hurt some even if you win."

"Look, we don't want to hurt our own friends," Orly said hotly. "It'd be different if we were fighting the Made Men with real swords. It'll be different *when* we do that, because surely the king'll attack someday soon. And the others will follow us when they see the danger's real."

"Cashel, do you agree?" Mab asked. "About it being different when they fight the Made Men?"

Cashel grimaced. She knew the answer, of course. "No, ma'am," he said, then meeting the eyes of the youths again. "Except then you'll be killed. I'm sorry, but you will."

He thought for a moment. The spectators had gone back to their own business now that the Sons weren't giving their dancing exhibition anymore. These fellows, these *boys*, knew there was a danger, they just didn't have anybody to teach them. And the rest of Ronn's citizens didn't even think there was danger.

"Look," Cashel said. "Herron—or Mab? Can you maybe hire soldiers? Enough to lead you, anyway? I mean, maybe the people here *would* follow if they had real soldiers to lead. But you need somebody to, well, get the rest of you started."

"We'll lead them!" Orly insisted. "When it's not our friends, we'll fight, and the other citizens will follow us!"

"Cashel's not your friend," Mab said. Cashel figured she was putting the sneer into her voice just to goad the others. It sure would've gotten *his* back up if it'd been directed at him. "Will you fight him?"

"He's bigger than any of us," said Enfero doubtfully. He was a lanky fellow, taller than Herron but not nearly as heavy. "He's a lot bigger."

"He's not bigger than all six of you together," said Mab. "Is that all right with you, Cashel?"

"Sure," he said, keeping his voice calm. He held his staff upright on his right side; now he tipped the lower end behind him so the upper ferrule was just about the height of his eyebrows.

Back in the borough, offering to take on six fellows with clubs would be asking for broken bones, but not here. Mab was teaching them what they needed to know before they got into a real fight with these Made Men. If they weren't willing to hear the words, then pounding the truth into them with a quarterstaff would do the job.

Stasslin cut at Cashel's head without warning. Cashel'd figured he might pull that. He shifted his right arm just a little so that the whistling wooden sword smacked into the end of the quarterstaff.

The sword flew off in the air while Stasslin yelped and grabbed his tingling sword hand with the other. He'd at least been trying, so Cashel hadn't let him smash his hand itself into the iron butt cap and break all his fingers. Still, Cashel wasn't feeling so kindly to a fellow who'd tried to sucker punch him that he didn't kick Stasslin just below the edge of his breastplate.

Cashel was barefoot, but he was generally barefoot, so his soles were tough as ox hide. Stasslin flew backward, hit the ground, and spewed up more breakfast than you ought to eat before you start a workout.

Cashel backed away. "Mab, you stay clear!" he said, but she was just a shimmer of light robes. All Cashel was really seeing right then were the five Sons still standing. "You, Herron! Get your gear on now while I give you the chance!"

Herron made as if to kneel, but that was a feint too, just like all the foot-stamping when the Sons "fought" each other. Well, you shouldn't trust the guy who's planning to whale the daylights out of you, but Cashel was finding all this pussyfooting around troublesome. If Herron didn't—

Herron knelt for real this time and slapped the helmet over his head so quick that he canted the noseguard over the corner of his left eye. He seized the double handgrip of his buckler and scrabbled for the wooden sword, grabbing it first by the wrong end.

Cashel shifted his quarterstaff crosswise before him, gripping it with his hands just more than shoulder's width out on the shaft. He hadn't had time to limber up properly, but he contented himself with a few twists and flexes instead of giving his staff the series of spins that he'd have liked to. He had too many opponents, and they were too close for that to be safe.

While Herron was getting himself back together, the other four Sons still upright stood with their swords and shields lifted but not doing anything. That was pretty much what Cashel'd figured would happen, though he'd been ready if they'd managed to show some spirit.

He didn't worry about Stasslin except for remembering where he was just as same as he'd need to for a section of tree trunk. After a kick in the belly like he'd taken, Stasslin wouldn't be leaving the field without a buddy to help him.

Herron got his sword right end to, then jumped back to put himself at the end of the tight line his friends had formed. Cashel stepped forward, shifting his grip again. He slammed his staff's left ferrule low into Herron's chest. The boy managed to get his shield in the way, but Cashel's straight thrust banged it out of the way without slowing.

Herron went over backward, throwing his sword and buckler out to opposite sides. There was a fist-sized dent in his breastplate, right over the pit of his stomach.

Enfero and Manza rushed Cashel together. They weren't coordinated enough to have planned it, but it was a good tactic anyhow. Because his left ferrule was leading, Cashel backpedaled and brought his right arm around widdershins, catching Manza on the left hip and flinging him into Enfero.

The two of them went down with a crash of metal. The sound seemed to have triggered Athan to leap forward. The Gods only knew what the fellow planned to do, but he managed to get his feet tangled with Manza's legs and tripped. That was better luck than he'd otherwise have had, because Cashel rapped him behind the ear with the shaft of the quarterstaff instead of catching him with the iron-shod tip.

Enfero raised his head. Cashel clipped him a good one, sending his dented helmet flying. Manza was clutching his left hip with both hands and moaning. Cashel hoped he hadn't broken the bone, but he didn't pull his blows in a fight.

Orly was the only one left. He'd raised his sword overhead like a torch to light his surroundings. He had a fixed look of horror on his face.

"I guess you can put that down, buddy," Cashel said, his voice a low growl. "I guess you can see it's all over."

"Kill the monsters!" Orly screamed, and charged straight forward. That was the first surprise Cashel'd had in the whole fight, but he brought his staff around low and swept the boy's legs out from under him, dropping him as neatly as a scythe does oats. Orly hit on his belly hard enough to knock the breath out of him. The sword flew out of his hand and clacked into the parapet. He tried to get up, but the best he could do was paw the ground while weeping with frustration.

"Hey, way to go, soldier boys!" shouted the man who'd made the earlier gibe. He began to clap.

Cashel strode toward him. "You want a chance?" he said in a savage voice nothing like the way he normally sounded. "They at least were willing to try. You want to show your girl what you're made of? Because just say the word, and I *will* show her!"

The man backed away in terror. He stumbled and almost fell.

"Boo!" shouted Cashel, waggling his quarterstaff overhead. The man gave a strangled cry and staggered off. The woman with him glanced over her shoulder to watch him go, then turned to stare at Cashel.

Cashel sank to one knee and butted the staff into the ground for an additional support. He'd been moving his considerable weight very fast, and he needed more air now than his lungs could take in even through his open mouth.

Mab walked over to Cashel and put a supportive hand on his shoulder. To the sprawled Sons she said, "You've learned the reality of what you claim you're willing to do. Go to your homes, now, when you're able to. The Councillors will be calling an emergency Assembly before the week's out, unless I'm badly mistaken. If you're really willing to be the heroes you claim you are, come to that Assembly. Ronn will need you."

The Sons didn't say anything, though Herron's lips moved as though he would've spoken if he could've drawn in a breath.

Mab nodded in approval. "Come, Cashel," she said. "You'll be ready for a meal, I suspect."

Sharina stood with Tenoctris in the small box projecting from the starboard prow of the *Star of Valles,* looking ahead as the ship rocked through slow swells on oars alone. The box—the ear timber—kept the outrigger from being smashed when the trireme rammed another ship.

The space was tight for even two slim women, but everything aboard a trireme was tight. At least there they weren't in the way of the crew and didn't risk being trampled by the soldiers who, less used to crowding than oarsmen, had left their benches and squeezed together on the decks, where they could stretch their legs.

Tenoctris held a small codex and was trying to read it in the fading light. Sharina had found that the ship's rise and fall seemed less uncomfortable if she looked at the horizon instead of down into a page on her lap.

The old wizard sighed and closed her book. "What do you know about the People, Sharina?" she asked. "The ones who invaded Ornifal. It's"—she smiled—"after my time, you see."

"I'm sorry, Tenoctris," Sharina said. "I know as little about Ornifal's history a generation ago as I do what was happening on the far side of the moon. I don't think Lord Waldron is much of a student of foreign cultures"—this was her turn to smile—"but some of the other officers may know something about the background to the invasion."

She looked forward again and pursed her lips. A few stars shone on the eastern horizon. There were two lookouts in the prow of the *Star of Valles,* clinging to the jib boom, but even so it'd soon be too dark to see shoals a safe distance ahead. Both Waldron and Bedrin were aboard the *Star of Valles.* The other five ships of the squadron followed in line, so that if the leader ran aground they'd at least be able to take off the crew and passengers.

It was still a dangerous proceeding, and Sharina knew that the way she'd forced Bedrin to put out later than he'd wanted to was part of the reason. In war, in life, you had to make the best decisions you could, even when none of the choices were good ones.

Something gleamed in the sea just ahead of the trireme's foaming bow wave. Sharina touched the older woman's hand. "Tenoctris?" she said. "Do you see—just ahead of us there?"

The shimmer broached and rode the trireme's bow wave for a moment, looking back over its shoulder. Looking back over *her* shoulder, for the figure was as distinctly female as she was human—save for the webs between her toes and fingers and the yellow-green sheen of her hair.

"She sees us!" the swimming figure called in delight, and she dived back into the sea.

"Tenoctris!" Sharina said. "She's a nymph! I saw a nymph swimming with us!"

The two sailors on lookout were muttering to one another, glancing sidelong at Sharina in the boxing just below them, but Tenoctris wore an expression of careful reserve. "Didn't you see her, Tenoctris?" Sharina said.

The nymph and two others curved up from the depths. As they swam, easily matching the speed of the laboring trireme, they chattered, "She sees us/Do you see us, missy?/Oh look at her hair/at her hair/at her golden hair!" Their words were as clear as the piercing notes of the time-keeper's flute in the stern, but Sharina realized she wasn't hearing them with her ears.

"I see something, dear," Tenoctris said. She bent forward; Sharina put a hand on her shoulder just in case the older woman managed to overbalance as she tried to glimpse what Sharina had said was there. "I see power, a great deal of power. Concentrated, flowing out of the depths and proceeding with us; but I don't see nymphs as nymphs, I'm afraid."

"But you're a wizard!" Sharina said desperately. She needed to have her vision affirmed—not because Tenoctris doubted her, but because she doubted herself. "I'm just a person!"

The nymphs curled beneath the surface again. This time Sharina followed their track into the depths, through water that was suddenly as clear as the air on a bright day. They rolled over and came up again, trailing bubbles and joined by three more of their kind. ". . . so lovely/so lovely/so lovely!" they caroled.

"You're a person who's been in places few humans go," Tenoctris said, straightening and giving Sharina a kindly smile. "Places I haven't been, many of them. That doesn't make you a wizard, but you shouldn't be surprised to find that you see things other people don't. Their minds haven't learned the tricks of observation that yours has."

"Your ladyship?" said one of the lookouts, leaning toward them over the bow railing. The sailor knew *of* ladies, though he might never before have been close enough to touch one. He didn't have any notion of the form of address proper to royalty, so he was making do as well as he could. "Please?"

"What?" said Sharina, looking up in surprise. The fellow was balding. He wore a gold ring through his right—and only—ear, and he spoke with a thick Sandrakkan accent. "You mean me?"

"Right, your ladyship," the sailor said. The other lookout was looking over his shoulder with a pained but hopeful expression. "Please? Did you call the Ladies down there to help us along?"

"You can see them?" Sharina said in relief. "The nymphs?"

"The Ladies, yes," the sailor said, relieved also not to be called down for speaking. He wouldn't use the word "nymph" though, preferring the euphemism. "I see them, and my mate D'vobin here sees them kinda."

"We been to sea all our lives, you see," the other lookout said, obviously relaxing. "You see a lot of things, mostly at night."

"We know the Ladies help sailors sometimes when they're, well, in the mood," the first man said. "And we were hoping, you know . . ."

"We can help you, missy!" a nymph called. "We can draw you to where you want ever so quickly. Would you like us to help you, missy?"

Sharina thought the speaker might be the first one she'd seen, but she couldn't be sure. There were twelve of them now, dancing around and below the trireme. The darkening sea had vanished, and the ship drifted over a bottom dressed in pearly light.

"For a price!" sang a chorus of nymphs, "For a price/price/price!" In a descant above them a solo voice trilled, "Such lovely hair . . ."

Commander Bedrin strode into the bow. Master Rincale, the sailing master of the *Star of Valles,* followed close behind. Lord Waldron was coming forward also, his face set like a granite cliff.

"What are you doing?" Bedrin demanded, glaring at Tenoctris. He let his gaze slide into the water, then jerked his eyes back. "What have you *done*? Are you responsible for this, wizard?"

"Lady Tenoctris is no more responsible for our visitors than I am, *Master* Bedrin," Sharina said, emphasizing her superior rank in a fashion she'd never have done if she weren't uncomfortable with what she was seeing in the water.

"We can help you, missy," said a nymph. "We can sweep you to your desire quickly, so very quickly."

"Quickly/quickly/very quickly," chorused her sisters in voices like silver bars ringing.

"Your highness, I'm sorry," Bedrin replied. He waved his hand toward the sea, making it clear that he was one of those who saw and heard the nymphs clearly. "I—it's getting dark, and the current's set against us. And now this, these."

Bedrin swallowed, grimaced, and said in a softer voice, "We honor the Ladies, of course, and we'd appreciate any help they offered us . . . but never would I *ask* them to involve themselves in the affairs of mere mortals like us."

"For a price . . . ," the nymphs sang. "For a little price, lovely missy."

"I see," said Sharina. She looked into the crystal, which gleamed where the sea ought to be. She imagined that her face looked much like Lord Waldron's. Still she—she grinned—knew her duty. "Ladies, what is your price to carry us to Valles safely, all five ships?"

"A small price/price/price . . . ," called the chorus.

"Your golden hair, missy," said the first nymph Sharina had seen in the water. "Only your lovely golden hair."

". . . hair/hair/hair . . . ," sang the others.

"All right," Sharina said, because there was no other answer in the kingdom's need. "Master Bedrin, you'd better inform the captains of the other vessels that we'll be getting help to reach Valles quickly."

Eleven of the nymphs had scattered laughingly when Sharina agreed, swimming with their whole bodies like otters as they swept into the far distance. The last spiraled down, snatched something from the glowing seafloor, and swirled back up in a smooth curve.

Sharina felt only minor pangs at the thought of losing her hair. She had to trust laughing, whimsical, *not human* creatures; but there was no choice.

"Yes, of course," said Bedrin, his tone that of a man who's been told he'll be executed in the morning. "I'll order the squadron to lie to. And for the men not to be concerned."

Bedrin strode back toward the stern, where the signal horn hung from a hook on the railing. He brushed Lord Waldron but seemed not to have noticed the grim warrior despite the contact.

Waldron met Sharina's eyes. "I don't see anything out there, your highness," he said in a tight voice. "But I know there is . . . something. It's wizardry, isn't it, your highness?"

"Something like that, milord," Sharina said. "It's an opportunity to get to Valles more quickly than the oarsmen alone could manage. I thought I should . . . I thought I *needed* to accept the offer when it was made."

"Yes, of course," Waldron said. He was looking at the horizon, now; or rather, trying not to look at their immediate surroundings. "For the kingdom's sake, we have to accept help from any quarter."

The horn called, two short notes and a long one. The ship's officers shouted orders, and the timekeeper shifted to the pairs of quick notes that signalled the oarsmen to ship their oars.

"Ah . . . ," said Tenoctris softly. "Yes, it's changing. . . ."

The nymphs who'd gone off were returning, leading in pairs and a triplet vast sinuous shapes. The nymph who'd stayed with the squadron sprang from the water like a trout leaping and caught the ear timber with one hand. Her other webbed hand held a flake of obsidian with an edge that looked sharp enough to cut sunbeams.

"Your lovely hair," the nymph murmured as she seated herself on top of the boxing and lifted a handful of Sharina's tresses. "Your lovely golden hair . . ."

Chapter Six

Ilna began to unknot her pattern now that she had no immediate use for it. "Who else is here inside your maze?" she said to the wizard on the floor. He'd risen onto one elbow, but Chalcus' rock-steady swordpoint kept him from trying to stand up.

"No one's here," the wizard said, looking at her for the first time. His gaze started angry and shifted very quickly to wariness. "Nobody should be able to enter. How did you get in?"

Ilna ignored the question as she looked around the room. The fellow's answer was probably true. There was a single wooden chair at the table under a side window, and though the bed frame along the opposite wall was a work of art in etched bronze, it was only wide enough for one.

Davus walked to the throne and set the two rocks he carried on the floor. He seated himself, closing his eyes and running his fingers along the ornate armrests. Ilna knew how hard and fibrous chalcedony was, so she marveled at the effort it must have taken to carve detailed scenes of men battling demons over every surface of the throne. On the left, men were winning; on the right, demons routed their human opponents.

The wizard noticed what Davus was doing. "Don't sit there!" he said in angry amazement. "You have no idea what you might do there by accident!"

"I'll do nothing here by accident," Davus said, his eyes still shut. He smiled at whatever it was his mind saw.

Chalcus relaxed slightly, raising his sword vertical but choosing not to sheathe it just yet. "You can get up, I think," he said pleasantly. "What would your name be, friend?"

"That's none of your business," the wizard muttered. He stood and dusted his palms together. He kept his eyes on the floor.

Ilna opened a freestanding cabinet. It held bread, cheese, and a variety of dried vegetables. She wondered how the fellow obtained them. There wasn't room in this clearing for a grainfield of any size, nor had she seen any sign of animals for milking.

"Well," said Chalcus, his tone still light but with an edge to it. He picked up the athame and appeared to examine the chip his blade had cut from the wood when he struck it out of the fellow's hand. "I thought it would be an alternative to cutting a grin in your throat so I could call you 'Smiler,' but we can manage that if you like."

"His name's Nergus but he prefers to be called Nergura," Davus said. Only his lips moved; to look at him, he might've been talking in his sleep. "He believes the seven letters have a secret significance, you see. He didn't want to tell you lest knowing his name give you power over him.'

Chalcus laughed, then tossed the athame into the fire. Nergura gave a strangled cry and lunged toward the hearth. He stopped when he found the sword edge barring his way.

"I have all the power I need over him already," Chalcus said, his voice as soft as a cobra's. "And people who take out a weapon when first they meet me can thank their stars if they lose nothing but that weapon by it. Eh, Master Nergura?"

The wizard shrugged with a sour expression and seemed to huddle into his robe. "What is it you want of me?" he said, looking again at the floor.

"Food and perhaps shelter," Ilna said. She lifted the pottery lid that covered the cistern in the corner opposite the cupboard. She didn't know how deep it was, but there was certainly water for the three of them. A bronze dipper hung from a cord within the shaft; she lowered it into the tank.

"And information, Master Nergura," Davus said, his fingers spread on the armrests. "Tell us about the present king and what happened to the Old King."

The wizard sighed. He leaned toward the hearth again, then caught himself when the sword twitched. "Let me swing my alembic off the fire," he said in a tone of anger suppressed by well-justified fear. "No more than that!"

"Go on, Master Nergura," said Chalcus, raising his blade vertical again. "You were going to tell us about the king."

The wizard pivoted the iron hearth crane so that the pot hanging from it was out in the room. The flames burned brighter now that the athame had ignited. He stepped back, grimaced, and walked deliberately to the wooden chair. He turned it to face into the room and sat down.

"The King . . . ?" Nergura said. "I suppose you can call it that if you like. The king that now exists isn't human. It was a beast, a pet I suppose, of the Old King who ruled this land in past ages."

"Davus?" Chalcus said. "Do you know of this pet of your king?"

"There was a creature," Davus said, leaning his head back against the chalcedony throne. "Supposedly from another world. It wasn't a pet, exactly. The king had gained his power through it. He kept the beast around afterward, though he needn't have done so."

"Well, he was a fool then," said Nergura, eyeing Davus sharply. "How is it you know about the Old King? Are you a wizard? You *must* be a wizard to have learned so much about the old times!"

"I'll let you be the only wizard here, Master Nergura," Davus said, his closed eyes lifted toward the roof. "For myself, I'm merely glad to be flesh and blood. I spent the past thousand years as a statue, it seems."

He paused, smiled wistfully, and added, "I wonder what I was thinking about while I was stone?"

"Aye, you can be the wizard," said Chalcus. He took the dipper of water, drained it, and handed it back to Ilna without letting his eyes slip from Nergura. "But you should recall that though I'm no wizard myself, I can make your head vanish from your shoulders in a heartbeat. Eh, my friend?"

"Yes, well . . . ," Nergura said. It obviously unsettled him to watch Davus' hands on the wax-smooth surface of the throne. "I said the Old

King was a fool not to have killed the creature when he no longer needed it. It happened because his power lay in a jewel on his brow."

Ilna refilled the dipper. She'd planned to offer it to Davus, but on consideration she drank the water herself. Davus was doing *something*. She didn't understand what, but she wouldn't have thanked anyone who broke her concentration while she was busy.

"Something happened," Nergura continued. "I haven't been able to learn precisely what—it was a thousand years ago, after all! There was an attack or at any rate a summons that drew the king's attention. Because he was focused on other affairs, the creature was able to steal his jewel, then kill him."

Ilna began slicing bread and cheese. She used her own paring knife instead of the longer—but dull—blade in the cupboard. The wizard glared at her for a moment, then looked at Chalcus, and said, "That's what the king deserved, since he should've killed the creature when he had the chance. Ever since, it's ruled this land. As much as anyone has."

Ilna offered Chalcus a slice of cheese on bread—good wheat bread and baked no later than the night before. He gestured it away without taking his eyes from the wizard. "What does this new king do with the land he rules, then?" he asked. "His yoke is light, you say?"

He'd sheathed his sword, but Nergura had seen the steel come out once. He didn't seem fool enough to chance anything that would cause Chalcus to clear his blade again.

"It doesn't do anything," the wizard said. "Mostly it stays in its Citadel and builds the walls higher. When it comes out, it wanders about and turns anyone it meets to stone. If there are reasons for what it does, they aren't human reasons."

Ilna heard the bitterness in Nergura's voice. She smiled faintly as she chewed bread and cheese made from cow milk, the latter a rarity in Barca's Hamlet. If this wizard had the power the alien creature had, he'd have used it. Looking at Nergura's scowling face, Ilna suspected the other inhabitants of the land were better off bearing a beast's random violence than they would be under him.

"Much goes on in the land that the Old King wouldn't have permitted," Davus said softly. His right thumb rubbed the glassy surface of the armrest.

"Who knows what the Old King would've allowed?" Nergura said sharply. "There's all manner of terrors walking the land now, and everyone is responsible for his own safety!"

Davus opened his eyes. He sat up straight, then rose from the throne with a graceful, controlled motion. He glanced at the stones he'd brought but smiled and left them on the floor.

"Yes, I see that's so," Davus said. His tone was pleasant, but there was an undertone to it that reminded Ilna of Chalcus when he was poised to explode into action. "How is it that you gain your information, Master Nergura?"

The wizard frowned. "Does it matter to you?" he said. "I drink herbal potions. They wouldn't do you any good, you know."

"I'm sure that's true," said Davus, sauntering toward the back door. "But I think I'll see what kind of herbs it is that you grow in your garden."

"You mustn't go—" the wizard said, bustling to put himself between Davus and the door. He shrieked as Chalcus pinched his earlobe between thumb and forefinger and jerked him back to where the sailor's dagger just pricked his cheek.

"Let's all go see the garden," Chalcus said. He and Davus exchanged glances. Davus smiled, opened the door, and stepped out with Ilna behind him. Chalcus brought up the rear, leading the faintly whimpering wizard.

Ilna supposed she'd been expecting an ordinary kitchen garden like those every housewife in Barca's Hamlet kept, fenced off so that the chickens wouldn't devour the new shoots. Instead she was looking at an orderly jungle. The air was warmer than that of the wasteland they'd crossed to reach Nergura's maze, and more surprisingly it was as humid as when the sun comes out after a summer shower.

None of the plants and shrubs were familiar. The tall tree near the back looked like a sugarberry, but the fruit was bluish, not red. Besides, the sugarberries shouldn't have been present at the same time as the flowers on the shrub near the door with figlike leaves. Why hadn't she seen the almost-sugarberry when they left the maze if not before they entered it?

A path of white gravel set in marl entered the garden. It branched before it vanished into the vegetation in the near distance. Ilna could see the tiled room of a gazebo or work shed beyond a stand of what she'd have called holly were it not for the round leaves; there might be other structures completely hidden by the foliage.

There might be any*thing* lurking in the foliage.

"Maybe we'll let our host lead, shall we, Master Davus?" suggested Chalcus, whose mind must've been turning in the same directions.

He tugged the wizard forward by the ear. Nergura yelped and cried and bent his face away from Chalcus to lessen the pain. "There's nothing here that can harm you!" he said in evident bitterness.

Davus must have agreed, for he sauntered up the path without waiting for Chalcus to push the wizard ahead of them. Ilna shrugged mentally. Davus seemed to know what he was doing—and anyway, Ilna had enough trouble making her own decisions. She wasn't about to start minding other people's business.

Davus reached the fork, rubbed the ball of his foot into the gravel, and turned to the right. Chalcus maneuvered the wizard in front of him so that he was sandwiched between the two men and let go of his ear. Gorgeous but unfamiliar flowers bordered the path. Beyond them were bushes with small leaves of a green so dark that an eye less well trained than Ilna's would've called them black.

They came to the tile-roofed shed Ilna'd seen from the door of the house. It was brick across the back with latticed end walls through which vines wound. The front facing the path was open. Tools leaned against the bricks on the left side or hung from pegs; drying racks reached from floor to ceiling on the right. Ilna heard a faint mewing sound and looked around for a cat.

"Yes, as I thought," Davus said, gesturing with one hand toward the vine. "How do you justify this, Master Wizard?"

"There's nothing to justify!" Nergura said, and the very violence of his tone proved he knew he was lying. Davus' face was hard; Chalcus smiled. Neither expression was one Ilna would've wanted directed at her.

The vine crawling up the lattice had a stem and leaves like a cucumber. Instead of simple sausage shapes the fruit was bulged and distorted till it looked like misshapen dolls of green clay. Ilna wondered if it was diseased. Certainly if a plant like that had come up in her garden, she'd have grubbed it out before—

Her skin flushed, then went cold. The lowest of the hanging poppets was moving its arms and legs.

"In my day, the king would've disagreed," Davus said. He lifted the topmost of the green homunculi. Touched, it began to squirm also. Davus gently set it back against the lattice and walked into the shed.

"The king is dead!" the wizard shouted. "It's every man for himself, now!"

"Ah, but *we're* not dead, my friend," Chalcus said, stroking Nergura's cheek with a first and middle finger. The wizard jerked as though he'd been burned. "Nor are you, as things now stand."

Three dolls like those on the vine hung from hooks on the wall between heavy shears and a bronze trowel. These were better formed in the sense of being more complete, though their proportions were those of a dwarf, and their faces looked indescribably ugly.

They mewed at Davus. He reached toward them. The nearest was formed like a female. She gripped Davus' index finger with both arms and tried to drag it toward her jaws to bite. He pulled his hand away.

"Every man for himself, you say, wizard?" Davus shouted. "*These* are men, as you well know. You hang them here till you're ready, and then you boil them down into an elixir that you drink for what you claim is wisdom. What sort of wisdom do you get by drinking the lives of men?"

"I had no choice!" Nergura said. "My safety depends on what the poppets' blood enables me to learn!"

"If you think you're safe now, wizard," said Ilna as she stepped between Davus and Nergura, "then you're a worse fool than I already believed."

She turned to Davus. "What now?" she said crisply. "Do we destroy the vines?"

"Or perhaps do we destroy the gardener?" said Chalcus. "For it seems to me that if we do that, no problem remains."

Davus sighed. In his anger he'd seemed a much bigger man, but now it drained out of him, leaving a stocky, tired-looking fellow wearing a tunic that was cut a little too closely around his chest.

"No," he said, "we'll not kill him. We'll free these sad, vicious creatures, because they're men; and we'll free Master Nergura, because he's a man as well. And then we'll leave here, because I don't choose to spend the night in a place that was built by that kind of wisdom."

Ilna took the trowel from its peg and walked out of the shed with it. "Yes," she said as she knelt and thrust the bronze blade into the soil near the base of the vine. "I couldn't agree more."

"I've arranged a reception in the palace courtyard, your highness," Earl Wildulf said. "Unless you prefer to see to your apartments, of course. I've ordered the rooms on the west side of the ground floor to be cleared for you. They're, ah, able to be separated from the rest of the building and the outside."

They're easily defensible, Garric translated silently. "No, your lordship," he said aloud. "A levee is an excellent idea. My staff can meet the officials with whom they'll be working out details of Sandrakkan's integration with the kingdom."

King Carus chuckled as he viewed the palace of the Earls of Sandrakkan through Garric's eyes. Though on an impressive scale, it'd been built with an eye to defense rather than pomp. The main door was too narrow to pass three men abreast, and the ground-floor windows started six feet above street level; the gray stone walls below were solid. A few gleaming streaks remained on the sides of standing seams to indicate that the lead roof had once been silvered, but not in a generation. The swags and cartouches forming a frieze between the second and third stories were bird-daubed and beginning to crumble.

Humans as well as time had damaged the building. Some of the grilles on the ground-floor windows had been replaced with others of a different and heavier pattern, and the stones of the door alcove showed signs of burning. They were granite, though, and hadn't been seriously damaged. Liane had said that there'd been months of rioting in Erdin before Wildulf had claimed the throne vacated by the slaughter at the Stone Wall.

The crush at the palace entrance forced Garric and the Earl to halt in the street. Wildulf rose in his stirrups, snarling, "What's the holdup! Sister take the fools! I'll have the skin of somebody's back!"

"I think the fault's mine, milord," Garric said smilingly. In all truth, he'd have been more comfortable on his own feet rather than on horseback. Fortunately, they'd barely ambled from the seafront, since the procession moved at the speed of the infantry. "Lord Attaper's men are making sure of the arrangements. They'll be in tents in the palace gardens to the rear, I believe."

"So I've been told," Wildulf agreed sourly, though he wasn't taking the situation as badly as Garric had feared he might. The earl might have figured out that with a large army on Volita the negotiations were going to go the way the royal officials intended they should. The more easily they were concluded, the quicker Garric and that army would be out of his hair.

Lord Attaper approached, talking over his shoulder to one of his own officers and a palace official. He broke away from them and said to Garric,

"Your highness, I believe everything's in readiness. You can enter anytime you please."

Wildulf's expression quivered between fury and amazement before settling on the latter. "You let him talk to you that way?" he demanded, as he and Garric dismounted.

"I'm ordinarily willing to listen to anybody who's polite and who's speaking in the course of his duties, milord," Garric said calmly.

He strode toward the entrance, smiling faintly. He knew that Wildulf probably thought the prince was weak because he didn't follow his own will without regard for his advisors' judgment. Well, you could find people of Wildulf's opinion in a peasant village, too; and the attitude didn't help them prosper.

With the front door open, Garric could see all the way from the street through into the gardens behind the palace. A pair of Blood Eagles with balls blunting their spearpoints stood at each archway—five of them that Garric could be sure of, but the number of people waiting in the central courtyard probably concealed more of them.

The walls of the vestibule were decorated with carvings instead of being frescoed. Garric smiled wryly, realizing he found the paintings of Valles and Carcosa to be more welcoming, more civilized, than these stones. He'd certainly learned to put on airs in the short time since he left a hamlet where most of the better houses were whitewashed over mud plaster.

Liane joined him as he entered the court. Grass grew from seams between the stone pavers, especially around the edges.

"His highness Prince Garric!" shouted a Blood Eagle noncom. Normally that duty would've gone to a palace usher, but lungs trained to call orders through the clash of battle made an impressive substitute.

Well over a hundred Sandrakkan nobles waited, the men wearing tunics and breeches of contrasting color. The dozen officials in bulky Ornifal court robes who'd arrived with Garric had begun to mingle.

Palace functionaries had placed serving tables between the arches along the left side for servants to dispense drinks. From the flushed look of some of the local men, the drinking had started well before the royal contingent arrived.

"Lord Tawnser is very drunk," Liane said as she curtsied to Garric. Her bright smile belied the concern in her low voice. "Attaper has men watching him, but be careful."

Garric scanned the crowd with a bland smile as though he were merely a friendly stranger surveying his surroundings. Tawnser, glaring from his one eye like an angry hawk, stood with several other grim-looking fellows by the serving tables. He was a tall man whose lean face might've been fairly attractive were it not for his expression and the scar across his forehead and cheek, punctuated by the patch covering his left eye socket.

"Well," Garric murmured back, "if only a handful of Sandrakkan's nobles are *that* hostile, I'll take it as a positive sign."

The two of them stepped forward, flanked by guards. Liane was guiding him with tiny gestures of the writing stylus in her left hand, though Garric doubted anybody else was aware of the fact. The three nobles who'd come to Volita to negotiate stood together with a certain distance between them and the other Sandrakkan courtiers. They'd straightened as Garric entered and now faced him with evident relief.

"There's resentment of the terms they've accepted," Liane muttered. "Only Lord Tawnser and a few of his cronies would've refused them, but the people who didn't have to make a choice are now saying that the envoys made the wrong one."

"Ah," said Garric. *Of course,* he thought. That was what people generally did, so he didn't suppose there was any point in thinking that they ought to behave in a different fashion.

"Lady Lelor," Garric said, nodding. He swept the two male envoys with his glance. "Milords. Perhaps you'd introduce me to some of your compatriots? They can see I don't have two heads, but I'd like them to be certain that I'm not a raving lunatic either."

There was a stir at the far end of the room. The pair of Blood Eagles guarding the corridor from the gardens snatched the balls from their spearheads. "Captain!" one shouted.

"That's the countess!" shouted Earl Wildulf. He pushed his way toward the arch like an angry ox from where he'd stopped to talk to a palace official about billeting arrangements while one of Tadai's senior aides watched sternly. "That's my wife, you Ornifal numbskull!"

Garric was moving forward as quickly as Wildulf. He was well aware of the weight of the sword at his left side, but his hand resisted Carus' impulse to draw it. There were plenty of bare weapons present already; one more in the prince's hand might spark the disaster Garric hoped to avoid.

He and Wildulf reached the back corridor together. Countess Balila had stopped when the guards shouted and raised their spears. She'd apparently changed into lighter garments, a violet tunic and a mantilla of purple lace, on returning from the seafront. She looked furious, and Garric couldn't blame her.

On the other hand, he didn't blame the soldiers either. Accompanying the countess were a strikingly ugly old woman—

"The wizard Dipsas," whispered Liane, who'd kept up with him.

—a little boy, naked except for gilt wings and a chaplet of roses—

"Cover your points again!" Garric said sharply. One of the guards was lifting his javelin to throw.

—and a bird taller than the countess. It had a huge hooked beak and clawed feet that could gut a horse with a single kick. It raised a tall crest—Garric saw where the feathers on Wildulf's helmet came from—and screamed, its tongue vibrating and its stub wings flaring out to the sides.

"The bird's Balila's pet," Liane said. "I should've warned you."

Duzi! But there's no accounting for taste, a thing Garric had known long years before he left Barca's Hamlet. Now that he had a moment to look, he saw that the huge bird wore a silver collar and that the cherub held the thin chain attached to it.

Earl Wildulf put his right arm about his wife, a gesture at once protective and possessive. Balila touched her husband's cheek with one hand, then reached back and stroked the throat of the great bird. It quieted, tucking its wings against its torso and closing its beak. After a moment, it folded the bronze feathers of its crest also.

"Odwinn, stand easy!" Lord Attaper said in a vicious snarl. "If you and Buros panic when somebody comes in with an oversized parrot, you've got no business in my regiment—or in Prince Garric's army, I dare say!"

The guards clashed their hobnails as they straightened to attention. They banged the butt spikes of their long javelins against the floor also, striking sparks. After a moment, one of the men snatched up the gilded wooden ball at his feet and stuck it back on his spear. Neither of them looked at their commander.

Garric bowed. "Countess Balila," he said, "I'm pleased to see you in a more congenial setting than the waterfront. And I'm very impressed by your pet here."

"Yes, Hero's a good friend," the countess said archly, continuing to stroke the bird's neck ruff with one hand while the other caressed the point of Earl Wildulf's jaw. The sight raised disquieting images in Garric's mind. "To those I deem worthy of his friendship, that is."

Garric stepped back into the courtyard to clear the doorway for the earl and countess. The little boy dropped the chain and ran past, giggling and waggling his head from side to side. He was certainly old enough to speak, but he didn't seem able to.

The bird had a certain beauty, but the wizard on the other side of Balila couldn't have been attractive even before time added its ravages to those of dissipation. Dipsas wore a peaked cap and a black robe of tightly woven wool with silk cuffs and collar. Garric couldn't claim to be an expert, but he suspected Ilna would approve the garments' workmanship. The woman's face, however, was cruel and petty both.

In Dipsas' right hand was an athame of black horn, carved with images of humans and beasts twined in sexual congress. Garric could imagine what Tenoctris would've said about the object, but he didn't need his friend's opinion to make his lip curl.

Dipsas met his gaze and smirked. "You feel my power, do you not, Prince Garric?" she said.

"I feel nothing but disgust," Garric said, blurting what he'd have managed to put a gloss on if the statement hadn't been so very true.

Dipsas glared and raised the athame, posing like an orator about to declaim. Garric turned his back deliberately. If the wizard tried to stab him with what was after all a horn knife, Lord Attaper would break at least her arm before she more than started the stroke.

Liane gave Garric an approving nod instead of grimacing at his outburst as he'd expected she would. Apparently her sense of decorum didn't require him to be diplomatic in the face of malicious filth.

Lord Tawnser glared from just over arm's length away, between the armored solidity of the Blood Eagles who'd been following Garric until he turned on his heel. Tawnser's face was flushed, all but the narrow white line of the scar. Two of the cronies he'd been drinking with were beside him, while the third followed a double pace back with a look of dawning concern.

"You prefer to threaten our women instead of facing our men in battle, is that it, Master Garric?" Tawnser said, his voice rising in both pitch and volume. "But maybe our pigs would be even more suitable. You *are* a swineherd from Haft, isn't that so?"

Lord Attaper turned with smooth grace. Instead of drawing his sword, he reached with both hands for Tawnser's throat. Garric grabbed Attaper's shoulder and jerked back with the effort he'd have used to turn a charging ox. It was enough, barely.

"Lord Wildulf!" Garric said without shifting his eyes from Tawnser's face. Attaper relaxed, but Garric didn't release him quite yet. "Put your puppy outdoors, or I'll put him out myself!"

The open courtyard was a sea of babbling excitement. Blood Eagles were shoving toward Garric from all the entrances, and somebody'd managed to overset one of the serving tables. The friends who'd been flanking Tawnser backed away suddenly. Even Tawnser himself looked shocked as his sodden brain replayed the words that'd come out of his mouth.

"Tawnser, you bloody fool!" Earl Wildulf snarled. He wasn't an intellectual giant, but he'd seen enough of war to know what would happen if real fighting started in a courtyard where only Garric and his guards had been allowed to carry weapons. "Get out of here and sober up. No, by the Shepherd—go back to your estates and don't leave them until I give you permission! Do you hear?"

Tawnser didn't move for a moment; his face could've been cast in glowing iron. He turned abruptly and strode toward one of the arches on the east side, shoving aside the people in his way with as little thought as a man walking through a field of waving oats.

The Blood Eagles crossed their spears to block that exit. "Let him go!" Garric called. The spears went vertical again. Tawnser stalked through, apparently oblivious of the guards and everyone else present. He disappeared into the hallway beyond.

Garric took a deep breath and let go of Attaper. Liane picked up the stylus she'd dropped when she drew her small, razor-sharp dagger. The knife was back in its ivory sheath now, wrapped invisibly in the lustrous silken folds of her sash.

Garric turned and gave Wildulf a trembling smile. "Well, milord," he said. "Now that we've taken care of that business, perhaps you'd be good enough to introduce me to your courtiers?"

It's good to have advisors who make sure the room you're going sleep in tonight is defensible, Garric thought; and, thinking that, broke into a broad, *real* smile.

The *Star of Valles* sailed through the void. Constellations blazed down on Sharina and up at her. That depended on whether she leaned back and looked at what should be the sky or craned her neck over the side to peer toward what'd been the depths of the sea.

She'd wrapped a shawl over her head. The air wasn't cold, but she wasn't used to feeling it on her bare scalp. She'd get used to it, she supposed, and of course her hair would grow back . . . but not as long as it had been. Not for a decade and more.

The rowers had shipped their oars and were sitting with the vessel's deck crew on the outriggers and narrow catwalks. In a reversal of the order of things before the *Star of Valles* left the waking world, the soldiers were mostly huddled in the hollow of the ship with their eyes cast down so that they could pretend they didn't know what was happening.

Sharina sat at the front of the starboard outrigger, overlooking Tenoctris in the ear timber and the nymph who perched on the frame of the box, talking to the old wizard. There wasn't room for three in such tight quarters, and in all truth Sharina felt nearly as queasy about the situation as the soldiers did.

She supposed that Tenoctris was able to see the nymph now, since they'd entered the void. She smiled to herself: it seemed a void to her human senses, but she didn't suppose it really was one. Certainly things lived in it, and swam. . . .

Master Rincale, the sailing master, chatted with sailors as he came forward. He nodded when he caught Sharina's eye; she smiled in response and looked forward again.

The worm about whose bluntly rounded head the trireme's anchor cable was tied had a broad, flat tail fin. Spines, scores of them, stuck out from its body. While the nymphs were harnessing the creature, Sharina had seen that conical teeth ringed its circular mouth. The worm undulated as it drew the *Star of Valles,* its tail fin driving up and down just beyond the vessel's bronze ram.

Sharina grimaced and turned away. Master Rincale leaned against the railing at her side. "A strange business, isn't it, your ladyship?" he said. "Or maybe it isn't for you. I suppose you've gotten used to this sort of thing in your, well, travels, so to speak."

"I wouldn't say I was used to it, Master Rincale," Sharina said, keeping her tone neutral. What did people think of her? *She* wasn't a wizard, she was the daughter of the innkeeper in Barca's Hamlet! Things had happened to her, that was all.

Sharina's eyes turned unbidden toward the huge worm. *Things are still happening to me.* She giggled. She supposed she must be on the edge of hysteria, but she preferred this reaction to the tinge of nausea the sight'd induced earlier.

Subsiding to a proper smile, Sharina said, "Your men are taking things well, I notice. I'm . . . well, frankly, Master Rincale, I had the impression sailors were likely to be superstitious. I thought that something like this would, well, disturb them."

Rincale laughed. "Superstitious, lady?" he repeated. "Oh, my, yes! The sea's bigger than any man, bigger than *all* men. Reason's all very well for landsmen, I suppose, but a sailor knows that reason won't get him anywhere but the bottom of the sea in a freak storm or the wind dragging his anchors toward a reef. There's not a man in the crew but has an amulet or a lucky garment or maybe"—the sailing master slid up the puffed sleeve of the tunic he wore to mark him as an officer—"a prayer tattooed on his wrist where the Gods can read it when he's too busy to pray properly himself. But why should we be afraid of the Ladies and their pets, princess? They came to help you, didn't they?"

"Yes, it seems so," Sharina said, though she wasn't sure that the nymphs would've appeared if she'd been a brunette like most women in Barca's Hamlet. The one shaving her said the blond hair would string the lyres they played to sailors on far rocky shores. . . .

"Mind," Rincale added, "we'll be telling our grandchildren about this, that you can bet your inheritance on. Anybody who's been to sea for a while has seen things, but *this*, well, my own wife'll think I'm lying and wonder why I didn't do a better job."

The nymph slipped from the ear timber with the fluidity of a drop of quicksilver. She dived deep under the ship, then curved upward to join the pair of her sisters who were guiding the great worm. Tenoctris watched her go before turning her face upward toward Sharina.

"Want to come on deck, milady?" Rincale offered cheerfully. "Blaskis and Ordos, get your asses outa the way so Lady Tenoctris has some room!"

Without waiting for an answer, the sailing master hopped onto the frame that the nymph had just vacated. Balancing on the balls of his feet alone, he gripped Tenoctris under the arms and lifted her like a woodpecker snatching a grub from its hole. Rincale was an older man, in his mid-fifties at least, but he'd obviously kept himself fit.

"Thank you," said Tenoctris, as Sharina helped set her on the deck. She gave Sharina a wry grin that showed how startled she'd been to come up in just that fashion. "I'd been wondering how I was going to get back here."

She tucked into her satchel the wax tablet on which she'd been taking notes during her discussion with the nymph, then resumed, "I'd been hoping to talk to you, Master Rincale. Do you know anything about the people, the People, who invaded Ornifal from the sea forty-nine years ago? You wouldn't have been present yourself, I suppose, but perhaps you've talked to some who were?"

"Oh, I was sailing with my da then, milady," Rincale said, smiling fondly with the memory. "Indeed I was. Had his own ship, he did, though that went to Foalz, my brother by his first wife."

Tenoctris nodded, probably believing as Sharina did, that the story would come out faster without interruptions intended to speed it along. "Yes, the People," Rincale said. "A right lot of liars they were, though"—he grinned broadly at Sharina—"I'm with my wife on this one. I can't imagine why they didn't tell a better one. You see—"

Rincale made a circular motion with his hand, gesturing to seaward. Well, it would've been seaward under normal conditions; at the moment it indicated a wasteland of stars.

"—the waters east of Ornifal, the seas, I mean?"

He paused to make sure these fine ladies understood so complicated a concept as "seas." Sharina, trying to keep the exasperation out of her voice, said, "Yes, we understand."

"Well, the People said," the sailing master explained, "the ones who weren't killed, I mean, that they live on a floating island that sometimes swings close to Ornifal and sometimes swings away. Now, that's nonsense. There's no island in the channel between Bight and Kepulacecil, there isn't and there wasn't then. East of the channel there's reefs that I wouldn't want to thread a fishing dory through, let alone an island. Wherever they come from, it wasn't from an island!"

"Perhaps," said Tenoctris carefully, "they didn't mean the island was floating in the sea."

"What?" Rincale said with a frown. "What else is there to float in, milady?"

Tenoctris pursed her lips, considering what to say. Sharina gestured toward the great worm swimming ahead of them.

"Oh . . . ," she said with a lopsided grin. "I think we could all imagine other places if we put our minds to it, Master Rincale."

"Ah," said the sailing master. "Ah. I hadn't thought of that."

The worm, undulating like the sea in a gentle breeze, swam onward through the stars.

"The Heroes, the men our friends are trying to emulate . . . ," Mab said, as she and Cashel sat at a table on the lowest of many terraces stepped up from the surface of a crystalline lake. Her hair was now a rich chestnut color, and she was nearly as tall as Cashel. "Were the great warriors who led the citizens of Ronn when the Made Men threatened the city in past ages. The last of them, Valeri, went down to the cavern where the Heroes sleep a hundred and fifty years ago."

The walls of Ronn slanted back on all sides like steeply sloped mountains, shading the lake's surface even though the sky above was still bright. Cashel saw brightly colored fish, the largest of them as long as he was tall, swimming lazily through the pure water. Occasionally one rose to gulp air, sending ripples across the shimmering surface.

"Valeri was a general?" Cashel said. Generals like Lord Waldron decided where to move troops and how to line them up—and how to feed them, besides, all sorts of things that Cashel couldn't even imagine doing. But Garric did them too. It was wonderful the things Garric could do even though he'd been raised in Barca's Hamlet the same as Cashel.

"Valeri was a Hero," Mab said, correcting him gently. "So far as generalship went, that was the queen's affair. There was no subtlety in the king and the minions of his creation, only numbers and savagery. Valeri *led*. The citizens of Ronn had weapons and the courage to fight; but without a leader, they would have huddled within the walls of the city, more fearful of making a mistake in their ignorance of war than they were of dying."

The water of the lake below had darkened to the point that the fish were no longer colors, merely darknesses beneath the shimmer of the reflected sky. Lights appeared in the lake or . . .

Could they be *under* the lake? Balls of blue and red and yellow moved slowly from the edges inward in curving lines. Each was an even distance behind the one that preceded it. Occasionally a great fish swam above a light and hid it for a moment the way a trailing cloud might block the sun.

"Young people with lanterns dance beneath the lake in the evenings," Mab said, pausing in her discussion of great issues to explain the thing that had Cashel's attention. "There's quite a lot of competition to get on the teams. The floor of the lake is diamond; the dancers are below it."

"Ah," said Cashel, leaning forward to take in the patterns that the lights wove. He couldn't see the dancers themselves, but the colored lanterns had a stately grace.

As he watched he realized that the movements of the fish weren't random either. Somebody who fights with a quarterstaff learns to see the rhythms of things that at first glance just seem to be happening. You learn that if you're going to win, anyhow. "Ah!"

He turned to Mab and smiled, feeling apologetic for not paying attention to what she'd been telling him. He'd listened, but he couldn't pretend he'd cared much about it.

"Mistress," he said, "it doesn't seem from what you tell me that Ronn has much needed heroes or armies either one in the past long while. Now that you do again, maybe they'll come along. Don't you think?"

"Ronn has had perfect peace for a hundred and fifty years," Mab said. "Ever since Valeri led her citizens to drive the Made Men back into the Great Ravine in the northern mountains. The people of Ronn didn't see the need of soldiers, and it seems the queen must not have seen a need either. People believe what they want to believe; even people who've proved themselves in the past to be wise and very powerful. You can be born brave or at least learn to act brave quickly enough; but nobody's born skillful with weapons. Those arts take longer to learn than the Sons have, or than Ronn has before she needs a leader."

Her smile took on a tinge of sadness; Cashel knew what she meant. Herron and his friends were puppies. Nice puppies, puppies that might grow up to be really good dogs. Trained right they'd be the kind of officials Garric wanted around him, bright active fellows with the good of the kingdom at heart.

They wouldn't be soldiers, though, any of them except maybe Stasslin. And Cashel didn't much like Stasslin as a person.

"The Sons would be willing to lead the people of Ronn," Mab said. "In their hearts, they really believe that's what they're going to do when the rest of the citizens realize their danger. And if that happened, they'd be killed at once, and everyone who followed them would be killed. They don't have the skills."

Cashel nodded. The Sons were young in a fashion that children brought up in the borough were never young. By the time you've survived three winters in a peasant village, you know things that the youth of Ronn had never been forced to learn.

"Ma'am . . . ?" Cashel said, his eyes on the dancers and the fish. The terraces were well filled with spectators, some foreign but mostly citizens of Ronn. From the talk he heard at nearby tables, the locals judged tiny variations from previous dances while Cashel himself was merely seeing the grace of the thing itself.

"Yes, Master Cashel," Mab said, her voice prodding politely so that he'd say what he was working himself up to.

He turned and faced her. He'd ever so much rather be fighting somebody, anybody, than having this conversation; but there he was, with no choice about it.

"Mistress," Cashel said, "if you're thinking I can lead your army, you're wrong—I can't. I wouldn't be any more use than the Sons were. I'm not afraid—and I'm not afraid to *fight*. But a man with a quarterstaff isn't much good against real soldiers, and I'd been no use at all with a sword."

"No, I wasn't thinking of that," Mab said with a dismissive wave of her left hand. Cashel wasn't sure whether his eyes were tricking him or if the fingernails really did make five rosy streaks in the air as they passed. "You're a stranger, Master Cashel. No matter what your skills were, the people of Ronn wouldn't follow you; and even you couldn't fight the Made Men alone."

Her expression changed to one that Cashel couldn't quite describe, serious and, well, affectionate at the same time. Mab touched the back of his hand and added, "Your pardon. You *would* fight the Made Men alone. But not even you could win."

"I guess I said that already," Cashel said. He was feeling even more uncomfortable than he'd been when he brought the subject up. "Look, mistress—what do you see as the way out of this? Because you do see something, you're not the sort to just wallow in how bad everything is, are you?"

Mab laughed, clapping her hands in delight at the joke. People at neighboring tables, toying with the remains of their meals or carafes of wine, glanced over in mild surprise.

"Oh, my, no, I'm not that, Master Cashel!" Mab said. "My hope, my plan if you want to put it that way"—she smiled in wry self-mockery—"is that the Heroes will awaken in their cavern and lead the people of Ronn against the king and his minions, his *monsters*. That the citizens of Ronn will destroy the enemies of the city and of all men finally instead of scotching them as so often in the past."

Cashel didn't say anything for a moment, just sat and thought about what she'd said. His staff leaned against the parapet beside him. He didn't pick it up, but he reached back with his right hand and ran his fingertips over the hickory.

"So you figure the Heroes have been sleeping, then?" he said. "Ah, how long would that have been for, ma'am? Because you said Valeri had gone down there. . . ."

"Yes, Valeri whom Dasborn brought up as his son and trained," Mab said. "Valeri with blood soaking through the bandage where a sword had found the joint between the halves of his cuirass. And before Dasborn, the twins Minon and Menon, blond and handsome as the very Gods till the day they went to cavern to sleep; Minon in his brother's arms, and Menon staggering despite his strength because of the shaft of the broken spear protruding from his thigh."

By then the sky was almost dark, but lights floated through the air above the tables. Although they were faint and the color of old parchment, Cashel could see his companion as clearly as he could've in a full moon.

"They're sleeping, mistress?" Cashel said quietly. "With wounds like those?"

"Minon and Menon were sister's sons to great Hrandis," Mab said, as though she hadn't heard the question. And perhaps she hadn't: she was looking down toward the diamond lake, but Cashel had the feeling her eyes were seeing much deeper than that, back in time as well as far into the core of the world.

"Hrandis was shorter than you," she continued, "but his shoulders were even broader. He swung an axe in either hand. When he led the citizens for the last time, he left a swath of the bodies of Made Men the width of both arms and his axe helves all the way from the walls of Ronn to where he fell at the mouth of the Great Ravine."

"Fell?" said Cashel. "Then Hrandis is . . . ?"

"Minon and Menon escorted their uncle to the cavern," Mab said, "holding his arms over their shoulders and walking on flowers and the rich garments the grateful citizens threw before their feet. Hrandis and his axes sleep there still; waiting for the city's greatest need, the legend says. Waiting as Virdin waits, the queen's first champion and Ronn's first Hero. Virdin whom the blades of the Made Men never touched, Virdin who went down to a well-earned rest in the cavern with his white beard spreading like a mountain cataract. Waiting for the city's need."

Cashel didn't speak. His fingers had been rubbing the familiar smoothness of the wood. Now he took the quarterstaff in both hands for comfort as he thought.

Mab gave a brittle laugh. "I think Ronn is in need now, don't you, Master Cashel?"

Before he could answer, she rose to her feet, as supple as an otter. "Come," Mab said in a cheerful tone. "The sun's down, so I can show you the way the Heroes guard the walls of the city yet today."

She took Cashel by the hand and guided him toward one of the platforms that effortlessly lifted Ronn's citizens through the city-mountain's many levels.

They'd found several coarse sacks hanging from the outer wall of the shed. Ilna had handled them; they told her of nothing worse than hot sun and the leaden exhaustion of the laborers who'd chopped the leaves from which the fibers were rotted before being woven. Now Chalcus carried the bread and cheese from Nergura's cupboard in one, leaving Davus' hands free to juggle three stones: two of them of a size to behead a pigeon if thrown accurately, the third big enough to dish in a man's skull.

Three homunculi, carrying the vine on which their siblings grew, trotted toward the east as soon as they were out of the maze. Ilna didn't see any advantage of the terrain in that direction instead of another, but the creatures seemed in no doubt. They went over a rise bristling with clumps of silkgrass and vanished from her life, except for the snatch of angry grumbling a vagrant breeze brought her a moment later.

Davus looked at Nergura, who'd stayed at the mouth of the maze as the three of them followed the homunculi out. He said, "You may think that you can catch them again if you hurry, wizard. If you do, I will come back for you."

"Let's go," said Chalcus quietly. "I'd like to get some distance on before we bed down for the night."

They started forward, walking abreast this time. Ilna was between the two men.

"Do you think you're better than me?" the wizard shouted. "Is that what you think?"

Ilna turned. "I know I'm not better than you," she said. "But I'd be worse yet if I said that what you were doing was no business of mine because you weren't doing it to me personally."

She and her companions started toward the Citadel again. The lowering sun turned the crystal into an orange-red blaze.

"From this valley they say you are leaving . . ." sang Chalcus in his lilting tenor. *"Do not hasten to bid me adieu . . ."*

Davus laughed and began to juggle his stones in an intricate pattern, and before long the maze and the wizard were out of sight behind them.

Chapter Seven

There's no call for concern," said Chalcus in the same light tone with which he'd been singing *I'm goin' away to Shengy,* "but I believe something's following us with such care that I've caught no more than a whisker here and there."

"I've thought there's something too," Ilna said, taking the silken lasso from around her waist. "I haven't seen anything I could point to, but the . . . well, I thought there was."

She couldn't say, "because of the way the clouds stand overhead," or "because of the way the tree roots crawl across the ground," and expect it to mean anything to people who weren't already disposed to trust her instinct for patterns. Chalcus *did* trust her; and so, apparently, did Davus. She didn't need to explain the things that shimmered on the surface of her mind.

They'd entered this valley around midafternoon. It was well watered, but the soil was a sickly yellow-gray and supported only coarse vegetation. Scrub oaks provided a welcome shade, and they'd been able to drink their fill from a little creek, but an enemy would find concealment easy. Shortly the sun would go down.

"It could be a jackal following us, hoping for scraps," Davus said conversationally. "There are jackals in these parts."

He let the two walnut-sized pebbles he'd been juggling along with a larger stone fly off to the side as he bent. He snatched a block of quartz out of the dirt, fist-sized and jagged.

"There's other things as well," Davus added, grinning at his companions. "Things that the jackals follow, hoping for scraps."

They saw the crops before they noticed the houses, a double handful of them on the other side of alternating fields of lentils and grain—oats, Ilna thought, but it might've been barley. The low buildings were made from chunks of pale limestone that weathered out of the ground. They were set on one another without mortar. Though the houses were close together, there wasn't a wall around the whole community.

A man with a girl of about ten at his side stepped between two houses and raised his hand. "Welcome, strangers!" he called. "We're just in from the fields. Come join us for dinner."

More people were appearing in the spaces between the dwellings. None of them were armed. A boy of three or so stared at Ilna, his thumb in his mouth. Suddenly he gave a cry of fear and ran behind a woman breast-feeding an infant. He continued to watch from between her legs.

"Since the king's law died with the Old King . . . ," Davus said. He fed a thumb-sized lump of chert into his pattern so that he looked like a juggler executing a complex pattern instead of a man ready to bash skulls by throwing stones. "I can't swear that their hospitality is more than a lure. But if something's prowling about us now, I'd as soon have stone walls around me in the dark."

The three of them continued to saunter forward together. Chalcus raised an eyebrow to Ilna. "Agreed," she said, looping the lasso back around her waist. It would shortly be too dark for her knotted patterns to be of much use, but the noose was no help at all against a whole villageful of people.

If they were enemies, which they certainly didn't seem to be.

"Thank you, good sir," Chalcus called cheerfully. "We're three travellers far from home who thought we were going to spend another night under the stars. Though we've no intention of putting you to trouble—we've slept rough in the past and can do so again."

"Why do you suppose they have no defenses?" said Davus, speaking quietly but without seeming furtive. "For I can tell you that even in my day, there were things in this part of the land that were less innocent than we are."

"Some claim there's a part of the world that the Gods bless and cherish," said Chalcus in a similar voice. "Mayhap they're right. Though the chance the likes of *me* would ever see such a spot, that I find hard to credit."

The field had been plowed, not planted in separate holes made with a dibble. A cow lowed, and as they walked toward the houses down three parallel furrows, Ilna caught the smell of cattle. There was also another animal odor, one she didn't recognize.

"I'm Polus," said the man who'd first greeted them. "This is my daughter Malia. Ah, are you traders? We don't get many traders here."

Polus wore a kilt and separate poncho, both of a vegetable fiber that Ilna hadn't seen before. The material had possibilities, but the workmanship was crude, and the embroidered decoration was childishly bad.

Ilna smiled minusculely. Not the sort of work she herself did as a child, of course.

"Not traders, just travellers on our way north," said Davus. He caught his small rock and a large one in his left hand. The other large one remained in his right. "If we could sleep in your cow byre tonight, we'd appreciate it."

They'd walked between two houses and found themselves on the front side of the village; the community, anyway—it wasn't half the size of Barca's Hamlet, which seemed tiny in recollection now that Ilna had experience of the largest cities in the Isles. The houses were built as single rooms on three sides of a square, around a courtyard of tamped earth. All the dwellings faced the same way.

Though there wasn't exactly a street, the long drystone corral ran parallel to the line of the dwellings at the distance of four or five double paces. Everyone in the community stood in that plaza, watching the strangers.

"We can provide you with a room to sleep in," Polus said. "There's one in Anga's house they could use, isn't there, Anga?"

"If they don't mind sharing with storage jars, I guess," said another man, stocky and heavily bearded. He rubbed his neck. "We'd be honored, I guess."

"And dinner, you'll have dinner, won't you?" asked the woman suckling the infant. She seemed to be Anga's wife; at any rate, she'd moved closer to him when he spoke, accompanied by the child still clinging to her legs. "That is, we don't have enough cooking, but others . . . ?"

She looked around at her neighbors. Ilna, following the woman's gaze up the plaza, saw a great cat holding a child between its paws.

Ilna dropped her knotted cords—only an owl could see well enough for her patterns to work in this half-light—and snatched the lasso free again. Chalcus had drawn both his sword and dagger in shimmering arcs, and Davus cocked the stone in his right hand back to throw.

"Wait!" cried Polus. "What's wrong?"

The cat got to its feet with lazy grace. The child, a girl of three or four, rubbed the creature's ear while continuing to stare at the strangers. It wasn't really a cat: its thick, jointed tail had a curved sting at the tip like a scorpion's. The lithe body was tawny, with gray-and-brown mottlings that almost perfectly mimicked the pattern of the corral against which it'd reclined with the child.

"The beast!" said Chalcus, lifting his chin to indicate the creature rather than using one or the other of the blades he held. A sword point was a threat even when meant only as a gesture.

"Why yes," said Polus. "He protects us. He's always lived here."

The cat sauntered toward the strangers, its head high and its long ears pricked up in interest. The boy hiding behind his mother suddenly darted back to the creature instead. He tugged at the long whiskers for a grip. The cat turned peevishly and licked the child's arm away, while the little girl on the other side said, "Don't pull, Ornon! Play nice, or I won't let you play at all!"

Chalcus sheathed his sword and, after a moment of consideration, his dagger as well. His hands remained close to the pommels, however. Ilna bunched the lasso in her hands, but she didn't loop it back around her waist.

"He eats porridge and offal when we slaughter a cow," said Anga's wife. "And he hunts for himself. There's deer and wild hogs in the valley."

"They'd eat half our crops if it weren't for him," Polus said. "And there's other things that'd find us sooner or later. They don't dare."

The cat, as Ilna'd decided she might as well call it, was nearly the height of a heifer at the shoulder, though of much rangier build. Two double paces short of Ilna it sat on its haunches and began to groom itself. Its eyeteeth were curved and as long as her index fingers. While it licked and combed itself with its dewclaws, one eye or the other remained on the newcomers.

"I've never seen a fellow who looked quite as this one does," said Chalcus, watching the cat as carefully as the cat watched them. "What is it that you call him?"

The cat suddenly shifted as smoothly as quicksilver flowing, bounding halfway up the plaza to where it flopped on its back. Children, all the children in the village who could walk, it seemed—cried out in delight and ran after it to throw themselves on its belly.

"Him?" said Polus, the village spokesman by default if not in more formal fashion. "We call him Friend, because he's the friend who keeps us safe."

"Such a creature is no friend to men," Davus said. He hadn't relaxed even as much as Chalcus and Ilna did. "I do not, I *will* not, believe that it can be."

Polus shrugged. "Folk in your land have different customs than ours," he said. "But please, it's getting dark. Won't you have bread and porridge with us?"

He gestured toward the central courtyard of the nearest house. Anga's wife had swung the infant over her shoulder to burp it. She trotted into the door in the left-hand wing, murmuring something like, "Not enough bowls!"

"Aye," said Chalcus, gesturing Ilna ahead of him into the open court. He smiled broadly. "If it won't offend you, though, we'll sit with our backs against the wall as we eat. I'd be pleased to be wrong, but I worry that your Friend is not necessarily our friend."

He laughed to make a joke of it; but it was no joke, as Ilna well knew.

The *Star of Valles* rocked as water coalesced out of the glowing stars beneath her keel. Sharina gripped the railing with one hand and put the other around Tenoctris' shoulders, just for safety's sake.

The four remaining vessels of the squadron settled with faint slapping sounds behind the flagship. The nymphs who'd been guiding the sea worm released the hawser. The great creature undulated toward the depths, growing faint and vanishing long before it could have drawn away in physical distance.

The eastern horizon—it was a shock to have a horizon again—was bright enough to hide the stars. Sharina thought the ship might be at the mouth of the River Val, but even in full daylight she wasn't enough of a pilot to be certain of one landfall against another.

"Come on, you lazy scuts!" Master Rincale shouted, dusting his palms together in enthusiasm as he strode sternward along the catwalk. "Oarsmen to your posts! We've got three leagues against the current before we dock in Valles! Move! Move! And you bloody landsmen, get your asses off the lower benches unless you're willing to pull oars!"

The sailors don't doubt where we are, Sharina thought.

The nymph rose toward them. At first she was only a glint in the water far below their keel, but she wriggled into full sight before Sharina had time to wonder what the object was. The nymph swam with her body and webbed feet, keeping her arms flattened back along her torso except when she wanted to turn abruptly in the water.

"This is as far as we will take you, missy," she called. Her eyes had the opalescence of pearl shell, and the pupils were slitted rather than round. "The water here hasn't enough salt for comfort, and going farther up the river's course would poison us. We have kept our bargain, missy, have we not?"

"You've kept your bargain," Sharina said, touching the hood covering her bare scalp instinctively. "Go with, with my blessing!"

She'd intended to say, "with the Lady's blessing," but she realized before the words left her tongue that these nymphs and the Goddess might be . . . not on the same side, say, even if they weren't enemies. The nymphs had helped Sharina and helped the kingdom; she didn't want to insult them.

"Perhaps we will sing to you someday, missy," the nymph called. She arrowed away, once waving back toward Sharina.

"We hope to sing for you, lovely missy," caroled the chorus of her sisters from invisibly far to seaward.

"Given who they are," said Tenoctris with a faint smile, "and where it is they sing, I rather hope that neither of us take them up on their offer. Though no doubt it was well-meant."

The soldiers and oarsmen were shifting places, the former with more enthusiasm than their relative clumsiness justified. The *Star of Valles* rocked side to side; common sailors, not just the officers, shouted curses at the landsmen. When Sharina glanced over the railing, she saw that all the narrow-hulled triremes were wobbling similarly.

Lord Waldron walked forward, looking haggard. He hadn't hidden in the belly of the ship the way most of his men did, but neither had he cared to stand in the prow and watch the great worm swim through the waste of stars.

"Your highness," he said in a tired voice, nodding in a sketch of a bow. "Lady Tenoctris. Your highness, I, ah . . . I'm in your debt for the time you've saved us in returning to Ornifal."

"We're all acting in the interests of the kingdom, Lord Waldron," Sharina said, trying to sound as cheerful as she'd been when her mind had settled down. She could see in the old warrior's haunted eyes how little he liked the means by which they'd voyaged, but he was too much of a man not to acknowledge the debt regardless.

"The kingdom?" Waldron said with a snort. "Oh, the army could serve the kingdom's need without having to hurry. I'd have to resign, of course, but your brother wouldn't have to look far for a replacement. If he even bothered! He's got a real man-of-war's head on his shoulders, Prince Garric does."

No, thought Sharina, smiling. *But he has a real man-of-war's ghost in his mind.*

Aloud she said, "Garric's very pleased that you're willing to undertake this dangerous task with minimal force, milord. He doesn't want to rule the Isles with his sword."

Waldron snorted again, this time in bitter humor. "Willing?" he said. "I'm forced to by the fact my cousin Bolor is an idiot. An idiot or a knowing traitor, and I prefer to believe the former. We bor-Warrimans have had our share of fools, but never before a traitor. If that's what Bolor is."

He took a deep breath, scanning the shore. The vessel's officers had sorted out the rowers by then. All the long oars were in position, hanging just above the water to either side of the hull.

"And aye, I know Prince Garric doesn't want to rule with his sword," Waldron went on. "His sword or his army's swords. He's the right king for the Isles now, your highness."

He turned and glared at Sharina as though he expected her to disagree. "He's the right king, wherever he was born or whoever his ancestors were," he said forcefully. "On my oath as a bor-Warriman!"

Bedrin and several of his aides were talking with the sailing master beneath the trireme's curving stern piece. Their voices rose, but the words were still unintelligible to Sharina in the bow. The trumpeter blew a signal. Three of the following vessels replied, but the last did not.

Bedrin snapped a command. The trumpeter signalled again, still without getting a response.

"This is where the People landed," Waldron said, gesturing toward the shore. "Back when I was an ensign in Lord Elphic's regiment."

He spoke in a tone of quiet reminiscence; partly, Sharina suspected, to calm himself by retreating into the past, where he could forget the voyage just ended. "Here at the mouth of the Val. They paddled their ships like canoes instead of rowing them, and the hulls were made of bronze instead of wood."

"Bronze?" said Sharina. "Weren't they awfully heavy, then?"

"Not particularly, no," Waldron said. "Except at the ribs and keel, the metal wasn't any thicker than your own skin, your highness."

He shrugged, and went on, "I don't know how they could've sailed boats like that any distance, the way the sea would've worked them up and down, but they got here somehow. Thousands of them. For a long time afterward, the price of bronze wasn't but half what it'd been in silver before all those boats were broken up and sold."

The last ship of the squadron finally replied with a quavering trumpet call. Bedrin shouted an order. The trumpet and curved horn called together.

The seated flutist began to play the rhythm of the stroke. The oars dipped down, splashed, and drew back in a bubbling surge. The *Star of Valles* started toward the river mouth hidden for the moment beneath a blanket of mist. The hull steadied as her speed reached that of a man walking at leisure.

"Why didn't the People go on up the river, milord?" Sharina said. The question had occurred to her, but primarily she asked to make Waldron more comfortable by ordinary talk and to settle herself as well. "There are only fishing villages and small pastures in the marshes on this part of the coast."

"I'm not a great lover of ships," Waldron said, smiling grimly to emphasize the degree to which he could put the statement more strongly. "But it was a good thing that we had ships on that day—had half a dozen triremes, at any rate, that Stronghand could crew and put in the water right away. It wasn't much of a fleet, but the People's boats were brittle as eggshells. They landed as soon as they reached Ornifal, because the Val is plenty deep enough to drown in—and that was the only choice, if the triremes caught them on the water."

The old warrior shook his head at the memory. "They came down on us so quickly, you see. There was next to no warning, then there they were, like cicadas coming out of the ground. Tens of thousands of them, all of them men. They had good swords and good armor, and they kept their ranks well. I wouldn't call them soldiers, rightly—they fought like they were hoeing rows of beans. But the city militia that stood between them and Valles was no better, and there wasn't time to raise the levy from all over the island."

The mist was no more than a faint haze when the *Star of Valles* drove into it, though it continued to curtain the shores while the squadron kept to the center of the channel. A few small boats were on the water. Men with clam rakes stood in them, watching the warships pass.

"We were the only real troops in the city, Lord Elphic's regiment," Waldron said. "Stronghand—though he was just Valence the Second at the time, he'd made a tour of his northern estates and we'd escorted him back to the capital. The People were marching up the right bank of the river, a quarter mile wide at low tide and only half that at high. They couldn't go inland because of the marshes."

The sun was visible over the hills to the east of the Val's boggy flood-plain. The mist had lifted, and the sound of cowbells drifted across the water. The *Star of Valles* cut the brown water at a fast walk, a good speed for her partial crew but not difficult to maintain over the short distance remaining before they docked at Valles.

"Stronghand put the city militia in the People's way just below the Pool," Waldron said, his voice strong and his face suffused with a harsh pride. Waldron didn't boast, but his whole personality was shaped by the certainty that he and his—the cavalry of Northern Ornifal—were the finest soldiers in the Isles. "North of there the channel's bounded by firm clay soil for leagues to either side. If the People got that far, they'd be able to use their numbers—and there were twenty thousand of them, maybe more."

"Who led the People?" Tenoctris asked. She'd taken a sliver of bamboo from her satchel, but she didn't seem to intend a spell; she was just holding the little wand between her index fingers while she listened to Waldron's memories. "Were you able to tell?"

"A wizard," Waldron said. He laughed. "And he was no general, that I can tell you, but he probably didn't think he needed to be with the numbers of men he had. He wasn't even with his army, but the prisoners told us later. He didn't have a name, at least to them: he was just the Master."

He looked at the right bank. Just to the north, the deep green of marsh grasses gave way to squared fields, varied by the type of crops and pasture. "Right there it was," he said, pointing with his right hand. The fingers of his left played with the pommel of his sword. "That's where they met the militia."

He lowered his arm and breathed deeply. "There was a barricade of sorts, carts with their wheels off mostly, but even so city folk couldn't have held them long. And then *we* came, Lord Elphic's regiment and Stronghand with us. We rode through the marshes on their flank. We had shepherds to guide us. The People didn't have time to form a shield wall against us, and after the front of their column stopped they were packed too tight to even use their swords. We mowed them down like barley till our swords were blunt. And then the tide came in."

Waldron slammed his right palm against the left, cracking like a thunderbolt. "They couldn't stand against us!" he said, his voice rising. "The militia slaughtered them at the barricade, and the tide didn't stop. The triremes rowed up and down the banks and swept them under, those our swords hadn't killed. There's never been such a day as the Battle of the Tides!"

Never for the young Waldron bor-Warriman, Sharina thought. And few enough such days anywhere, this side of Hell. She'd seen war, but it was still hard to imagine death on the scale of the barley harvest: the mud and water both bloody red and rafts of corpses drifting out to sea on the current. Mouths open, eyes staring, bodies already beginning to bloat with the gases of decay. Tens of thousands of corpses . . .

"You mentioned talking to prisoners, Lord Waldron," Tenoctris asked. She didn't seem as distressed at Waldron's account as Sharina was. Perhaps at Tenoctris' age, the awareness that everyone dies was so constant a companion that death even in wholesale lots no longer had the horror Sharina felt. "Is it possible that any remain for me to examine?"

"We captured some," Waldron said, staring far into the past. "It didn't seem like many, but there must've been thousands by the end. They were willing to talk, but they really didn't know much. From what I was told, at least. I didn't talk to any of them myself."

The *Star of Valles* had entered the Pool, the basin just south of Valles where the current grew sluggish. There the big freighters unloaded their cargo onto barges for transport the rest of the way to the city. It included naval installations also, and a pair of triremes were exercising in the broad waters. The trumpeter beside Bedrin in the stern blew a signal to the guardships, but the squadron didn't slow.

Waldron turned away from the rail to face the women for the first time since he'd begun to reminisce. "I had seventeen men in my troop when the battle started," he said in a different tone of voice from the one he'd used during the previous portion of the story. "There were three of us left at the end, and only my standard-bearer was still mounted. He'd have given me his horse, but I couldn't have lifted myself into the saddle. I was so tired. I've never in my life else been so tired. They carried me back to Valles in a wagon, and it was a week before I could raise my sword arm above my shoulder, it'd cramped so badly."

"And the prisoners?" Tenoctris said. She didn't sound peevish, but she was quietly determined to get an answer.

"They died," Waldron said. He shrugged and smiled faintly. "Oh, I don't mean we killed them. I don't think anybody who'd been in the fighting had the energy left to do that. But they sort of ran down. They didn't eat, not enough at least, and they even seemed to forget to drink. Mostly they just sat. They'd answer questions, not that they knew much except that their Master had sent them to capture Valles, then go on to conquer the whole island. There'd be more of them coming soon, or so they said; but no more did. And in a few weeks they were all dead. Or so I was told."

Waldron held out his right arm. He repeatedly made a fist, then relaxed it, as if he were working out the swelling and numbness of a long battle.

"Stronghand's councillors, the ones who survived, summoned the levy," he said, his mind slipping again into the past. "The king himself didn't leave his bed for three months, and he was never the same man again. Even when he was sober, and that was rare. But the People never returned."

The horns and trumpets of the whole squadron began to call, waking echoes from the Valles riverfront. A watchman at the naval dock rang his bronze alarm gong in reply.

"Never . . . ," Lord Waldron whispered.

"At least until now," said Tenoctris, echoing the words that had formed in Sharina's mind.

Garric awakened; Liane had touched his cheek. When she felt him twitch she whispered, "Quietly. Garric, I see light coming through the wall there." She pointed.

Garric's sword belt hung from the head of the bed on his side. He got up in his bare feet and drew the long sword with only the least hiss of the blade's chine on the bronze plate protecting the mouth of the scabbard.

A three-wick oil lamp hung from a wall bracket, but the only wick lighted when they went to bed had burned to a blue ember. It was dark enough in the bedchamber that Garric should've been able to see light coming from any other source—and he didn't.

The suite he and Liane shared had been used for storage until only hours before the royal contingent arrived at the earl's palace. It'd suffered severe water damage some decades ago, very possibly around the time the previous earl died along with his hopes of kingship at the Stone Wall. The frescoed plaster above the wainscotting had fallen, leaving rough brick walls, and the wood had warped in many places also. The damage hadn't been repaired immediately, so the unused room had attracted unused objects the way silt settles to the bottom of a pond.

"There, do you see it?" Liane said. She'd pulled on her left slipper. She pointed again with the other, then slid it on also; she hadn't been raised a peasant and gone barefoot eight months of the year. "Just a faint line."

Garric still didn't see anything, but he didn't see any reason to say that. He could trust Liane. He stepped to the lamp and filled it from the ewer of oil in the alcove beneath the bracket, being careful not to submerge the ember of wick yet remaining.

Normally that'd be the job of the servant sleeping in the small room off the bedchamber, but Garric preferred privacy to having somebody perform tasks he could handle perfectly well himself. He'd had plenty of experience in his father's inn, after all.

As the flame brightened, Garric looked around the room. He found what he needed immediately, as he'd expected he would. The palace servants who'd been told to prepare the room for guests wouldn't have had time to do a careful job even if they'd been willing to make the effort.

The skirts of the bed covered a considerable quantity of trash they'd found easier to hide than to bundle up and carry out. One of the objects was a half pike whose shaft had begun to split where the head was riveted onto it.

Garric sheathed his sword, then buckled it around his waist. Liane had donned an outer tunic over the one she'd slept in. "What should I do?" she asked.

"Bring the lamp closer," Garric said as he fished out the half pike. Though it was an ornate thing intended for show rather than serious use, it'd do for his purposes. He thrust the point into the wainscotting and struck brick immediately.

"More to the right," Liane directed, unhooking the lamp from the bracket.

Garric slammed the pike into the wainscotting again. This time the rusty head scrunched through not only the paneling but also the structure inside. He twisted, splitting the panel. Behind was a low doorway, blocked with wattle and daub on a frame of poles.

Garric set down the half pike and wrenched the panel free with his hands. He was as quiet as possible, knowing that if the guards in the hallway outside heard wood tearing, they'd be through the door even if they had to smash it down.

Since Garric became Prince Garric, he spent too much of his life being protected from the unusual. This was something he'd handle himself until he found some greater threat than a doorway plugged in the distant past. The withies were cracklingly brittle.

The wattle had shrunk as it dried, and the remains of the clay that'd filled it shook away as Garric wrestled out the plug. There was a draft, faint but cool. He stepped back, dusting his palms against one another, and Liane thrust the lamp into the opening.

"There's steps going down," she said. "Farther than the light shows."

Garric squatted beside her to look. He grinned, laid his hand on the half pike, and said, "It looks a little tight for this, don't you think? I think my sword's the better choice."

He rose and drew his sword again. Liane balanced the half pike in her left hand and said, "I'll carry the spontoon in case there's something blocking the passage. Though the shaft's split so badly that it probably wouldn't work as a lever on any serious obstacle."

She slipped through the opening, using the pikeshaft to support her as she dropped nearly her full height to where the steps started. A foundation wall for the present palace rested on what would've been the upper portion of an ancient staircase.

"Hey!" said Garric in surprise. "I'll lead, and I'll take the lamp too."

"No," said Liane. "This leaves you free to deal with anything waiting around a landing or a corner."

Garric made a sour face but followed as Liane started down the steps. The staircase was wide enough for two, but only barely. If he were attacked unexpectedly, the lamp would be a serious hindrance; though he didn't like to think of killing an enemy whose weapon was stuck in Liane either.

In his mind Carus, who'd watched silently to that moment, murmured, *Sometimes there's no really good way to do it. It's just that simple.*

"This building's built over one that was destroyed a thousand years ago," Garric said. "We must be in part of the cellars of the earlier palace that didn't completely collapse. I don't see how there can be light here that you saw, though."

"Neither do I," said Liane quietly. Her voice whispered an accompaniment to itself between the narrow walls of the passage. "Unless fungus glows on the walls, but it doesn't seem . . ."

The steps ended on a concrete floor that hadn't been finished or even properly leveled. They'd reached the subcellars of the original palace.

Storage jars had been placed upright along the section of wall opposite, their narrow bases sunk in a stone-curbed sandbox. All but one had broken in the violence that brought down all the building to their right. Liane raised the lamp, but it could only hint at the thoroughness of the destruction.

Garric heard water dripping; it seemed to come from below where he stood. He frowned, turning slowly and letting his other senses tell him what his eyes couldn't in this gloom. The hairs fringing the shell of his ears felt an air current too faint to be called a breeze.

He walked slowly toward the corner to the right. It was a shadowed mass of rubble by the flickering lamplight. His shadow shifted around him as Liane stepped to his side with the lamp high. At the end of the vast room the debris sloped not only inward but to the side as well: the shock had dropped part of a foundation wall into a natural cave.

"How far do you suppose . . . ," Garric said, then swallowed the rest of the question. It was one of those silly things you said—or caught yourself before you said, if you kept control of your tongue—when you wanted to make noise because you were afraid.

Liane had no better way than he did of telling how deep the cave might be. The faint air current suggested it went on some distance, but a crack too tight for a mouse would still let air through.

"Well, we can go a little . . . ," Liane said. She stepped onto a broken chunk of concrete, planting the butt of the pikestaff farther down the slope like a walking stick. The block shifted under her weight and slid, gathering lesser debris and sending a cloud of dust up the scree. Liane twisted after it.

Garric grabbed her shoulder with his left hand. The lamp flew from her grasp and shattered. Its wick faded into a blue spark far down the slope of rubble, then went out.

Garric hugged her to him. "Love," he said. "Love. Is your ankle all right? I can carry you if you've turned it."

"I'm fine," Liane said, but she held him tightly for a long moment. "I'm a fool not to have brought rushlights instead of the lamp! They'd still burn if I dropped one."

"I think we've seen enough for one night," Garric said, pleased in his heart that he had an excuse for not going farther with what was either a pointless exercise or a very dangerous one. "Here, give me the pike and I'll feel our way back to the stairs."

In the morning—later in the morning, he supposed—he might send a squad of soldiers here to explore with pine torches or rushlights as Liane suggested, dried fennel stalks whose spongy pith had been soaked with tallow. This jaunt had been enough to satisfy his desire to do something real instead of talking interminably and 'looking regal,' whatever that meant.

"I'll guide us," Liane said. "You keep your sword out. Anyway, it shouldn't be difficult. The floor was clear enough."

She walked briskly with Garric's left hand on her shoulder, tapping the staff but obviously following her instincts rather than needing the help. She had as good a sense of direction within buildings as Garric did in the woods. At the stairs she continued to lead, but without Garric to boost her she'd have had a difficult time getting through an opening at the height of her head.

As Liane scrambled back into their room, Garric turned and listened. Somewhere in the distance water dripped, or perhaps he was imagining that it did.

There *was* a glow, though, from the subcellar or perhaps from beyond it. It was fainter than starlight, but he could make out the flat arch over the bottom of the stairs.

"Here," said Liane. She set the pike crosswise in the opening, braced against the wall on either side. Garric gripped the shaft with his free hand and tugged to make sure it would hold. Then he shot his sword back into its scabbard and pulled himself up by the strength of both arms and the soles of his feet on the wall.

The moon had risen since they'd started down the opening; Garric's eyes, adapted to pitch darkness, gave him a good view of the unfamiliar room. He lifted the clothespress that held his regalia and straddle-walked to the opening, where he set it down as quietly as he could.

"There," he said, stepping back to view his handiwork. "Now I think we can get some sleep."

"Will it hold?" Liane said doubtfully.

Garric laughed. "Not against a serious threat," he said, "but it'll make a good deal of noise if somebody slides it back. And if that happens—"

He drew his sword with a *sring!* and an arc of shimmering moonlight.

"—I'll have something to say about it even before the guards get here."

Still chuckling, he led Liane to the bed. Suddenly, getting more sleep wasn't the first thing on his mind.

Cashel'd always had a good head for heights, so the view at night from Ronn's north parapet thrilled rather than frightened him. He bent over the edge, feeling the force of the wind that rushed up the wall's slope. It brought with it dry odors and hinted mystery.

A patchwork of lights gleamed at every level of the city, the suites of residents still awake. The outside stairs were pastel zigzags against the general darkness.

He turned; Mab was watching him with an amused expression. The night was moonless, but drifting glows like those he'd seen on the terraces over the diamond lake were enough to keep the scattered strollers there on the topmost plaza from walking into one another.

Mab was shorter than she'd been when they left the terrace. Though he couldn't be sure in this light, he thought her hair'd changed color too.

She pointed to the nearest of the lights; it floated obediently closer. "They'll brighten enough for you to read by," she said.

Cashel smiled. "Well, not me, ma'am," he said. "But if I could read, I'm sure they would."

For the first time since he'd met her, Mab lost her self-composure. "I didn't . . . ," she said with a look of shocked surprise. Instead of finishing whatever she'd started to say, she went on, "You've had a hard life, haven't you, Cashel?"

He thought about the question instead of just blurting an answer, but it came out the same way anyhow. "No, ma'am," he said. "I don't guess I have. Not for me, I mean."

Mab quirked a smile at him. "No?" she said. "Well, perhaps you haven't, then. I believe your mother would've wished things had been otherwise for you; though a more learned upbringing might've left you less able to aid Ronn in her present plight."

Cashel laughed. "Oh, mistress!" he said. "You wouldn't say that if you'd met my friend Garric! He can read and write like any city-bred scholar, but he can knock any man in the borough silly with a quarterstaff. Besides me, of course."

Cashel had room here, so purely for the joy of it he stepped clear of the woman and started a series of exercises with his staff. He made slow circles at first, in front of him and overhead; then he crossed his grip to reverse direction, spinning the heavy hickory faster.

Only when Cashel was sure he had the rhythm and he'd warmed the kinks out of his muscles, did he start doing fancy tricks. He fed the staff around his body sunwise, then widdershins, and when he had it around in front of him again he spun it between his legs and caught it over his head. That was one where you could do yourself a world of hurt if your timing was just the least hair off.

There were more people coming over to watch him now. Mab had brought a yellow light to hover overhead, brighter than the others drifting over the plaza. If Cashel hadn't already gotten into the feel of the thing, the spectators would've embarrassed him, but as it was he was glad for their eyes. He was good at this, better than any man in the borough and any man he'd met since leaving the borough. He wasn't going to pretend that wasn't so.

Cashel capped the show with the things that were more than just tricks—the moves you made in a bout or a fight for real, if you were good enough. He spun the staff overhead. When the smooth hickory was a blur of soft light, he jumped beneath it and let it pull *him* so that he was facing the other way, then jumped again and returned to the way he'd been standing before.

Cashel's weight slowed the staff so he could slam it to a dead stop upright beside him. He was sweating and gasping in deep breaths, but he was as happy as he'd been since he walked into the hillside with Mab.

The spectators raised their hands over their heads and clapped them together. There were really a lot of them, more than he'd realized while he was exercising.

Mab stepped to Cashel's side, touched his right hand, and with gentle pressure turned him so that everybody could see his face. It was a little embarrassing, but mostly he was proud.

Mab pointed to the bright fairy light directly overhead. It went out, returning the two of them to darkness and privacy. The spectators drifted away.

"Now," she said, "we'll watch what I brought you here to see. It's time."

As she spoke, a male Councillor stepped through an arched doorway that came from the interior of the city. He murmured a word, beating time in the air with an athame of zebra-striped wood. Beside him appeared the lighted figure—no, it was a figure of light!—of a warrior in steel armor.

Blond hair spilled from under the figure's helmet and fell across its polished shoulderpieces. It was oversized, half again as tall as Cashel and taller than any living man he'd seen, but it wasn't a fanciful giant like the trumpeter who'd greeted the dawn.

"That was Valeri," Mab said. "The queen formed his image after he went down to the cavern to sleep. The Councillors cause the image to walk the parapet every night; it and the other Heroes."

Cashel watched the figure go by, moving at the speed of the wizardling who walked beside it. The image's legs scissored, and its head turned like that of a real man looking toward the mountains as he sauntered along. The body looked solid, but it was too clear to be real. It looked like it would in daylight, but there wasn't any light there except for the floating glows. When the figure passed through a planter of roses, it did just that—passed through them.

"There's nothing on this plaza that's higher than the parapet," Mab said as she and Cashel followed the warrior's image into the distance. "Someone watching from the mountains, even if he were able to bring objects closer with wizardry or mechanick arts, would see only what appeared to be Valeri walking the battlements."

Another Councillor came through the arch. This time it was the woman who'd spoken when age prevented her chief from addressing the Assembly.

"They're honoring the people who saved the city?" Cashel said. "I've seen statues in Valles and other places too, but those're mostly bronze. The ones I've seen."

Instead of an athame this Councillor held a flight feather from the wing of some great bird. She beat time with it, and at every stroke it changed color: from purple to orange, and back again with the next stroke. Each step she cried, *"Misauda!"*

"It's not for honor's sake, Cashel," Mab said. "I'm afraid most of the citizens couldn't tell you the names of the Heroes, even though their images walk the parapet every night. But if the people of Ronn have forgotten the Heroes, their enemies have not. Every time the Made Men marched against the city, one Hero or the next drove them back with slaughter that left the bare ground red. Even a hundred and fifty years haven't been enough to erase the terror of Valeri sweeping almost to the heart of the king's power."

Two figures of light stepped through the archway, seemingly arm in arm. Cashel could see that the elbow of the figure on the inside actually passed through the jamb of dark crystal. They were taller than real men, though perhaps not quite as tall as the image of Valeri had been. One had fair hair and the other was a dark brunette, but apart from that they were as like as the two eyes of an owl.

"Minon and Menon," Mab said, as the phantasms of light walked past. "Few cities have had a champion as great as either of them, and in Ronn they were both together till the day Minon carried his brother down to the cavern and the sleep they now share."

One of the images carried a broad-bladed halberd. The other wore a long, straight sword and carried a shield broad enough to cover two: the blazon on its face was a double-headed eagle. They were turned toward one another, and their smiling lips moved as though they were talking.

"The king created the Made Men," Mab said, "and he rules them—to a point. But not all his threats and promises have been enough to convince his creatures to attack again while the Heroes walk the parapet of Ronn."

"But they aren't real," Cashel said, nodding as the twins passed on at the pace of the wizard walking beside their images. "They can't defend the city."

"They're semblances," Mab said, "but their semblance alone is enough to protect Ronn so long as memory of real slaughter remains; as it does."

Two Councillors, a young woman and a boy of scarcely Cashel's age, came through the doorway. They chanted; the boy's voice was nervously high and loud enough that Cashel heard the word *sabaoth*. As they beat the air together with their athames, a lanky, rawboned figure appeared. It was so tall that it had to duck to clear the high arch.

"That's Virdin," said Mab, "as he was when he was a youth. No minion of the king nor *all* the minions of the king could stand against him during the long life before he went to the cavern."

Cashel had noticed without giving particular thought to the matter that the citizens of Ronn kept some distance from the parapet. The wizards and the figures they controlled passed outside of them. It was with surprise, then, that he saw a group of stooping men come up an outside staircase and place themselves directly in the path the image of Virdin must take. Two carried between them what looked like a large oval mirror.

"Mab?" said Cashel, bracing his legs for better support and spreading his hands into a fighting grip on his quarterstaff. "What're those fellows doing? There, by the—"

"Citizens of Ronn!" Mab shouted. "The Made Men are attacking!"

At the sound of her cry, four of the newcomers drew curved swords. They were pale as soured milk, and the pupils of their eyes were empty.

The other two turned, holding the mirror between them. Face on, Cashel saw a hideously misshapen man reflected in the mirror's surface. Beyond him was a sea of creatures like the few who'd climbed the walls, manlike but not men.

"Citizens of Ronn!" Mab said. "The Made Men are here, and they bring their wizard-king with them! Rally for your lives!"

The figure on the mirror's surface raised an athame of human rib; his albino creatures scuttled toward Cashel with their swords raised.

Chapter Eight

A *t least I'm warmed up,* Cashel thought, but the truth was it never took him long to get moving in a fight. With the smile that thought brought to his lips, he stepped into the Made Men with his staff spinning.

Four swordsmen who knew what they were doing—any four veterans in the royal army, say—could've cut him to collops in their initial rush. Two who were really skilled could do the same, men like Chalcus or like Garric when his warrior ancestor was in charge. But these Made Men—well, they were willing to fight, which put them one up on the Sons of the Heroes, but there wasn't much to choose between those boys and these fungus-white creatures for skill.

Curved swords lent themselves to wide, flashy flourishes, which the Made Men did a lot of. Cashel chose, feinted toward the pair in the middle, and brought the quarterstaff out of its spin in a thrust at the creature on the left end. The iron butt cap crushed the Made Man's forehead.

Instead of flying backward from the force of the blow, the Made Man spasmed to the side. Its sword, held in a literal death grip, clinked and sparked on the plaza.

The two young Councillors lost the rhythm of their chant and cried out in surprise. The male threw himself in front of his partner, holding his long ivory wand as a club. The image of Virdin stepped halfway through the mirror, then faded like a lump of salt dropped into water.

The Made Man beside Cashel's first victim had flinched away from the feint. Though still off-balance, it slashed sidewise at Cashel. He stepped back, recovering his quarterstaff in a widdershins arc. The blood-smeared butt cap rapped the back of the Made Man's head.

Though not as spectacular as the first stroke, it was equally effective. The creature sprawled with its skull dished in, across the path of its two fellows as they rushed Cashel together. They fell.

Cashel put his left foot on the sword hand of the nearer of the pair that'd tripped, pinning it hopelessly against the hard surface. While the one his weight held mewed and squirmed like a broken-backed snake, Cashel stabbed like he was flounder gigging, breaking the neck of the farther

Made Man. A moment later Cashel's fourth judicious stroke *did* break the back of the creature he stood on.

He paused to suck air through his open mouth, wheezing like a foundered horse. While the fight lasted—all the few seconds that the fight lasted—he'd seen nothing but the four swordsmen coming at him, moving in discrete intervals of time. Now everything expanded back to normal and speeded up again.

Age had so wizened the man in the mirror that even standing he was doubled over like a frog. He pointed his curved athame at Mab as his lips twisted over words of power. No sound passed the surface of the mirror, but spears of red and blue wizardlight stabbed out—

To meet the shield Mab's hands wove in the air before her. The bolts blasted upward, spreading and fading to a dim pastel fog above which the stars faded.

Cashel sized up the situation. He spun his quarterstaff before him, then stepped onto the quivering body of one of the creatures he'd slain.

The surviving Made Men dropped the mirror and tried to draw their swords. Cashel crushed the chest of the nearer, flinging its body over the parapet.

"*Remiel!*" Mab shouted. "*Nemiel!*"

The mirror fell flat to the ground. All but a sliver of Cashel's mind was focused on his staff and the way the remaining Made Man was trying to duck. That small part expected the mirror to shatter when it hit. Instead the plate bounced upright. For an instant the king at its heart looked squarely at Cashel rather than at Mab. The king's eyes were glowing blacknesses brighter than the hottest forge, and his athame pointed.

"*Lemiel!*" said Mab.

The mirror disintegrated, falling as dust instead of breaking into visible pieces. The last of the Made Men leaped for the stairs up which it had come. Cashel stepped through the shimmering ruin and struck the creature. His quarterstaff broke its hips rather than its chest as he'd intended, but the weight of the blow hurled it well out from the side of Ronn. Cashel wasn't sure how far below the ground was, but it was surely miles rather than furlongs.

The fight was over. Cashel sank to his knees, gasping and blowing. He'd have fallen on his face if he hadn't planted his staff straight up and down to support his sagging torso.

Behind him Mab cried in a voice of despair, "The king's now proved to his creatures that the Heroes walking the walls of Ronn are phantasms. They'll attack soon, perhaps in a matter of days!"

Cashel's vision blurred momentarily. Colors faded to shades of gray, then slowly steadied and returned to their soft pastel hues.

"Lord Ardane and Lady Thaida!" Mab said. Her voice had become firm and imperative. The wailing despair of a moment ago had faded into the past. "Summon your fellow Councillors and call an emergency Assembly at once. The king and his creatures are coming. If Ronn isn't ready to receive them, may the Gods have mercy on the city and her residents; for be assured, the king will have none!"

"It's been months since I've seen the palace," Sharina said, as an usher led her, Waldron, and—just behind in a sedan chair—Tenoctris through the walled compound that encircled a sprawling collection of buildings on the northern edge of Valles. "It's completely different now."

They were approaching the Chancellery, the largest single structure in the compound. It'd been reroofed with tiles whose red hadn't had time to soften in the sun, and the grounds in front had been cleaned to display the mosaic pavement underlying what Sharina remembered as an expanse of sod and leaf litter. She'd never have imagined it—

"A waste of money better spent on the army, I'd say," Waldron muttered. He glanced at the pair of workmen repairing a corner of the mosaic, rebuilding with new tesserae the picture of a fox leaping at a quail. "A waste of men who could be holding spears, too."

Sharina smiled. The landscaping had run riot during the last decade of Valence the Third's reign, and many of the separate bungalows had fallen into ruin. The effort being expended on reversing the decay since Garric became regent was a paradigm for the even greater efforts the new administration was making to recover the kingdom's unity.

"People can't really comprehend the changes in something as large as the Kingdom of the Isles," she said. "They can see the changes here in the palace, though, and they're changes for the better. It's worth the money, milord."

Chancellor Royhas stood at the main entrance alone. There were guards for the building, but Royhas didn't presume to meet Princess Sharina and Lord Waldron with a retinue when they'd arrived without one.

Royhas was the quietly competent man who'd led the conspiracy that made Garric regent when the king's mind gave way under the threats facing him. He'd acted for the sake of the Isles, certainly; and in his own interest, because Royhas and all the members of the royal court faced death if the kingdom tottered to total collapse. But he'd acted for the sake of Valence the Third as well, saving his friend the king from the certain destruction to which his own inability to act doomed him.

Today Royhas looked worn. His cheeks sagged, and his eyes had dark circles. While he hadn't made a fetish of physical fitness the way Waldron did, he'd struck Sharina as remarkably healthy-looking for a man whose duties didn't involve physical exercise. Strain had robbed him of that.

"I don't know what wind brought you here at this moment, your highness," Royhas said, bowing to Sharina, "but it was a fair one. And you, milord—"

He clasped arms with Waldron, who'd winced at mention of their passage to Ornifal.

"—you're even more welcome. Did you bring the whole army? There've been terrible developments. My dispatches won't have had time to reach Erdin, but—"

"We know about the imposter Valgard," Waldron said. He'd allowed the Chancellor's greeting, but he remained stiffly unbending to discourage further intimacy. The army commander generally didn't like either civilians or nobles from the mercantile families of Valles, and he didn't like Royhas as an individual. "And I know about my cousin Bolor's involvement. As for the army, I'm here with sufficient troops for the purpose; you needn't trouble yourself on that matter."

Royhas stepped back. He gave Waldron a smile of wry amusement that brought the familiar glow of health back to his face. "Milord," he said, "it's still a pleasure to see you. But please, won't you all join me in my private office, where we can discuss the details?"

He bowed again to Sharina, said, "If I may precede you, your highness?" and, without really waiting for an answer, led his guests through the central hall. It was lined with batteries of low-ranking clerks reading out names and numbers as they copied them into ledgers. The noise reminded Sharina of feeding chickens at the kitchen door of her father's inn: a thin, purposeless babble that vanished even as it was spoken.

A light well in the center of the room provided illumination during daylight. On this fine day, the roof transoms of bull's-eye glass set in lead frames were swung back. To the sides of the central hall were the offices of senior clerks. Every door was open so that the officials within could catch a glimpse of Princess Sharina.

If they'd seen me two years ago in Barca's Hamlet, Sharina thought, *they wouldn't have paid me any more notice than they would the table.* And that was very likely true, but it didn't mean there was anything wrong with the officials' behavior—at either time. You couldn't understand anything apart from its surroundings.

The buildings in the palace compound sprawled rather than rising as they'd have had to do in the heart of the city. Royhas' office was on the upper of the two floors running the width of the back. Its pillared loggia overlooked an enclosed garden set off from the rest of the grounds so that the Chancellor could entertain ranking visitors among flowers and statuary if he chose.

Sharina helped Tenoctris to a place on the loggia, then seated herself beside the older woman. The chairs had frames of bronze filigree with wicker cushions, artistic and comfortable but unlikely to be harmed if a storm blew up before the servants got them inside. They were arranged in an arc so that those seated could see one another while looking out onto the garden.

It was a civilized and peaceful setting in which to hold tense discussions. Sharina noted again that Royhas was a very intelligent man in addition to being wealthy and wellborn.

Royhas took the end chair to the left. "I'm glad you know about the situation," he said bluntly, "because I knew almost nothing about it until ten days ago. There were rumors that another son of Valence Stronghand was returning to take the throne—silly nonsense, but widespread. Reports came from the city markets and in from outlying districts as well. Then real trouble started. Royal officials in the north were set upon—beaten and driven out. Even a few imprisoned I gather."

" 'Royal officials,' " Waldron repeated. "You mean tax gatherers."

Royhas looked at him with a determinedly blank expression. "Yes," he said. "Officials who collect the taxes out of which the royal army is paid, if you like. That was rebellion or next to it. In the eastern districts it's approaching anarchy—bandits, really. The gangs have gathered every bad man in the island as well as a lot of farm laborers who decided burning the squire's fields was better fun than stacking his ricks in the hot sun.

Some of the bands are supposed to be large—several hundred apiece, though I doubt there's anything like that number of armed men in them."

"What about the army?" Waldron demanded. "You have four regiments. What have they accomplished?"

"Nothing," said Royhas. "Because I haven't dared use them."

He raised his hand to silence the retort on the tip of Waldron's tongue. "Not because I didn't trust the troops, milord," he said, "but because I didn't trust myself to lead them. And before you ask—I didn't trust any of the regimental commanders to lead the force in my place. As a matter of fact, I don't trust Lord Titer's loyalty, nor do I—"

He leaned toward the army commander to add emphasis without raising his voice.

"—trust Lord Olinus' ability to find his ass with both hands. I'm very glad to see *you*, milord, however many troops you've brought with you."

Lord Waldron relaxed abruptly and barked a laugh. "Well, to tell the truth," he said, "when I was deciding who'd go with me to settle the rebellion in the west and who'd stay in Valles where nothing was going to happen, I may have left the garrison here a little short of brilliance. I ask your pardon for that, milord, but I'll try to correct it now."

Servants hovered at the back of the room with trays and pitchers, but Royhas hadn't ordered them forward, so they had no choice but to wait. He glanced over his shoulder, making sure the servants were still out of earshot, and said, "Whereas I assure you, milord, that the financial staff accompanying Prince Garric *is* skilled to the point of brilliance. That's because Lord Tadai is quite as capable of running the Chancellery as I am—and he'd be trying to do just that if he were in Valles, which praise the Lady he is not. But I understand the choice you faced; and as you say, you're here to deal with the problem now."

Lord Waldron rose. "All right, Royhas," he said. "I think we understand each other. I'll call a military council and put some spine into the garrison, then we'll see about this Valgard. And if Titer's the problem you think he is, I'll sort him out myself!"

He bowed curtly to the seated Chancellor and started toward the door. Only then did he remember that Sharina was the highest-ranking person in the room—and save for Valence, pottering about somewhere in the palace, the highest-ranking person on Ornifal. Waldron clacked his boots to a halt and stood stiff as a pikestaff.

"Good luck with your business, milord," Sharina said, smiling at his back. "I'd appreciate a report when you've had a chance to appraise the situation."

"Yes, your highness," Waldron said, too embarrassed by his gaffe to face her. "With your leave." He clicked his heels again, then strode out of the room much faster than he'd entered.

Royhas, smiling also, turned to Sharina. "Your highness," he said, "what do you wish of me?"

"Just to carry on as you've been doing, milord," Sharina said. "I think—and my brother thought—that I'll be of most use to you if I'm simply seen in public. In Valles to begin with, but perhaps we'll be able to widen our range later as Waldron gets the security situation under control. And of course"—she looked at Tenoctris—"support Lady Tenoctris in whatever fashion she wants. Is there anything . . . ?"

Tenoctris nodded. "Yes," she said. "Since this Valgard is said to be the son of Stronghand, I'd like to see Stronghand's burial place. Is that possible?"

"Easily," said the Chancellor, nodding approval. "It's on the Caldar Road, following the left bank of the Val just north of the city proper. Perhaps you'd like to accompany her, your highness? It's precisely the sort of public event you suggested making."

"Yes," said Sharina, rising to her feet. She offered Tenoctris a hand, though the older woman seemed her best sprightly self and didn't need the help. "But I want to see King Valence first."

She smiled wryly in response to the others' looks of surprise. "I suppose it's silly," she explained, "but I'd like to hear what the king himself thinks about the notion that he has a half brother."

Ilna turned at the northern edge of the flax field. The villagers had cut patches of scrub for firewood beyond here, but the terrain was basically natural. "Thank you again for your hospitality!" she called.

Polus and another of the men hoeing among the lentil fields to the south raised their heads and waved. The other men just continued working.

"I wish we could've paid them," Ilna said, more to herself than her companions. "It was good to sleep with a roof overhead again."

It was odd to find that she missed a roof, but she did. She'd grown up in an massive Old Kingdom mill, the oldest and most solid building in

Barca's Hamlet. Her brother was in the sheepfold or out in the pastures as many nights as he wasn't, but Ilna herself hadn't slept under the stars until she left home.

"It didn't seem they'd have had much use for money even if we'd been carrying our purses," Chalcus said. "Though coins make pretty bangles, which I'd judge our hostess wouldn't have turned down."

"This village seems to exist apart from the world," said Davus thoughtfully. "They'll forget us completely in a few days, I suspect. Maybe they've forgotten us already, most of them."

"Well, it's in the back of beyond," Chalcus commented. His blades were sheathed, but he kept his head moving in a fairly successful attempt to look in all directions. "I didn't see anything in the village that hadn't been made there, with the exception of a few iron knives and some perfume bottles."

"Yes," said Davus, "but it shouldn't be *that* isolated. There's enough here to draw more than half a dozen peddlers over the course of . . . how long would you say? A generation at least."

The women were back among the houses, preparing meals for their households. Simple as the food was, it required a great deal of effort. The oats were parched, then ground with the lentils and boiled as porridge. There was no miller; the work was done by individual housewives, grinding with pestles in bowls whose coarse inner surfaces were as effective as a stone and easier to manufacture.

Ilna'd found the porridge filling and quite tasty for one meal. It was likely to pall as a steady diet, though, even for a person like her, who ate to live instead of the other way around.

Preparing cloth seemed to take up the rest of the women's time. They rotted the flax stems in water, then separated the useful fibers from the pulp by a process not very different from the way they turned oats into porridge. After they'd spun the flax into linen thread, they wove it much the same way as Ilna did wool.

She tried not to be overly critical—the villagers had been extremely kind to her and her companions, after all—but their weaving didn't impress her. It was all very well to say that they lacked Ilna's advantage of having the wide world to measure themselves against; but the truth was, these women were simply sloppy.

"The cat keeps folk away, do you think?" Chalcus said in his usual pleasant tenor, calm and cheerful in this as in almost all things. "I'd thought we'd hear it snuffling about us in the night, but there were only the crickets and a nightjar. And no cat to greet us this morning, neither."

Davus took off the length of linen that Polus' wife had given him; for a sash, he'd said, but now he looped it and dropped one of his fist-sized stones into its pocket. "Not in the village, at least," he said as he began to spin the simple sling in a lazy circle at his side.

They entered open forest, walking between pines and broad-leafed trees a little taller than the scrub near the village. The land was rising. Ilna didn't fancy herself as a woodsman, but she judged it shouldn't be long before they were out of the valley.

She weighed the choices, then put the hank of yarn back in her sleeve and readied the noose. Of course she might be quite wrong in her concerns. . . .

"There may be people just that innocent," Chalcus said, his sword and dagger drawn. "What would an old pirate know of basic goodness, eh? And I surely grant they might not know what their friend the cat—"

Ilna was watching the pattern a juniper's branches wove as the breeze ruffled them. "*Now,* I think," she said.

As she spoke the cat pounced from an outcrop three man lengths ahead, unseen to the instant it moved. Its forelegs were flared, and its silver-gray claws were each the length of a man's finger.

She saw Davus move from the corner of her eye, but the lump of quartz was only a flicker. The sound of stone hitting bone was like a sledge on timber. The cat convulsed with a squall like nothing of flesh and blood. It'd been leaping for Chalcus. Momentum carried it toward the sailor, but it doubled up and pawed at its shattered left eye socket.

Chalcus dodged, slipping the curved sword in and out. His steel lifted a fluff of mottled fur from the thing's throat, then a spurt of blood.

The cat struck the ground and got its feet under it, twisting its body to the right like an eel. The scorpion tail snapped forward like a catapult releasing.

Ilna's noose settled about the stinger and drew taut. The force of the cat's stroke jerked her off her feet, but the needle tip ejected its yellow poison into the air instead of Chalcus' throat. He thrust again, this time piercing the creature's right eye.

"Get clear!" Chalcus shouted, glancing to see where Ilna was. "It'll bleed out, I swear on my hopes of dying in a bed!"

The blinded cat sprang toward the sound of his voice. Chalcus had made a flat-footed jump downslope that put a thigh-thick tree bole between him and the cat. Ilna let go of her end of the lasso—it was good for nothing but to lead the beast toward her—and rolled in the opposite direction.

The cat's hearing must've been demonically good, because it twisted again, this time toward the scrunch of the coarse soil under her hips. Bright blood from the slit in its neck spurted farther than a man could reach.

Chalcus cried out, lunging toward the creature behind the point of his outstretched sword. He needn't have worried: a second rock smacked the cat between the ruined eye sockets, crushing the skull.

The missile ricocheted high in the air, its white quartz surface flecked with blood. The cat went suddenly limp. It slithered downslope a few feet, dead and as harmless as a rug.

"I think we should leave this place quickly," said Chalcus. The quaver in his voice was mainly from the deep breaths he was dragging into his lungs.

"A moment," said Ilna, gasping also. She rested on all fours, keeping the pressure off her chest and diaphragm so that nothing hindered her breathing. "I don't want to leave my noose, but I think I'll wait a trifle before I retrieve it."

Though the monster was dead beyond question, its jointed tail moved spasmodically. Every time it jerked forward, the hooked sting spurted another firkin of venom.

"Yes," said Chalcus softly. "I'd say I owe that rope my life; which I'd laugh at if I had my breath, for I never thought I'd find a noose my friend."

And they all three gasped with laughter, at the joke and with a touch of madness as well.

"Duzi!" said Garric as he caught his first sight of the Temple of the Shepherd Who Overwhelms. "I've never seen a temple so big!"

"In most cities the priesthoods of the Lady and the Shepherd are rivals," Liane said as she walked at his side. Garric had insisted she accompany him, for her knowledge—as now—as well as for the calm her presence brought him. "Here in Erdin, worship and wealth go almost entirely to the Shepherd. The Lady's only temple is on the waterfront for travellers from other islands."

The flight of ten broad steps to the plinth on which the temple stood was on a scale with the building itself, far too high for a man to walk. Squads of trumpeters in priestly robes stood on the ends of each step. They began to call as Garric, Liane, and their guards approached. The notes rose because the instruments shortened by a hand's breadth at each stage.

Spectators filled the plaza and the buildings surrounding it. It wasn't a happy crowd like those that'd greeted Garric in Valles and Carcosa, but it was at least grudgingly respectful. Many in Erdin might think—or at least say—that their city was greater than Valles and by rights should rule the Isles, but in their hearts they were impressed that the Prince of Haft had dared to come to them.

"Aye, and they're impressed by the size of the fleet and army billeted on Volita," growled the image of King Carus. *"Don't think you'd get this peaceful a reception if that weren't in the minds of everybody with brains enough to pull on his tunic right side to."*

Garric grinned. That was probably so, but it was acceptable. The people of Sandrakkan would learn in good time the advantages of being part of a unified kingdom standing against massed Evil. For now, all that mattered was that they acquiesced.

The Blood Eagles marched in two sections, ahead of and behind Garric. There were fewer than two hundred men present because of losses in recent fighting, men detached for duty in Ornifal with Sharina and Valence, and the fact that Attaper hadn't had leisure to train volunteers from the line regiments to his exacting standards.

That there *were* volunteers—more than enough to bring the Blood Eagles to peacetime strength of five hundred—was a mystery Garric still couldn't fathom. Everyone in the royal army had seen how extremely dangerous it was to guard a prince who led from the front in the fiercest battles the Isles had known for a thousand years. Nonetheless, many of them begged for a chance to wear the black armor.

In his mind, Carus chuckled. *"Aye, lad,"* he said. *"And you could be back in Valles running the government while folk like Waldron and Attaper lead the armies, not so? But you wouldn't be kin to me if you were."*

From a distance the actual stairs up to the temple looked like a narrow line separating the two halves of the stepped base, but in reality they were twenty feet wide. The altar was on the broad plinth in front of the building rather than inside. The small fire on it sent a trail of smoke into the sky.

Lady Lelor and two male assistants waited at one side in full regalia, including jewel-encrusted shepherd's crooks. Across the ornately carved altar from her stood Lord, soon to be formally Earl, Wildulf and his wife. The plaza behind them, all the way back to the temple façade, was crowded with Sandrakkan nobles wearing elaborate costumes.

"Only about two-thirds of the nobility is present," Liane said. She was speaking in a louder-than-normal voice, though her words were for Garric alone. It required a near shout to be heard over the vast crowd, even in the intervals between trumpet calls. "Some are ill, but a number of the most powerful have retired to their estates to see what happens."

"But Wildulf called a levy of all his forces in case it came to a fight, didn't he?" Garric said in puzzlement.

"Yes, he did," Liane agreed with prim amusement. "And some of his vassals are just as unhappy with his rule as Bolor seems to be with yours, your highness."

Garric chuckled at his own naïveté. It was easy to assume that the other fellow didn't have the same sort of problems that you did. Wildulf had had to fight for his throne after the Stone Wall. Of *course*—now that Garric thought about it—there were going to be powerful people who'd be pleased if Wildulf lost power and his head along with it, even if it took an army from Ornifal to bring the change to pass.

The trumpets blew a final call, all of them together, as Garric and Liane reached the last flight of steps to the plinth. Liane wasn't panting—Garric couldn't imagine her doing something so unladylike—but her face was set in a fashion that indicated she wasn't happy about the situation.

"I should've thought of the height of the steps when we decided that Prince Garric would march in state from the palace while Lord Wildulf waited for him!" she growled under her breath. Then, in a slightly less irritated tone, "It was still the right decision, but I see now why Wildulf's envoys didn't argue with me."

They stepped onto the plinth. The Blood Eagles who'd formed a line between the altar and the Sandrakkan courtiers shouted, "The Isles!" and their comrades coming up the stairs in ranks of four, repeated, "The Isles!"

The sound of two hundred men in the midst of so many might have been lost, but the Blaise regiment under Lord Rosen in the plaza took up the cry also, hammering their spears against the bosses of their round shields. That was enough to trigger some of the crowd, then more of it in waves, a blurry but positive cheer: "The Isles-s-s . . ."

This is working, Garric thought as he raised his right arm overhead, fist clenched. He wore high boots like a horseman, with breeches and a short blue tunic whose puffed sleeves were gathered at the wrist. He slung his long sword on a shoulder belt, but he had neither body armor nor a helmet, only the simple gold diadem of Old Kingdom monarchs.

Garric had dressed for the occasion as King Carus might've done a thousand years before. Most of the spectators wouldn't know that—but all but the most ignorant understood that he wasn't wearing Valles court robes. Their earl was submitting himself to a greater authority backed by the threat of force—but it was the authority of the Isles, not of Ornifal.

"The Isles!" Garric shouted. To his amazement his voice echoed back to him. The plaza was brilliantly designed so that the temple steps acted as megaphone for anyone speaking from the plinth, and the façade of the palace on the other side formed a sounding board.

The crowd, most of the local civilians as well as the royal soldiers, cheered louder. *This is really working. . . .*

Garric turned to face Lady Lelor. The priestess with a bland expression dipped her crook but didn't curtsey as she'd been directed to do. She was pushing it, acknowledging royal authority over her temple—but only barely. And she was going to get away with it because Prince Garric couldn't make a scene without more provocation than that.

He grinned, and the king in his mind grinned also. *"She's got balls, that one,"* Carus muttered approvingly.

One of Lelor's assistants stepped forward, holding a plush cushion on which rested a strikingly ugly crown of garnets set in heavy gold. Garric lifted the massive thing, thought *Better the Earls of Sandrakkan than I,* and turned to Wildulf. The soon-to-be-earl looked glumly resigned, like a traveller caught in a storm many miles from shelter.

"Kneel, milord," Garric said, "and receive your charge as representative of the kingdom on Sandrakkan!"

Wildulf knelt. As he did so, Garric caught Lady Balila's expression for an instant before she wiped it blank again. He hadn't seen such malevolence since the day a poisonous snake struck for his life.

Garric felt his skin quiver as though lightning had struck a nearby tree, but his face remained unmoved. He stepped forward, the crown outstretched. The second male priest dropped frankincense and nard on the fire. Mixed with the aromatics was something that made the flame sparkle and lifted a plume of bright yellow smoke.

Wildulf had an unexpected bald spot in the middle of his scalp. Garric set the crown on his head carefully, and cried, "Arise Wildulf, Earl of Sandrakkan!"

The sky darkened. Garric and everyone else in the great plaza looked upward. A cinder-black cloud had appeared as suddenly as a thunderbolt. It spread, forming into the shape of a vast, shambling demon. A woman screamed, and a thousand throats took up her terror.

Garric had his sword out though he didn't remember unsheathing it. Instinct wanted to put him between Liane and the creature of smoke and darkness, but since it was in the sky, he couldn't really do that.

The shape spread wider. No sunlight leaked through the form though the heavens surrounding remained bright morning. The misshapen head turned and the right arm reached down toward the altar, spreading clawed fingers. The crowd surged away. Garric, glancing into the plaza, was glad to see that the Blaise regiment held, although its ranks had become disordered.

It didn't occur to Garric to run. There was nowhere *to* run. If he was going to die, then it might as well be with his feet planted and his face to the enemy.

The shape vanished, not the way a cloud dissipates but instead like a soap bubble—in the sky one instant, then gone utterly. A few flickers of blackness, what would've been sparks if they hadn't been the absence of light; then not even that.

"It's the Ornifal oppressor behind the portent!" Lord Tawnser shouted in a voice as jagged as a saw blade. He pointed his whole arm toward Garric, his good eye blazing with fury. "It's the tyrant Garric summoning his monsters to destroy Erdin! Death to the Ornifal tyrant before he destroys us!"

"Get that man!" shouted Attaper, but Tawnser was already gone, vanishing around the corner of the temple porch.

A squad of Blood Eagles started forward. They'd already snatched the blunts off their spears. Sandrakkan courtiers milled, some picking themselves up from the pavement, where they'd flattened when the shape appeared.

"No!" bellowed Garric as he would've called across the pasture south of Barca's Hamlet. "Don't chase him! Let him go!"

What he'd have really liked would be for Lord Tawnser to slip and break his neck. The chance of that happening was very slight, but it was more probable than any good result of scattering handfuls of royal troops through the streets of a hostile city.

Lord Attaper must've come to the same conclusion as soon as thought had a chance to overrule reflex. He ordered, "Return to ranks!" even as his soldiers glanced back to see if they should obey Garric. They were beyond question loyal to their prince, but they took direction from their own commander.

Lady Lelor and her two aides stood close together. Her face was set, and she didn't appear to see Garric when her eyes swept over him. The courtiers, led by Earl Wildulf and his wife, were streaming down the broad steps of the temple. They didn't look back at Garric, or if they did, their gaze slid quickly away when he tried to meet their eyes.

In the plaza the crowd disappeared like a chalk drawing in the rain. From a dozen corners came the faint echo of, "Down with the Ornifal oppressors!"

Chapter Nine

Earl Wildulf greeted Garric at the door of his suite with an unintended belch that embarrassed the black scowl off his face. He'd been drinking and still held the silver-mounted bison horn full of ale because he couldn't put it down. His hand gripped the flaring lip, and its long tapering length rested on his forearm.

"Milord, he insisted!" the commander of the squad on guard said quickly. He kept his eye on the horn with a degree of concern that suggested he thought it might be slung at him.

"He's the prince, you backwoods numbskull!" snarled Lord Attaper, who'd taken charge of the escort personally when he learned that Garric intended to interview the earl in his apartments. "And the only reason the prince didn't have us use *your* head to batter the door down is that he is a more forgiving man than I am!"

"Gently, milord," Garric said. "Earl Wildulf, I'd like to talk with you privately about what happened this afternoon."

Generally Attaper was perfectly professional, but the business at the coronation had rattled him. He knew how dangerous it would've been if the whole city had turned on the "Ornifal oppressors," and he seemed to have taken as a personal failure the fact it hadn't been possible to capture Lord Tawnser. Attaper really *had* come very close to letting out his anger and frustration when a mercenary in Sandrakkan pay denied the Prince of the Isles access.

Wildulf snorted. "Talk?" he said bitterly. "All right, we'll talk. Are you behind those accursed demons in the sky?"

"No, milord, I am not," Garric said evenly. "My understanding is that they've been appearing since long before my companions and I arrived on Sandrakkan. Now, shall we sit down and talk like gentlemen?"

Garric didn't add an "or else," because he was trying hard to calm the situation instead of fanning Wildulf's anger and resentment . . . and fear, no doubt, as there was good reason for fear. He found it very hard to keep a bridle on an angry retort, though, since he'd been frightened too. Who wouldn't feel frightened, watching a smear of evil blackness reaching down out of the sky for him?

The earl's suite was a south-facing bay, a central space surrounded by three wedge-shaped rooms where the occupant could determine how much breeze and light he wanted at any time of day. Wildulf huddled in the central round. The outer rooms were shuttered and curtained, so the only illumination was by narrow clerestory windows of ribbed glass. Garric would've been luxuriating in the returned sunlight if he hadn't needed to see Wildulf, but he understood perfectly why the earl wanted to avoid all sight of the sky for a time.

A pair of sad, nervous servants stood against a wall. They watched with silent concern as Garric and his guards followed Wildulf into the suite.

There was a square table in the middle of the room. The top was patterned marble, pretty enough to be decorative but able to function for meals and conferences as the need might be. Liane had explained that Sandrakkan etiquette was based on circles of intimacy. Visitors of the very highest rank were admitted to the bedchamber, which therefore had the most ornate and expensive decoration in the house.

Garric hadn't brought Liane with him. This discussion was between men.

"Ah," said Wildulf. He gestured to the bench across the table from where he'd been sitting. "Ah, be seated, your highness. I, ah, there's wine if you'd like. And I'm drinking ale, though I don't suppose . . ."

When the earl hadn't appeared at the planned reception in the court-yard—the countess and her wizard were present, and about half the nobles who'd attended the coronation—Garric had decided to go find him.

Wildulf couldn't ignore what was going on. If he tried to, Garric didn't dare let him.

"Where I was born, on Haft," Garric said as he pulled the bench a lit-tle out from the table before sitting down, "Sandrakkan ale was the drink of the Gods according to the folks who'd travelled enough to have drunk it. I'd like some—but in a mug, if you please."

He added the last with a grin and a nod to the earl's drinking horn. Wildulf turned to bark an order at the servants, but one of them was already bringing Garric a goblet of carnelian carved with ivy leaves and berries. A far cry from the masars of polished elmwood in which Reise served customers in his taproom in Barca's Hamlet; but the ale was smooth. When he drank it, Garric thought of other men all over the Isles drinking similar beer and dealing with the problems that were just as important to them as his were to him.

Wildulf took a deep draft from his horn. "I suppose you think I'm a coward," he said with a morose belligerency. "Because those cursed clouds scare me. Scare me!"

"Well, they scare me too," Garric said. "Maybe it's just a cloud, but you can't tell me it doesn't mean something—and mean something bad. There's evil in this world, milord. It doesn't like men, and it'll wipe us away if we don't fight it with all the strength there's in us."

"I'm not afraid of anything I can fight!" Wildulf said. "Only—"

He looked at Garric, drank, and went on, "What good's my sword against a cloud, eh? Tell me that!"

Garric nodded. "Milord, I can't give you an answer to that," he said. "But there's a place for swords. And if men stand together, then we have only the monsters to worry about. If you stand with me and with Count

Lerdoc of Blaise and with all the other rulers. Working together, for the sake of our families and our subjects and of mankind."

He sipped and smiled. The ale was good beyond question, but maybe it was too good for a boy raised on dark germander bitters brewed in a peasant community where hops were an expensive import.

"Milord," Garric continued, "if we fight each other, the blackness that waits outside will take us all, sure as death. For a thousand years the separate Isles have been squabbling with one another, holding each other back. That's going to stop now, either because we stop it ourselves or because the Dark comes in from outside and stops everything. Come with me to the reception. Stand beside me, and know that I'll stand beside you with all the strength the Shepherd gives me. For mankind's sake."

Wildulf drank and dropped his empty horn to clatter on the table. He rose to his feet. "Right," he said. "We'll go. Now!"

Instead of leaving through the formal entrance to the suite, Wildulf strode toward the back stairway obviously intended for servants. When Attaper realized what was happening, he spoke a curt order that sent two Blood Eagles sprinting ahead with a clatter from their hobnails and their skirts of studded-leather straps. He himself followed Garric as Garric followed Earl Wildulf: the stairs were too narrow for two to walk abreast.

At the bottom, four landings below his suite, the Blood Eagles stepped aside so that Earl Wildulf could push back a hanging woven from coarse grasses. The squad of guards at the entrance stepped aside, then stiffened when they saw Garric following. Attaper glowered at them as he fell into step at Garric's side.

They were in a service hall. To the left were the palace's inside kitchens, while on the right were the backs of tables placed in arches of the central courtyard as they had been during the reception of the previous day.

A senior household functionary wearing a silken snood noticed the earl and his unexpected entourage. She snapped an order. All the servitors turned and bowed, some of them dropping or spilling food and beverages.

Wildulf ignored them as he strode through an archway that wasn't blocked, but Garric offered servants a smile and a dip of his head. He'd served guests in the inn for too many years not to think of servants as human beings.

The nobles and officials already in the courtyard turned with a flutter of sound to greet the newcomers. It was like watching brightly colored

geese change direction, the heads twisting around first, the bodies following. The locals were even more rigidly segregated from the royal officials
than they had been the day before.

They'd all been watching something on the other side of the courtyard. The crowd parted as Wildulf stepped through, with Garric pointedly
at his side.

The focus of attention had been a tented table on which dozens of
small figures moved. *A puppet show,* Garric thought . . . but they weren't
puppets, they were live mice and frogs, wearing armor and standing on
their hind legs as they battled with tiny swords. Wizardlight, faint azure
sparkles, danced over the helmets and sword points.

Lest there be any doubt that they weren't illusions, a number of fighters sprawled dead or dying on the stage. A frog leaked pale blood from a
throat wound, its broad mouth opening and closing spasmodically. Nearby
was a mouse whose belly had spilled intestines for a hand's breadth before
death stiffened its little limbs.

Countess Balila's great bird prowled behind the stage, fluffing its stub
wings and making angry metallic sounds deep in its throat. It smelled the
blood and didn't like it—

Any better than did Garric.

Balila herself stood beside the stage with the naked cherub prattling at
her feet. She spoke through the side of the tent, then gave Garric a cold
smile, and said, "Does our entertainment impress you, your highness?"

The wizardlight vanished. The frogs and mice reverted to their natural
selves, capering and rolling in desperate attempts to free themselves from
the equipment hooked about them. Their terrified squeaks would've
roused pity in a butcher's heart.

Dipsas stepped out of the tent. She looked worn, but her eyes were
feverishly bright. The reptile-scale athame hung loosely from her right
hand.

"Your entertainment disgusts me!" Garric said. He spoke much louder
than he'd intended, but he didn't regret the outburst. Liane was at his side,
touching his arm to reassure herself and him as well.

"Aye, he's right," Wildulf said. In the heat of the moment, Garric had
forgotten the earl's presence. "You! You're a wizard, you say?"

Dipsas backed from the threat in Wildulf's voice, looking surprised
and frightened like a rat startled in the middle of a large room. In her place
the countess said, "She's a great wizard!"

"Then let her do something about those *damned* clouds!" Wildulf said. "Portents or not, I want them stopped. And you, wizard"—he groped unconsciously at the place on his belt where the hilt would be if he were wearing a sword—"if I thought for an instant that you *were* behind those things, if I ever learn that, your best hope is for a quick death. Because you'll be luckier than you deserve if I grant you that kindness."

"She's not responsible, Wildulf!" Balila cried. "Lady Dipsas is going to save us and get you your deserts! You'll see. You'll all"—she turned and swept Garric with a blazing glance—"see. You will!"

The countess laid an arm around Dipsas' shoulders. She walked through another archway, half-hugging and half-supporting the old wizard. The bird thrust out its black tongue in a hissing *skreek!* and stalked off behind them. When the cherub noticed they were leaving, he burbled in terror and followed—stumbling and paddling forward, half the time on all fours.

Garric hugged Liane close without taking his eyes off Balila and her wizard until they'd disappeared from sight. In a quiet voice, he said, "Do you suppose Dipsas is behind the portents? Or whatever the clouds are?"

"I don't know," Liane murmured. "But I'll have more information shortly, I believe."

A few of the frogs and mice were still pawing at the fine wire screen closing the front of the stage, but for the most part they'd subsided into trembling misery against the walls of the enclosure. Occasionally a mouse flailed against its armor, then gave a whimpering squeal and stopped.

I understand how they feel, Garric thought; but he didn't allow the words to reach his lips.

The wall stretched east and west to both horizons. It was stone and taller than a man—taller than either of Ilna's companions, at any rate. They could easily climb over, but the watchtowers every few furlongs were obviously intended to prevent that from happening without discussion.

A wooden trumpet called from the nearest tower. It was a blat of sound, not in any sense music, but it seemed to have done the job. A gong rang from the manor house that sprawled on the opposite ridge. Ilna could see the figures of men running toward the stables.

Chalcus waved his left arm enthusiastically. "May as well convince them we're friendly," he said in a cheerful tone. "And I surely am friendly, since I see how many of them there are: and them having bows too, or I'll be pleasantly surprised."

They started down the slope of sharp-edged grass and flowers on central spikes. The plantings on the other side of the wall were darker green. The figures working among the rows straightened to watch the strangers until the wall cut off further view.

"The fields are irrigated," Davus said. He held a fist-sized rock in his right hand, but he didn't convert his sash into a sling for the moment. Like Chalcus—and Ilna herself, of course—he was of the mind that fighting was a last resort against such obvious power. "There must be several hundred people in the community. Maybe more, depending on how far north it stretches where we can't see."

"Is there a habit of being hospitable to wandering strangers here, Master Davus?" Chalcus asked. "Strangers who come in peace, I mean, of course."

Davus shrugged. "In my day the Old King enforced such a custom," he said. "But my day is long past, as we all know."

The estate's southern gate was hung in a high archway, but there were no guard towers; nor was the wall wide enough to stand on and throw things down on an attacker. Even Ilna—not by any stretch of the imagination a soldier—could see that it would be impossible to defend from a single determined person with a hatchet, at least until after he'd managed to whittle his way through a gate leaf.

As they approached, Ilna walked a little ahead of the men flanking her. Chalcus could be charming, but looking harmless was completely beyond him. Davus, she'd begun to realize, wasn't any better in that respect, for all that she couldn't have asked for a more polite and pleasant companion.

The gate creaked inward, then jerked open farther. The tall leaves hogged, so the inward corners plowed curving furrows in the ground. Two horsemen with swords and quivers of short javelins rather than arrows hanging from their saddles rode through. They pulled up just outside the enclosure, trying to look menacing, while the four men who'd opened the gate remounted and followed them.

When all six were in a line, a man so fat that Ilna felt sorry for his poor horse—he'd have done better on an ox—came out, keeping carefully behind the others. This last fellow wore a sword, but he looked as though the horse would be more dangerous wielding it.

He was overdressed and badly dressed, both. His cloak was of blue wool dyed in several different lots, and his black tunic had started to fade in patches. Both were embroidered with gold thread. The seamstress who'd worked on the left side of the garments was skilled enough to receive Ilna's silent approval, but that only served to point out the childish incompetence of the two different hands who'd done the rest of the embroidery.

The leader of the six horsemen wore a mail shirt and trailed a red pennant from the peak of his helmet. He looked at the fat man, then glowered at Ilna, and said, "Get on with you! Lord Ramelus doesn't allow vagabonds on his land!"

Ilna smiled faintly. She was thinking of how this flunky in armor would look dangling by his own intestines from a limb of one of the chestnut trees growing beside the manor house.

"We're travellers, not vagabonds," she said in a mild voice, hoping that her smile had been misinterpreted. "We'd appreciate a little food and drink, but we're more than willing to work for our keep."

She glanced at her companions, keeping her face bland. Chalcus grinned engagingly at a pair of the mounted men; Davus was digging at the ground with his big toe. To a stranger he'd look embarrassed, but Ilna noticed that he'd uncovered a wedge-shaped shard of limestone. A piece like that could very nearly decapitate a man if it was well thrown.

The chief guard glanced again to the fat man, who was obviously Lord Ramelus. Ramelus frowned, then said in a squeakier voice than his bulk suggested, "They can have water, Gallen. We don't need their labor—or their presence here, either one."

"All right, Lord Ramelus says you can have water," Gallen said, twisting to get the skin of water slung from the back of his saddle where it balanced the sheaf of javelins.

Ilna smiled again, her fingers weaving a pattern of cords. It struck her as amusing that Lord Ramelus and his flunkies were just as safe as they thought they were, but only because she and her companions didn't *want* to kill them all. It would've been quite simple, at least if Davus was what she thought he was; and possible even if he wasn't, given Chalcus' skills and her own.

But they weren't going to do that. There were far too many men— and women too, hurling loom weights and wielding turnspits—in the community for the three of them to take their simple needs by force, even if they'd killed the leader and his immediate guards. No, there were better ways to get food and something better than a drink of water from a sheep-skin bottle.

The horseman leaned forward, holding out the skin. Ilna reached up, but instead of taking the water from him she spread the pattern she'd just knotted, saying, "I can weave a hanging that will make everybody who sees it feel better about themselves and their neighbors."

"Oh!" said Gallen, staring transfixed. The waterskin slipped slowly forward, forgotten in his amazement. "Oh, milady, that's wonderful—"

"What is?" Lord Ramelus demanded. "What are you doing there, Gallen? Seifert, what's Gallen doing?"

Ilna folded the pattern between her palms. It was a little thing, nothing of lasting effect, but Gallen groaned when it vanished.

"I can weave a hanging that will make your subjects happier, milord," Ilna said, stepping around the head of Gallen's mount so that she could meet Ramelus' eyes. The horse whickered; she touched its muzzle with her left fingertips. "For that we'll have food and drink while we're here, and another portion of food and drink to carry us on our way when I've finished the task to your satisfaction. Do you agree?"

"What is that?" Ramelus demanded. "The thing in your hands—show it to me!"

Ilna walked through the line of guards, stretching the pattern between her thumbs and forefingers again. Ramelus squinted, but he was apparently nearsighted. He leaned slightly forward in the saddle; he was too heavy and awkward to bend down the way a more supple rider might've done. "Hand it up!" he ordered in irritation.

Ilna frowned minusculely. "It only works if I keep the tension cor-rect," she said. "The one I'll weave for you will be larger. It'll be able to hang in the open air and still have its proper effect."

Ramelus glared at her, then dismounted with a degree of care worthy of masons lowering a keystone into an arch. Wheezing slightly, he stepped around his horse and peered at the pattern in Ilna's spread hands.

For a moment, Ramelus' expression became hostile, even angry. It softened but almost instantly shifted to one of shielded cunning. Ilna folded her pattern and, by straightening, implied a greater separation between them than the distance itself involved.

The quickly knotted design lost its positive effect on a spectator who'd stared at it for a few minutes, but Ilna really could weave a larger panel that would act more subtly and for as long as it hung. Of course she could do that: she'd said she could, hadn't she?

"You're a wizard," Ramelus said, breathing hard and looking at her with an expression she couldn't read—couldn't read and probably didn't want to read.

"No," Ilna said. "I'm a weaver. If your women will loan me a loom—"

All the garments she saw were homespun, with the possible exceptions of the lord's own cloak and tunic.

"—I can do a thing like this—"

She held up the hank of cords that her fingers had already picked out again.

"—on a larger scale. For our keep while we stay here, a day or so should be enough; and for supplies to go off with, which we'll do as soon as I've finished the design to your satisfaction."

The horsemen had crowded together to hear their commander trying to describe what he'd seen in Ilna's pattern. In fact he hadn't seen anything, for all that he was waving his hands to suggest shapes and objects. All it'd been was a feeling of bliss and beauty, the sort of pleasure some people said they remembered from dreams.

Ilna wouldn't know of her own experience, of course. Mostly she didn't remember dreams at all, and when she did they were of a very different sort.

"Food and drink for you, that's your price?" Ramelus said. "That's what you said."

Ilna looked at him without affection. The landowner reminded her of her uncle Katchin, the wealthiest man in Barca's Hamlet and easily the most disliked. Katchin had boasted of his own dignity and importance; but in his heart he'd known he was a joke to his neighbors, albeit a joke they told behind his back for fear of his malice.

"Food and drink for the three of us," Ilna said in a cold voice, seeing the cheat in the words. That was like Katchin also: the letter of the law, but by policy veering as far from justice as that law permitted him. "Space in a manger to sleep if you choose, though we can do without that. And food and drink for the three of us when we go off—tomorrow, I would hope, but whenever that is."

"Done!" Ramelus said. He clasped hands with her to seal the bargain. He looked around him at his guards. "You're all witnesses!"

In gripping the landowner's hand, Ilna let her fingertips caress the embroidered sleeve of his tunic. *He's going to cheat us,* she thought. *For no reason other than to prove to his tenants that he can cheat a stranger and get away with it.*

She backed away, dusting her palms together and smiling as she watched Ramelus struggle to mount his horse. Ramelus planned to cheat, and she planned to keep her word. And there was no doubt in Ilna's mind that she would have the better part of the bargain.

Either the dome of Ronn's vast Assembly Hall had become perfectly clear, or it'd somehow been slid off to the sides since Cashel was there that morning. The moon was overhead and looked bigger than he was used to seeing it. Nobody had a better chance to study the night sky than a shepherd. Maybe that had something to do with the dome, if the dome was still there.

"Citizens of Ronn!" said the female wizard. She seemed to've become leader of the Council of the Wise for all intents and purposes. The old man hunched in his chair, his limbs drawn up to his body like a dead spider. "We and our city face the greatest danger of all time!"

Mab, at this moment a slender, gray-haired woman, sniffed, and said tartly, "Councillor Oursa is getting a little above herself if she believes she knows what the future will bring. And if she means, 'the greatest danger in the past thousand years,' that's true only because of our weakness, not the enemy's strength."

"The images of the Heroes no longer protect our walls," Oursa said. "We must protect ourselves!"

Cashel tried to imagine Oursa and the other Councillors waving swords as the Made Men charged across a field at them. The thought made him smile, which seemed to bother the people nearby in the big hall. For some reason everybody around him and Mab was looking at them instead of up at the stage.

The Councillor's voice sounded from the air like she was standing just arm's length away, the way all the speakers had in the morning levee. The light was the same way, kind of: everything in the room, the walls and floor and even the air itself, glowed. No part of it was brighter than a firefly's tail, but from everything together Cashel could see all over just the same as he would during daylight.

There was a whisper of sound, nothing that the room picked up so that everybody could hear, though. Suddenly a voice rang out, "How can we protect ourselves? *We* don't know how to fight!"

Cashel saw the Sons of the Heroes coming toward him and Mab through the crowd. Herron turned toward the stage and shouted a reply. His words vanished in the great room, smoothed away by the air—though as close as the boy was, Cashel figured he should've been able to hear normally. He wondered just what—or who—decided what was said that was worth other people listening to.

Mab slashed her right hand through the air in a gesture that suggested more than it showed. A dazzle of wizardlight the same sapphire color as her nails struck skyward, calling the attention of everyone in the chamber to her. In a ringing voice, she cried, "Your homes still hold the weapons and armor of your grandfathers' grandfathers. Go back to your hearths. Get the swords and spears of your forefathers and face the Made Men!"

In place of the night sky, the air above the hall showed giant images of what'd happened on the ramparts earlier: the Made Men coming on, and Cashel knocking them down with short, quick strokes that each ended an opponent with the certainty of a thunderbolt. Cashel'd never seen himself moving like that, from the outside. His lips pursed. He wasn't one to give himself praise—but judging what he saw with a critical eye, the first thing that went through his mind was that *he* wouldn't look forward to fighting somebody as good as the fellow he was watching.

Again there was a whisper of response, the brilliantly clothed folk of Ronn talking among themselves. The Sons clustered around Cashel and Mab, their expressions a mix of hopeful and frightened. Cashel understood: this was the big chance they'd hoped for, trained for; but they must have a good notion, at least since he'd taken them apart with his quarterstaff that afternoon, that they weren't up to the job they'd set themselves.

"We don't know how to fight!" the voice of the Assembly said. The Council of the Wise remained silent on the stage, the woman still standing but none of them trying to lead the discussion. "The big stranger fought the Made Men. Will he fight them for us again?"

Cashel gripped his quarterstaff harder. Everybody was looking at him. Everybody: the floor of the assembly hall wasn't flat anymore, it sloped up in every direction like a bowl with him in the center, and Duzi knew how many people staring. He supposed it was some trick of the light, or else the

Councillors were more powerful wizards than he'd been thinking they were. Regardless, it was happening, and he sure didn't like it.

"Tell them, Cashel," Mab said with her cool smile. She spoke to him alone, her hands tented before her. No matter what the rest of her appearance was, Cashel could always tell Mab by those dazzling fingernails. "Tell them what you think."

This is none of my business! Cashel thought. But because he was more angry than he was embarrassed, he blurted aloud, "You people can fight these Made Men yourselves! You saw them up there——"

He waved his left hand toward where the images had stepped and swung; the moon was back now.

"They can't fight, they're no more real soldiers than you are. If you've got swords, get them. When the Made Men attack you just *fight*. That's all you have to do."

"We need a leader," the assembly said. Some*body,* some individual, had spoken the words, but they were what the whole huge gathering thought. "In the past, the Heroes led the citizens of Ronn. Give us a Hero. Let the stranger lead us!"

Cashel looked at the faces, the tense and frightened faces, staring down at him. Suddenly he smiled. The answer was simple and so obvious that he didn't need the verbal push Mab was opening her mouth to provide.

"I can't lead you," Cashel said, "because you wouldn't follow me. You need one of your own people to lead, if you mean really lead and not stand out in front till I'm hacked to death and the rest of you turn and run."

He knew he was being more honest than they were going to like hearing. While Cashel wasn't as bad as his sister about not caring whom his words hurt—nobody else was as bad as Ilna that way—he knew this was one of those cases where folks had to understand the truth. If they didn't really understand instead of just hearing words in a way that let them ignore them, they *were* going to die or face whatever other thing the king and his monsters decided to do instead of kill them.

"We'll lead you!" Herron cried, his right arm raised with the fist clenched. He'd been shouting, Cashel could see. When his voice boomed through the hall, he looked as though he'd been dropped into ice water. Stumbling on his tongue he managed to add, "The S-sons will lead you!"

"You're only boys!" replied the Assembly; the massed faces staring down at Herron. The people sounded irritated but not too much so, much the way adults would be when a child piped up in the middle of a serious discussion.

They're as old as I am! Cashel thought, but he didn't say that or anything because the Assembly was right. Cashel couldn't lead Ronn because he wasn't part of Ronn; the Sons couldn't lead because they weren't fit to lead.

"Master Herron?" Mab said, speaking for the Assembly in a tone of cool superiority. "Are you and your friends willing to serve the city by doing something that *is* within your powers? Are you willing to wake the Heroes in their cavern?"

The Sons went slack-faced in amazement. Enfero in particular had the look of a rabbit frozen by the eyes of a viper.

"You said you'd face the king and his Made Men," Mab said. Her words seemed carved from blocks of ice. "Do you have the courage to face the dark? Or are you little boys who'll shiver in the sunlight till the darkness comes to you?"

"We'll go," Orly said in an angry voice. "We'll find nothing but dust and bones, *I* think, but we're not afraid!"

"Yes, we'll go," Herron said to Mab, suddenly calm. "You'll lead us, mistress?"

"Of course," said Mab. "And I believe Master Cashel will accompany you as well, will you not, Cashel?"

Cashel wished there weren't all those faces looking down at him with desperate expressions, but he couldn't help that there were. "I said I'd help, didn't I?" he muttered, scowling because he sounded ill-tempered when he was really just embarrassed. "Anyway, I will. I'd be glad to."

And that much was true. If it really was a dangerous place to go, then maybe he could be of some real help for the first time since he came here to Ronn.

"Funny," said Trooper Lires, looking to both sides of the flagstone path with his usual bright interest. He grinned at Sharina to show he was speaking as much to her as he was to his fellow Blood Eagles. "In the old days there'd be half the clerks in the palace camped out here, hoping to get the king to sign something or do who knows what. It just about never happened, mind."

"Lires," said Undercaptain Ascor, "the less talk about what happened here in the old days, the better I'll like it."

"Right, Cap'n," the trooper said. Perhaps he was mildly abashed, though Sharina couldn't be sure. The Blood Eagles were chosen from the line regiments on the basis of courage, military skills, and complete loyalty to whomever they were guarding. Social graces and the willingness to bow and scrape to their superiors weren't high in the selection criteria.

Sharina and her escort came around a high wall of prickly euonymus to see a low brick residence set near the wall of the palace compound. Two Blood Eagles were at the front door, alerted by the ringing of hobnails on the path. They smiled to see their fellows. "Hey, Ascor," one of them said. "I thought you guys were off in Carcosa still."

Valence the Third had retired to this bungalow, within the palace grounds but at a distance from the Chancellery, while he was still as much of a ruler as the kingdom had. In the final days of his rule, he'd turned to wizardry and an alliance with black Evil to preserve his power. When his closest friends had transferred real power to Garric with themselves as his advisors, Valence had sunk into religious mania and guilt over what he'd done and allowed to be done.

"No, we're with her highness the princess here," the captain said. "She needs to talk to himself-as-was. Any problem with that?"

"Not if he's sober enough to talk," the other guard said. "Which he generally is, not that he has much call to be. He spends most days with a couple old friends. They're with him now."

So speaking, the guard pulled the door open, and called through, "Your highness? Princess Sharina's here to see you."

He nodded the newcomers forward. Ascor and Lires stepped inside ahead of Sharina, while the rest of her escort waited outside with their fellows.

There was no doorman in the anteroom, though with guards outside there didn't need to be. Sharina didn't see servants in the bungalow's single large room either, however.

Valence had just thrown the dice and was moving his pieces on the board, playing Bandits with two cronies. One was a former courtier named Geddes who hadn't been important enough either to promote or to imprison when Garric became prince, the other a very old man named Rylon who'd been chamberlain a decade before. At a sideboard stood Lord Lichter—still the royal chaplain, Sharina supposed, since nobody'd bothered to replace him.

The four men looked around in dull surprise. Valence frowned, then reached again for the game piece he'd begun to advance.

Ascor sized up the situation and thumped his heels on the thick carpeting. "Princess Sharina of Haft!" he announced loudly. That brought two startled servants out of a side chamber, tripping over one another. The male still held the jam-filled pastry his face showed he'd been in the process of eating.

Sharina pointed at them. With the anger of a woman who knew from personal experience how servants were supposed to behave, she said, "You two! Report yourselves to the chamberlain *now*. I'll discuss your situation with him later."

She knew it was a trivial thing to become exercised about, but the room was filthy, and the servants obviously thieves as well as lazy pigs. Part of the reason the kingdom was in its present dreadful state was that for too long people had shown as little concern for mankind as a whole as a ewe has for the pasture where she grazes and voids her bowels.

The male servant opened his purple mouth to protest. The woman, though wearing silk tunics that she couldn't have purchased on her salary, at least showed the judgment to slap him on the ear and pull him back into the room from which they'd come. Presumably there was a back hall to the anteroom.

"Well, well, well," said Rylon, chuckling. "About time somebody put 'em in their place. Yes, indeed."

Sharina curtsied to the king. "Your majesty," she said, "please forgive this intrusion. I want to ask some questions about your father."

"Do I know you?" Valence said, blinking at her. He leaned back in his chair and finally took his hand off the game piece.

The room was dim, though it'd be hours before there was a need to light the hanging lamps. The windows were shuttered, but the large skylight was open; the cypresses planted around the bungalow screened but didn't block the westering sun.

"Of course you know her, Valence," Lord Geddes said. "She's the sister of the boy who's running things now, Prince Garric."

Geddes' bland face clouded. "That's right, isn't it, dear?" he said. "Prince Garric's sister?"

"Yes, milord," Sharina said. It wouldn't do any good to lose her temper in frustration. Besides, the situation was better than she'd thought it might be: Valence could've sunk too deep in prayer and flagellation to respond to her at all. He'd certainly been headed in that direction when she'd seen him most recently, some months earlier. "A man claiming to be your half brother Valgard is stirring up trouble. Witnesses say he looks very much like Stronghand. Did you ever hear your father speak of another son?"

"Another son?" Valence said, frowning. "I don't think so. But to tell the truth, I kept away from my father as much as I could. He was an angry man. He threw things a lot, though he couldn't throw them very well."

He tittered. "'Stronghand' indeed!" he said, lifting the wine carafe from the tub of water on the fourth side of the table where they were playing. "Half the time he trembled so badly he had to have a servant hold the cup to his lips. Stronghand!"

The carafe was empty. "Lichter!" Valence said peevishly. "Dip us some more wine, won't you? That's a good fellow."

The chaplain took the carafe in his left hand and with the other pulled open the lower portion of the sideboard. It was a large drawer instead of a door panel. Inside were two open storage jars with wine thieves, narrow bronze pitchers with vertical handles, hanging from their rims.

"More Caecuban, Valence?" Lichter asked. He began to dip red wine into the carafe without waiting for an answer.

"Stronghand," Geddes said in a musing tone. "Goodness, it's been years since I thought about him. And you say"—he turned quizzically to Sharina—"that he had another son, dearie? Goodness, goodness."

"I asked if you'd ever *heard* of Valence Stronghand having a son named Valgard," Sharina corrected the courtier firmly. "Even a rumor or a joke about a younger son. Supposedly Valgard was born to a female prisoner captured after the Battle of the Tides, though those present say all the People were men."

"*After* the Battle of the Tides?" Rylan said. "Oh, my goodness me! Well, it wouldn't really matter if the prisoners were men or women *after* the battle, would it? Oh my goodness, no!"

The old chamberlain started to laugh but quickly collapsed into a paroxysm of coughing. He raised his goblet; it was empty. Patting his chest with his left hand, he held the goblet out demandingly. Lichter took it from him, poured wine from the refilled carafe, and set the goblet in front of Rylan before passing the carafe to Valence.

"What do you mean about it not mattering whether the prisoners were men or women?" Sharina said. She didn't let her voice rise, but she knew her tone had lost the pleasant warmth with which she'd begun the conversation. "Your majesty, gentlemen, this is really very important. There's a serious danger to the kingdom. And thus to your lives, you see."

Lord Lichter cleared his throat, turning toward one of the frescoes set in the center of decorative frames. This particular one was a male centaur carrying a woman over his shoulder as he galloped away. The woman, bare-breasted, with the remainder of her garments streaming behind her, reached out desperately toward the viewer.

"Well, you see . . . ," he said. "It's not the sort of thing that got talked about, of course, but many people knew. In a palace, well, things get around. The *place* Stronghand was wounded, you see . . ."

Valence drank deeply. When the chaplain's voice trailed off, the king looked directly at Sharina.

"Whatever else my father might be doing after the Battle of the Tides," he said in a harsh, challenging voice, "he wasn't fathering children. Because that spearpoint didn't leave him anything to father them with. Do you understand?"

Lord Geddes shook his head sadly. His eyes were on the game board, but his mind was in a distant place. "You can't really blame the old fellow for being angry most of the time, can you?" he said.

"By the Shepherd!" said Lires. "You sure can't."

Chapter Ten

Ilna finished warping the table loom she'd borrowed from Malaha and Mostera, the sisters who squatted across from her staring. They were the chief weavers at the manor—the Abode of Ramelus, according to Ramelus himself and his henchmen, though Ilna'd heard others call it only "the big house."

The sisters were short, dumpy women past middle age, dressed in hooded black robes. There was little to choose between them in appearance, but Malaha seemed excited by the chance to see what the outsider was going to do, while Mostera glared with the fury of a priestess watching her altar defiled.

Ilna smiled faintly. Though she wasn't going to defile anything, what she planned to make fabric do that day was at the edge of what she considered proper. She'd promised to bring a feeling of joy in those who viewed the result, and so she would, but . . .

The manor house was a sprawling thing that tried to look like more than it was. Originally it must've been a rectangle of one story and perhaps a loft. Ramelus had built it to two stories and a false front to the north with pillars all the way up; wings had since spread to either side. Ilna couldn't imagine who Ramelus expected to impress, but perhaps it was just for himself. He seemed like a man who thought about himself most of the time, if not all of it.

The courtyard behind the house was formed by lines of stables and workshops rather than colonnades like the front. Women in a line under a pole-framed tile roof were preparing food for the evening meal, while across from them other women washed clothing in large vats carved from limestone. The blacksmith was repairing tools in his forge at the back of the court, near the bread ovens. The *cling* of his hammer and the wheeze of the bellows worked by two of his assistants were regular interruptions to the chirps of playing children.

The gray yarn Ilna was using for the warp was of goat hair. The individual strands were longer and finer than the sheep's wool she'd more often worked with, but—like human hairs—they weren't as tightly coiled. The difference in texture was part of the pattern. Everything was part of the pattern, the height of the sun, the haze of dust in the air, even the noisy flutter of sparrows squabbling for grain fallen in the courtyard.

Ilna checked her weft yarn, touching each loaded bobbin instead of merely looking at them. The feel told her things that eyes, even her eyes, couldn't see. She smiled as her fingertips read the future.

She didn't fit in with other human beings. Either they saw too little truth, or their world held truths that were merely fancies to Ilna os-Kenset. But threads and fabrics spoke to her, and they never ever lied.

The weft threads already on the bobbins were wool of various weights and colors: bleached white, indigo blue, and three different shades of gray.

The grays were each the natural color of a particular sheep, the darkest nearly black.

A final hank of weft thread was drying in the sun. Ilna had simmered more of the gray goat hair in raspberry pulp, the waste left in the bag after the kitchen staff made jelly. The yarn was now a soft pink that seemed to cling to the eyes even after one looked away.

She touched the yarn she'd dyed. It was dry already: though bright, the sun wasn't particularly hot, but the air sucked all moisture out of the thread. Ilna took the hank from the cleft stick on which she'd hung it and began to wind it onto a bobbin.

"You're a fool if you use that for your pattern, woman," Mostera growled. There was worry as well as challenge in her tone.

"Now, maybe the foreign lady has a trick we don't know of, darling," Malaha said, pursing her lips into a fishlike expression that apparently was meant to be a smile. "Is that so, Mistress Ilna?"

Ilna sniffed. "Whatever I may know about dyes and yarns that you don't," she said, "doesn't matter. The pattern I've chosen is probably beyond your ability to plan, but I suspect either of you could weave it yourselves if you watch me carefully the first time."

"Such a fine lady," Mostera sneered. "I don't think! A vagabond come traipsing up to the big house without so much as a spare tunic."

"Watch and learn, mistress," said Ilna mildly as she twisted the shed and ran her shuttle through the warp for the first time.

Davus stood in the center of a group of house servants, each wearing a headband of wool dyed with indigo. He was juggling fist-sized stones, more of them than Ilna could've counted easily even had they been lined up on the ground before her. He had at least three separate sequences in the air at the same time. She couldn't predict the patterns Davus was weaving, but she could *see* them clearly.

The indigo headbands were rank insignia as well as a uniform to set the indoor personnel off from the field hands. The highest servants present, the steward and chief cook, had bright blue bands of first-quality dye. Ordinary servants had duller bands from the second quality of the plant, while the scullery maids and potboys wore bands the color of gray mud with only the slightest hint of blue.

Ilna brought her shuttle across the loom, moving as swiftly and gracefully as Davus was spinning his stones skyward. She'd noticed that he not only kept within sight, he always had at least one eye on her—though his audience probably thought he was wholly focused on his juggling.

Ilna doubted that Davus watched what the stones were doing at all—or needed to, any more than she needed to look at the yarn as she fed it through the warp. She smiled, feeling the future as it wove onward.

"I suppose that's where your Lord Ramelus sits when he addresses you?" Ilna said, nodding toward the ornate chair in a three-walled kiosk behind the house proper. The shelter had blue-glazed tiles on the outside and a tree-of-life pattern enclosing the throne. The roof was of ordinary terra-cotta roof tiles, their faded orange color a painful contrast with the walls.

The kiosk's workmanship wasn't very good to begin with, nor had it been kept up well. Where tiles had fallen off, Ilna saw they'd been laid over a core of wattle and daub.

"Oh, yes," Malaha said cheerfully. "Every day at midday. Everybody gathers here in the courtyard, and he dispenses justice. Well, the herdsmen and the men working in the New Fields in the north, they don't come in except on every Ninth Day, but everybody else does."

What he calls justice, Ilna thought, and thought also that Ramelus' version of justice wasn't something she'd care to count on.

"He likes to have people whipped," Mostera said. "Sometimes he whips them himself. If he doesn't like the cloth you weave, mistress, he'll have you whipped."

"I expect that he'll like my pattern," Ilna said with a faint smile. She glanced toward Chalcus, singing to the women doing laundry and to many of the children besides. *And I don't think Ramelus or any man will whip me while I live and while Chalcus lives.*

The breeze shifted from east to west, bringing a snatch of his song, *". . . in its worst despair, still ponder o'er the past . . ."* Chalcus was accompanying himself on an odd little instrument that he must've borrowed here, a lyre of sorts made by stringing gut across the humped shell of a tortoise.

Ilna's hands slid across the loom, beating the fabric at the short intervals required by the speed at which it was growing. "Oh, she's wonderful, Mostera!" Malaha murmured. "Mistress, you're a wonderful weaver."

Ilna smiled faintly. She didn't need these women to tell her that, but she wouldn't pretend she didn't like to get praise. Her eyes were unfocused, while in her mind she watched what would happen to the fabric in a few weeks or a month.

"She can weave, I'll grant," Mostera said. She didn't share Malaha's enthusiasm, but neither was the statement grudging; and for that Ilna felt a tinge of respect. She'd praised others for the sake of truth, even when it tore her heart out to do so. A weaker person might've deluded herself that Lady Liane bos-Benliman wasn't a worthy mate for Garric, but Ilna hadn't permitted herself to do that . . .

"Lord Ramelus could have you or me or any of us whipped," Mostera said in a distant tone. "He's a great man, and he'd be the first to tell you so. But he couldn't, I think, do anything so great as weaving the cloth on your loom, Mistress Ilna."

Across the courtyard Chalcus sang, *"For mem'ry is the only friend—"*

Ilna said nothing, but she smiled more broadly.

"—that grief can call its own."

Cashel had thought that if he maybe squinted a little, he could imagine that the Sons of the Heroes were really soldiers. It didn't work. Sure, they wore swords and armor as they listened to Mab explain what they were getting into, but they didn't hold themselves right. They weren't poised like people whose job was standing shoulder to shoulder and killing other people. That's what a soldier was, after all, and by now Cashel had met his share of them.

"The queen's power is from the air and light," Mab said, standing as the others watched in a half circle around her. The Sons were on crystal benches under a canopy of ferns; Cashel squatted at the right end beside Herron, where he could see all his companions out of the corner of his eye. "The king's power is strongest in earth and water, so it was natural that when the queen drove him out of Ronn, some remnants of his influence would linger in the lowest levels of the city."

Mab made an angry gesture with her left hand: red sparks danced angrily in the air.

"Natural," she repeated, "but very unfortunate. Because the queen was exhausted from the battle—and I have to say, arrogant with her victory—she failed to wipe Ronn clean of contamination when she could've done so with relative ease. She didn't, and by that she failed her duty and failed the city."

"The queen's a great wizard and a great *person*." Orly said in glowering discomfort. "She's kept Ronn safe for a thousand years. You shouldn't talk about her that way!"

"If she hadn't vanished," Herron said, "then we'd still be safe."

"You weren't safe while the queen was present, Master Herron," Mab said with a dismissive snort. "Or she wouldn't *have* vanished, would she? If you're afraid of straight talking, then how do you expect to face the things you'll meet on the way to the Shrine of the Heroes?"

Cashel smiled though he knew he shouldn't have. Right then Mab looked like she was a girl no older than the Sons themselves. She had blue eyes and fluffy blond hair, just as cute as you could ask for. Her tongue and her temper hadn't changed from what they'd been earlier, though.

Herron grimaced and hung his head. "I just meant . . . ," he muttered; but what he'd meant was obvious—"The queen didn't fail us!"—and obviously false. Herron had sense enough to swallow the remainder of his words.

"The armies of Made Men are a spectacular threat, but perhaps not the most dangerous one," Mab resumed in a softer tone. "The king's power has been increasing *in* Ronn ever since he was driven out. The Heroes have defeated his creatures repeatedly, but those defeats don't change the way darkness and night have slowly spread upward from the living rock beneath the city. By now they lurk at the edges of the crystal plazas open to the sun."

"Mistress?" said Enfero. His head was bandaged from where Cashel'd smacked him with the quarterstaff. "How can we fight that? How can we fight things that I don't even see?"

Mab twisted her face toward him like a hawk sighting prey; then the cold anger in her eyes melted. "You can't fight a fog, Master Enfero," she said mildly. "The queen will have to burn that away after she returns. Perhaps she'll have learned to do it properly this time, to sear the very rock clean of the taint of evil. But before the queen can return, the citizens of Ronn must defeat the army of Made Men massing on the plain outside. And to do that you six, and Master Cashel, and I, must wake the Heroes."

Cashel cleared his throat. "What's to stop us going down to this cavern, ma'am?" he asked, concentrating really hard on the wad of wool he rubbed along the smooth length of his quarterstaff. "Just bad feelings, like you were saying? Or are the Made Men going to be waiting for us when we get lower down?"

Mab looked at him and laughed, though the sound didn't have much joke to it. "You don't believe in bad feelings, in a miasma of evil, is that it, Master Cashel?" she said.

Cashel shrugged. "I believe, I guess," he said, "if you tell me it's so, ma'am. But I don't"—he raised his eyes to meet hers—"figure it's going to stop me."

Cashel looked down the line of the Sons, all of them staring at him. "Look," he said, then paused to frown. It was *really* important that they understand what he was about to tell them, but he'd never been good at words. "A lot of times it's really hard. The sun's hot, and you ache all over, and it doesn't seem like anybody really cares anyhow. But you've got to go on and finish it anyway, just slogging on."

He shrugged, his hands spread on the quarterstaff. "You've got to finish it," he repeated, "because otherwise it's still there to do. For you, or anyway for somebody, and you're the one whose job it was. Right? Because we've told everybody this is our job, going down to wake the Heroes."

"If there's any such thing!" Orly burst out. "If the Heroes *are* sleeping, if there's even a cavern! Nobody of all the people alive in Ronn today has seen it, you know."

"We don't need to worry about that," Cashel said.

"Don't worry?" Stasslin sneered. "Of course it's a worry! If there aren't any Heroes, then we can't wake them!"

"*We* don't need to worry," said Cashel, raising his voice just a little more than he had to so that they could all hear him clearly, "because that's not our job. Our job is to go down and do what we can. If there's no cavern or no Heroes, that's not our fault. So we don't need to worry about it."

Enfero suddenly laughed. "He's right," he said. "We only need to worry about *our* task. The questions as to whether our task is impossible or even pointless—those matters aren't our concern. Master Cashel's logic is impeccable."

"Are the Made Men in the lower levels?" Ather asked, unconsciously rubbing the bruises he'd taken when Cashel demonstrated what he could do with a quarterstaff. "You didn't answer that, milady."

Mab whisked her brilliant blue fingernails through the air. "No," she said. "We won't find Made Men. The king can't physically enter Ronn, except over the walls if he defeats Ronn's army. But his power influences the growth of things already in the city, and that increases the deeper we go. We'll have more to deal with than bad dreams."

For some minutes Cashel had been hearing chants and a sibilant ringing sound. Now a line of young people wound into the shady garden area, spinning and whirling as they followed one another. The men held tambourines, which they slapped overhead, while the women shook castanets to the same wild rhythm. As they danced they sang, "... *Our Mother Queen leads us to a seat and bids us sit, she gives us nectar in a golden cup* ..."

Mab fell silent, following the dancers with her eyes till the last of them jingled his way out of sight again. Cashel didn't try to count them, but there were at least as many as he had fingers on both hands. Their cheerful voices faded slowly.

Mab turned again to face her companions. A cold smile spread across her lips. She said, "As you see, the citizens of our city depend on us ... though they aren't aware of the fact. Unless we succeed in waking the Heroes, there'll shortly be no dancers waking the sun, and perhaps no sun at all for Ronn."

Cashel got up with the smooth grace of a gymnast, holding his staff out before him to balance the weight of his body as his knees straightened. "Well, ma'am," he said, smiling also. "We already said we were going to do that, right?"

"Yes," said Herron, lurching to his feet more clumsily than Cashel had but with a frown of fierce determination. "We did. Because it's our job."

Cashel smiled more broadly. It seemed like they'd understood what he was trying to tell them after all.

Sharina's first thought was that the wooded hill to the right of the road was steep-sided and oddly symmetrical. Then she realized it was artficial.

"That's the tomb," said Undercaptain Ascor, riding alongside the carriage Sharina and Tenoctris shared. "We used to escort the king here on Commemoration Day to make sacrifices. Though he gave that up the last couple years before, you know, your brother took over."

The Mausoleum of the bor-Torials, the family of the Dukes of Ornifal who'd for the past several generations claimed the kingship of the Isles as well, was a mound more than a hundred feet high. The plantings, cypresses interspersed with plane trees, were on four ascending terraces; at the top was a statue that, though large, was beyond Sharina's ability to identify at this distance.

A brick wall separated the grounds from road traffic. There was a keeper's house and a barred iron gate through which Sharina saw neatly tended vines mixed with the olive trees that would shade the grapes from the direct summer sun.

The gates were open. The twenty-odd horsemen who'd ridden on ahead to prepare for Sharina's arrival were talking volubly to one another within, still mounted. Sharina's escort was a company Waldron had brought from Volita. They'd originally been cavalry but had converted to infantry when Prince Garric refused to take horses when he sailed west across the Inner Sea. They'd remounted as soon as they returned to Ornifal and were revelling in the experience.

The mausoleum was designed to receive royal parties as large or larger than Sharina's. Immediately inside the gate was a cobbled plaza. A flagstone path curved through the vineyard and up the mound; along it were statues of the dukes interred here. Stronghand, at the end of the line, was a powerful man whose features showed determination and a hint of cruelty.

A husky, grizzled civilian in his sixties stood at the door of the house, talking easily with the officer who commanded the troops. From a gable window, a much younger woman suckling an infant peered at the soldiers in obvious concern.

The carriage swung around in the plaza. Sharina reached for the door latch, but the postillion had already jumped off his horse to forestall her; a second servant was handing Tenoctris out on the other side. The civilian stepped forward and bowed deeply, watched intently by the squad of Blood Eagles who'd dismounted as soon as the carriage stopped.

"Your highness," he said as he rose from his practiced bow, "I'm Master Madder. Madder the Master Gardener, if you'll allow me. Please accept this gift from your new ancestors."

He handed Ascor a squat, narrow-necked bottle with a black glaze. "The finest wine on Ornifal," Madder said proudly. "That was laid down fifty-one years ago, when your adoptive grandfather Valence the Second took the throne!"

"I'd like that, if you don't mind," Tenoctris said unexpectedly. Ascor looked at her, then to Sharina—who nodded. If the wizard was making sense of this, she was in a better place than Sharina. Ascor gave her the wine bottle with a bow of deference.

"I've kept the burial precincts of the bor-Torials for forty-two years," Madder continued, "through good times and the recent lean years as well. I want to express my joy, my *great* joy, that you and your royal brother are making the tomb of your adoptive family your own!"

"Ah . . ." said Sharina, taken completely aback. There was no doubt Madder's enthusiasm was real: the only time she'd seen a happier expression was on a young wife holding her firstborn. "That is, my brother hasn't made a final decision on our . . . ah."

She cleared her throat. "Master Madder," she resumed, forcing her mind back into the track it'd been following during the whole drive from the palace. "Lady Tenoctris—"

Sharina nodded toward the wizard, safely out of the vehicle. The servant was holding her satchel. She smiled brightly to Madder.

"—and I would like to view the burial chamber of Valence Stronghand. Will you guide us there, please."

A habit of polite deference almost twisted Sharina's words into a question: "Might we see his tomb?" for example. In fact it didn't matter what the gardener's feelings were, and anything but a flat statement would dishonestly imply that Madder had a choice. Sharina'd arrived with a company of soldiers and the needs of the kingdom to tend to.

"I'd like to determine whether someone has worked a contagion spell," Tenoctris explained, smiling again, "connecting the person posing as Stronghand's son with Stronghand himself. I'm not very powerful, so I'd like to be as close as possible to one terminus of the spell. If there's a spell, that is."

Sharina cringed inside, thinking about how nervous wizardry made most ordinary people. Tenoctris was an unworldly person, a scholar rather than a public figure. Though she knew intellectually that people were squeamish, she had a tendency to explain things that might better have gone unsaid.

Madder merely nodded approvingly. "Yes indeed," he said. "Tombs draw wizards, always have, and where in the Isles is there a finer tomb than the Mausoleum of the bor-Torials? Why, if I had a copper for every wizard I've chased out of here over the years, I'd be a wealthy man."

"Well, you're not chasing Lady Tenoctris out," said Ascor firmly. "And if you don't watch your tongue, you'll find it hard chasing anything because your legs'll be broken. Get moving, fellow!"

"What?" Madder said in surprise. "Oh, of course, of course."

The gardener bowed again, to Tenoctris, then a second time to Sharina. "I didn't mean you, your highness and milady," he explained. "Why, you're family, of course. My, my, I'll be happy to show you. That is, you'd like me to lead?"

"If you would," Sharina said mildly, amused at Ascor's puzzled expression. He and the gardener had been talking at cross-purposes, but they were obviously both enthusiastic about helping Sharina do anything she wanted.

Madder trotted off along the path through the vineyard. "I remember Lady Indra," he said over his shoulder with a chuckle. "She was a cousin of the Stronghand's wife, I believe, back when I was still an apprentice. Every week she'd arrive with a different wizard. Once there was a Dalopan with a bone through his nose, if you can imagine that. Mad about horse racing, Lady Indra was, and no hand at all at picking horses."

He shook his head reminiscently. "No hand at picking wizards to help her either, it seemed," he added. "But that never stopped her trying."

Sharina looked about her as she followed the gardener. The plantings were very extensive, at least half an acre of grapes and olives. A workman pruning the lower limbs of an olive tree with a billhook paused and stared at the procession—a squad of soldiers; Madder, the two women, and the Blood Eagles; and the rest of the troops—then hurriedly lowered his eyes and went back to work. Madder was used to royalty visiting the mausoleum, but the younger staff obviously were not.

"I'm surprised at the type of plantings, Master Madder," Sharina called to the man stumping along in front of her. "I'd have expected the tomb to be landscaped, but with flowers and funerary shrubs, yews and myrtle and the like. This is a working vineyard."

"Oh, by the Lady, yes, your highness!" Madder said cheerfully. "You're from the west, aren't you? Haft, I believe? I've heard they do things different there, but on Ornifal we like our tombs to pay for their own upkeep. Our vintage is famous. What doesn't go for libations—or went in the days the family visited regularly, as I hope you'll do now that you're here—we sell for the staff's pay and the supplies we need."

They'd reached the point the path began to curve up the mound proper. Lires put a hand on the gardener's shoulder and slowed him with a significant nod at Tenoctris, who was showing signs of strain.

The path curved as it climbed. Masonry arches were set into the mound. The doors hanging in the first two were of iron with a patina of rust; the third was iron-strapped wood. Cypress, Sharina thought, but even so decay had eaten into the lower edge of the panel. The bronze nameplate was too corroded to read.

"The twins Attistus and Porra," Madder said, noticing Sharina's interest. "And both of Porra's wives, I believe, though I'd have to check the records on that. They were cousins of the reigning duke, that was Valbrun, but he adopted them as his heirs."

The gardener chuckled. "Teaches you humility, this job does," he went on. "Both of them died before Valbrun. It was his own son Valtor who succeeded. Yes sir, humble!"

"My experience," Tenoctris said in a cheerful tone, "is that life by itself is sufficient to do that. The more I learn, the more wonderful and complex the universe beyond what I know becomes."

"That pleases you, Tenoctris," Sharina said; there was no mistaking the tone of the other woman's voice. "Why? I mean, you're pleased at your ignorance, that's what you're saying, isn't it?"

Tenoctris laughed. "Yes indeed, dear," she said. "That means I'll never run out of things to learn, you see. *That* would be quite an awful business, don't you think?"

Sharina laughed also. "I never thought about it," she said. "I suppose I never thought there was any risk of it happening."

They were more than halfway up the side of the mound. When Sharina glanced outward, she found herself looking over the tops of cypresses planted on the level ground at the base. They were at the back of the tomb, with a view to the east toward the gymnasium built by a victorious general of several generations earlier. Men were running and vaulting in the courtyard, while a larger number lounged under the porticoes built on three sides of the open area. The two-story building forming the entrance had been faced with colored marble, but many slabs had cracked off without being replaced.

"The next alcove is Stronghand's," the gardener said, looking over his shoulder toward the women. "I remember his funeral. My, that was a wonderful day. A splendid pageant!"

"This one's been broken open," called the file closer who commanded the leading squad of soldiers. He and his men drew their swords, the long cavalry blades they'd retained when the regiment officially became infantry. "Woo-ie! *She*'s been dead a while, I guess!"

"What!" Madder cried. "No, that can't be!"

The gardener pushed through the troops, oblivious of the risk that he'd slice himself on a bare blade. He gave a wordless cry, threw his hands in the air, and fell to his knees.

The Blood Eagles locked shields in front of Sharina and Tenoctris. "Let me by!" the old wizard said. She tapped the rim of Ascor's helmet with the bamboo sliver she'd taken from her sleeve. "In Wisdom's *name*, sir, you're preventing me from doing the one thing that may be of service!"

"Captain Ascor," Sharina said in a tone of aristocratic command. "You and Trooper Lires will please escort us to the alcove immediately."

"All right, soldiers!" Ascor snapped, placing his right hand on a horseman's shoulder and shifting him sideways. "Out of the way of her highness. Now!"

With the pair of Blood Eagles preceding them, Sharina and Tenoctris entered the burial alcove. The walls were covered with slabs of marble, probably a veneer over brick or concrete. Benches faced one another along the sidewalls; on each was a bronze coffin.

The old wizard frowned and half turned. "Please," she said in what for her was a peevish tone. "Don't block the light."

"You heard the lady!" Ascor snarled. In all likelihood the soldiers shuffling for a look inside hadn't heard Tenoctris, but they certainly heard Ascor. "Move it back *now* so her highness can see what's going on!"

Sharina felt a moment's surprise that the spectators outside really did back away so that sufficient light penetrated the alcove. She'd been thinking in terms of what would've happened back in Barca's Hamlet—basically nothing, except those in back would've shoved forward harder. *These* men were disciplined soldiers.

Both coffins had been wrenched open; the lids lay askew, half-blocking the already narrow aisle between the benches. The one on the right held a woman. The bronze must have fitted tightly enough to slow decay in the decades since her burial: dried flesh and even some of the skin clothed the skull, pulling the jaws open as if to scream. Her hair had continued to grow for a time after death but without the normal pigment; it formed a red-gold mass.

The other coffin was empty. Tenoctris touched the velvet lining with the bamboo sliver, her lips pursed in an expression of bright interest.

"Oh, this is terrible!" said Madder, who'd entered behind the women. "How could this have happened?"

"Yes, I was wondering the same thing," said Tenoctris. "There must have been a good deal of noise, even though this alcove is on the opposite side of the mound from your dwelling. Could the persons who did this have climbed over the wall, do you think?"

"No," said the gardener forcefully. "No. Not without our noticing it, I mean."

He grimaced. "I'll admit it's been months since me or the staff have been up the mound proper," he said. "Some of the oleander needs pruning bad, I saw that on the way up, and I apologize. But the vineyard we work on daily, and the tracks'd show up in the dirt if nothing else. They must've *flown* in—oh!"

"Go on, Master Madder," Tenoctris said. "Did you see something flying over the mausoleum?"

"No, no, it's not that," Madder said, kneading his forehead with callused fingers as though squeezing the thoughts into line. "Only a month ago—no, I'm a liar, longer than that, it must be near two, and at the dark of the moon. We all had dreams, me and the mistress and the three boys who sleep in the shed too. And in the morning, the gates were unlocked."

"What do you mean by dreams?" Tenoctris said. She touched the satchel Sharina had taken from the servant when they started up the mound, but she moved her hand away immediately.

"Bad dreams," Madder said. "I can't tell you more than that—and I wouldn't if I could, they were *bad*."

He rubbed his forehead again and shrugged. "We searched, I don't mean we didn't," he said. "We get plenty people trying to climb the walls and steal fruit, you bet, and they don't try again after they heal from the first beating. But nothing was gone—"

He looked up sharply. "I could tell, you know," he added belligerently. "You may think I couldn't, but I know my crop!"

"I'm sure you do," Tenoctris said calmly. "But you didn't go up to the tombs themselves?"

"No, milady," Madder said with another scowl of inward-directed anger. "No, I surely didn't. It's not like foreign parts, you know—there's nothing in the coffins but the bodies."

"Yes, of course," Tenoctris agreed. "The wealth of the dead, like their temporal power, remains with their heirs."

She smiled, but her face had the look of someone viewing a future that held a great deal of difficulty. "The trouble is," Tenoctris continued, "that there's other kinds of power than that granted by money and political position. It would appear that a wizard with the ability to cast a spell of deep sleep was looking for Stronghand's body in order to get additional power. And it would seem that he's gotten it."

"You'll be well paid for this," Garric said to the pair of servants who'd just given him and Liane their outer clothes. He took the rear pair of handles of the handbarrow heaped with used bedding.

The young male servant blinked and swallowed, looking terrified. Garric didn't suppose the fellow was afraid of anything in particular, but he was obviously concerned that anything so unusual meant some formless disaster was waiting to pounce. The middle-aged female sniffed, and said, "I hope I know my duty well enough to do it without thinking your highness needs to pay me extra!"

"Even so," said Liane, taking the front handles. She unlatched the door and stepped into the hallway, her head bowed.

It was drizzling outside, so the servants'd had an excuse to raise the hoods of their short gray capes. The guards had still checked them when they came down the hall with clean bedding—but they wouldn't, Garric hoped, bother to do that again when the servants left.

Garric pulled the door to behind him as he followed Liane out. A three-wick lamp hung over the doorway. It was placed to illuminate the faces of people coming from either direction down the hallway, while those beneath it remained in shadow.

The guards were discussing the upcoming wrestling match between a Blood Eagle file closer and a Blaise armsman from Lord Rosen's regiment. They didn't pay any attention to the servants leaving the royal apartments and shuffling down the hall.

"What they oughta do," one of the Blood Eagles said, as Garric and Liane rounded the corner at the slow pace of tired servants, "is let us fight the local talent with training swords. That'd show 'em what's what!"

"That'd be the quickest way to start a for-real war, at any rate," said the ghost of King Carus, shaking his head with a rueful smile. *"And I wouldn't be surprised if Gyganes—"*

Carus knew all the Blood Eagles by name, as well as virtually every other soldier in the royal army whose name Garric had heard even once. It was an ability Garric doubted he'd have been able to equal if he'd made it his life's work.

"—*knew that just as well as I do. Of course, we can't have common soldiers deciding policy for the kingdom, and it's nice that the ruler isn't spoiling for a fight either. The way I was when I was king.*"

Grinning along with his ancestor, Garric said to Liane in a low voice, "It's a pretty pass when the fellow who's supposed to be running the kingdom has to sneak out of his room, or he wouldn't be allowed to go."

They walked more briskly now that they were out of sight of the guards. These corridors made do with a lamp at each corner, and those would burn down by morning.

"*I'm* not sure you should go," said Liane. "My agent certainly thinks the business is dangerous, and he's not easily alarmed."

"If there's wizardry involved . . . ," Garric said. "And there is, Dipsas is a wizard, and what else'd she be doing in the vaults under the palace? If there's wizardry, then nobody's more fit than you and I to judge what's going on. Except for Tenoctris, of course, and if she were here, I'd insist on going with her or sending Cashel."

"I'm not disagreeing," Liane said, looking over her shoulder to smile at him. "I'm just saying that I understand why others might."

She paused by a door covered by a swatch of age-rotted tapestry nailed to the jamb and transom. "This is the room," she said, then tapped twice on the wood—with the ivory hilt of the little dagger Garric had seen her kill with, he realized.

The door swung outward, frame and all. There was no light inside. "Watch the hole!" an unfamiliar male voice whispered. "Half the floor's gone in here, that's why they closed it."

Liane slipped in, elbowing the door wider: they couldn't leave the load of washing out in the hall without attracting attention. Garric followed, closing the panel behind him. The shutter of a dark lantern scraped open. The light of the single candle behind a lens of thin horn blazed like a burst of sunlight.

"Who's he?" the voice demanded; a sharp-featured youth in the bleached-white tunic of Earl Wildulf's palace servants, Garric saw. "You weren't supposed to bring anybody. Anybody!"

"You know who I am," Garric said. "Now tell us where Dipsas and the countess go at night."

The room contained a broken bed frame and a litter of smaller objects, but it wasn't completely filled with junk the way the suite turned over to Garric had been. The floor, concrete poured over a lattice of withies, had sagged when a supporting beam gave way; half the slab had then collapsed into the darkness beneath. The response of whoever was in charge of palace maintenance at the time had been to close the room instead of trying to repair it.

When Garric glanced into the hole, he could understand why nobody'd wanted to work down there. He grinned. He wasn't looking forward to it himself.

"You weren't supposed to tell anybody who I am!" the youth said peevishly to Liane. "My life's in danger, you know that!"

"All our lives are in danger," Liane said calmly. "Yours will be in less danger if you stop angering me when time is so short. Where does the wizard go?"

The spy twisted his mouth as if for another complaint, then caught himself with a shrug. "Right," he said. "Right, and anyway, what's done is done."

He pointed his thumb toward the hole where the floor had been. "I've left markers on the walls with mushroom spores. When your eyes adjust, you'll see them. It's not the same path Dipsas takes at the start—it's a rabbit warren down there, there's tunnels off every direction and I don't know where half of 'em go. Anyway, you'll join her route about two levels down."

"Won't Dipsas see the markings and know someone has followed her?" Liane said with a frown.

"No, they take lamps, her and the countess," the spy explained. "If there's any light at all, you can't see my marks. And even if they did—"

He shrugged again. "Chances are they'd figure it was natural, it seems to me. You get that sort of glow in caves. That's where I gather the mushrooms."

"Then you'd better close your lantern," Garric said, "so our eyes can adapt. They're there tonight, Dipsas and Balila?"

"Right," the spy said, sliding the cover over the lens. The smell of hot iron and candle smoke was suddenly more noticeable, though that was probably because Garric's eyes no longer distracted him from the odors. "They started down at their usual time, an hour ago. I've followed them three times when I wasn't on duty, and they always go the same place."

The spy made a sound with his cheek as though he'd tasted something sour. "The bird and that jabbering little moron the countess keeps with her, they went too," he said. "They always do. I don't understand why. I *don't*."

He's frightened, Garric realized. *But not, I think, by anything he could put a name to.*

"He seems a sensible fellow," Carus remarked with his usual grin. It was always daylight at the place where he stood in Garric's mind. *"So perhaps he just doesn't like wizards."*

"I see a glow down there," Liane said, her voice calm, but perhaps too calm.

"There's a ladder here to take you down the first part," the spy said, sounding embarrassed. "Look, I can't go with you tonight, I'm on duty in the message room. I ought to be there now."

"No one's asking you to come," Garric said. He shifted the belt holding his dagger so that it was over the borrowed tunic instead of under it. His sword was too long to conceal from the guards, and in the close confines of the tunnels a dagger might be more useful anyway. "You've done your job, and more."

"It's really pretty clear," the spy said. The door opened. As his silhouette slipped into the hallway, he added, "You shouldn't have trouble."

"I'll lead," said Liane. Garric heard the *tick* of the long reed she'd concealed on the handbarrow, then the creak of the ladder as it settled under the girl's slight weight.

Garric followed, smiling as he thought of the way he had to sneak around in order to carry out a task he really was the best available person for. He hadn't seriously thought of forbidding Liane to come, though he was frightened at the risk to her. She'd been in worse places than this was likely to be, and she'd likely put herself in worse ones yet as long as she survived: for the kingdom's sake and mankind's sake.

A life spent hiding until Evil triumphed wasn't a life of safety in any real sense. Garric wouldn't order Liane to waste her abilities in that fashion, any more than he was going to allow his well-meaning guards and advisors to force him to twiddle his thumbs.

He could see the markings clearly, irregular bars of yellow-green that didn't illuminate any more than themselves. The floor at the base of the ladder was firm but scattered with bits of something that scrunched beneath his feet—fallen plaster, perhaps, or tesserae loosened from an ancient mosaic.

Liane handed him one end of her sash, several times normal length but hidden till then beneath the tunic she'd gathered above it. "Ready?" she asked.

"Ready," said Garric, and drew the dagger. He might have done better to keep his hand free, but for the moment the hilt gave him a little extra confidence as they started into the near darkness.

When Garric got used to it, he *did* find it surprisingly easy to navigate through the cellars. The phosphorescent markings were adequate, each within sight of the ones before and after it. Even more important, the path itself was clear. The spy must've spent considerable effort preparing the route instead of simply scouting and marking it.

"He's a good man," Garric said aloud.

"All Liane's people are," said Carus, grinning like a bear in a honey tree. *"Between her and Tenoctris, I've had to change my opinion of wizards and spymasters both!"*

"He had reason to be angry," Liane said, her reed brushing across the ground ahead of her with a *tick-tick-tick*. "But I couldn't warn him that you'd be with me. Just in case he were caught, you know."

Garric hadn't known. He'd never really thought about the problems of not knowing whom to trust. Now that he *did* think about it, he realized that meant you could never trust anyone. How could Liane live in that world, at least part of the time?

They reached a blank wall where a glow faintly arrowed toward stairs to the left. They were brick and solid despite a crack splitting them in the middle. Their thin marble veneer had flaked away dangerously, but somebody—presumably the spy—had swept the broken slabs to either side.

"Did he say how far it is?" Garric asked, more for companionship than a need for an answer. The spy'd laid out the route while Dipsas and Balila were above ground, so he could use a lantern without risk of being seen. Garric and Liane couldn't take that chance, so the fact they needed total darkness to see the markings wasn't a handicap.

"He said it took him half an hour," Liane said. "I don't know the distance—it doesn't really matter, I suppose. Of course it'll take us longer."

But not a lot longer, Garric suspected. Liane was walking with a confidence he wouldn't have been able to equal if he'd been in front. She showed no more hesitation than if she were stepping across a drawing room at midday. Either Liane was certain of her agent and that the reed she tapped ahead of her would give sufficient warning, or she acted as though she were certain.

The latter was more likely, and it showed quite amazing courage. Little things like risking a bad fall in the dark were harder to achieve than great flashy ones like charging a dangerous enemy. The big ones you did with a kind of madness seething in your blood to overcome normal concerns, but Liane's steady courage was the sort you had to find on your own.

The sound of their feet and breathing changed. The walls had closed in, and the markers were painted on living rock. Garric touched the wall. They were in a tunnel bored with crude tools, hammers and drills made by grinding sand into the softer limestone.

The atmosphere shifted again; echoes became a distant whisper. The markings were on glass-smooth flow rock, the pearly deposit that formed stalactites when it dripped from the cave roof instead of in sheets over the walls. Besides the echoes, Garric heard another thing, or thought he did.

"Pause a moment," he said. He bent and laid his left palm on the cave floor, finding it faintly warm. Through the rock shivered a slow rumble that was neither his imagination nor the sound of blood in his own ears.

"All right," he said, straightening and gripping Liane's sash firmly again.

"It's real, then?" she asked as she strode ahead again. They were clearly going down, but Garric couldn't be sure how steep the slope was.

"I think so," Garric said. "But I don't know what it is."

Liane gave a laugh that didn't seem forced. "Well, perhaps we'll learn," she said. "That's what we're here for, after all."

The cave narrowed; the right side had been improved by tools, but the left was natural. Garric touched a few threads, remains of fabric caught where tools had left a sharp fracture in the rock.

"There's light ahead," Liane whispered. Garric could see it too, though the glow was so faint that it turned Liane's form into a wraith instead of a silhouette. They continued on, down a short flight of steps broken into the stone with hammers and levers. The tip of a deer-antler pick remained in the crack where it'd broken off unguessably far in the past.

"And voices," Garric whispered back. He looped the sash over Liane's shoulder so that it wouldn't drag on the ground and trip one of them, then let go of it. She'd shifted the reed to her left hand, holding it at the balance.

The words were more distinct than they ought to be. *A trick of the echoes?* Garric could make out syllables and sometimes whole snatches of the chant; enough to know he was listening to words of power, not the speech of human beings.

The light came through a natural crack widened into an egg-shaped opening large enough for a human. Even Liane would have to hunch to enter, though. They crept close on either side and peered into a large natural cavern.

The lamp must've been in a niche in the limestone wall, but it was out of sight from where Garric knelt. Countess Balila sat with the light over her shoulder, writing with quick, firm strokes on a tablet. As Garric watched, she flipped over one of the several waxed leaves and started on the next.

"Ouer sechan libara," thundered a voice. It must be shockingly loud in the cavern because the flame of the unseen lamp shivered in time with the syllables, but Garric heard the word only as a faint, *"Amounabreo."*

The bodiless voice stilled. Dipsas sat before a figure drawn in the center of the plug of black volcanic rock that formed the floor of the cavern. She chanted an invocation, her athame dipping and rising like a drinking bird. The wizard's voice seemed as loud as that which had spoken the response, but Garric couldn't make out the words.

The little cherub was playing with his toes near the countess; his wings of stiffened and gilded linen wobbled in the lamplight. He suddenly lost interest in his game and tugged at the hem of his mistress's outer tunic. She twitched it away from him, continuing to watch the wizard with the focus of a kestrel hovering above movement in the grass.

Dipsas swayed and would've fallen if she hadn't slapped both hands down on the figure. The athame lay before her; lamplight gave its polished, carven surface the look of rippling blackness, unformed evil.

"Chauboe!" said the voice with the power of a distant avalanche. The cherub threw himself on his belly and squirmed over the rock, his eyes shut and his mouth twisted into a squall of terror lost in the response.

"Adeta mesou!" said the voice. The light dimmed as though the first gust of a storm had struck the lamp.

Balila's great bird had been pacing on the other side of the cavern, visible to Garric except when it was at the end of its circuit. It stopped and backed against the rock, flaring its crest and wings. It raised its hooked beak toward the roof and shrieked, its black tongue quivering but the sound inaudible.

The thundering response cut off. Echoes of the bird's cry and the child's terror rang about Garric and Liane.

The lamplight slowly steadied. The wizard remained as she'd been, sagging onto her hands. The countess let her stylus drop. The open leaves of her notebook swung lazily on the leather hinges.

Garric took a deep breath. Closing his eyes, he whispered to Liane, "We'd better leave now. They'll have the lamp."

"Yes," she said. "But I don't think Dipsas will be moving very quickly."

"I don't know that I will either," Garric said as he rose to his feet. "Even though I was just listening, and that to the last part of it."

He thought of Carus' loathing for wizards. That opinion wasn't justified in the case of Tenoctris—but for the most part, Garric was inclined to agree.

Ilna set down the bowl that she'd polished with a piece of wheat bread, getting the last of the stew of lentils and barley in chicken broth. Glancing to either side where Chalcus and Davus were finishing their meals, she chewed the bread. So far as she was concerned, it was even tastier than the meat stew.

Ilna had kept poultry at home in Barca's Hamlet, pigeons and occasionally chickens, and Cashel not infrequently knocked over a squirrel or rabbit with a rock. Meat was a luxury, but not an unthinkable one.

Nobody in the borough raised wheat, though, so not even the wealthiest of her neighbors had bread like this unless they travelled. Ilna disliked most of the things she'd found in the world beyond Barca's Hamlet, but wheat bread was an exception.

She grinned at herself: she'd disliked most of the things she'd grown up with also. Occasionally she tried to convince herself that perhaps she was wrong about the world or at least needlessly uncharitable. She could never sustain the notion for long, though.

"Well, you've eaten now," Lord Ramelus said, standing across the table from her and glaring with his fists on his hips. "How much longer will it take you to finish the pattern?"

"Not long," said Ilna calmly. Ramelus reminded her of the fable of the frog who tried to make himself bigger than the ox by puffing himself up—till he burst. "When my companions have eaten their fill—"

"As indeed I have, your lordship," Chalcus said, rising to his feet with his usual ease. "And a fine meal it was, I must say."

The three of them ate at a trestle table on the porch of the western side-building. Chalcus had chosen the spot. Behind them was a storage shed, closed and locked; most of the side-buildings were open sheds. While Ilna didn't imagine they'd been in any real danger of being attacked from behind, it obviously affected how comfortable Chalcus felt when he was among people who weren't his friends.

"And I as well," said Davus, getting up also. The three fist-sized rocks that he'd been juggling before the meal was served were lined up on the table beside his empty bowl and beer mug. "Your lordship is extremely generous to wayfaring strangers. The Old King would've approved."

Ramelus scowled. Seifert sniggered. The landowner turned in barely contained fury, which the guard defused by twisting his grin into an expression of funereal sadness.

Ilna had declared that Ramelus must provide a meal—with meat *and* wheat bread, though the demand for meat was more to irritate their host than because she needed it—before she gave the fabric its finishing touches. He'd obeyed—with extremely bad grace, but obeyed—because the partial pattern he'd seen over Ilna's shoulder had given him an inkling of how effective the finished design might be.

"I've fed you," Ramelus snapped. "Now, do what you promised. If you try to gull me, you'll regret it—that I promise you!"

"I'll give you what I swore to give you," Ilna said. "A hanging that makes most of those who see it happier. I'll follow the rules you set. Depend on it!"

The last sounded more like a threat—which it was—than Ilna'd intended, but Ramelus was too caught up in his own importance to pay attention to anybody else. "See that you do!" he said.

Ilna stepped to the nearby table where she'd left her loom. Her two companions came with her as naturally as her tunic swirled—and almost as closely, too. Peasants who'd been staring in wonderment at the pattern moved back like little fish when a pike darts toward them.

Ilna ran her fingers over the heddles of the borrowed loom. It was a good one, a loom she wouldn't have minded owning herself.

She smiled as she made the final adjustments to her pattern, thread by thread: craft was in the craftsman, of course, not in her tools. And this particular work was a piece of craftsmanship that showed all there was that mattered in Ilna os-Kenset, the skill and the sense of justice as well. Charity was a fine thing, no doubt, but it wasn't a virtue Ilna claimed or even really desired.

Mostera gasped in wonder as she saw what Ilna was creating. She and her sister might be the only spectators who realized that the fabric was a double weave with different patterns on the front and back. Ordinarily Ilna would've opened the finished piece at one selvedge to double the width of the finished cloth, but in this case she'd picked up threads from the underlayer to deliberately bind the patterns together. And when she was done—

Ilna beat the fabric one last time, then withdrew the bar and paused. Her arms and shoulders were stiff. There was quite a lot going on with this business. Weaving itself was physical effort, particularly at the speed at which Ilna accomplished it, but there was more to her art than that. Everything had to be paid for, which was exactly the way it should be.

"You're a demon," Malaha whispered. "You're not human!"

"I'm human," Ilna said as she began to knot off her fabric. She'd deliberately left the selvedges long to make it easier to hang the piece above Ramelus' throne. She looked Malaha in the face, and added, "There was a time that I was much worse than any demon, but I've always been human."

Mostera put her hand on her sister's. Neither of them spoke.

Ilna smiled, nodded, and stretched the fabric out toward Lord Ramelus. "I've met my obligation," she said, a statement instead of pretending there was any doubt of the fact.

The chief of the landowner's bodyguards muttered what was a curse by the words of it, a prayer in its tone. Even Ramelus drew in a breath of amazement.

The pattern was abstract both visually and in emotional effect. A bed of earth tones and grays zigzagged up the fabric till at midpoint the yarn dyed with berry pulp appeared—a few pink flecks, then a ripple, and from there to the top a hinted outline picked out by the insistence of the color rather than the weight of the line.

When Ilna looked at the pattern she saw, she *felt,* a spring morning in

Barca's Hamlet. Dawn was rising over the Inner Sea, and she had no pressing task in hand. Others who viewed it would feel other things. From the expressions on the faces of Ramelus and his guards, Ilna herself would find some of those things distasteful or even disgusting.

But it wasn't her task to edit the fantasies of her fellow humans. As she'd said to Malaha, she had enough on her own conscience.

"Wonderful!" a peasant shouted. Half the large crowd chorused, "Wonderful!" or started to cheer. Ramelus looked stricken, sick and angry and uncertain—but drawn despite himself by what he saw in the fabric.

Ilna folded the panel closed. "Master Chalcus?" she said, nodding to the man at her side. "The posts of the chair back—the throne there in the kiosk? I believe this is sized to their span. Please tie it there."

She handed the fabric to Chalcus but looked at Ramelus. "Do you agree, sir?" she said.

The landowner had regained his composure after the pattern was folded away. "Yes," he muttered hoarsely. He cleared his throat, and said in a firmer tone, "Yes, all right, put it there. Put it up behind me."

There was a whisper of sound throughout the crowd, wonder and a delight that verged in some cases on awe. Ilna smiled bitterly. Her skill was a wonderful thing, no doubt about that; but she wondered how these peasants would react if they learned that the skill had been purchased at the cost of the weaver's soul?

Well, she had her soul back now. Worse for wear, of course, but the lesson that she must *never* lose control was worth the damage. Ilna wasn't enough of an optimist to imagine that there was no worse error she could've fallen into had she not learned from that one.

The chair's gilded finials were an eagle on one side, a lion's head on the other. Chalcus hopped onto the chair seat, but even so he had to stretch to reach them. When he did, he tied the panel in place with quick knots.

"And now, Master Ramelus," Ilna said. "The agreement was for our meals while I worked on the panel, and food for our journey when I completed it satisfactorily."

"Yes," said the landowner, clearing his throat again. He looked at his guards, and said in a harsh voice, "Three of you watch the one behind us!"

"There's no need for that," Ilna said steadily. "Chalcus, come stand by me. Ramelus is nervous with you behind him."

"Tsk," said Chalcus, dropping to the ground so smoothly that his feet didn't kick up dust. He smiled with engaging innocence as he walked through the locals to Ilna's side. "Does he imagine I'd besmirch my honor by stabbing a man in the back? Dearie dearie me."

Ramelus looked half-puzzled, half-incensed. He apparently wasn't sure whether Chalcus was mocking him, which meant he had even less intelligence than Ilna's previous low opinion had assigned him. She had no doubt that in his day Chalcus had killed people from behind, people who were sleeping, people who were praying on their knees . . .

Nor did she doubt that Chalcus could sweep away Ramelus and his guards, face on and smiling. But it wouldn't come to that, not this time.

So thinking, Ilna smiled also. The expression made Ramelus blink, which suggested he might not be entirely a fool after all.

"The rest of the bargain if you please, Master Ramelus," Ilna said calmly. The peasants had mostly turned to stare at the hanging. At noon the roof would shade it, but now the afternoon sun made the pink blaze.

The landowner's face settled into a scowl. "Food, yes," he said. "Food for your further journey."

He took from his belt a purse of embroidered silk, obviously prepared for this moment, and shook its contents into his palm. "A barley corn, a lentil, and a chickpea," he said loudly. "We didn't discuss quantity, you'll recall!"

"I recall," Ilna said, smiling a little broader. "This is your choice, Master Ramelus?"

"It's the bargain we made!" Ramelus said. He tossed the three seeds on the table beside the empty loom. "If you didn't think about what you were saying, that's no business of mine."

Ilna raised the chickpea between her thumb and forefinger, looked at it, and set it back on the tabletop. "Then we've each kept our bargain according to our codes," she said. She nodded toward the throne, flashing the smile again. "I expect my pattern will bring a good deal of pleasure for as long as it remains here."

She glanced at her companions. "Let us leave this place," she said. She walked forward; Chalcus fell into step, keeping between Ilna and the guards surrounding the landowner.

Instead of joining them, Davus stood arms akimbo. In a clear, challenging voice, he said, "This is injustice, Lord Ramelus."

"I kept my bargain!" Ramelus said. "If I'm too smart for you, that's too bad for you!"

"This is injustice," Davus repeated. The peasants, all but an old woman who still stared at the fabric, watched the interchange in a mixture of fear and anticipation. "In the days of the Old King, you would be a block of basalt and a warning to others."

"He's threatening me!" Ramelus said, his voice rising. "Gallen, he threatened me! Deal with him!"

"I don't threaten you," Davus said, upright as a stone pillar. "We'll all leave this place, because that's the desire of Mistress Ilna, whom you cheated by your injustice. That is so, mistress?"

"Yes," said Ilna. "And I would prefer to be leaving now, Master Davus."

"Leave him be, friend Davus," Chalcus said in a tone of quiet urgency. "It's the lady's choice. And Davus? I won't have you put *her* life at risk for anything so empty as justice."

Davus laughed suddenly. "Indeed, friend," he said, sauntering out from behind the table and touching Chalcus by the shoulder. "Though I'm less ready than you to call justice empty."

"As am I," said Ilna tartly, "but we've done all we need to preserve it here."

She looked at Ramelus. He responded by stepping behind Seifert and tugging another guard over into an actual human barrier. The utter *fool*.

"Master Ramelus," Ilna said. This wasn't a man whom she would address as "Lord," not though the choice was impalement. "I wish you all deserved pleasure from the panel I've woven for your community."

Then to her companions, "Come." She strode off along the path curving around the house and continuing north through the barley and wheat. The men fell in step—but behind her, not at her side.

"I didn't see any bows, did you, Davus?" Chalcus said in a cheery voice. "Though I didn't see any sign of them having the balls to try us, either."

"With this sash I can outrange a bow," Davus replied in similar apparent unconcern. "But I too doubt we need worry."

But they were walking behind her. Just in case. Ilna's mind wavered toward anger at being coddled, then decided to see the humor of it and chuckled instead.

They were past the house; none of the peasants or servants were close enough to overhear. Without turning her head but loudly enough for her companions to catch the words, Ilna said, "I suppose you're wondering why I walked away from that?"

"Yes, dear one," said Chalcus. "But I knew you had your reasons."

"Yes," she agreed. "If Ramelus had kept the spirit of the agreement instead of the word alone, I'd have told you to turn the fabric over so that the other side was toward those looking at it."

"But mistress," Davus said with quiet puzzlement in his voice, "the pattern's everything you said it was. To me, at least. I don't know that it'd please others as it did me, but I could *feel* a grotto in the side of a mountain with a waterfall rushing past the opening."

"That was what you saw?" Chalcus said in surprise. "I was on a ship. We'd come through a storm, and a rainbow filled the horizon ahead."

"Yes, you're both correct," Ilna said. She took the hank of yarn from her sleeve and began knotting a pattern that would show them what she meant. "For now. But the design on the back of the cloth is in permanent dyes. The pink on the front will fade into the natural gray of the yarn in a few weeks, there in the sun as it is."

"Ah, you lovely darling!" Chalcus said. "So for his cleverness, Lord Ramelus will be left with no pattern in a short time, is that it?"

Ilna snorted. "Oh, no," she said. "There'll still be a pattern, and it'll still give pleasure, I'm sure, to most of those who see it. But what that pattern is—"

She straightened her hands out, stretching taut her knotted design. Swinging it left, then right, she showed both men what she'd done.

Chalcus caroled in delight; a moment later, Davus burst out with a guffaw of laughter so loud that it startled into flight a covey of quail that'd been hiding unseen among the dark green barley till that moment. Still laughing, Davus bent to pick up a pebble.

"Lord Ramelus himself!" Chalcus said. "And naked as the day he was born!"

"Yes," said Ilna, picking her design back to bare yarn with quick, fastidious movements. "The woven pattern takes effect more slowly, and I don't think Ramelus himself will ever see it. But everyone else will, and once they've seen that image they'll never be able to look at Ramelus without seeing it again."

In a cool tone Ilna added, "I thought he might change his mind there at the very end. After all his own people were angry, and what did a few firkins of pulse and grain matter to him? But in truth, and though I'm sure

I should wish I was a better person—*I don't mind missing a meal or two for the sake of serving out that self-important toad.*"

The men laughed again. They continued laughing in bursts until the manor's pompous façade had dipped beneath a rolling hill of barley behind them. After a time Chalcus began to sing, *"From this valley they say you are going. . . ."*

"We will miss your bright eyes and sweet smile . . . ," Davus chimed in, to Ilna's great surprise. His baritone made a pleasant undertone to the sailor's light tenor.

Chapter Eleven

Though her mounted escort was quite willing to clear a path, Sharina was content that the carriage proceed back to the palace at the speed of ordinary traffic. They were returning by the next radial street to the east of the river. That was partly to spread Princess Sharina's public presence more widely through the city—but also partly, Sharina suspected, because Undercaptain Ascor hadn't wanted to risk an enemy preparing an ambush along the route they'd taken before.

Tenoctris sat on the opposite bench of the compartment with a lap desk across her knees. She'd checked several documents from her satchel as they rode along. Sharina had her finger in a scroll even then to mark a place, though she was pretty sure the old wizard didn't need it anymore.

At present Tenoctris was murmuring an incantation above a seven-pointed figure she'd sketched on her desk. It must take enormous concentration to manage that in a rocking vehicle, but Sharina had already learned that doing *anything* well took concentration. A fuzz of scarlet wizardlight pulsed above the heptagram, barely visible even in the shade of the compartment.

Sharina smiled and drew a bamboo sliver from the wizard's satchel. She marked the place in the scroll with it, then leaned out the window. By supporting herself with an arm, she kept from being bounced hard into the frame. Even at a walking pace, the iron-shod carriage wheels banged sparks from the cobblestones. She'd as soon have been on foot, though that wasn't comfortable on stone either.

The Blood Eagle riding on the carriage step glanced at her, then returned to checking his side of the road for threats. Sharina didn't recall the soldier's name. She frowned: she should learn who all her guards were. It was the least she could do for men ready to throw themselves between her and danger at the first opportunity.

This route passed through an affluent suburb instead of the concentration of commercial buildings across the river. The residences were single-family dwellings rather than apartment blocks, though the fronts at street level were rented to shops, taverns, and restaurants. By then Sharina had been inside enough expensive city homes to know that the family rooms would face the courtyard and gardens inside.

Among the residences stood a small temple. It must be very old, because the sides were of stuccoed brick—only the façade had a marble veneer. It was well kept, which was unusual for a neighborhood temple. The stone was white instead of gray from ages of city grime, and two workmen on a scaffold were touching up the pediment reliefs with red and blue paint.

"Stop!" said Tenoctris suddenly. "Where are we? Stop, please, there's something wrong!"

Sharina glanced over her shoulder. Tenoctris still held the sliver she'd been using as a wand, but the desk had slipped off her lap. Her face had the wide-eyed look of someone awakened from a nightmare.

Sharina stuck her head out. "Stop the coach!" she shouted. She didn't know if the driver could hear her over the rumble of the tires.

She'd have opened the door, but the guard was in the way. Instead, she wormed her whole torso through the window, and said, "Stop now!"

"Whoa!" bellowed Undercaptain Ascor, riding on the driver's bench. He grabbed the reins and heaved back hard. Unlike the driver, he didn't have gauntlets. Nobles generally had experience with horses, driving them as well as riding, while in Barca's Hamlet nobody did; even the plowing was done by oxen.

The two horses rose onto their haunches, protesting with shrill whickers. The carriage bumped them from behind, slamming them forward in the traces. The off mare skidded and almost lost her footing. Behind the vehicle, the cavalry escort milled and shouted curses.

The guard jumped to the pavement. One of his fellows on the roof handed down the shield and javelin he hadn't been able to hold while he rode on the step. Sharina flung open the carriage door.

"What's happening, your highness?" Ascor demanded. He looked back toward the commander of the escort, who was shouting questions. In a wholly different voice, he snarled, "Shut your bloody mouth, you baboon! I'm talking to the princess!"

"Tenoctris?" Sharina said. The wizard had edged to the door to get out, so Sharina hopped down to give her room.

"Is there a temple?" Tenoctris said. "Yes, there it is! Please, I want to go into it. I think there's something very wrong. There's forces here that aren't natural. And I think it's a recent thing as well."

"Second platoon, dismount!" the escort commander said, as Sharina helped Tenoctris out of the carriage. The Blood Eagles who'd been on the roof of the vehicle were forcing back the servants. Both groups were trying to do their jobs, but because the thing happening—whatever it was— was unexpected, the soldiers had decided that civilians no longer had any business with the two women.

Ascor raised an eyebrow toward Sharina; she nodded. "Right, let's take a look," Ascor said. "Straight up the steps, your highness?"

"Yes, if you please," said Tenoctris, replying to Sharina's glance. The entourage started forward like a wave curling shoreward. The escort led and swept to either side, while the black-armored bodyguards formed an inner casing around the nugget of the two women in the center.

The temple was less than forty feet across. An altar stood in front of a simple three-step base up to a porch supported by six unfluted pillars. Instead of a slotted screen in front of the sanctum, allowing those outside to see the God's statue, there was a two-valve wooden door.

The painters turned to look at the commotion in the street. Together they dropped down the ropes to the temple porch instead of lowering the scaffold in normal fashion. One called a warning in a language Sharina didn't recognize.

"Hold where you are!" Ascor said. He and his men held close to the women—meaning they were moving no faster than Tenoctris could shuffle—but the troopers of the escort broke into a run.

The temple door opened, allowing the workmen to dart inside. Another man looked out through the crack in the door. He had regular features, but his skin was white. His hair was an almost invisible blond, and the irises of his eyes were so pale they almost merged with his corneas.

The temple door slammed.

"By the Lady!" shouted the commander of the escort. "I've seen those devils before! That was one of the People, boys!"

"Master Cashel," Enfero whispered. He didn't point, but his eyes were on Mab as she and Herron discussed the food they'd carry. "She is the same one, isn't she? Mab, I mean?"

Cashel followed the boy's line of sight. He frowned, because there didn't seem to be any doubt.

"Sure," he said. "I mean, she doesn't ever look the same twice running, but the way she moves is always the same. And besides, there's her fingernails."

They'd gathered on Ronn's highest terrace, going over their baggage. To the north were the hills, black even with the sun on them. There were citizens all around, more people maybe than had been in the Assembly Hall the night before. This whole crowd had come to see the Sons leaving, if you could really call it leaving when they were just going down to the cellars of the building they lived in.

Granted it was a really big building.

"Lots of women in Ronn paint their nails that way," Orly protested. The Sons carried real swords, but they weren't wearing armor. Mab had said it'd just be in the way on this trip. "Most of them do, in fact."

Orly and Stasslin had been standing close enough to overhear. From the way they'd glanced at each other before Enfero spoke, the three of them had talked the question over between themselves.

"Not like hers," Cashel said. Sometimes people played games with words, thinking they were making fun of him. Maybe that was happening here, because surely even city folk could see the difference between the enamel other women used and Mab's fingers shining like light itself.

Right then Mab had gray hair and a slim, straight build—something like what Ilna might look like in thirty or forty years, Cashel guessed. When she pointed, her nails seemed to trail a path even through the bright sunlight.

"Master Cashel?" Enfero said again. "We thought that maybe there were different women using the same name instead of one person with different looks. But you don't think that's what it is?"

"No," Cashel said. "I don't."

He cleared his throat, and went on, "But if it was that way, I guess it'd be even better having that many more people on our side. Wizards, that is. We might want them."

Orly burst into laughter. "You're a wonderful philosopher, Master Cashel," he said. "Always driving straight to the heart of the problem."

Cashel wasn't sure whether Orly was mocking him, so he got out his pad of wool and began polishing his quarterstaff. It really didn't seem like mocking, but Cashel couldn't see what else it could be. He wasn't a scholar, that was sure; and he was pretty sure a philosopher was a scholar.

Mab and Herron walked over. Athan and Manza, who'd been listening to their argument, followed in their wake. "I've convinced Master Herron that though he feels strong enough to carry a whole mountain of equipment now," Mab said, "this will very quickly change. You're better off with a knapsack of food and your swords. Even those will be heavy enough by the second day."

"But how do we sleep, then?" Stasslin said in frowning surprise. "We're not going to find bedding on the way, are we?"

"No, you're not," Mab said, with a smile that reminded Cashel of his sister's expression when she was talking to a fool. "But it never gets very cold in the lower levels, quite the contrary in fact. I believe you'll find you can make do when you're tired enough. Which you will be."

Cashel put the wool away. "How much food do you figure, ma'am?" he asked, paying attention for the first time to the pile of things Herron had been planning to take.

He grinned too. There were cots in that pile, and more cookware than Ilna had in her whole kitchen in Barca's Hamlet. And there was heaven knows what all else.

"Three days' supply," Mab said. "That should get us there and partway back if things go as I expect. I've prepared packs for all of you."

She nodded toward another, smaller collection. The lined-up knapsacks were of some slick black fabric that Ilna'd like to see. Maybe he'd be able to take some back for her when all this was over. "Including you, Cashel," Mab said.

Cashel patted the big leather wallet on his belt with a broad grin. He'd filled it with bread and cheese after the meal they'd just eaten.

"Ma'am," he said, "I'm used to carrying my meals like this. Straps on my back might get in the way if, you know, I had to do something."

He didn't much like the local cheese, even though he'd found it filling. It didn't have much spirit to it. Cashel had grown up on whey cheese because it was cheap. The cakes were flat and so hard that you had to moisten them to bite off a chunk. Most folks wouldn't have liked whey cheese, he supposed, but a mouthful then would've taken Cashel back to where life was simpler.

His face'd sobered, but now he grinned again. The quarterstaff in his hand was a better memory for the purpose, he guessed. Life was always simple enough when he had a chance to use his quarterstaff.

"Take your packs then, Sons of the Heroes," Mab said to the youths. She was smiling, but the expression was as sad as anything he'd seen on her face during their short acquaintance. "Take your packs, and may whatever Gods there are help you and help Ronn."

Mab started toward the shaft that would take them to bedrock, as far as she'd said it was safe to descend that way. To get lower, they'd walk.

The Sons shuffled to the knapsacks, hesitating to choose among things that Cashel was pretty sure were all the same. When they saw Mab well ahead of them, walking through the crowd that'd opened for her, each snatched up a pack and carried it by the straps without waiting to put it on properly. Cashel followed behind. He glanced repeatedly over his shoulder though he didn't figure there was going to be any problem, at least until they'd gotten out of the shaft.

The people of Ronn started to cheer: a few voices at first, and then the whole huge crowd. They shrieked all sorts of things from, "Hurrah!" to "May the Gods bless and keep you!" It was easy to shout, of course, and it really didn't mean much; but the Sons' shoulders straightened, and their strides grew quicker as they stepped onto the platform waiting to take them down.

Cheering didn't mean much; but maybe it was the one thing the citizens of Ronn could do that would save these poor hopeful boys; and through them, the city. Cashel beamed like the sun overhead as he followed his companions on the first stage of their journey away from that sun—and perhaps back.

The wind was fitfully from the north. Ilna and her companions had smelled woodsmoke for most of the morning as they tramped across the rolling plain, but they were nearly on the little community before Ilna realized that the smoke rose not from cookfires but from the crushed remains of the houses.

Then she smelled death: recent, but it'd been a hot day, and the slaughter was very considerable. The chest-high drystone wall around the whole community was slammed inward at the south end, overthrown with a violence that'd flung stones the size of a man's chest a double pace from where they'd lain in the wall.

There'd been four stone houses with thatched roofs, round-ended and longer than they were broad. The track of destruction, which began at the outer wall, continued through the houses, smashing them into total ruin. At the north end of the community the wall was opened again, this time outward. The creature had departed, leaving only death and wreckage behind.

"I pray that the Gods are real," said Davus harshly. "So that they can build a Hell to hold the thing that now reigns as king but does not do a king's duty to the land!"

Birds rose from their feast, mostly crows and vultures but including a few cranes, whose long beaks would've found food others couldn't reach. Squawks of peevish anger replaced the muted caws and clucks Ilna'd heard as she approached. There'd been enough carrion for all in the village, so the scavengers hadn't needed to fight.

Davus placed a stone in the pocket of his sash and prepared to sling it. Chalcus touched his arm. "Save it," he said. "We don't want to eat them, and we can't kill them all. It's better not to start."

Davus shuddered but nodded agreement. They'd reached the hole in the wall, but none of them chose to enter.

"It was bad luck," Davus said quietly. "It must've come in the last watch of the night. Everyone would've been asleep. There'd have been no warning."

"What 'it'?" Ilna said. "What did this?"

"A troll like the one we waked from the bluffs," Davus said. "Very possibly the same troll."

He looked at the village a moment longer, then rubbed his eyes with both hands. "Trolls hate all life that isn't stone like them," he said. "They don't move very fast, as you saw, and they're stupid. The villagers could've led it away if they'd seen it coming, tricked it into following one of them who'd have hidden when he'd drawn it out of sight. It was just bad luck."

Two houses had burned out completely when the thatch was crushed down onto remains of the hearthfires. The other two had not, but the troll's slashing stone arms had made a job of destroying them. Ilna remembered the way the creature had paused to smash to splinters the tree it'd chanced against as it staggered away from the cliff.

Here the victims had been sheep and humans. The troll had held a man—she thought it had been a man—by the ankles and flailed him several times against the compound wall. Everything upward from mid-chest was splashed over the stones or on the ground outside.

Ilna thought of suggesting burying the remains, but there were scores like him in or around the other huts. They simply didn't have time.

And anyway, it was just meat. That was the only way to think about what had happened here.

Chalcus shrugged. "You two go on around and find a place to camp. Get a fire started."

He nodded to the flattened hamlet, then added "I'll find us something to eat."

"What is it that you mean to do?" Davus said. His voice was low, but it was no more calm than the growl of a dog about to lunge—and no more friendly.

"Gently, friend," Chalcus said as if he was stroking a child. "There'll be stored grain that we can take with no harm to those who stored it, I think. No meat, not even what might've been cured beforetimes. Eh?"

"Sorry," said Davus. "I'm on edge, and it makes me foolish. Sorry."

Davus started off, skirting the wall to the left. A pine grew from between two exposed blocks of stone. The lower half of one slab was dark with seeping moisture.

"Chalcus?" Ilna said. "We can do without the food, you know."

"Aye, love, I know that," the sailor said. He gave her a lopsided smile and nodded to the ruins. The birds were settling again, having decided the humans weren't enough of a threat to interfere with a feast like the present one. "I don't mind. I've seen worse, you know."

His mobile, laughing face was briefly that of a man dead for a month. "I've done worse, truth to tell; though those days are behind me now. Or so I hope."

He patted her hip gently. "Go help Davus with the fire, and I'll be along in a little bit with the makings of ash cake, as we have no pot for porridge."

Ilna touched Chalcus on the cheek, then rejoined Davus, who waited a little way along. Meeting Davus' still, observant eyes, she blurted, "He's a *good* man." She knew she sounded defensive, and she hated the weakness that had driven her to speak.

"Yes," said Davus, seeming to transfer his attention to the three chips of quartz he was juggling. "And if the truth were known, it might be that a wrathful man like me has more on his conscience than Master Chalcus does"—he met Ilna's eyes—"black though the sins of his former life may have been."

He understands, Ilna thought. And because Davus understood, it was just possible that what he said was literally true; as it might have been for Ilna herself—black though the sins of Chalcus' former life undoubtedly were.

"What's there to be done about a creature that did this?" Ilna said, nodding toward the ruin as they passed its northern edge. "What can be done to a troll?"

"By ordinary folk?" Davus said, quirking a smile. "By you or me? Little enough, I fear. Run away, for it's not quick. Lure it off and hide, as the folk here might've done; for trolls aren't bright either."

The pine's branches for a man's height up the trunk were dead. Davus eyed them, then gripped one at midpoint and snapped it cleanly. He squatted and with a frost-split hammerstone began pounding the wood to kindling.

"But the Old King . . . ," Davus continued, as Ilna examined the spring. There was a basin under the seepage, a quite adequate one as soon as she cleaned out the leaf litter. "He had a jewel over his forehead. It gave him power over stone, control of all sorts: power to direct and to loose and to bind."

He looked up and added, "The Old King would've changed the troll back to a boulder. If it hadn't gotten far from the cliffs—and trolls generally didn't get far in his day—he'd have sent it back to those cliffs first. Letting it be with its kind, you see, so long as it couldn't harm men."

"What happened to the jewel?" Ilna said. The slaughter that'd happened here, massacre of the village, must've bothered her more than she cared to realize. When she heard her words, she knew the answer and spoke it: "The new king has it. The creature, Nergura said it was."

Davus struck sparks expertly into his pile of tinder, using a flint and a thumb-sized crystal of fool's gold that he must've found unnoticed along the way. He smiled in satisfaction at the smoke twisting from his fireset, then looked at Ilna, and said, "Yes, the creature. In a manner of speaking I suppose it's only fair. The jewel is the creature's own egg, you see."

"Egg?" Ilna repeated sharply. "Then it's going to hatch into more of the things?"

Davus bent over, feeding larger fragments of the branch to the wood fibers that he'd used for tinder. He chuckled. "No," he said, "not that one, any more than the hen's egg you boil for dinner is going to start clucking. The power is there regardless, but trying to use it with the egg still alive is"—the chuckle returned, deeper and grim as a death knell—"a good way to guarantee that you'll not live to the end of the spell yourself. Or at least that was the story that people told in my day."

Ilna looked over her shoulder. Chalcus was leaving the hamlet with a jaunty step and a basket balanced on his left shoulder.

"Ah, we'll feast like lords and ladies tonight, my friends!" the sailor called when he found Ilna's eyes on him. "Wheat and beans and *honey,* a whole comb, wrapped in a palm frond and fit for the greatest king in all this fine world, I'm sure!"

"Perhaps the Old King spared the mother because he'd slain her child, the egg," Davus said softly as he built up the fire. "That's the sort of thing a man might do but a king should not, allowing sentiment to affect his rule. Who knows what's in a man's heart?"

"Who indeed," Ilna said. "He was a sentimentalist, your Old King?"

"Him?" Davus scoffed. "Not him! He was a choleric fellow with a quick tongue and a hard hand. But justice mattered to him, and perhaps his sense of what was just led him into the error of sparing an enemy."

"If that's what happened," said Ilna, "then his choice had a bad result; but not so bad, I think, as the result of deciding to ignore justice."

She rose to her feet smiling—broadly for her—and took the basket of scavenged foodstuffs from Chalcus. She had to believe in justice, because without a sense of justice there was no difference between the Ilna os-Kenset of today and the woman who'd come back from Hell, bringing that Hell along with her.

If that was the case, then Ilna and all the world besides were better off dead.

Garric, bending over the pile of clean linens folded on the handbarrow, followed Liane along the corridor. Though it was still an hour short of dawn, most of the hall lamps had burned to glows.

Garric was surprised to see that lamp above the door to his own suite was as dim as the others. The Blood Eagles were usually much more punctilious about their duties—and lighting the faces of those approaching Prince Garric's room was very much a part of their duties.

"This isn't right," said Carus, quizzical and mildly irritated at a failure of discipline. Then, in a voice without any emotion at all, he said, *"It's an ambush, but don't run, on your life don't run; they've got javelins, and you've only got a dagger."*

But my sword's in the anteroom of the suite, Garric thought. Using the linens for cover as he continued to pace forward, he slid the dagger out from under his tunic and held it flat beneath the left pole of the barrow. *Perhaps they'll wait for us to enter instead of attacking in the corridor, where they might be interrupted.*

The eight guards were twenty feet away and, as Carus noted, all but the undercaptain commanding the squad had javelins. If Garric and Liane turned to run, they'd be spitted like chickens for roasting before they got three steps toward safety at the turn of the hallway.

"When you get the door unlatched," Garric muttered, hoping that Liane could make out his words, "get in and get clear."

"All right," Liane whispered back. Her pace, a sullen shuffle, didn't change.

The watch would've changed at midnight, so the features beneath the black helmets properly weren't those of the Blood Eagles on duty when he and Liane went out. Garric, watching as best he could with his face bent down, didn't recognize any of them.

"They're none of them men I've ever seen before. The uniforms are right, but they're not Blood Eagles," Carus said, seeing through Garric's eyes. That put the seal on what Garric had known in his heart—in the pit of his stomach—already.

The guards were all watching him. That wasn't right: two men should've been looking the other way down the corridor in case the "servants" were a deliberate distraction.

Garric had expected to be recognized on his return tonight—well, this morning—despite the proper pass stamped with the wax bulla of his personal secretary, Liane bos-Benliman. Being identified at that point wouldn't have mattered much. Attaper would probably hear about it and complain in forceful terms about what Garric had done, but he couldn't stop what'd already happened. Garric *hadn't* expected the guards to be waiting for him, though. But of course these weren't guards.

Liane held out the pass, a palm-sized potsherd with the information brushed in ink on the inner side. She bent her head away with the shy propriety of a modest girl meeting a group of men.

The man wearing the white horsehair crest of an officer grunted, "Go on." He didn't touch the pass or demand that Liane and Garric look him in the eye.

Garric caught the scent of decay. It was very faint, but he was sure of it.

"Dead men," Carus said, his image tense and grinning. *"Cattle and horses smell different, not so bad; but dead mules stink even worse."*

Liane reached for the latch lever calmly, then snatched it down and leaped inside. Laundry spilled from the handbarrow as Garric followed her, dropping the handles so that his dagger was free.

He tried to slam the door shut behind him but a heavy body hit it from the other side before the latch clicked. An arm pushed through the gap, swinging a sword blindly.

Garric slashed through the elbow tendons. The forearm sagged at the joint, then dropped to the floor. The muscles were rotten tatters hanging from the bones, oozing putrescent fluid.

Garric's sword dangled in its scabbard from the back of the chair in which a servant was intended to sit in case the prince needed something during the night. As Garric reached across his body to draw the longer weapon, the weight of several men crashed into the door panel. They threw him backward, off-balance with the tip of the blade still caught in the sheath. Three black-armored guards shoved in, one slightly in front. His javelin was raised to thrust through Garric's chest.

Liane hurled the bedroom lamp into the guard's face. Oil splashed as the three-headed silver dragon bounced away. The one lighted wick didn't ignite the spilled fuel, but it blinded the guard for the instant Garric needed to stab up through his throat.

Garric's dagger point jammed in the guard's spine at the base of the skull. He let go of the hilt and grabbed the chair with his left hand, then skipped backward into the doorway between the anteroom and the main part of the suite. He had the sword clear now.

The guard with the dagger in his throat fell forward. The appearance of normal flesh sloughed away, leaving a corpse so decayed that both arms separated from the shoulder blades when the torso hit the floor.

Two more guards came on, their spears raised over their shoulders. The remainder of the detachment bunched behind them. The one on the left thrust. Garric caught the javelin point on the chair seat. He twisted chair and spear to the right as he lunged low, stabbing the other guard beneath the cuirass.

His sword grated into the hip joint. On a human enemy—and the guards *weren't* human, whatever they'd been in life—Garric's thrust would've severed the great artery in the thigh. He jerked his point free in a gush of decay, not blood, but the effect seemed to be the same: the guard's body rotated as his leg collapsed. It was a rotted corpse by the time it hit the floor.

Thought would've made Garric retreat a step into the bedroom so that he could use the doorway to constrict his enemies. He wasn't thinking. There wasn't time for thought, only for the instincts his warrior ancestor had honed in vicious battles a millennium past. He drove forward again, hacking through the leg of the guard who'd let go of his stuck javelin to draw his sword. Garric's stroke threw the guard sideways, over the body of his fellow. The fluids of their decay mixed as their stinking corpses partially disintegrated.

Then Garric jumped back. He was gasping through his open mouth, and his lungs were on fire. Guards pushed forward, slipping on the bodies of those who'd been in the lead.

"Watch out!" Liane screamed. She and the male servant banged the door into its jamb, brushing Garric's left arm because he wasn't quick enough to get clear. The female servant slid the bar through the staples.

Bodies hit the door from the other side, but the panel was sturdy and through-bolts anchored the staples. Garric bent forward to breathe with the least constriction. Liane and the servants were doing something, sliding a couch against the door, he supposed, but all he saw for the moment was the blurred grain of the cherrywood door panel. There was nothing he needed to see just then, so his body was putting all its effort into recovering in order to meet the next test.

Sharper blows shook the door. A spear butt squealed through a crack, which widened as the guard levered his shaft sideways. A sword and another spear butt struck the panel together, breaking a board out of the core, which had been covered on both sides by veneer.

250 / D a v i d   D r a k e

Garric backed a step. A guard reached through the opening to pull the bar. Garric thrust, aiming for his throat. His point glanced off the flare of the guard's helmet but gashed flesh through the shoulder straps. The arm jerked back quickly.

Two more guards rammed the door with their shoulders. The panel bowed inward between the upper and lower cross braces. Garric lifted the chair to use it as a shield again. The javelin had cracked the seat, only half remained attached to the back.

Guards smashed through the door, swords raised. Liane hurled a quilt over the first pair. Garric thrust home and jerked his blade free in a cloud of white goosedown. His ears rang with shouts and the thunder of his own blood.

Garric backed and stabbed again, hitting a gorget but punching through the thin bronze in a gush of foulness. The guard collapsed, but the anteroom was full of black-armored bodies. There were more in the hall trying to force their way in. It was going to be over very quickly.

Garric stepped forward again, his legs wobbly but his decay-smeared blade thrusting straight for the next guard in the doorway. This one parried expertly, locking Garric's crossguard with his own. Garric tried to knee the guard in the groin, but his bare foot slipped in fetor and he went down instead. It was over now beyond question, but Garric dropped the chair and seized the guard's sword wrist with his left hand.

"Your highness!" Lord Attaper cried. "Your highness!"

Garric's eyes focused: he was struggling with the commander of his bodyguards. The other men, in the anteroom and now slipping past Garric and Attaper to search for further dangers within the suite, were real Blood Eagles. In the corridor behind, Blaise armsmen shouted questions.

Garric tried to wheeze a greeting. The word wouldn't come out. He'd have fallen sideways if Attaper hadn't held him up.

"What in the Sister's name is going on!" Attaper said.

Garric could only shake his head. He was smiling, though. The only thing he was sure of was that he was still alive; but that in itself was reason to smile.

Chapter Twelve

I swear I didn't have anything to do with it!" Earl Wildulf said, sweating profusely. He tried to drink but found his mug empty. With his face twisted into a snarl he turned to shout at the servants whose job it was to keep those at the table supplied—and remembered that Garric hadn't permitted servants into the conference room.

Wildulf got up and stepped to the wine jars along the wall, repeating, but in a chastened voice, "I *swear* I didn't."

"I assure you, milord," Garric said, "that nobody in this room believes that you called up a squad of corpses to murder me."

"I wouldn't be so sure about your wife, though," Attaper said, with a grim eye on the earl. "Or that wizard of hers, anyway."

"Balila wouldn't have done that!" Wildulf snapped, though the anger in his voice as he filled his mug proved that he'd been thinking the same thing. Instead of mixing water in equal or greater amount with the wine in normal fashion, he slurped down half of what he'd just poured straight. Even angry and defensive, he hadn't bothered to deny the accusation leveled at Dipsas.

"Countess Balila and her wizard weren't involved in the attack," Liane said calmly, sorting through documents she'd taken out of the traveling desk. It was the only thing she'd brought from the suite that she and Garric had abandoned for what had been an office corridor on the second floor.

Liane half smiled. "I don't say that out of any affection for Mistress Dipsas. Blaming the wrong party prevents us from identifying the real threat, and I have trustworthy information as to where those two ladies were tonight."

They were in what had been the private office of Earl Wildulf's treasurer, a commoner named Ardnon who probably wouldn't be best pleased in the morning when he learned that his Bureau of Revenue had been ousted to provide living quarters for Prince Garric and the entire detachment of Blood Eagles accompanying him. The troops were cleaning out the other rooms on the corridor, and from what Garric had seen they were doing so with greater thoroughness than care. Desks, files, and other furnishings were all going into the back stairwell, leaving Attaper's men only one direction to guard.

Wildulf himself and Marshal Renold were the sole Sandrakkan officials present, facing not only Garric and his councillors but six Blood Eagles as well. The earl kept trying to grasp his sword hilt. The guards had disarmed him and Renold; every time Wildulf's hand closed on nothing, rage flushed his face.

"My men were asleep," Attaper growled, looking through a window out over the dark city. His profile was stony. "The real midnight relief, I mean. Look, I'm not making excuses, but"—he grimaced and forced himself to meet Garric's eyes—"I think there must've been wizardry involved. Somebody got in and took their weapons and equipment without them waking up. I can't believe they were just derelict."

"Of course there was wizardry!" Garric said. "No blame attaches to you or your men, milord. And I need scarcely point out that you *did* save my life and Lady Liane's. I was on my last legs when you arrived to finish the assassins."

He wished now that he'd kept Tenoctris by him. Though the Shepherd alone knew what was going on in Ornifal. He'd weighed the choices when he sent Tenoctris with Sharina and Waldron, and the chances were still good he'd made the right decision.

Attaper looked like a rocky crag trying to smile. "I don't know about your legs, your highness," he said, "but your hands were still in good shape. I have the bruises"—he raised his right wrist, which Garric had grabbed as he tried to wrest away Attaper's sword—"to prove it."

"Do we know who the attackers were?" said Lord Tadai, cutting through an exchange that was so far removed from his life that he thought it was meaningless. "That is, they were dead men who, I gather, didn't look dead at the time, but surely the bodies came from somewhere?"

"Serjeant Bastin was talking to an old buddy who's serving in the local garrison," Lord Rosen said unexpectedly. "The fellow says he recognized one of them as a housebreaker who'd been hung three months back. The body'd have been buried in the potter's field or whatever they call it here in Erdin."

Marshal Renold nodded glumly. "The Sister's Hundred, west of the city wall," he said. "All unclaimed bodies go there, not just people who're executed. They're dumped in a trench and covered at nightfall every day. Nobody'd notice if a few were taken out after dark."

"Wizardry!" Wildulf said, half-despairing and half-furious. Lord Attaper nodded forcefully in agreement

Liane looked up from the beechwood notebook she'd been reading, holding it close to the light of the candle lamp she'd set on the table before her. "Earl Wildulf?" she said. "Two years ago"—when Liane was being taught at Mistress Gudea's Academy for Girls, here in Erdin—"the best collection of Old Kingdom manuscripts in Erdin was the library attached to the Temple of the Shielding Shepherd. Is that still the case?"

Garric noticed that Liane dismissed empty complaints about wizardry as brusquely as Lord Tadai had trampled through the camaraderie of warriors reliving past battles. She and Tadai were correct, of course: there was serious business to conduct and no time for small talk. Yet it was small talk that eased the friction of folk squeezed together in hard times, and these times were hard beyond question.

He grinned wryly. Sometimes it was a mistake to be too correct.

"Library?" the earl repeated, frowning as he tried to get his mind around the concept. "I don't know. Renold, do you . . . ?"

"I could ask someone," the marshal said, frowning in turn. "My wife's secretary, he's the sort who'd know, I think."

"I think we can take it that there've been no changes in governmental policy toward the library since you left Erdin, milady," Garric said, grinning a little wider. "And I assume a major fire would've attracted attention also. Are you looking for a particular document?"

"I hope there may be more information on the cataclysm that struck Erdin a thousand years ago," Liane said. "Besides the Bridge Island account, that is. Perhaps if we knew more about what happened then, we'd have a better notion of what we're facing today."

Her reserved stiffness melted in a smile. "I can't help with wizardry," she said, sweeping her gaze across the room. "But I can search records as well as Tenoctris, or almost as well. And it's *something* to do."

"Yes," said Garric. *Something to do instead of waiting for an enemy to strike again from the darkness.* "Yes indeed."

He rose to his feet. Dawn was breaking, turning pink the side of the building visible through the west-facing windows. "I don't think there's anything more to be gained by discussing what happened tonight," he said.

"Last night. Lady Liane, do you want to wait till later in the day to visit the library, or—"

"No," said Liane forcefully. She cleared her throat, and went on, "That is, I certainly don't intend to go to bed. I wouldn't be able to sleep. Though I'll need the help of the library staff, and they won't be present at this hour, I'm sure."

"Nor could I sleep," said Garric. He'd only napped before going down into the caves beneath the palace, and he'd fought an exhausting battle besides; but he *certainly* wouldn't sleep just yet. "But I would like to bathe. With luck"—he nodded to Wildulf, who he thought would understand "—I'll scrub off some of the memories as well as what splashed me during the fight."

He looked around the room more generally. "Lord Tadai, Admiral Zettin," he said. "You and your staffs will continue working with Earl Wildulf and his officials on the details of Sandrakkan's return to full membership in the kingdom. If there're any questions for me, I'll deal with them when I return from the Temple of the Shielding Shepherd, where I'll be accompanying Lady Liane."

"And where I'll be accompanying both of you," said Lord Attaper grimly. "And every bloody one of my men will be with us!"

Cashel wasn't afraid of heights—or long drops either, which'd been more to the point when he gathered guillemot eggs on the sheer islets off the coast of Haft. Even so it made his lips purse to look down from the top of the . . . well, what would you call it?

"Ma'am?" he said aloud. "Mistress Mab? Is this a cave we're going down into?"

"An artificial cave," Mab said. "It was the Lower Commons, back in the days when men lived on these levels. The Upper Commons is the plaza on the roof of the city, and the king carved this from the fabric of mountain itself while he was building the Ronn."

The Sons had been looking down into the cavern, all but Manza, who'd taken one glance and jerked back from the railing. When Mab spoke, they'd turned to watch her instead. None of them spoke, but they didn't look comfortable.

Truth to tell, Cashel didn't like the view either. It was less the height than the shadows, gray on gray on gray—and none of them soft shades like those of a normal twilight.

Aloud he said, "Well, there's water, at least. I could use a drink."

"After I purify it," Mab said in a thin undertone. "This high it might be all right; but again, it might not. I don't care to take chances."

So speaking, she took what seemed a flat disk from the purse on her belt and gave it a shake. The plate slipped into a cup, its slanting walls locked open in tiny steps.

Mab walked toward the watercourse that cascaded over the rim of the gallery and fell by a series of pools into the far distance. Cashel followed, balancing his staff crossways before him. As he'd expected, the Sons fell in behind—Herron leading and the rest following after.

He looked across the cavern again. He wasn't sure he could see the other side, the place was that big, but white arrows in the distance were the flumes of more little cataracts like the one near where they'd come out of the rock-cut tunnel leading from the shaft that'd dropped them through the crystal part of Ronn.

The great cavity wasn't completely empty, though: paths slanted out into it. Some were wide enough for a cart, often with water running through a channel down the middle, but a lot of them looked so narrow that people'd have to walk one ahead of another. Sometimes they crossed each other like the cords of a spiderweb, and generally they dropped either by gentle ramps or a flight of stairs and another waterfall.

The Sons were whispering among themselves, wondering if they'd be going down that way soon. Cashel supposed they would, though of course Mab might have another notion entirely. He didn't bother asking her; they'd learn soon enough.

Mab knelt at a stone coping more like the mill flume in Barca's Hamlet than a stream bank. She dipped her cup full of water. It looked clear as it ran down the channel—you could see bits of leaf litter from the upper levels tumbling along in the swift current—but it started to bubble when it filled the cup. Cashel smelled brimstone and a hint of decay.

Mab held the cup out in her right hand and stroked the air with her left index finger. Cashel could've repeated the pattern himself—he was good with those things, just as good as Ilna, though he didn't have his sister's feeling for fabrics.

He couldn't have described what he saw in words, though, and he wasn't sure that even somebody who really *knew* words like Garric and Sharina could've done that thing. Mab's tracery was something that you had to feel, not hear about.

The water flashed red. A skim of ice appeared on the top. For just an instant the veins in the ice were the same as the figure Mab had drawn. The bad smell vanished like thistledown in a flame.

Mab handed the cup to Cashel, smiling archly. He took it and sipped; the ice had melted to a rind even before his lips touched it.

He wasn't sure what the water'd taste like, not that it really mattered. On hot summer days while plowing he'd drunk ditchwater, kneeling beside his oxen. In fact it was cool and sparkled, as refreshing as a long draft of bitters from Reise's inn. His eyes met Mab's; her smile had grown wider, like she knew what he'd been wondering.

"Really good, ma'am," he said, turning to hand the cup to Herron.

"You've only had a mouthful," Mab said. "Drink more."

"Ma'am, there's a lot of us," Cashel said. "And it's not a big cup."

"Nor has it gone down any from the drink you've taken, you might notice," Mab replied tartly. "Drink your fill, then pass it on."

Cashel couldn't help looking into the cup, but that was just reflex: if Mab said he could walk over the edge of this gallery without falling, it'd be the truth. He drank more, not his fill but three big swallows taken slowly. Then he passed the cup to Herron, saying, "Don't drink too much the first time, any of you. We'll pass it around again, after the first settles in our stomachs."

The Sons drank deeply, ignoring his advice. Well, he'd thought they would. It shouldn't matter.

"When we start down," Mab said as the cup went to Orly, the last, "be careful of what you may meet. And, of course, don't fall. The paths are solid, but the railings may not be. They weren't part of the king's plan, and the citizens who added them after the king's exile weren't able to build for the ages the way he'd done."

"Why did you tell us not to wear our armor if we're going to be meeting the Made Men?" Stasslin asked. Cashel wouldn't have used that tone to anybody, let alone the lady who was helping them.

Cashel had one butt of his quarterstaff on the floor by his right foot. He leaned the staff forward, and said in a loud voice, "I'll have another drink now, Orly, if you're done with the water."

Orly had paused with the cup halfway to his lips. Instead of handing it to Cashel, he said, "She didn't say we'd be fighting Made Men, Stasslin. She said to be careful."

"Yes," said Mab. She looked at Stasslin with a cold expression much more threatening than Orly's anger. "If you're going to put words in someone's mouth, make them pleasant ones; boy."

The deliberate pause before 'boy' made Stasslin flush. "Look, I just meant . . . ," he began, and stopped, probably because he couldn't think of where to go from there.

Cashel took the cup from Orly's hand, mostly to cool things off a bit. He drank, and said, "Stasslin, I learned when I was a boy that if you're stupid, you're best off keeping your mouth shut. I try to live by that."

Cashel offered the cup to Herron, who waved it away. "Anybody want more?" he said. Nobody spoke.

"Then we're ready to start down," Mab said. She gestured to a path, one of the wider ones, that slid into the cavern some fifty double paces away on the other side of the little creek. With her left hand she lifted the cup from Cashel's hand and folded it flat again. Though she didn't pour out the water first, nothing splashed on the pavement.

There was a humpbacked bridge over the creek, but Cashel jumped the channel since it wasn't as wide as he was tall. He glanced back as Mab followed, then frowned in surprise. She didn't jump, exactly; at least it didn't look like she had. She scissored her legs and she was across, that was all.

The Sons were all going to the bridge, so Cashel and Mab walked to the path alone. "Who told you you were stupid, Cashel?" she asked.

"Lots of people, ma'am," Cashel said. He let a slow grin spread over his face. "Not after I got my growth, though. Not twice, anyhow."

"Sometimes people need to have their errors beaten out of them," Mab said in a quiet voice trembling over fury. "I'm afraid there aren't enough of us to do all the necessary beating, but we have to try."

Cashel looked at her in concern, but her face was calm enough. They'd reached the walkway before the others, so he paused.

Mab nodded. "Yes, we'll wait," she said. Pointing down, she added, "Do you see the fish hanging in the air below that broad catwalk? Midway to the surface."

Cashel squinted to see better. "I think so, yes," he said. It was fish-shaped, anyway, but as far down as it was it must've been bigger than he was. It was moving, squirming furiously and rising headfirst toward the path. That wasn't just a trick of the bad light.

He puzzled the question through in his mind, and asked, "Ma'am, do fish fly in this place?"

"No, though we may well see stranger things," Mab said. "There!"

A spider dropped along a strand of silk unseen in the dimness, scrabbled at the fish for a moment with its four front legs, and climbed quickly out of sight again beneath the walkway. The fish resumed its jerky upward journey, but it'd stopped wriggling.

"The king's influence has leaked into these lower levels during the millennium of his exile," Mab said. "The way filth drains into the bilges of a ship. Neither the king nor his creations have entered Ronn, not yet; but here in the lower levels the insects and plants and the fish in the ornamental pools have changed. In the directions that the king would've wished."

The Sons had caught up to them again. They'd been whispering among themselves as they crossed the bridge, but now they fell silent as they listened to Mab and Cashel.

Cashel looked at them, feeling his face grow harder than usual when his eyes fell on Stasslin. The burly Son frowned for an instant, but then looked away.

What good would your breastplate be if that spider grabbed you? Cashel thought, but he didn't say anything. The spider and the prey it'd netted in one of the pools were out of sight, and scaring the Sons worse than they already were wouldn't help anything.

Cashel smiled in sudden warmth. Aloud he said, "You fellows aren't used to this sort of thing. You're doing real good."

"Watch yourselves," Mab said again, nodding to the Sons as a group, then to Cashel. She stepped onto the walkway. It spiraled down for quite some distance, then split into three separate paths that slanted off. Cashel put himself a half step ahead of her, where he could move fast without having to worry about friends being in the way of his staff.

"Mistress Mab?" said Orly. He seemed to be the one who did the most thinking. "You said the lower levels are turning into the way the king would have them. But the king *built* Ronn, didn't he? And he didn't build it like this."

"The king was a very great wizard," Mab said. "Was and is. Greater than the queen in many ways: he could create what she could only maintain. But the king had to change things in order to live, and eventually he changed himself. He couldn't turn himself back, any more than an addled egg can become fresh again. And so the queen ousted him, for the sake of Ronn and the citizens of Ronn."

Cashel saw movement on a distant catwalk. He thought it was water flowing till it raised its head and tasted the air with its tongue. After a moment it slithered out of sight among the trees of a hanging garden.

Well, he'd seen snakes before. Never one that size, though, as far as he could remember.

"The king came from the earth and created Ronn," Mab said. Her voice was clearer than it should've been with this huge emptiness around them to drink the words. "But the queen came from Ronn itself."

"And the queen's gone," said Herron harshly. "It's up to us, now."

"It's up to us," Mab repeated in the same flat, clear voice as before. Cashel wasn't sure she was agreeing, exactly.

Stepping out a little farther ahead, Cashel began to spin his quarterstaff slowly to loosen his muscles. Something passed overhead. He heard Enfero gasp in surprise, but Mab didn't speak. He continued to spin, a little faster each time he crossed his wrists.

He guessed Mab would warn them if there was going to be a fight. And though Cashel wasn't sure about the Sons beyond figuring that they'd try, *he* knew what to do in a fight.

Smiling, content as he usually was, Cashel began feeding his spinning staff before and behind him in a careful, complicated pattern like what Mab had done to clear the water.

Oh, yes. Cashel was *certain* sure he knew about fights.

"There's people on the sand spit," Ilna said, speaking in a low voice. The creek they'd been following much of the afternoon forked there. Though the shallow channels weren't real protection, the freshly deposited sand at the upstream end would be more comfortable than a camp hacked out of the willows and sedges lining both banks. "Making supper, it seems."

"I don't smell smoke," Chalcus said. His hands weren't on his sword and dagger, but his voice had the peculiar lightness that meant the blades would be clear at the first hint of a threat. "There's four of them, and a dozen donkeys—one's strayed downstream."

"They're not people," Davus said, cold and hard and certain. "Not any longer, at least. The new king's been this way."

Instead of relaxing, Chalcus rose onto his toes and looked about them. They were on an animal trail that came into sight of the water only at fords: the vegetation was much heavier at the streamside than a double pace back from it. Even so, Ilna doubted that her friend could see anything that'd been hidden while he stood flat-footed.

She understood why Chalcus was—in his way—nervous, though. What use was a sword against a creature that turned its victims into stone?

Davus splashed through the stream. He held a chip of patterned obsidian in his left hand, but as a talisman rather than a weapon. His thumb rubbed the smooth stone, and his face was set in lines as hard as those of the statues on the sand.

Chalcus nodded Ilna across; she waded over quickly. The water was only knee deep, but the strong current made her tug up her tunic. She didn't mind the hem being wet, but the fabric might give the stream purchase enough to pull her down.

Chalcus waited till Ilna was on the sand, then followed. He watched their backs with a faint false smile. If Davus was right, mere sight of the creature and its jewel was enough to turn the victim to stone, so it didn't seem to Ilna that keeping a close lookout was a useful defense. There were other dangers in this land, of course.

And perhaps Chalcus thought that if he were turned to stone, it would give her warning to escape. Her lips tightened at the thought. As if she'd run!

The Citadel—the tall basalt spike whose crystal crown flared and twisted into fanciful shapes—loomed not very far away. Ilna hadn't learned to judge distances, growing up as she did in a small hamlet that she'd never expected to leave. The new king's victims hadn't been looking that way, however.

Something had come down the creek from the west. The wayfarers were preparing supper. Two men had risen, their hands on a sword hilt in the one case, a spear too heavy for easy throwing in the other. A third had gone to settle the tethered donkeys, which must've become restive, while the last had remained squatting by the fire.

And so they remained, figures of coarse black stone. Their clothing had rotted off, all but a few tatters where the cloth was doubled, and the blades of their weapons were lumps of rust.

Chalcus dug his bare toe into the hearth. Sand half covered the ring of stones and the feet of the man who'd been watching the fire, but Chalcus turned up a layer of ash beneath. It'd burned itself out, whenever the thing happened. Years ago.

Davus knelt by a pile of flat black boulders near the stone donkeys, running his fingertips over them as Ilna might have done with a complex tapestry. Ilna frowned at the blocks, puzzling as to where they came from. They were basalt, not the limestone that cropped out of the brush in this—

Oh. They were leather packsaddles, turned to stone by chance or whim at the same time the creature had petrified the men who owned them.

"Ilna, dear heart?" Chalcus said, looking about them with a smile as bright and hard as the glint of faceted diamond. "You brought Master Davus back from the black, stony place that these poor fellows are in now. Might it be that you could do the same for them?"

The statues—they'd been merchants, Ilna supposed—were utter strangers; and though Chalcus was no longer the red-handed pirate he'd once been, she'd seen him viewing a bloody shambles with no greater concern than a sawyer has for cut timber. The difference here, the reason there was a real plea in his falsely cheerful voice, was that he knew the victims weren't dead. They were living men, inside a prison that had been their own flesh.

"I'm sorry," Ilna said. "The vines around Davus told me where to cut. I can't see the patterns here. Not in stone."

Davus poised his chip of obsidian like a writing stylus, then tapped once on the uppermost packsaddle. There was a slight click, no more, and the thin slab that'd been the flap cracked away in a single sheet. A shower of wheat kernels spilled out, golden in the sunlight and far more welcome than bullion would've been. Ilna's belly growled in anticipation.

Davus rose and faced his companions. He wasn't smiling, but he seemed satisfied. "They've been sealed better than any storage jar," he said. "Mistress, if you can manage flat bread, I'll take a handful"—so speaking, he bent and scooped up a little of the bright grain—"and see if I can't bait some quail in for a meat course, eh?"

"Yes, of course," Ilna said, looking for stones she could use to grind the grain. She was hungry enough that she didn't think she'd take the time to parch it first. A packsaddle would do fine for the lower stone . . .

Chalcus began gathering brush for the fire, his face immobile. Occasionally he had to use his knife, a crudeness that the fine steel didn't deserve; but these were hard times, for people as well as for blades.

Davus spread grain at several places where the bank was open and in sight of the sand spit; then he crossed back. Pausing, he looked up at the spire of black and crystal not far to the north.

"I don't know why the creature would come down from his Citadel," he said musingly. "The Old King walked the land at intervals to mete out justice."

He gave his companions a lopsided smile. "His version of justice, of course. Perhaps the new king does the same. These poor devils may have offended in a fashion that no human being could understand."

Ilna had expected the broken flap to be uselessly brittle, but on trying she found it quite sturdy enough to grind the hard kernels against the block beneath. Davus must have tapped with the skill of a diamond cutter to split it so easily.

"How will we enter the Citadel, friend Davus?" Chalcus asked, feeding fuel to the fire he'd just sparked. "If we're to climb that wall of rock, I'll say that it's a task that lies beyond me."

"And it's certainly beyond me," Ilna said. "Though I'll try if I must, of course."

"Of course," Chalcus murmured. "Though you hate stone; and if there were a thing you feared beyond your own self, dear one, that would be stone as well."

He glanced over his shoulder at her. He was hard and knew very well how hard she too was; but Ilna's breath still caught with the warm certainty that this man, this *man,* loved her.

"There's an internal passage from the base to the crown," Davus said. "A natural vent originally, I'm told, but improved over the years. The route shouldn't be a problem in itself."

"Is it guarded?" Chalcus said, his voice returning to its natural lilt. Ilna smiled to hear the tone. There might shortly be better work for his blades than willow stems.

"There'll be someone there," Davus said, standing with his hands together at his waist, looking down the trail. "It won't be easy dealing with her."

Ilna looked at the tree lying in the streambed. It'd been a palm, but the fronds had long vanished, and the trunk was crumbling. Originally it must've fallen across the path, but travellers like the ones frozen here had wrested it out of the way of their donkeys.

On it, looking back at her with sightless eyes, was a lizard. Like the humans, it'd been turned to stone.

"We'll deal," said Chalcus with bloody cheerfulness.

"It depends," said Davus, "on just how skillful we are."

As he spoke, he flung a pebble sidearm. Not one but two decapitated quail shot into the air in a scatter of feathers, dust, and their own spouting blood.

"It depends . . . ," Davus repeated. This time there was no doubt of the satisfaction in his voice.

Sharina wasn't sure that she and Tenoctris had any business thrusting themselves into a group of armored men rushing to assault a building. Tenoctris obviously felt otherwise: she was trotting toward the temple at the best speed her old legs could manage.

Sharina threw the older woman's left arm over her own shoulders and grabbed her around the waist with her right hand. If she was that determined, there was no choice for a friend but to help.

Stretching herself, Sharina was able to join the second line of soldiers as they ran up the temple steps. Five Blood Eagles formed an arc in front of them, with Lires watching their backs. Ascor seemed to view his job as protecting Princess Sharina while she went about her business instead of preventing her from doing that business.

A squad of regulars had paused to wrench the hearthstone from the altar; they started up the steps with it. The slab was a thick piece of fine-grained limestone, blackened in the center and burned slightly concave. It weighed as much as any four of them put together.

The troops chopping at the temple door with their swords backed away at a shout from their commander. The soldiers carrying the block of stone staggered onto the porch, paused to organize, and lunged forward on command. They smashed the square stone battering ram corner first into the door, where the leaves joined.

The doors sprang partway open but caught on the crossbar and staples, which the blow had bent but not broken. The altar top slipped from the hands of the men wielding it, dropping to the porch edgewise before toppling to the left. The troops shouted warnings and jumped in various directions, one of them tripping on his own feet. He slipped beneath the falling slab, but another soldier grabbed his belt and jerked him clear just in time.

A pale figure inside the temple tried to push the leaves closed. A soldier thrust his sword out to stop him. A javelin thrown by a man who'd just reached the porch glanced off the swordsman's helmet, knocking him silly, but then catching its proper target in the throat.

The troops who'd carried the altar top hit the doors again with their boots or shoulders. They struck in near unison though they didn't have any formal coordination so far as Sharina could tell. The leaves flew back.

Inside were three People, two in tunics with drawn swords. The third lay on his back, clutching at the spear that'd killed him. The first soldiers through the door chopped the People down. It wasn't a fight, even though the troops had dropped their shields to lift the hearth.

As the leading soldiers entered, Sharina carried Tenoctris inside also. The ring of Blood Eagles, now shield to shield, kept them as safe from jostling as they'd have been in the middle of an empty plaza.

The cult statue was wooden and only slightly greater than life-size, an old image that hadn't been replaced when the temple was repaired. There was a door to the right of the statue, ajar when the troops burst in. A man came through it, another of the People. He was older than the others, unarmed, and wore a ring with a brilliant sapphire on his right index finger. When he saw the troops, he turned to flee.

A thrown javelin caught the man in the middle of the back, flinging him down the stairs he'd ascended. The blood that sprayed from his mouth was the bright orange-red like that of an ordinary man speared through the lungs.

Soldiers charged into the cellars, sounding like a wagonful of old iron tipping even before one stumbled. He and half a dozen of those ahead of him crashed through the railing.

Sharina halted in the middle of the sanctum, holding the older woman back. "Tenoctris, we can't go down now," she said.

"But I want to see what they're doing there!" Tenoctris said. "I'm afraid it'll be smashed if we wait."

"*We'll* be smashed if we don't wait," Sharina said. "I'm sorry, we can't."

Ascor nodded strong agreement. "We'll get you there when things settle a bit, milady," he said, his lips close to the old wizard's ear to be heard over the racket.

From the cellars came shouts, mostly unintelligible but one very clear, "Got 'em got 'em got 'em! They's dead! The ones as was painting is dead!"

"Oh!" said Tenoctris. "Oh, I did hope we'd capture living prisoners. That would have been helpful."

Additional troops were still trying to force their way down the stairs. *Are they insane?* Sharina thought. And in a way they were: they were soldiers ignited by battle. Fear and bloodlust drowned their ability to think.

Aloud she said, "Ascor, where's the commander? I need the commander."

"Captain Rowning!" Ascor bellowed. "Here to the princess! Now! Now!"

Sharina couldn't see who he was shouting at. The Blood Eagles stood in a tight circle around her and Tenoctris, their shields raised to fend line soldiers away from them.

An officer who seemed old for his modest rank stepped close to the circle of guards. "Your highness?" he said, peering between the shoulders of Ascor and Lires. "Your highness, you shouldn't be here! It's far too dangerous!"

"The only danger at present is that we're going to be trampled to death by your men!" Sharina flared. "Get them out before they destroy information we need to save the kingdom!"

Captain Rowning recoiled in shock. "Your highness!" he said.

Sharina felt her gut knot in self-disgust at what she'd just said. Rowning's troops had reacted splendidly in an unexpected situation. She shouldn't have let her fear and anger cause her to lash out that way.

"Captain," she said, "you've done very well, very well indeed. But please bring your men up from the cellars now."

Rowning turned to the signaller at his side, a cornicene whose horn curved around his body instead of the trumpeter normally attached to an infantry unit. "Sessir," he said, "sound recall!"

The signaller blew a long note followed by three quick ones, then repeated the call. His mouthpiece was bone, not brass like the horn itself: he might have to use it in the dead of winter. The horn calls rattled the roof tiles.

Though Sharina didn't see how anybody could tell what the signal was supposed to be through the blurring echoes, troops stopped shoving forward. After a moment they began to back out of the sanctum. Men returned from the cellars, some of them helping along fellows who'd fallen under booted feet.

The sanctum had nearly emptied, and the last of the soldiers were straggling up the stairs. "Ah, your highness?" said Captain Rowning, hesitant because of Sharina's snarl. "What would you like me to, ah, do? Now, I mean."

"Leave a squad here, and you accompany me into the cellars," Sharina said in quick assessment. "If you'd be so good."

She didn't especially want the captain present, but he'd be pleased at the invitation. She owed him that and more for her outburst.

"I'm honored, your highness!" Rowning said, his expression opening brightly like a lotus flower at dawn.

"Hey, troop!" Lires called to the last soldier coming up from the cellars. "What did ye do for light down there? There's lanterns?"

"Huh?" said the soldier. "No, it's windows, like, in the ceiling. There's plenty light, though. No problem there."

Rowning drew his sword and trotted down the steps, apparently worried that Sharina would withdraw her offer. Ascor raised an eyebrow to Sharina for instructions, then muttered, "Let's go," to his men.

"Tenoctris, hold my shoulders," Sharina said, stepping in front of the wizard. The stairs were narrow, and the soldiers rushing down them had ripped the railing away. It'd been a sturdy one, judging from how thick the upper bracket with its tag of broken pole was.

Twenty steps led to a floor of poured concrete. Looking down as she descended, Sharina saw six troughs of bright gray zinc along the wall on the street side of the single room. Sealed storage jars, wide-mouthed and each big enough to hold several bushels of grain, stood opposite them, and in the middle was a long limestone table. The tabletop had originally been smooth and probably white, but now stains and blade scratches covered it. It'd been used for surgery—or butchering.

The room was better lighted than the sanctum above. Slabs of crystal around the edges of the coffered ceiling flooded down a cold, milky light. The panels on the south, the street side, were brighter than others.

Tenoctris looked at them with interest. "That isn't wizardry," she said, "but it's quite clever. Sunlight's led down through blocks of glass from the roof, I suppose. I saw a device like that on Yole in my own day, in an underground chamber built by one of the duke's ancestors."

A corpse lay between the table's two slab supports. He'd been one of the lookouts pretending to be painting. His partner was huddled just behind him. They'd been hacked to pieces by soldiers who'd found no better way to slake their bloodlust.

Tenoctris sighed. "Well," she murmured, "it can't be helped."

"Captain Rowning?" Sharina said. "These are ordinary men, are they not? Not People, I mean."

"Right," Rowning said. He'd sheathed his sword and was using his dagger to pry at the tar sealing the ceramic stopper onto a storage jar. "They couldn't put People out where they'd be seen, your highness. Once you get a look at them, it's like Serians—you don't have any trouble telling what they are the next time. And there's a lot of folk here in Valles who saw them after the Battle of the Tides. Or in it, for that matter, with all the militia who fought that day."

Rowning popped the plug off the jar. He looked in, sniffed, and stuck his dagger down inside. The dagger point drew up a slab of flesh as broad and flat as a napkin. It was pink and fresh-looking but it didn't have blood vessels.

"By the Lady!" Rowning said. "What's this? Is it human? *Is* it?"

He twitched the dagger, slapping the flesh against the wall. It slipped down with a sucking sound. Rowning's face had a look of horror. That struck Sharina as incongruous in the midst of slaughtered men who'd been human beyond question.

Tenoctris knelt beside the third body, the member of the People whom the javelin had thrown down the stairs. A pair of Blood Eagles bracketed her to keep others from bumping the frail old woman.

She looked over her shoulder at Rowning. "No more than the People themselves are," she said. Smiling wider, she added, "But no less, of course. I think this is Hani's workroom. Here in Valles, of course. There'd have to be a much larger installation to create as many People as were in the army that invaded Ornifal before."

Rowning jerked back from the jar, his dagger poised to slash at anything that came out of it to touch him. "Bloody *Hell!*" a Blood Eagle rasped under his breath.

"Create?" Sharina said, staring at the People's leader. She edged back unconsciously, much as Rowning had done. "Then they're not human?"

"Human?" Tenoctris repeated with a grimace. She lifted the corpse's hand and looked at the big ring on its finger. "Dear, I don't know how to answer that. What I'm sure of is that Hani or someone else, some wizard, builds the People from materials like those"—she nodded to the jars—"instead of them being born the way you and I were." Tenoctris smiled with a vagary of thought, and added, "A very long time ago, in my case."

Ascor glared at the dead leader of the People. "I suppose they could sneak into Valles without being noticed," he said grudgingly. "But what were they here *for?*"

Tenoctris pulled the ring from the corpse's finger, twisting it one way and then back to loosen it. "I suspect they might have known something about the theft of Stronghand's body," she said, holding the ring to the light. "I'd have questioned them about it if I had a chance."

"Sorry, milady," Captain Rowning muttered. He started to wipe his blade on the skirt of his outer tunic, then thought again. He turned and, with a grimace of fury, hurled the dagger point first into the stairs. It drove deep into a tread and hummed for a moment with the violence of the stroke.

Lires prodded the leader's corpse with his boot. "I'm not sorry they're dead," he said conversationally. "I guess you and her highness'll figure things out, milady."

Sharina looked at Tenoctris, then at the soldier. She felt a rush of relief. "Yes, I agree with Trooper Lires," she said. "With both parts of what he said. What do we do now, Tenoctris?"

Tenoctris rose to her feet, helped by one of the Blood Eagles. She smiled also.

"Speaking as a human being," she said, "I don't think creatures like the People should exist, nor that humans should help accomplish purposes that certainly aren't meant to benefit mankind. A scholar would have a more detached viewpoint, but one can't be a scholar always."

She handed the ring to Sharina. The sapphire was as large as her little fingernail and seemed to be perfect. It was set in dense gray metal, lustrous but heavier than silver.

"Sharina," the wizard said, "your eyes are younger than mine. Can you make out what's written around the bezel?"

Sharina adjusted the ring against the angle of the light. There were tiny letters encircling the sapphire; at first glance she'd taken them for brushed ornamentation.

"It's in the Old Script," she said. "I think . . . *Ereschigal aktiophi*—"

"Sharina, stop!" Tenoctris cried. "Don't read—"

But the words of power had already gripped Sharina's tongue. The stone's facets threw dazzling highlights across the cellars.

"*Berbiti baui*—" Sharina shouted, her lips speaking the words despite her mind's desperate attempt to control them. Tenoctris covered the ring with her own hands, but the light burned through her flesh and through the fabric of the waking world.

"*Io!*" Sharina shouted, spinning down into a vortex of adamantine light.

Chapter Thirteen

reschigal aktiophi! thundered from no human throat. The words of power filled Sharina's mind as she whirled out of the cellars, out of Valles, out of the sidereal universe.

Berbiti baui—

She still held the ring. Tenoctris had vanished into the white mist. Everything had vanished except Sharina herself and the clothes she was wearing.

Io!

The ring couldn't have been a trap. It was a tool meant to carry the user from where he was, where she was, to another place. It was a tool but not Sharina's tool, and she didn't know how to use it properly.

Ereschigal—

Beneath Sharina a plateau rose through the white mist, an island lapped by a sea of clouds. Squared fields covered the rolling surface, and many of the gleaming watercourses feeding or fed by the lake in the center were laid out in straight lines also.

Aktiophi—

The island swelled quickly beneath her. A building of polished marble with a two-story colonnade lay beside the lake, embracing half the shore in its spreading wings. Sharina didn't see any other structures, but except for wooded stretches along the canal margins, the whole surface appeared to be under cultivation.

Berbiti—

The ground was a hundred feet below, fifty feet below, twenty feet below. Pale men bent over their hoes in fields of squash shaded by maize. The laborers didn't look up.

Baui—

The laborers weren't men. They were People, wizard-made creations. The People captured in the Battle of the Tides had said they came from a floating island . . .

Io!

Sharina landed so lightly that her sandals barely sank into the soft earth. Then she fell backward.

A horn called.

Ilna stared at the Citadel, feeling impressed the way she'd been the first time she'd looked west over the Outer Sea from the heights above Carcosa. A thick growth of hardwoods and pine covered the base of the spire, but from midpoint the rock was bare and black and as sheer as a house wall.

It was beyond her to judge how tall the thing was, but it was very tall. The crystal crown overhung the basalt, though from this angle Ilna saw only the glittering points and arcs that projected beyond the black shaft.

Chalcus was standing arms akimbo, leaning back from the waist to view the Citadel instead of just tilting his neck. He straightened and barked a laugh, "I'm happy that we're not going up the outside of *that,* dear heart," he said. "I've known a few men who could manage it—or could've, for most of them are dead now—but I wasn't among them."

Davus smiled and set down the three rocks he'd carried as weapons. He took the bit of snowflake obsidian from a fold of his sash, caressing it with his thumb.

"Don't claim you're happy till you've seen what the choice is," Davus said, in a voice as wan as his smile. "But it's the choice regardless, I'm afraid."

He nodded to the right. "Time we get to it," he added as he started off in the direction he'd indicated.

There wasn't a path, even an animal track, but because the ground was stony, the undergrowth was too sparse to be a barrier. "I hear the sea," Chalcus called from behind Ilna, sounding surprised.

"Aye," replied Davus over his shoulder. "A lake, more properly, but too broad to see the other side."

"Well, perhaps we'll be able to do that from the top, eh, my friend?" Chalcus said, with a laugh. "We'll learn when we're there, shall we?"

"Not even from the top," Davus replied. "Which I'll willingly prove to you, Master Chalcus, as soon as we have no greater demands on our attention."

They came out of the woods onto rock bare even of leaf litter. The basalt was rippled like pond ice. It'd weathered into shades of lighter and darker grays, with patches of the original black where winter had cracked a flake loose. Ahead was the ragged edge of a cliff overlooking water that the sunlight turned a chalky ultramarine; to the left rose the chimney-straight shaft of the Citadel, splotched here and there with blue-gray lichen.

In the basalt wall was an oval hole taller than a man. The lower half was blocked with squared stones set in mortar. Over the wall, her arms crossed before her, a bare-breasted woman watched the companions with a thin smile.

"Did that come by nature or did someone, a wizard mayhap, drill it, eh?" Chalcus said as he surveyed what was clearly the next stage on their journey. He grinned like a jester, his hands on his hips.

"The hole's natural," Davus said, rubbing the obsidian again before slipping it back into his sash. "The lady there that we must treat with is another matter. The Citadel draws in a great deal of power. Part of it leaks back down this channel; and for that reason alone, she'd be uncanny. Her name is Arrea."

"Is she human?" Ilna asked bluntly. Her fingers were knotting cords without any specific intent.

"Less than many of us, I'm afraid," Davus said. "But we need her permission to go further."

"Well, there's ways and ways of treating with a lady," Chalcus said, sauntering forward. Though his clothes were worn by the hard journey, he was every inch the gallant as he said, "So, Milady Arrea, you see before you travellers who want only your good wishes as we pass by to deal with the tenant above. I trust you'll grant us that slight boon."

"For a price," the woman said. Her voice was clear with a pleasant sibilance. She shrugged her shoulders, sending waves down her long, coppery hair. "Everything for a price, traveller. And for that great thing you ask, a great price."

Ilna walked forward also, keeping a little back from Chalcus and a double pace to his left. She knew how wide a swath a blade swept when wielded in the flashy, curving style the sailor favored.

Davus, an equal distance to the sailor's right, tossed his obsidian point high in the air. "Arrea bargains from the certain knowledge," he said, "that killing her would close the passage. She'll bargain hard, of that I have no doubt."

He turned up his other hand: the point dropped into it. His nonchalant gaze had been on Arrea the whole time, without so much as a glance to judge the trajectory of the bit of stone.

Chalcus looked at his companion with a blank expression that hinted nothing of the fury Ilna was sure lay beneath it. Davus had blandly removed any chance they had to bargain. That would've disturbed Ilna also if she'd had only the words on the surface to go by, but she felt what she did not hear—a pattern weaving, subtle and deep.

"Certain, you say, my dear friend?" Chalcus said, his voice a song like the ringing whisper of a blade drawn from its scabbard.

"As certain as the rock"—Davus rubbed the ball of his right foot against the basalt, an oddly sensuous gesture—"beneath us, friend Chalcus," he replied. "We must find the price she demands, not the one we wish to pay. Whatever that demand may be."

"Then for Merota's sake . . . ," Chalcus said, suddenly relaxing. "That is what we shall find. What is your great price, milady?"

Arrea laughed in a voice as cold as the winter moon. "I need a task performed," she said. "Look into the sea and tell me what you see. It may be that none of you is fit to carry it out."

"I've looked at water before," said Chalcus as he swaggered to the edge. "So far I can go with you, milady."

Davus walked after him, tossing and catching the chip of stone as if his hands were wholly separate from the man himself. He glanced at Ilna with a soft expression, then turned to Chalcus and twisted his mouth into a broader, harder smile.

Ilna faced Arrea squarely. It was like looking at a snake, though the woman's features had the chiseled beauty of a temple statue. Ilna turned and followed her companions. Behind them, Arrea laughed triumphantly.

The men were looking down from the cliff. The fierce updraft ruffled their hair into the liquid curves of candleflames. Ilna stepped between them and peered over, holding her tunic to her thighs with her hands.

The cliff was sheer—undercut, even—but at present the lake a furlong below had only waves enough to dapple the light reflecting from it. It was deep, much deeper than the Inner Sea off Barca's Hamlet.

Chalcus scowled, then composed his face into a smile and looked over his shoulder at Arrea. "I look and I see water, milady. Water and a bird in the distance, a very large bird to look as big as a gull within bowshot but in fact be so far away. Is that what we're to see?"

Ilna frowned. In a voice meant for the sailor's ears alone, she said, "Surely she means the cloud there in the water, don't you think? That cloud in the depths, and the silk strands glued to the rock and running down to it."

Wrist-thick cords, tens and tens of them, were anchored to the rock face for as far as Ilna could see in either direction. They looked like the lines supporting a spider's web, but these were as heavy as a ship's cordage. They slanted toward the water and wove themselves into a hollow tube just above the surface.

"What is it, dear heart?" he said, obviously puzzled. "The water's clear as a baby's conscience, I'd have said."

"Davus, what do you see?" Ilna said, irritated to hear a desperate undertone to her voice. "There, where I'm pointing? And the lines running down to it!"

"I see nothing, mistress," Davus said calmly. "The same nothing that Master Chalcus sees. But if you see something, then it's there and it's you who must go the next part of the way."

He stepped back so that he could look straight at Chalcus without Ilna between them. He crossed his arms behind his back, leaving his chest open to a blow or a sword thrust. "As I feared might be the case, though I hoped it would not. Still, the price is the price; and it has to be paid."

Ilna turned and walked the ten double paces back to where Arrea faced them over the masonry wall. She could've shouted to the other, but Ilna didn't like to raise her voice, particularly when she was angry.

She grinned. She had more experience with being angry than most people did—or anybody should, she supposed.

"I see a cloud in the water," Ilna said. "A cloud or a silk bag, I suppose it must be, since silk cords hold it to the cliff. Is that what you wanted to know?"

Instead of answering directly, Arrea gave her a broad, tight-lipped grin, and said, "You'll do, then. It's not a sack, it's a cocoon. In it you'll find a

274 / David Drake

for you and your friends."

"I can see the cords," Ilna said, speaking in a cold tone to hide the anger blazing within her. "That doesn't mean that I can breathe water, mistress. Nor can I swim!"

That last was a little more tart than she'd intended. She *couldn't* swim, and the thought of suffocating as the waters closed over her filled her with a disgust that wasn't the same as fearing to die.

"The larva needs air," Arrea said in an arch tone. "It's a white bloated thing with no eyes and no limbs and no mind, so it will neither know nor care that you're breathing some of what was meant for it."

"And has it a mouth, milady?" said Chalcus, come to Ilna's side now as she had come to his. "A mouth to swallow those who've come to steal its jewels?"

Arrea laughed. "Have you nothing to worry about on your own account, Master Chalcus?" she said. "The larva is squirming blubber that eats nothing and knows nothing about the jewel. It will not be aware that your slip of a girl here has come and gone."

"On your life!" Chalcus said, the planes of his face rigid.

Arrea laughed again.

Ilna turned on her heel and walked to the cliff, eyeing the task she'd taken on herself. Davus, who hadn't moved from the edge, said, "The threads weave themselves into a floor you can walk on before you're a hundred feet out, and they twist over in a tube well above the water."

"And the larva isn't a danger?" Chalcus said, come up on Ilna's other side.

"Not the larva," Davus said, "but there may be parasites in the cocoon sucking its blood."

He shrugged. "They're not lions or wolves, Master Chalcus," he said. "There'll be danger, but there's danger in life. And we cannot go in her place or even go with her, because we're blind to what must be seen."

"Yes," said Ilna. "And while I regret seeming to agree with Arrea, whom I neither like nor trust—"

Chalcus chuckled and even Davus, who hadn't known Ilna long, smiled.

Ilna grinned also, pleased that the unplanned joke had broken the tension. "Yes, I suppose that does put Arrea with the great majority of the people I've met," she agreed. "Nonetheless, I don't see that my going down to a room in the sea, for that's all it is, is so greatly more dangerous than your waiting for me up here."

"We'll keep our eyes open," Chalcus said. He stepped close and kissed her, then turned. "I'll watch our backs, Master Davus," he said. "You keep an eye on her and tell me if there's anything I should do. That way we'll come out all right, I think; or anyway, come out best."

"Right," said Davus, fitting a good-sized rock into the pocket of his sash. He swung it idly, watching the far horizon where the bird soared.

Ilna touched the nearest line, attached only a hand's breadth below the top of the cliff where she was standing. The cord appeared to have melted onto the stone in a splotch wider than Ilna could circle with both hands. Given that the strand was strong enough to tow a trireme, and as best Ilna could estimate there were more strands than there were rowers in that trireme, the risks she was taking didn't include the chance of the cocoon breaking loose with her in it.

Turning backward and wrapping her legs around the silk, she started down. The slope was gradual and the cord so thick that she could probably have walked it like a rope dancer, but she didn't need to do so.

That would've been showing off, behavior Ilna disliked and particularly disliked in herself. Besides, her companions both knew what she really was, and respected her, for what she was and—she felt—despite it.

I know what I am too. And if there was a God to forgive me, I would still never forgive myself.

Above her Chalcus began to sing, "*Don't bury me here, in the cold gray sea. . . .*"

"*Where the seagulls cry . . . ,*" Davus joined in with his pleasant baritone.

Ilna reached a point that three strands joined. She turned and stood, walking down the widening pavement and luxuriating in the feel of the silk against her soles.

"*. . . so mournfully . . . ,*" her companions sang.

Ilna began to laugh, a thing she did rarely and would never have imagined doing under the present circumstances. She'd been alone most of her life, for all that there'd generally been people about her.

She wasn't alone anymore.

———

Just ahead of Cashel the cavern narrowed to a knife-edge. The walls stepped back a bit at every level rising to the dimly glimpsed ceiling, but down where he followed Mab and the Sons it was going to be tight. Cashel figured he'd have room to spin his quarterstaff crossways but only just, and that because a staff didn't wobble when *he* spun it, the way it did for most folks.

"Mistress Mab?" he said. "Ought I to lead here, or maybe . . . ?"

He stopped because he didn't even know how to ask the question. Truth to tell, it seemed to Cashel he ought to be *all* places in the line, since the only direction he didn't worry about things coming at them from was up through the floor. And if there turned out to be a floor grate in the crevice, he'd be looking down between his feet too.

"I'll make a light and lead, Cashel," Mab said. "Shall we have . . ."

She made a sign in the air before her with her right hand; a blob of blue wizardlight bloomed. After an instant's pause, Mab signed again, this time with her left hand and a completely different gesture. Red light swelled beside the blue.

"The crimson, I think," Mab said. The blue light vanished, and the red flooded soft color over everything within a stone's throw ahead of and behind her. "Neither's more natural than the other, but the crimson makes things look more natural to our human senses, don't you think?"

"Thanks for giving us light, mistress," Herron said. All the Sons had taken to carrying their swords in their hands instead of wearing them in their belt scabbards, but only Herron held his with the point up, where it might be good for something against a sudden attack. "I was . . . I wondered how much darker it was going to get."

"Algae grows over the light pipes," Mab said, not sounding very concerned about it. "It's natural, but the way it grows isn't."

"Like the mushrooms we saw," Orly said.

"And the rosebush that tried to follow us," said Enfero.

And also like the big spider you didn't see, Cashel thought. *And probably a lot of things I didn't see besides.*

But he didn't say any of that aloud. They were decent boys, trying hard to be brave doing something they didn't begin to understand. Cashel didn't understand either, but he was used to that, and the Sons weren't.

"I see something," Orly said. "On the fifth terrace above us. To the left."

He pointed with his sword, then jerked it back. Cashel guessed he was afraid of calling attention to himself.

"They're white!" Stasslin said. "It's the Made Men!"

Cashel saw not figures but the pale shadows of figures, watching from just above where the glow lighted. There were a lot of them, many times more than he could count without a tally stick. They moved back and forth along the edge overlooking the crevice.

Stasslin turned to face Mab. In the tone of angry accusation that seemed to be pretty usual for him, he said, "You told us the Made Men couldn't get in, but here they are waiting!"

Before Cashel could act, Mab flicked her left index finger. The rosy haze expanded suddenly, filling the whole vast cavern and the passage ahead. A tree frog hung with its mouth open on the wall just below the terrace where the figures'd been, blinking at the light. Its webbed feet were much broader than those of frogs Cashel was used to, and its body was as large as a lamb's.

But the figures had vanished.

Mab shrank the light down to what it'd been a moment earlier. Cashel couldn't see the big frog anymore, but the white shapes came capering back.

"The Made Men were gone," Athan said, "and now they're there again."

"They never existed except as ghosts in your minds," Mab said coldly. "They have no physical presence, and they can do you no physical harm."

She looked at Stasslin and smiled. Her lips could've cut glass.

Stasslin glowered and turned his head away. "I didn't know!" he said in an angry voice. "I'm not afraid of ghosts."

"There's reason to fear these," Mab said, her voice gentler as she glanced across all those with her. "The king's spirit never really left these depths, and in the past decades his power here has increased to levels it's not reached in a thousand years. He can't touch your bodies, but he can trick your minds into seeing things that aren't there. He can make you feel things that're to his benefit. Not your benefit or the benefit of the citizens of Ronn."

"Lady Mab," said Herron, pretty much succeeding in keeping his voice steady. "What are we supposed to do?"

Mab smiled and raised an eyebrow at Cashel, passing the question to him. He shrugged, uncomfortable with everybody looking at him; but that'd happened to him before, and worse things had happened too. And the answer was always the same.

"We go on," Cashel said. "We go to the Shrine of the Heroes, and we wake them to come back with us."

He cleared his throat. "Or anyway, we try."

"Yes," said Mab, "that's what we'll do. As I said, I'll lead."

She walked forward, the light moving with her step by step. Several of the Sons started after her right away, but Herron glanced over his shoulder at Cashel.

Cashel smiled, pleased that Herron'd been concerned about him. They were good boys; most of them, anyhow.

"I'll bring up the back, Herron," he said. "That gives me a little more space if I need it."

So speaking, he spun his staff slowly. Just the simple sunwise turning made him feel better right away, so he crossed his arms behind him and reversed his spin to widdershins.

The Sons all gasped. Cashel didn't see why. He was showing his skill, but these fellows didn't know enough about quarterstaves to see that.

Then he brought the hickory around before him again. The ferrules were trailing blue wizardlight.

"Oh," Cashel said, feeling his cheeks flush. He twisted his staff to a halt and butted it on the ground beside him.

"Master Cashel, how did you do that?" Manza said in amazement. The Sons were staring at him. Mab watched too, but she had a crooked smile.

"He's a wizard, Manza!" Enfero snapped at his friend. "How else would he do it?"

"I'm not a wizard!" Cashel said, looking at the deep passage they were supposed to be going down. "Anyway, let's get going."

He made a shooing motion with his free hand. Since he wanted to be at the back of the line, he couldn't very well stride off down the crevice the way he'd have done otherwise to get them moving. He felt like Stasslin had a moment ago, embarrassed at what he'd done and having no idea what to say about it. He didn't understand the power that came over him sometimes, but he *wasn't* a wizard.

Mab walked on. The Sons followed, most of them right on her heels, though Herron and Stasslin both tried to keep a decent separation. Cashel couldn't pretend he liked Stasslin—and unlike Ilna, Cashel generally found he *did* like people—but even Stasslin was doing his best. That counted for more than the results did.

Well, it did to Cashel. Ilna, well, Ilna didn't have much time for failure either, even when it was somebody besides herself who was failing.

"Master Cashel believes a wizard is a person who uses spells and symbols to work changes in the waking world," Mab said. She spoke in a normal voice without looking back over her shoulder, but Cashel at the end of the line heard her clearly. "That defines many wizards, of course."

They were well within the crevice, now. The walls oozed, but the way the drops ran made Cashel wonder if they were something thicker than water. The floor was slimy, and the air had the musty closeness of something long dead but covered up. He remembered the time he'd opened the tarred seal of a storage jar and found that a rat had managed to hop in with the oats before the jar was closed the August before.

He heard something ahead, different from the dismal *plink* of water falling into water. One of the Sons was whimpering. There weren't any words to what was coming out of his mouth, just cold misery.

"They're up above us again," Manza said. "They're coming closer, I think."

"They aren't there!" Athan said. His head was bent forward as if he needed to watch his feet for every step. "Just don't look, and they'll go away!"

"They will *not* go away," said Mab. "But they can't do you physical harm. Follow me, and we'll make it through."

One of the Sons clustering close behind her turned. Hard to tell what he was thinking, but when he saw Cashel bringing up the back with his quarterstaff across his body—and across the width of the crevice, which was just as tight as it'd looked before they entered—he jerked his face forward again and kept on the way he'd been going.

Cashel wouldn't have sworn which of them it'd been; and anyway, Orly needn't be ashamed for being scared. He'd proved he was brave when he'd charged Cashel on the exercise ground after seeing what the quarterstaff'd done to his friends.

They walked on, surrounded by Mab's light. Cashel knew from watching other wizards that it was a lot of work to keep up a steady thing like that light. Mab didn't seem to show the strain. She'd walked and talked with them just like always, but she must feel like she was carrying a load of timber.

Yes, that was pretty impressive; but in the long run it wouldn't make any difference. The light would go out, and Mab would sink under the effort, fall down right here in the ooze and darkness. She'd be the lucky one. Cashel and the Sons wouldn't die right away, but there wasn't anywhere for them to go, neither forward nor back. They'd die slowly, covered by the slime that was slowly filling the crevice. It'd fill the greater hall in back of them, and eventually slime would own all the places that men had been.

The world would be a better place when slime filled it.

He stumbled into Enfero, who'd knelt on the narrow path and was weeping. Though Cashel's eyes were open, he'd been putting one foot in front of the other, scarcely aware of his surroundings. The collision shocked him back to the present. Though the light was no fainter than before, it was losing the rosy tinge. It turned the stone walls and the thin-stemmed plants that still lifted their leaves in hope a pale gray.

Cashel grabbed Enfero by the back of the collar, lifting him and shoving him forward. "Get on!" he said. "Keep walking! It's not time for us to die yet!"

At another time the words would've bothered Cashel to hear from anybody's mouth, let alone his own. Now it was the only truth in the world: they had to go on till they died and the world died and the sun grew cold. Cashel didn't know why that was, but he generally couldn't answer questions starting with "Why?" He just did the thing that'd been set him.

Stasslin hacked at the wall beside him. His sword made a nasty clang.

"It won't spark!" Stasslin cried. "It won't *spark!*"

Nor did it, maybe because of the slime that covered the stone. Stasslin struck three times more; then his sword broke just above the guard. The blade flew off, and Stasslin flung the hilt after it.

Enfero was marching forward again. He'd lost his sword too, either back where he'd knelt or maybe earlier that that. That didn't matter: the swords weren't good for anything. Nothing was, not even Cashel's quarterstaff.

Furious at the hopelessness of it all, Cashel whirled his staff before him. It moved sluggishly like he was trying to spin it underwater. Something *ripped* sizzlingly; a brilliant azure flash lighted the crevice. Momentarily, just for a heartbeat, the feeling of despair lifted.

Cashel spun the staff again. This time it moved the way it usually did, sliding through the air in an arc as pointless as the one the sun made every day: rising and setting, looking down on lands that slowly crumbled; sinking into a sea of cold gray slime that rose till the sun itself drowned in darkness.

The Sons stopped where they were, whining like a litter of puppies. Cashel set his staff crossways, and shouted, "Go on!"

He shoved them forward. Altogether they weighed much more than he did, but that didn't matter in Cashel's current temper. It was like dragging a bullock—and he'd done that, more by determination than by main force, hauling against the rope and, every time the beast relaxed, jerking it a further hand's breadth on.

"Go on, you puppies!" Cashel said. "We've got to keep going till we die. Walk on!"

The Sons gave before him, stumbling on again. They didn't have the will to resist. There *was* no will that could've resisted Cashel's at that moment. He'd go on and go on, driving them with him till they all died.

They came out from the crevice between the down-tapering walls. They were now in a natural cave, a huge bubble in the rock. There were no crystal windows from there to the surface, not even those smeared over with algae. The glow shimmering from between Mab's hands was the only light in these depths, and that was as faint as the sky an hour before winter dawn.

The walls had the layering of natural rock; stalactites pointed the distant roof. Across the great opening was a bronze door, impressive but smaller than those of some temples Cashel had seen in the waking world.

"Come!" said Mab, her voice shrill. She hobbled toward the doorway, taking full steps with her right leg but only half steps with her left. At some time during the journey she'd become an ancient harridan, toothless and hunching under the weight of years.

What was the truth of her? Cashel wondered, but the answer didn't matter because nothing mattered in a world that was merely a prelude to the end.

The Sons hesitated, their heads bent. "Get moving, you!" Cashel said. "Soon we can die, but not yet!" The boys obeyed because they didn't have the strength to do anything else.

Mab reached the bronze door. Close up, it was larger than Cashel'd thought from across the cave. The metal was perfectly smooth except for the line down the center where the panels joined.

She raised her hands. The light she'd projected to that moment vanished; the dark closed in, complete. *Now we can die,* Cashel thought in a great wave of relief.

"Cashel, keep them off me," said a voice from the blackness. It must be Mab, but it sounded like a little girl. A frightened little girl.

"There's nothing I can do," Cashel said, too bleak to be angry, but he turned his back to the door and gave his staff a trial spin. First he rotated it widdershins, but that wasn't right, didn't *feel* right. He reversed the spin, turning the shaft sunwise, a little quicker each time and with all the power of his thick wrists behind it.

The touch of the hickory, smooth and familiar, reminded Cashel of times that things *did* matter. Things like the sun and the way clouds piled up before a storm; and love, his for Sharina and the heart-stopping wonder of hers for Cashel or-Kenset. He didn't feel those things, but he viewed them in memory as if in a mirror of black glass.

The quarterstaff spun. He brought it overhead, then shifted it before him again because that was what felt right. He couldn't see anything, and there was nothing in the darkness to touch, but the spinning wood calmed him, and the thrum of the staff as it sliced arcs from the air quieted the Sons' whimpers.

Mab spoke in an undertone. Hissing wizardlight, red weaving with blue, glanced from the bronze and threw back the endless night for a few moments more.

Cashel had his rhythm. He kept the staff spinning, feeling the weight of what he couldn't see and knowing he was pressing back on it. He gasped with laughter. It was a fight after all, even though he didn't know what he was fighting. That didn't matter: a fight was a fight, and he'd win it or die.

"*Brimaio thiahiao . . . ,*" Mab said. Cashel didn't look behind him, but he heard metal squeal on metal and the bronze valves begin to rumble open. "*Chermari!*"

"Get in there, you Sons of Heroes!" Cashel said. The pressure was driving him backward, and the quarterstaff turned in treacle, not air; but it turned. "Get in while I hold them!"

There was a shuffle behind him. He kept the staff spinning, though it felt as if he was turning millstones against all the force of the flume.

"Cashel, *now!*" Mab cried. But he couldn't take another step back.

They had him in their power, the things he'd been fighting. They hemmed him before and behind and there was no way—

Brilliant bolts of wizardlight, blue, then red, flashed before him. The concussions threw him backward, faceup on a stone pavement. For a moment there was darkness again, but this time it was filled with the savage leering faces of white things that weren't men.

Then the bronze doors slammed shut, and Cashel's mind surrendered him to sleep.

Garric looked at the reading room's painted ceiling. On it a gorgeous fresco showed the Shepherd in a wolfskin cape standing against the lightning-shot storm clouds in one corner. He carried a crook to help him lift bogged animals rather than the simple staff that shepherds used on Haft. The rest of the painting was of vineyards and merchant ships, shops and a procession of city officials: all under the Shepherd's shielding presence.

"There's not a soldier in the whole picture," Carus observed from Garric's mind with a grin. *"It must've been painted by a priest. Or a woman."*

That depends on the woman, Garric thought, glancing at Liane as she turned pages quickly. Liane never hesitated to deal with reality. The realities of the present, when the powers on which the cosmos turned were rising to their thousand-year peak, certainly included soldiers.

The stresses twisting the world affected ordinary people as well as wizards. Lust and greed and anger were never far beneath the surface of human interactions, but the membrane between those emotions and civilization had thinned.

"The painting must've been cleaned recently," Garric said to Attaper, standing at his side. "The paint's very bright, though I'd imagine it dates from hundreds of years ago."

Attaper glanced up and grunted. He returned to glowering at the priests entering and leaving the room.

Garric smiled faintly. The Blood Eagle commander wasn't an art lover, and he'd been understandably nervous ever since Garric announced he was crossing to Erdin with limited forces. This trip added another level to Attaper's concern. The Temple of the Shielding Shepherd was a mile from the palace.

Attaper and Garric stood near the eastern reading table, where Liane turned the pages of a vellum-bound codex. Across the room a squad of Blood Eagles guarded the trio of priest/librarians—two old men and an eager young woman with very short hair. They were fetching books Liane had asked for, either by name or, more often, by subject.

Some of the works were in the reading room's ceiling-high wall cases, but for the most part the priests had to go through the gilt-arched doorway, past more Blood Eagles, to other portions of the library. When they returned they set their finds on the west table, from which soldiers carried them to Liane.

The process seemed cumbersome and silly to Garric, but it didn't slow Liane's search and it made Attaper happy. Well, a little less unhappy. Besides, deep in a corner of Garric's mind was the recollection of the things in the semblance of men that'd attacked him and Liane in the night. Attaper was there to vouch for the identity of his troops, but who would know if a seeming librarian was human?

Liane read swiftly, a page half-lifted to turn against the moment she finished the one she was scanning. "No," she muttered. "No, not that—"

She flipped the page. Her face was set in stern lines. She didn't look so much angry as like a judge preparing to deliver deservedly harsh punishment. Even so, it was disconcertingly different from any of Liane's normal expressions. Garric kept his eyes on other things instead of making himself uncomfortable by watching her.

"—either!"

Instead of glazed casements, the windows across the room's southern and northern walls were covered with vertical strips of bleached parchment sewn together at the edges. They lighted the reading tables well, but the illumination was softer than glass would've provided.

Liane closed the book she'd been using. Though frustrated, she treated the volume with the respect due its age instead of banging it shut. She opened a waiting scroll. The temple librarians had already untied its cords of gold-colored silk for her.

Attaper cleared his throat. "Ah . . ." he said. "You're something of a scholar yourself, aren't you, your highness?"

Meaning, "Why are you standing here with your thumb up your ass instead of helping her?" Garric translated mentally. Aloud he said, "Yes, I am, but in this kind of research two people would just get in each other's way. Much of it's a matter of remembering what one writer said and connecting it with an item from somewhere else. All the information has to be in the same place."

He tapped his temple, smiling. "In the same mind, that is."

The image of King Carus chuckled at him. *"Don't expect me to help you there,"* he said. *"The best use I found for a book in my own day was to prop up a wobbly table leg."*

"Ah!" Liane said. "Garric, read this."

She thrust the scroll she'd been reading toward Garric in her left hand while with her right index finger she worked down through the stack of codices that she'd reviewed earlier in the morning. When Garric hesitated a moment, Liane waggled the scroll impatiently. He took it, freeing her hands to lift the top three books off her pile and retrieve the second from the bottom.

Garric cleared his throat. Attaper was looking toward the door with the forced nonchalance of a man who was determined not to have seen or heard something that would otherwise be embarrassing.

"It's from the annals of a temple or possibly a city," Garric said to Attaper, holding the document by both winding sticks. A full two columns were open between them. "It's headed Sixteen, that'd be Year Sixteen of someone's reign—"

"Aguar the Fourth, Earl of Sandrakkan," Liane said as, with forceful impatience, she turned the pages of the book she'd chosen. "He acceded at about the time Carus became King of the Isles. And the document is the *Chronicle of Sandrakkan* compiled at Kremsa, sixty miles east of Erdin. I'm looking for something I found in the *Chronicle* compiled at Erdin during Aguar's reign."

Garric waited a moment to make sure Liane wasn't going to interject something more. She continued to page through the codex in silence. Catching Attaper's eye, Garric read, " 'In this year a great pirate host came from the Outer Sea and took Erdin. They dwelt in the city for eleven months, and in the twelfth month Earl Aguar attacked them from the Island, that'd be Volita, with a great . . . ' "

He paused, changing the angle of the document to the light. The ink was sepia and the parchment had yellowed over the centuries, making the contrast less than ideal. " 'A great band of warriors,' I think this must be," Garric resumed, " 'whom his advisor Dromillac had brought to him with his, that is, its leader, the band's leader, a man of great power. The band of warriors, the army, split the earth and cast the pirates into the Underworld.'"

"The priest who wrote the Kremsa *Chronicle* . . . ," Liane said, relaxed again now that she'd found the place she was looking for and was marking it with her finger, "was afraid to use the word 'wizard'. 'A man of great power,' is his code for wizard, I believe. Now here's a passage from the Erdin *Chronicle*, 'And Earl Afrase died, and his son Aguar succeeded. Aguar was a great warrior but an unlucky ruler, and he was too beholden to the wizard Dromillac who came to him out of Dalopo—or some said out of the Underworld, for they thought him a demon.'"

"What does that book say about the pirates, milady?" Attaper said, frowning as he considered what he'd just heard.

"Nothing, because there's a five-year gap starting in the fifteenth year of Aguar's reign and continuing through the second year of his successor Afrase the Third," said Liane with a smile of triumph. "Which is exactly what you'd expect if the Kremsa account is true, because the priests of the Erdin temple would've had to flee if pirates captured the city. If they even survived."

"Liane," Garric said, frowning at the passage he'd just read to Attaper, "I understood this as 'large band of warriors,' but what it actually says is 'a large warrior.' If Dromillac was a wizard, is it possible that he brought a giant to help Aguar? And what I read as 'the leader of the band' could be another wizard, a wizard who controlled a giant."

"Yes," Liane said, nodding three times quickly to emphasize her agreement. "That'd explain why Tenoctris said Volita is a focus of power still, even after a thousand years. But Garric—I read the passage the same way you did at first, 'cast the pirates into the Underworld,' as meaning 'killed them.' But what if . . . Garric, Dromillac was a wizard and probably so was the ally he brought to Volita to help him. What if they cast the pirates *under*ground literally? Under where the palace now is built."

"And they're coming back up," Garric said, speaking the words to see how they sounded. "The pirates are coming back from underground after a thousand years. I don't see how men could live . . . but there would've been a wizard with the pirates too, wouldn't there? Even so, how could they *live* underground?"

The two male librarians came through the cordon of guards carrying a roll of oxhide that was almost too heavy for them. The female librarian following saw Garric's frown of puzzlement. She said, "It's a map of Sandrakkan, your highness. It was copied from a marble original that was destroyed in the palace at the end of the Old Kingdom."

Attaper glared at the priests, then looked from Liane to Garric, and said, "Your highness, were these pirates like the People who attacked Ornifal from the sea in Stronghand's time? Because those were led by a wizard, and they weren't, well, ordinary men."

He cleared his throat, and added, "Of course, I don't mean they could live in caves underground. But nobody was sure where they really came from, because there isn't any island where they said it was."

"It's . . . ," Garric said. He meant to go on, ". . . a thousand years, so there can't be a connection," and of course it *was* a thousand years. But that was true whether you connected the pirates who attacked Sandrakkan here in the West at the end of the Old Kingdom with the People who'd fallen on Ornifal in the past generation, or if you were suggesting that those pirates might still be alive in the caverns beneath Erdin.

Which he and Liane had both thought of as soon as they read the passages in the *Chronicles*. And both might be true.

"I don't know, milord," Garric said instead. "It's at least possible. As possible as anything else I can come up with now."

"Garric," said Liane. She paused and dabbed her tongue to her lips, less to wet them than to give herself time to order her words. "If it required a wizard to defeat the pirates the first time . . . a pair of wizards, if we understand the *Chronicles* correctly. Should you recall Tenoctris from Ornifal, do you think?"

Garric looked at her as he thought. Then he grinned. There were side effects that he couldn't possibly guess no matter which choice or *what* choice he made. Liane was trying to follow every thread back to what would be the right answer, the perfect answer. She had a splendid mind, but no human being was capable of carrying out the task she'd set herself. There wasn't a perfect answer, period.

"No, love," he said. "I shouldn't."

Attaper's eyes flicked between them as if he were watching a handball match, while the ancient king in Garric's mind grinned. "We had good reason to send Tenoctris with Lord Waldron," Garric continued. "Nothing we've learned or guessed here changes that. While I'd very much like to have Tenoctris' advice right now, she'd be the first to say that summoning warrior giants is beyond her. If they're what's required, I'm afraid we'll have to find them on our own."

There was a jangle in the hallway; the guards stiffened. Garric found his hand going to his sword pommel by reflex.

He and Carus grinned together. The reflex was that of the king, but there'd been times Garric had found it the difference between life and death.

"Between your death and somebody else's, I'd put it," Carus said, laughing with his usual good humor. *"And I'll always pick somebody else for the job of dying, having done it once myself."*

The noise was one of the soldiers who'd been stationed outside the temple double-timing down the hall, his equipment and studded apron clattering. Priests peering in at the visiting prince jumped out of the way. The Blood Eagle's shield banged clear one who didn't jump fast enough.

Attaper placed himself slightly forward of Garric. "What's the trouble, Muns?" he asked, louder than a normal speaking voice.

"Sir, there's people gathering down the streets outside," Muns said, halting in the archway with the troops on guard there instead of coming through. "It's not a mob yet, not exactly, but I think we'd best get back to the palace."

He paused. Attaper turned to Garric with his mouth open, but before he could speak, Muns added, "Sir? I think I saw that one-eyed scut as made the trouble at the coronation. I think he's leading them."

"I should've put my sword through Tawnser when he first turned his one bloody eye on me!" Attaper snarled. He looked at the three librarians, then pointed to the woman.

"You!" he said. She drew herself up sharply, as anyone would at Attaper's tone; Garric felt his own back straighten instinctively. "We came in by the front entrance, but there's a back way, isn't there? Come on, where's the back way?"

The librarian blinked. "Yes, of course," she said, "you entered from Factors' Square, but there's the door onto Lantern Street. I'll take you."

"Right," Attaper said. "Muns, tell Undercaptain Fiers to hold the front as long as he can with his section, but to send the rest of the regiment to me at the Lantern Street entrance. Go!"

He scowled, and muttered to Garric, "I figure we'll need everybody we've got available, and we'll be bloody lucky if we don't need more. A mile to go through somebody else's city!"

They followed the librarian at a quick trot. The parties of Blood Eagles guarding corridor intersections fell in behind at Attaper's barked commands. They'd already snatched off the gilt balls that blunted their spearpoints.

If the mob was gathering on side streets until it was fully prepared to attack, it wasn't really a mob. And if Lord Tawnser had arranged things so neatly at the front of the temple, Garric doubted that he'd have neglected the back entrance too. But it was the best choice available.

"There!" the librarian cried, pointing down a short hall to a door lighted by a transom glazed with bull's-eye glass. An attendant was dozing in the corner. He jumped up with a shout of terror when Garric and the leading Blood Eagles crashed along the corridor at him. The soldiers' hobnails sparked on the stone floor.

"The Cattle Market's on this side!" said Liane from Garric's heel. "It's near Erdin's north gate!"

"Keep behind me!" Garric snapped, as Attaper lifted the crossbar from its staples. Garric pushed the door open with his left hand; his sword was bare in his right. He and Attaper stepped through the doorway together.

Lantern Street was a narrow alley facing the twenty-foot-high stone terrace that supported the Cattle Market, a plaza surrounded by stalls for beasts who'd been separated after sale. The street was empty, but the terrace was full of people, most of them men, and all armed.

The mob gave a shout of bloody triumph. Garric and Attaper threw themselves backward, shoving against the troops who'd started to follow them. A shower of stones and roof tiles arched downward. Garric slammed the door just as the missiles thundered into it. A javelin hit the panel hard enough to thrust its quivering tip a hand's breadth into the temple.

Attaper touched the steel with a fingertip to damp it for examination. "From the earl's arsenal, or I miss my bet," he said.

"Some of the people in Erdin who don't like us are bound to be soldiers," Garric said with a lopsided grin. It seemed odd to be coolly rational at a time like this, but there was no time they'd need cool reason more. "It doesn't mean that Wildulf himself is a traitor."

Though his wife Balila—that was another matter.

"Leave a squad here," Garric went on, taking charge because in a fight he trusted his judgment and his ancestor's instincts further than he did those of anyone else present. "The rest of us will take our stand at the front where we're above anybody who comes at us. Trying to get out that gauntlet would be suicide."

As Attaper turned the troops around with a great deal of shouting and clanging in the strait surroundings, Liane leaned close to Garric's ear, and said, "Perhaps we can signal Lord Rosen from the roof."

"We'll hope so," Garric said grimly. "Because if there are as many people in front as there were waiting for us in the market, we're *not* getting out of here on our own."

Chapter Fourteen

Here," said Liane. She handed Garric a white priestly robe that she'd snatched from the flat of cleaned clothing two servants were carrying toward the suites on the second floor.

A passing soldier swiped at them with his javelin. The servants yelped protest and scrambled up the stairs. It wasn't a serious blow, but it'd reminded the civilians that the priorities had just changed.

"I can't sneak out wearing this!" Garric said in amazement. "I can't! I won't!"

They'd reached the front of the wing they'd been in—to the right of the temple and set forward of it. Most of the volumes were held in the wing that balanced this one across the open plaza with the altar. Undercaptain Fiers had drawn up his thirty men across the front of the plaza, looking down the broad steps to Factors Square.

"She's right," said Attaper unexpectedly. "If they see Prince Garric, they'll attack. If they're afraid you're sneaking out some other way, it'll keep them off-balance."

In a snarl, he added, "And I bloody wish there *was* some other way out!"

"Right," Garric muttered, sheathing his sword to throw the robe around him. It was cut to lace up the front—which he didn't bother with—instead of pulling it on overhead, so it wouldn't be hard to shrug off when he needed his arms free. He'd let personal pride get in the way of assessing the situation. He didn't need the image of Carus in his mind, nodding ruefully, to know how dangerous that could be.

Fortunately, he had Liane and Attaper to advise him—two people who didn't let *his* personal pride affect them in the least. Garric grinned as he hoisted himself on top of the altar. Waist high, it gave him a view over the heads of the Blood Eagles trotting onto the plaza to form with the section already there.

Five streets fed into Factors' Square. Each was filled with people holding weapons and missiles. The front ranks were burly men wrapped in cloaks, which in this warm weather were almost certainly meant to conceal body armor. As the Blood Eagles fell into ranks, a concealed gong sent a piercing, plangent note through the whole district. The crowd shouted and surged forward into the square.

Attaper called an order. The Blood Eagles lifted their rectangular shields so that the upper edge was just beneath each man's chin strap. They were in close order, which meant only two ranks; the men in the second rank cocked their javelins to throw, while those in front held theirs underhand so that the mob faced a hedge of points.

"Don't loose!" Garric shouted. "Don't throw your javelins!"

He had fewer than a hundred and fifty Blood Eagles. The mob—which certainly included soldiers—was thousands strong. The troops might be able to hold the temple or at least one wing of it for some while, but Garric could already see torches made from pine knots and oil-soaked rags flaring in the midst of the crowd.

Liane saw and understood the torches also. "Garric, they're ready to burn down the finest collection of Old Kingdom texts west of Valles just to kill us!" she said. Then, in a tone as hard as the *skritch* of a knife on a whetstone, she added, "If Tawnser's captured alive, he mustn't be pardoned. Garric, a barbarian like that isn't fit to live!'

Despite the situation, Garric smiled at her vehemence. Of course there were probably better reasons to hang Tawnser than his willingness to burn books, but none of them touched Liane's soul as deeply as that one—or Garric's either.

Tawnser stood on an overturned wagon at the back of the square, shouting orders through a bronze speaking horn. He'd obviously planned the attack carefully—and he'd had considerable *time* to plan it, which was the most puzzling part of the business. Garric and Liane hadn't decided to visit the temple until that morning, but Tawnser's preparations must've taken days.

"He's a wizard who can predict the future," Liane said, addressing the same problem. "Or he's being aided by one."

"And I'd venture a guess about who the wizard is," Garric agreed grimly. "Well, there'll be time enough for Dipsas later."

The mob surged to the bottom of the temple steps, but, as Garric expected, they didn't charge home against the shield wall. Instead they halted, shouting threats and curses.

The men in the front rank carried swords, but from the mass of civilians behind them came a shower of tiles and paving stones. For the most part the Blood Eagles' shields shrugged the missiles off, but a man in the second rank sprawled backward with a crash of equipment. His dented helmet rolled away from him.

Garric sized up the situation, saw that it wouldn't change for the better, and made his decision. He shouted. "Attaper, we—"

Realizing he couldn't convey his intentions by bellowing from where he was, Garric jumped off the altar and stepped to his commander's side. His timing was good: an arrow snapped through the air close to where he'd been. There was an archer in the crowd. That posed problems much more serious than hand-flung stones.

"Attaper, we're going to have to cut our way through them now!" Garric said as calmly as he could over the mob's shouting. "Withdraw the squad you left at the back door, then we'll—"

"They'll stay, your highness," Attaper said. "It's the only way we can keep from being surrounded before we're clear of the square."

"I won't leave them to die!" Garric said.

"It's their *job,* your highness, and they'll do it!" Attaper said. Then with a look of anguish he added, "My son Attarus commands them. They'll stand till they die, as their duty requires!"

Garric stood for a heartbeat frozen in horror. Then he said, parroting the words of the warrior ghost in his mind, "Yes. All javelins together, then wade into them with swords. Echelon back from the regimental standard"—the center of the front rank—"by squads. We'll head down Carriage Street. I know it's the way we came, but it's wider than the others by half, and we need the width. On your command, milord!"

Many of those in the mob had come with baskets of stones, but even so, the volleys of missiles had by then slackened. Attaper opened his mouth to shout his orders.

The bright sky dimmed with the suddenness of a door closing.

Garric and everyone else in the square looked up. A cloud as opaque as chimney soot was swelling across the sun.

"Abracadabra!" Liane shouted, as the crowd sucked in its breath. Garric looked over his shoulder. She was standing on the altar now, both arms stretched toward the sky.

An arrow arched toward Liane, but it wobbled and went wide. The archer must've been drawing his bow when the apparition appeared above him. He'd simply let go of the cord instead of loosing his shot properly.

"Demon, I command thee, strike my enemies!" Liane cried. *"Hic haec hoc!"*

The mob gave a collective scream. At the rear Lord Tawnser was trying to keep control, but not even the speaking tube could give his voice authority.

"All ranks!" Lord Attaper bawled. *"Throw on command, throw!"*

Garric doubted that the Blood Eagles could really hear their commander's words over the tumult, but they were so well trained that a hint was enough. The javelins went up over the right shoulders of every man still standing, then snapped forward with the authority of strong arms and long practice. The front of the mob—the soldiers, the cutthroats, the thugs who'd break heads for fun if no one was willing to pay them for the work—went down like wheat in a reaper's cradle.

"At 'em, boys!" Garric shouted, ripping off his priestly robe to draw his sword again. Through his willing lips, King Carus added, "Haft and the Isles!"

The ghostly cloud had smothered the rioters' courage, and the javelins smashed them like thistledown in a sleet storm. Only the mob's own numbers and the narrow streets leading out of the square kept it from dispersing instantly. The troops surged down the temple steps in perfect unison, moving like a hammer dressed in black armor.

For a moment the urge to slaughter threw a red mist over Garric's mind. He was Carus the Warrior King, about to stride through the streets of a rebel city, the tip of his long sword slinging blood at every stroke.

But he wasn't Carus—

Erdin wasn't a rebel city unless he made it one by a massacre here—

And Garric had seen enough dead men to want to avoid seeing more of them when he could avoid it.

"Use the flat of your swords!" Garric shouted as he followed the Blood Eagles down the steps. "Don't kill anybody who isn't trying to fight! Knock 'em down and let 'em tell their stories when they wake up!"

It wasn't exactly being softhearted, but—there were men and there were monsters. The only way the kingdom would survive—and mankind itself would survive—was if all men stayed together.

Though Garric had to agree with Liane: there were a few men like Lord Tawnser whose actions had made them monsters.

Tawnser was still trying to rally the mob, but nobody was paying attention to him. The wagon he'd overturned to serve as his command post rocked like a ship in the storm as desperate rioters forced their way by it. When it gave a particularly violent lurch, Tawnser flung away the speaking horn and jumped off the other side of the wagon, out of sight.

Garric hadn't been sure the Blood Eagles would obey his order, but all the strokes he saw as he stood on the bottom step to check the advancing lines were with the flats, not the edges, of the blades. The troops didn't even push as hard as Garric knew they could. They were aware that panicked congestion at the mouth of the streets leaving the square could be as lethal as swords.

Being knocked down by a steel club or a shield boss was a hard lesson, but it was a survivable one. Some of the Blood Eagles had even retrieved javelins from the heavies who'd fallen in the front row of the mob. They were using the shafts as batons against the scalps and shoulders of those fleeing.

"Not every regiment would take that order," said the image of Carus, watching with a mixture of pride and a frustrated urge to kill. *"And not every king would've been smart enough to give it in the first place."*

Carus laughed and threw his hands behind him. That was a gesture he must've used in life when circumstances prevented him from following his violent instincts.

Garric hadn't worried about the apparition in the sky while he had pressing business with the mob, but that seemed to be under control. He glanced up at a cloud whose writhing, smoky tentacles mimicked a giant ammonite. They, the Great Ones of the Deep, had a close link with black wizardry. The apparition was so savagely evil that Garric raised his sword, a pointless but instinctive response.

Breathing through his open mouth, Garric looked down to the square. He knew the cloud was probably harmless, but it horrified him to look at. Better a shambles of moaning, bleeding human beings . . .

Lord Tawnser was escaping. A confederate had lowered a rope to him from the roof of a three-story building. Tawnser'd lost the black cape he'd worn as a backdrop, but his scarlet tunic and breeches showed vividly as he climbed the wall of weathered brick.

Garric was sure he'd capture Tawnser eventually. But as long as the mad nobleman was alive, his venomous hatred would poison Sandrakkan's relationship with the kingdom. This riot wouldn't be the last trouble he'd rouse.

Lord Attaper had been with his men. Now he came back to join Garric on the step, from which he could judge the Blood Eagles' progress. Attaper's boots were blood-splashed, and from the smear on his blade, he'd used it to thrust, not club.

"There were Sandrakkan soldiers in the mob," Carus explained hard-faced. *"Which makes them mutineers by my lights, since Wildulf's accepted you as king. I think Attaper sees that the same way as I do."*

Garric grimaced, but what's done is done—and he was pretty sure that none of his advisors, Liane included, would've agreed with him about sparing traitorous soldiers. A battle wasn't the same as an execution, at least so far as the public had to know.

"I didn't know your . . . ," Attaper said. He glanced sidelong at Liane, still on the altar with her arms raised. "I didn't realize that Lady Liane was a wizard, your highness."

"She's not," said Garric.

"But I saw—" Attaper said. "Your highness, there she is!"

"There she is, shouting gibberish and playacting," Garric said. "Knowing that that lot"—he nodded to remnants of the mob, climbing over the bodies of those crushed trying to leave the square—"would panic if they thought she controlled the vision, which she can't any better than you could."

Blinking away emotion, Garric added, "There's not a smarter person in all the Isles, Attaper. And maybe not a braver one either, to dare to look at that thing in the sky!"

In the wrack of injured civilians behind the double line of troops was the archer, a sturdy-looking countryman. He must've slipped and been trampled in the mob's sudden rush to escape, because he was well back of where the volley of javelins had landed. The bow lay several feet away, but the quiver hanging from his belt was certain identification.

"She was *playing?*" Lord Attaper said in amazement that seemed tinged with anger. The apparition had frightened him as surely as it did Garric, and the notion that a wellborn girl had the wit and courage to toy with that fear was at best embarrassing.

Garric didn't answer. He sprinted across the plaza, sheathing his sword as he ran. He had to dodge fallen bodies. Once he jumped over a woman in tawdry clothing who screamed curses as she clutched her wrenched knee. Garric had learned about armies and swordsmanship from his ancestor Carus, but as a shepherd boy on Haft he'd had plenty of opportunity to become a skilled archer.

He picked up the bow. It was a simple weapon, a staff of seasoned yew without the layers of horn and sinew that would've made it more powerful but also more delicate. A compound bow might not have survived being trampled, but this self bow and its horsehair cord were none the worse for the experience.

It was a hunter's weapon. The staff was only four feet from tip to tip so that the man using it could slip through dense brush, but it was thick and a powerful weapon in the hands of an archer strong enough to use it.

Garric nocked an arrow from the fallen man's quiver. It had a head like a knitting needle instead of the flaring barbs of a hunting arrow: the archer had thought he might have to shoot through a breastplate, so he'd come with bodkin points instead of broadheads.

Garric held the bow cord to his right ear. He no longer heard the shouts and screams filling the square. He was in a world of his own, his eyes focused on his arrowhead, silhouetted against the scarlet blur of Lord Tawnser's tunic. He threw his weight onto his left arm, bending the bowstaff instead of drawing the cord as easterners were taught to do; he loosed as part of the same smooth motion.

The stiff cord snapped painfully against Garric's left wrist—he wasn't wearing a bracer. He reached to his belt to draw out the next arrow, then remembered that he wasn't shooting at a predator back in the borough, that it wasn't his bow, and that he wasn't a shepherd anymore.

Tawnser had almost reached the roof; men were leaning over the coping to pull him the last of the way to safety. He flung his hands in the air and dropped backward into the square.

Garric threw down the bow; he swayed for a moment. He'd acted by instinct, and only now was he able to understand exactly what he'd done.

"You got him, your highness!" Attaper shouted beside him. "Good shot, your highness, a shot worth everything else that's happened today!"

A man who was alive is now dead, thought Garric, suddenly sick. *A man whom I killed.*

"We've got to get to him before the body's stripped!" Liane cried from Garric's other side. "He may have important documents!"

The three of them ran together toward where the rebel leader had fallen. The rioters who could move under their own power were out of the square by now. Sections of Blood Eagles who'd chased them a little way down the connecting streets were returning. Their officers weren't going to let them disperse in a city which, if not wholly hostile, certainly wasn't friendly to them.

Lord Tawnser lay on his back with a surprised expression. The arrowpoint glittered a hand's breadth out of his breastbone. There wasn't much blood, but the arrow had broken his spine when it struck.

"That was too quick for a man like him!" Attaper said, as Liane undid the clasp of Tawnser's purse.

Garric looked down. "Milord," he said, "for the sake of the kingdom I'm glad he's dead. But I'm sorry I killed him or ever killed a human being; and the kingdom isn't served by even a bad man dying slowly."

"Here, Garric!" Liane said, holding up a slip of parchment. "It's as we thought!"

Garric forced his mind from the memory of a dead man falling down the side of a building. The note read, GARRIC WHO CALLS HIMSELF YOUR PRINCE WILL BE AT THE TEMPLE OF THE SHIELDING SHEPHERD TOMORROW MORNING WITH A FEW SOLDIERS. IF YOU'RE A MAN AND A PATRIOT, SERVE HIM AS HE DESERVES. There was no signature, but the broken wax closure had been sealed with a stamped design.

"That's two intertwined serpents," Liane explained. "It's Dipsas' seal."

"Lord Attaper," Garric said, steadying his voice as he spoke, "we'll return to the palace with all deliberate speed. And then we'll discuss what happened here with a wizard named Dipsas."

He couldn't keep another wave of bloodlust from trembling across the surface of his mind as he thought about the woman responsible for this.

Cashel opened his eyes. He'd gotten barely a glimpse of the cave as he fell into it backward, but he knew he couldn't be there now.

He was in a hall whose sharply peaked ceiling was higher than any place he'd been in. A line of stone-framed windows just below the roof trusses flooded light onto the tapestries along the walls. The hangings on the west were brilliant, and even those in morning shadow gleamed with threads of gold and silver shot through the silk. Ilna would *love* to see those.

"Come join us," said the eldest of the six men on the other side of a table long enough to seat many, many more than those present. It ran down the center of the hall beneath the ridgepole, nearly end to end of the big room. The men sat midway along the table's length. The speaker gestured toward the short bench across from him.

"Yes sir," Cashel said. He wore his tunics but didn't have his quarterstaff with him. The lack didn't bother him as much as he'd have expected it to. "Sir, where am I?"

He didn't ask who the men were, because he already knew that. He'd seen their images walking the battlements of Ronn when he was with Mab.

Virdin, the first of Ronn's champions, had spoken. To his right were the twins Menon and Minon, laughing at some joke between them as they watched Cashel over their wine cups. At that end of the row was Valeri, lanky and glaring as fierce as a seawolf at Cashel.

The images of the two warriors on Virdin's left hadn't come by before the Made Men attacked, but Hrandis had to be the squat man, broader even than Cashel. That made the man beside him Dasborn, who had long limbs and a swordsman's wrists.

"You're in the Cavern of the Heroes, Cashel," one of the twins said. Cashel couldn't tell them apart, and he doubted their mother could've done that either.

"The real Cavern," his brother said, grinning broadly. "Not the hole in the rock that people see beneath Ronn."

Big Hrandis poured wine from a ewer into the rock crystal cup waiting in front of Cashel. "You had a hard trip here, I'll warrant," he said, in a voice that rumbled like distant thunder. "Have some of this."

Cashel touched the cup. It felt solid, but . . . "Is it real?" he asked.

"It's as real as we are," said Dasborn, with a sardonic grin that made Cashel think of Garric's father Reise. Reise had more education than just about anybody, but there was a sadness under even the jokes he told. "Or as real as you are in this place, if you prefer."

Valeri looked at Virdin, and said with a sneer, "She sent us a talky one, didn't she? I'd have thought she could do better."

"If you've got a problem with talk, Valeri," the twin nearest him said with a hard grin, "then you can stop making so much empty talk yourself."

Cashel drank to separate himself from the bickering. He supposed these fellows had been together a long time. Folks can get on each other's nerves, even when they're all heroes.

Because he was thinking about something else, Cashel gulped down more wine than he'd meant to. It prickled; he hunched forward and made a muffled *whuff!*

Duzi, he'd barely kept from sneezing the wine back out his nose! That'd have given Valeri something to sneer at, wouldn't it?

Virdin leaned back on his bench. He had a full white beard, but the lean face it framed looked like that of somebody younger by far. "What do you think of the men you came with, Cashel?" he asked.

"The boys, you mean, Virdin," Valeri said. "By Ronn, what a litter of puppies!"

"You were young yourself once, Valeri," Dasborn said, looking down the table with a deliberately blank face. Now that he'd met the Heroes, Cashel didn't doubt they were all their reputations said they were; but Dasborn was the one he'd watch closest if Fate put him on the wrong side of them. Dasborn was the sort who made up his mind without any sign at all—then acted, quick and cold as a housewife wringing the neck of the chicken for dinner.

"I was young," said Valeri, "but I was never like that. If I'd been like that, I'd have hanged myself!"

Cashel drank again, then cleared his throat loudly. The wine was well enough, he supposed; but he preferred beer, and the cup had a gold rim besides. Cashel didn't like the taste of metal with his drink. Even the tarred leather jacks he and Ilna used at home would be better, if he couldn't get a wooden masar instead.

"They're a good lot," he said, looking straight at Virdin so it wouldn't seem like he was picking a fight with Valeri. He wasn't afraid of Valeri, mind; but it wasn't in Cashel's nature to quarrel if he could avoid it.

"They're young, sure, but they're braver than it maybe seems just to come down here when it's all so different from anything they know. They're willing, I guess I mean."

"Willing?" said Hrandis, filling Cashel's cup again. Cashel didn't realize he'd drunk as much as he had. It did seem to perk him up some. "Are they willing to die for Ronn, Cashel?"

Cashel took a drink and swirled it in his mouth while he frowned over his answer. He swallowed and met Hrandis' eyes again. "I think they are, sir," he said. "They'd say they were, I know. But . . ."

He scrunched his face up over something he felt but couldn't point to. He couldn't say it so another person would believe him if they weren't disposed to.

"Sir, I don't think they know what that means," he said.

Dasborn laughed in honest amusement. "When we were their age," he said, "we didn't know either. But we know now."

"Aye," said Valeri. "We know a lot of things. Now."

Hrandis shrugged. "Ronn needed us," he said. "The citizens needed us. That's all that mattered."

Valeri looked at him. "Is it?" he said harshly. "Do you believe that, Hrandis?"

"Yes he does," said Dasborn. He smiled faintly, cruelly. "And so do you, Valeri, or you wouldn't be here."

"They've agreed," said one of the twins. "They're here, and they're agreed. It doesn't matter what they understand."

"We didn't understand, but we're here," said his brother. He looked at Virdin, and added, "Tell him the rest, Virdin. That's all that remains to do."

"Yes, I suppose it is," the white-bearded man said. "Go back to what men think is the Cavern, Cashel. You'll find your companions sleeping there. They'll awaken when you arrive. Tell them to take up the arms they find in the chamber with them. Do you understand?"

"Yes sir," Cashel said. He didn't know how he was supposed to go back to where the Sons were, but he supposed Virdin or whoever'd brought him here would take care of returning him also. "What do I do then?"

Dasborn laughed. "There's nothing more for you to do, Cashel," he said. "You'll have saved Ronn for the last time—if the city can be saved."

"You can go now, Cashel," old Virdin said. He raised his hand in a salute.

The vast hall shrank down to the size of a pinhead, then vanished. Cashel lay on his back in a chamber.

He sat up. The room was lighted only by a rosy haze between Mab's left thumb and forefinger. The Sons slept on the stone floor.

Along the walls were six sets of armor. They stood as monuments to the skeletons lying beneath them.

Ilna kept her eyes on the horizon and let her feet choose a path down the lines anchoring the larva to the cliff. Usually silk carried the imprint of the tiny fingers of children who'd unwrapped the cocoons, then spun the long threads into yarn. Despite how thick the ropes were, they owed nothing to human involvement.

Spider silk carried with it a hunger as fierce as the noonday sun. Worms, though, both the little ones the Serians fed on mulberry leaves in the world Ilna knew and this huge one in the sea, had no desire save to exist. They and their silk were as bland as flour paste.

Ilna smiled. Worms had no personalities and no reason to exist—except that they created the most lustrous and beautiful thread in the world. That couldn't be of interest to the worms themselves. Only when Ilna felt whimsical—as now—did she imagine that there might be something in the universe greater than individual worms and sheep and humans.

More lines in bundles of three joined the ones she walked on. Sheets of steel-strong gauze bound the heavy strands together, twisting them into a trough that closed on itself near the surface of the water to become a tube. Ilna knew through the certain witness of her feet that the worm was no more intelligent than the silk it'd spun, yet how *could* the perfection of this creation not involve will and understanding?

She laughed again. There was no answer that her reason would accept. Therefore, there was no answer.

Because she was looking outward, not down, Ilna noticed that the bird had changed its pattern from the slow circuits it'd been making on the horizon. Its wings stroked the air in slow unison, like the oars of a great warship making the first efforts toward driving the vessel into motion from a wallowing halt. The bird was so far away that it didn't swell in size even though it was flying directly toward her.

She frowned, but the bird's actions no longer mattered. The anchor cords and their wrapper of silk completed the tunnel. She entered, leaning against an outrushing breeze. It carried with it the ripeness of a plowed field fertilized with some indefinable manure. The light dimmed to that of an overcast morning.

Ilna walked downward. The footing was springy but agreeably firm. The light continued to dim, but her eyes adapted to it. The tube had a slight curve as it flattened from a slope to a plane, so she couldn't see the open sky when she glanced over her shoulder.

No matter. Her duty lay deeper, not up from where she'd come.

The wind soughed, rushing past her as if glad to be gone. Its odor was thick and unfamiliar but not anything a peasant woman found offensive. The tanyard in Barca's Hamlet cured hides with manure and lye. It was downwind of the houses when the breeze came from the sea, as it normally did; but sometimes the wind changed.

Ilna walked on. Some light still pierced the layer of water overhead, but it was a pale blue that made her hands look like those of a month-dead corpse. She smiled. That could be true, a month or so from this moment or the next. . . .

Without warning she entered the larva's chamber. From the cliff above it'd looked like a spindle of yarn. Seeing it from the inside, she thought that somehow she'd taken a wrong turning that brought her to a place she'd never imagined. Only when her eyes absorbed the pattern did she understand the nature of the cocoon.

The interior was dimpled where lines attached to cables above and to rocks on the seafloor beneath pulled the skin outward. Otherwise, the weight of water would flatten the bag and its occupants.

The larva was the size of a building, the size of a ship: a smooth mass moving with the slow majesty of a summer cloud. In direct sun its skin would be white with brown mottlings, but here the background was the leprous color of fungus on a tomb.

It lay in a pool of its own wastes. Hard-shelled, eyeless creatures browsed the fluid, their hairlike legs stirring the surface.

The larva's movements were as slow as the pulse in a sleeping lizard's throat, but when its head lifted slightly Ilna caught the needle-sharp flash of the jewel she'd come for. The creature shifted again, hiding the jewel, but now Ilna understood why there were highlights reflected onto the curved silken surface at the far end of the chamber.

And naturally, it *would* be at the other end. Having come this far to fetch the jewel, Ilna wasn't going to complain about walking another furlong—even if she had to do so over the back of a giant worm.

The first problem was getting *onto* the worm's back. It was easily twice, perhaps even three times, her height. From where Ilna stood the curve swelled out like the face of an undershot cliff. That meant she'd have to climb the cocoon and drop onto the creature.

Ilna turned her head, eyeing, then touching the silken wall. Immediately her stomach settled, though she hadn't been aware that she was queasy before then. The larva's movements made the whole cocoon undulate slowly. Ilna didn't like the feel of a ship at sea, and this was worse—more like being in the guts of a snake. Focusing on fabric, even a fabric woven by a worm, brought the universe into a perspective Ilna was comfortable with.

The bag had several layers, each formed from three different sizes of thread: thumb-thick lines that alone or in bundles provided strength; straw-thick cords that formed a close framework within the heavy supports; and finally sheets of gossamer to cover the framework and make the bag watertight. Ilna thrust her left hand into the fabric, forcing the gossamer aside with her fingers to seize one of the heavy lines. When she was sure she had it, she reached a little higher and gripped with her right hand.

Kicking holds for her bare feet, Ilna walked and pulled her way up the side as if she was climbing a silk net. It wasn't especially difficult even when she got high enough that the bag's curve meant that she was hanging upside down. Ilna was a good deal stronger than she was heavy, and this was only for a brief time anyway.

She looked down, then pulled her feet free. Her toes dangled close to the larva's back. If she slipped off the slick, pulsing body when she let go—and she might—she'd still scarcely injure herself on the yielding surface below. Though it would be unpleasant.

Ilna's mouth formed into a hard smile again. She *wanted* to be punished when she made a mistake. It made it less likely that she'd do the same thing again. Falling into a pool of worm dung certainly qualified as punishment.

She dangled for a moment, then dropped. Her weight dimpled the worm's flesh. Slow ripples quivered out from her feet, reflecting and cancelling one another as they proceeded down the white surface.

The nearest brown blotch was only a double pace from Ilna. It shifted slightly and focused six glittering eyes on her. What she'd thought was a skin discoloration was instead a flat parasite the size of a half cape. Its beak was driven deep into the worm's white flesh.

There were more parasites than Ilna could count on both hands. They formed a diamond pattern across the larva's back, as regular as the studs an artisan might hammer into a leather box for decoration. Here the reason for the spacing was a matter not of craft but of survival: the parasites were territorial as serpents, each claiming an expanse of the worm's flesh sufficient to feed it to breeding age.

The nearest parasite withdrew a beak the length of a man's forearm from the worm's flesh; a drop of clear fluid oozed up before the wound puckered shut. All down the worm's back other parasites were moving, restive because of the disturbance to their careful hierarchy.

Beak lifted, the nearest parasite squirmed toward Ilna, the human who'd invaded its territory. It moved on more tiny legs than she could count.

Sharina got up from the ground. She'd landed without the forward momentum she'd been braced for. She'd been as active as that of any boy in the borough before she became a princess, but the reflexes she'd developed running and jumping had played her false. The mechanism the ring used to bring her here wasn't bound by the laws of the waking world.

Men—People—were hoeing their way down every row of the broad field in which she'd landed. They were bent over their work, but the nearest were only twenty feet away. They came toward her a chop at a time.

Sharina looked for a weapon. The hoes had sturdy shafts and wedge-shaped bronze heads that could cut flesh as well as the roots of weeds. If she pretended to be submissive, she might have a chance to grab a hoe and—

The workers paid her no more attention than the corn and the peavines did. They worked forward, intent on their tasks and never looking above the earth they were cultivating. Sharina stepped aside cautiously, feeling the muscles of her abdomen tense. She expected that at any instant one or the other of the men passing her would turn and grab her.

They didn't. They hoed on with no sound except the *chk! chk!* of their tools and the occasional cling of bronze on a pebble.

A horn trilled a long, silvery note. It seemed to be far in the distance, but Sharina didn't know how sound travelled in this place. She looked at the ring. If she began to read the legend on the bezel, would it take her back to Valles or . . . ?

Sharina slipped the ring onto her left thumb, where she wouldn't lose it. "Or," was too likely for her to take the risk just yet. She'd been many places, in the waking world and out of it, since leaving Barca's Hamlet. This island wasn't where she wanted to be, but experience had taught her that things could've been worse. Leaping somewhere at random might very well drop her into one of those worse alternatives.

Sharina looked around. From what she'd seen as she descended to the island, most of the surface was more or less the same as her immediate surroundings. Their fields ran between a pair of irrigation channels marked by the pale fronds of the weeping willows growing on their margins.

The land wasn't as dead flat as it'd seemed from above. The surface rolled enough that Sharina could see at most a couple furlongs to the right, the direction of the lake and building she'd seen in the center of the island. Her only choices other than the fields were that building or the shore. The latter'd looked like it was lapped by clouds, not a sea of water, but Sharina understood little enough about this island that she wasn't going to jump to conclusions—especially to one that made it more likely that she was trapped.

She smiled as she jogged down the row, passing through the line of workers. They gave her no more notice than they had before. Her being trapped was likely enough already.

At least she wouldn't starve: she snapped off a pea pod as she ran and popped it whole into her mouth, the way she'd have done as a child when she was cultivating the inn garden. The peas were ripe and crunched tastily. Pausing—the workers were far behind her already—she gathered a handful and trotted onward, eating them.

The horn called again. It seemed closer this time.

Sharina looked over her shoulder, but all she see were the green billows of the maize. She frowned, going over her choices as she continued to jog through the grain.

The field ended ten strides ahead in an irregular line of willows and mimosas, a natural watercourse instead of a man-made canal. The horn sounded, by now in the near distance; another replied from much farther away to Sharina's right.

She reached the creek. Its pebble bottom was clearly visible through the turbulence caused by larger rocks breaking the surface of the water. The banks of the stream were low, though undercut, and the channel was never more than eight feet across.

Instead of leaping the creek and continuing on, Sharina lifted herself into the crotch of a willow and scrambled up one of steeply slanting main branches. It took her thirty feet into the air before it began to wobble dangerously from her weight. Gripping the slick bark with both hands, she paused, calming her quick breaths. By craning her neck she found an opening through which she could look back the way she'd come while remaining concealed behind the curtain of fronds hanging from higher branches,.

The laborers continued hoeing their way down the field in as good order as a rank of Garric's pikemen. They seemed to have no more minds than ripples on a pond did: and like the ripples, they moved forward in perfect unison.

The horn called. Sharina slitted her eyes, but there was nothing to see in the direction of the sound. She was about to drop to the ground and resume running when a man wearing a helmet and polished breastplate came over the swell of the earth.

He was mounted on a two-legged lizard with a tail twice the length of the torso to balance its neck and long skull. The beast raised its head and licked the air the way a snake does, scenting prey. Its jaws hung slightly open, baring a saw-edged mouthful of teeth.

The lizard whuffed, then strode forward again. It moved like a grackle, bobbing its head back and forth, but each stride was ten feet long. The man on its back raised a bronze trumpet to his lips and blew another trembling call.

Sharina found her hands gripping the branch tighter than she needed just to hold on. "Lady," she prayed in a whisper, "if it is Your will, help me in this danger."

She slid back down the tree, making her plans. Whether or not the Great Gods helped her, she'd be helping herself to the best of her ability.

Chapter Fifteen

M a'am?" Cashel said, meeting Mab's eyes. Softly crimson wizardlight wrapped her, like a tree in deep fog silhouetted against the sunrise. She looked like a middle-aged woman, pudgy but not fat. Her expression was coldly cynical like Ilna's on a bad day; which for Ilna had been more days than not.

"Wake them, Cashel," Mab said. "That's what you were told to do, isn't it?"

"Yeah," he said. He glanced at the equipment along the back wall, facing the door. "And to tell them to put on the armor there."

The Sons slept more soundly than people sprawled on a stone floor ought to do. Cashel guessed something was going on with them besides just being tired and sleeping. Maybe they were having the sort of meeting he'd had with the Heroes, but he kinda doubted that.

In the Sons' minds, the Heroes were the next thing to Gods. Cashel knew enough about people to understand that real heroes were more apt to be men like Ilna's friend Chalcus than they were to be saints. These boys hadn't been out in the world enough to know that, and it might discourage them to meet those six hard men.

"Rise and shine!" Cashel said in a loud voice. The Sons stirred, but they didn't open their eyes.

Cashel frowned. He banged his quarterstaff against the inside of the door, noting with surprise that the ferrule struck sparks of blue wizardlight from the bronze.

"Wakey, wakey!" he said. Only by a heartbeat did he keep from adding, "You'll get no breakfast, you lazy woollies!" as he'd have done with a flock of sheep slow to leave their byre in the morning.

The Sons were alert now, sitting up or at least rolling to one arm. "How long have I been sleeping?" Enfero asked plaintively.

Cashel took out his wad of raw wool and began polishing his quarterstaff. People asked a lot of questions that didn't make any difference. That was all right, he supposed, but it didn't mean he needed to answer them.

Rubbing down the staff was more than just filling time. Cashel hadn't really done anything with the staff during the journey, just spun it through the air in much the fashion he did most days for exercise. The air he was spinning it in was something he didn't like the memory of, though. If he cleaned nothing but the surface of his mind with the wool, then it was a good thing to've done.

Orly got to his feet, slowly and carefully. "We're up, Master Cashel," he said. "What do we do now?"

"We were supposed to wake the Heroes," said Stasslin. His voice started accusingly, but the peevish tone bled away as his eyes moved from Mab to Cashel, then settled between them. "There's nobody here to wake. Unless that's them."

He gestured. "The bones."

"You're to put the armor on," Cashel said. "And the swords, I guess."

He looked at the equipment, which hadn't interested him a lot until then. He'd never worn armor nor had any truck with weapons beyond a quarterstaff. The knife he'd carried all the years he could remember was a tool for trimming leather or picking a stone from the hoof of a plow ox, not something he'd ever thought of stabbing somebody with.

This was fancy stuff, though. Cashel didn't see much point in the engraving and gold inlays, but the quality showed in the falling-water sheen of the swordblades and the way the axe heads were shrunk onto the helves instead of just being wedged in place.

"It won't fit us," Herron said. He glanced down at the sword belt he'd unbuckled when he curled up on the floor to sleep, then looked again to Cashel. "Will it, Master Cashel?"

"It will fit you," Mab said. "Well enough. Put the armor on, Sons of the Heroes."

Orly looked at her with an expression Cashel couldn't read. "Yes," he said. "It's what we came here for. Isn't it, milady?"

"You came here to save Ronn from the king and his creatures," said Mab. "For that you must put on the armor."

"I thought we came to wake the Heroes," Athan objected with a whine, but he stepped to the set of equipment on the right end of the line and began to examine it.

The gear varied in style and decoration. Each place had a helmet, but these ranged from the simple iron pot that Herron set carefully on his head to the ornately chased and gilded pair that Enfero and Manza chose.

Cashel stood uncertain as the Sons armed themselves. He glanced at

Mab. She crooked a finger to bring him silently to her side, then laid her free hand in the crook of his elbow as they watched together.

Five of the sets included shields. The last had instead two short-hafted axes; that had been Hrandis' equipment, Cashel supposed. Stasslin lifted Hrandis' cuirass of riveted iron bands from the rack on which it hung, muttering, "This'll never fit any of us. . . ."

He closed the piece around him and it did fit, fit the way a scabbard fits the sword it was made for. Something had changed, but Cashel couldn't swear whether the difference was in the armor or the body of the man wearing it.

"Somebody help me with these laces," Athan said. His cuirass had a sleeve of mail to cover the right arm. He was trying to do something with it one-handed and, of course, failing. "Dasborn, help me, will you?"

Cashel started forward. Mab gripped his arm to prevent him.

"Come on, Dasborn!" Athan said, but it wasn't Athan's voice. "I didn't come back so I could die of old age."

"What would you know about dying of old age, Valeri?" Enfero—or was it Manza?—said.

"Maybe he's been talking to Virdin," said . . . said his brother. Neither man was Enfero or Manza now.

Orly had slid on a coat of mail with a silver wash that made it shimmer like a moonlit lake. He finished buckling the crossed shoulder belts that held his long sword and dagger, then walked over to the man who used to be Athan.

"You'd be in a hurry on the way to your execution, Valeri," he said, taking his companion's sleeve in one hand and reeving a thong through the rings above, then below, the elbow. He'd gathered the metal fabric so that it wouldn't bind if the man wearing it swung his sword violently.

"We all were, weren't we?" said Stasslin, wearing Hrandis' black armor. "What else did we ever get from being Heroes?"

"We got the eyes of every man in Ronn," said one of the twins.

"And especially every woman in Ronn!" said his brother. "Oh, those were the days, weren't they?"

"We did our duty," said Herron's body speaking in Virdin's calm, reasonable voice. "There isn't any pay for that—not the honor, not any of the rest. It was our job, and we did it. And we'll do it again."

The swords were racked apart from their belts and scabbards. Athan held Valeri's blade up in the shimmering light for examination, then sheathed it with the absently smooth motion Cashel had seen skilled swordsmen like Garric and Chalcus display.

Athan couldn't have handled a sword like that if he'd practiced all his life. It took more than work: you had to have the sort of understanding of what you were doing that Cashel did with his quarterstaff. The Sons of the Heroes were . . . gone, maybe dead; Cashel didn't know where the boys were now or if they'd ever come back. These men in armor were the Heroes themselves.

"So," said one of the twins to Mab. "Who are you?"

"You know who she is," Hrandis said. "Who else could she be in this place?"

"I've never seen her look like this," the other twin said. He walked a few steps to the side.

"It doesn't matter what I look like," Mab said, smiling faintly as she turned, keeping her face toward the twin who was trying to view her profile. "It doesn't even matter who I am, Menon. What matters—"

She swept the whole band with her glance. She'd been playing before. Now each word came out like the thump of a door closing, without music or doubt: "What matters is that none of you is a wizard, and Ronn will need a wizard's help as well as your own if the city is to survive."

Dasborn laughed. "The citizens thought I was hard," he said, looking around his fellows. "It must've been the same for all of you in your day. But they didn't know what hard really was, because they only saw surfaces."

He bowed to Mab, and went on, "We didn't serve you, milady, we served Ronn and her people. But it was an honor to serve *with* you, and I'm pleased to be doing that again."

"He speaks for all of us, I think," Virdin said. "Anybody disagree?"

"We're here, aren't we?" Valeri snapped. He hunched, settling his cuirass to ride more comfortably on his shoulders. "Let's get on with it."

"One thing first," Virdin said, turning to Cashel. The Hero's features were those of Herron, but nobody could've mistaken the boy from sunlit Ronn for the man who faced Cashel now.

"You're a stranger, Master Cashel," Virdin said. "You've done a man's duty to come to this place to wake us, but you have no business with what comes next. Go home with our thanks and the thanks of the city."

"I've come this far," Cashel said, facing the men in armor. "I guess I'll go the rest of the way with you."

"This is Ronn's business," Hrandis said, his eyes on Mab. "Ours and the citizens. He doesn't belong."

"He belongs," Mab said. "He's said he's willing to accompany us, and he doesn't say things he doesn't mean."

Cashel smiled. "No ma'am," he said, his voice husky. "I don't."

"I want Cashel with me," Mab said. "He's made it his business. He belongs with me, and with us."

"All right," said Valeri. "We've talked enough."

He turned and touched the great bronze door where the valves met in the middle. It opened with the soundless majesty of sunrise. Drawing their swords and Hrandis lifting his two axes, the Heroes stepped from the temple.

Darkness fled before them.

Sharina knelt and picked up one of the larger stream-washed stones. It was some dense pinkish rock, about the size of both her fists clenched.

The lizard was hunting her by smell. She wasn't sure she'd gain by walking downwind with the stream, but it was something she *could* do. The water wasn't deep, but the bottom was dangerously slick, especially when cold water had numbed the soles of her feet. She'd like to have run, but that wasn't possible.

Sharina's silken inner tunic had long sleeves. As she paced over the smooth, algae-haired stones, she ripped the right sleeve off at the shoulder seam to create a fabric tube. She knotted the wrist end into a bag, then dropped the stone into it. That gave her a mace of sorts, easier to hold than the bare stone and much harder-hitting.

She continued on. The nearest horn called, followed at intervals by horns at a greater distance to either side.

The willows and mimosas were a good screen against anybody looking her way from the fields, but they wouldn't hide Sharina if the rider reached the creek and chose to follow it. That's what he *would* do almost certainly, if his mount lost the scent. The lizard's long legs could in a few minutes go farther up- and downstream than Sharina could walk before the hunter arrived.

She glanced through the mimosa stems toward the cultivated field. She'd reached the edge where an irrigation channel separated the maize and beans from a field of dark green rape. The rider wasn't in sight yet, but he would be soon.

The builders had stubbed the irrigation channel off just short of the creek so that the measured water didn't drain away. Trees must sprout along the channel's margin, but they'd been trimmed away; cattails grew from the muddy bottom, however. Without hesitating Sharina scrambled out of the creek and across the short stretch of waste ground, then threw herself into the channel. It was shallow, but she could wriggle down into the soft bottom to conceal herself among the cattails. The standing water was blood-warm and opaque with mud.

Sharina lay down full length and settled a mat of leaves from last year's growth over her head. She hoped she'd covered her blond hair completely, but she'd decided that she had to keep her eyes above water so that she could see. Settling her breathing again, she waited.

What would Cashel do if he were there with her? Hide in the ditch, she supposed, just as she was doing. There was no other choice, not against the band of hunters coursing her. She could hear the horn calls coming closer. She might escape the nearest rider, but she didn't see how she could get off the island without using the ring and taking her chances with where it sent her. Nothing Cashel could do would change that.

But she'd feel better with Cashel beside her. Things were never hopeless if Cashel was there with you.

Sharina grinned, the way Cashel'd expect her to do. She shifted to grip her mace's silken shaft with both hands. Things weren't hopeless now, either.

The horn sounded from where she'd entered the stream. After a brief pause, Sharina heard loud splashes mixed with the clack of stones being knocked together by the weight of the great lizard. Chance or instinct had caused the hunter to turn downstream, the correct direction.

Well, Sharina couldn't do anything until he'd come past her. That made his choice her good luck, didn't it?

And perhaps it did, but she wouldn't pretend that she really *felt* that way about it.

The hunter came closer, though Sharina still couldn't see him. There was a *Braaaa!* from the lizard's throat, a startled, "Ho! Ho!" from the rider, then a sloshing like a waterfall. The beast had slipped.

"Up!" the rider called. "Come, come up!"

The scene was *wrong,* but it took Sharina a moment to understand how. She was expecting a torrent of shouted curses. She'd never met a human, no matter how saintly, who wouldn't have reacted excitedly to that dangerous fall. The People appeared to have no more emotions than dung beetles did.

The lizard's head and clawed right foot slid into her field of vision over the creek bank. The beast lurched forward in the rainbow spray as its tail lashed the water for balance. Its pebbled skin was pale gray with darker stripes that looked purple when the light was on them.

The rider'd been lying close over his mount's long neck. He straightened, looking first forward, then back the way he'd come. He clucked the lizard into motion, holding the reins in his left hand and raising his trumpet to his lips with his right. He blew his long, soughing call as he strode past the ditch where Sharina lay. The lizard cast its head from side to side, obviously restive.

The saddle was over the lizard's hips, more than six feet in the air. Its high crupper would, incidentally, protect the rider against a blow from behind.

As the lizard's head swung away from Sharina, she came out of the cattails swinging her stone mace from left to right. She was two strides from the hunter. He dropped the trumpet onto its neck chain and snatched at the long-shafted trident upright in a saddle scabbard.

The mace struck the center of the rider's polished bronze breastplate, just below the ribs. It bonged, dishing in the thin metal and throwing the rider out of the saddle. He tumbled backward, hitting the ground with a crash; his helmet fell off.

Sharina caught the left stirrup. She couldn't stay hidden in this place. She supposed she'd be better off mounted. She wasn't planning, just reacting, but she didn't have enough information *or* time to do better.

The lizard twisted its head back to bite her; it couldn't quite reach. Its breath, stinking of dead meat, made her gag.

The saddle was high and narrow, like a mule's only much larger. A downward extension formed a mounting step below the stirrup. Sharina put her right foot into it. As she did, the lizard sidled away and tried to snap at her again.

She still held the mace in her right hand, gripping it close to the stone. She batted the beast's snout. It squealed like steam from under a pot lid and hopped sideways, dragging Sharina with it.

The rider lay faceup on the ground. His eyes were open, but his only movement was to move his lips like a carp sucking air. The stone had caught him in the pit of the stomach, knocking the wind out of him despite his armor.

Sharina tried to pull herself into the saddle. She had her right foot on the step and held the stirrup in her left hand. From the way it was laid out, she was meant to lift her left foot into the stirrup, grip a bronze handle below the horn with her left hand, and lift herself aboard. She was perfectly capable of doing that—if the lizard stopped hopping away for the three seconds or so it'd take!

A horn sounded, a quick *Heep! Heep! Heep!* rather than the long calls she'd heard before. The lizard sidled, twisting. Loping down the waste ground on Sharina's side of the creek was another of the lizard-riding hunters, with his horn to his lips. She grimaced in frustration, making one last attempt to get—

The lizard had been easing forward at the same time that it moved sideways. Sharina, her attention fixed on mounting, hadn't noticed what was happening. She jumped, her left foot lifting for the stirrup, and her left shoulder slammed into the trunk of a willow as big around as her body.

She recoiled backward and dropped to the ground, her body a white flash of pain in a cocoon of numbness. The lizard, having finally brushed her off, capered away and turned with a hoot of delight.

The second hunter leaned from his saddle and thrust his trident down, pinning the skirts of Sharina's tunics to the ground. Leaning on the shaft to hold it in place, the hunter blew the quick three-note call, then repeated it.

Two more hunters rode up. One dismounted and rolled Sharina onto her stomach. When he jerked her arms behind her back, the pain in her left shoulder turned the world into white haze. He tied her wrists efficiently, then turned her faceup again.

The third rider bent over his saddle horn to check on the hunter Sharina'd disabled. The injured man was doing something with his hands, maybe trying to unbuckle his dented cuirass. The third rider straightened and clucked his lizard over to the first man's mount, catching its reins without difficulty.

Sharina's head had hit the willow also, though she hadn't noticed it until the pulsing agony in her shoulder subsided a trifle. She hadn't had an inkling that the tree was there till the instant she slammed into it. . . .

Her captors turned to look to the left, the direction from which they'd come. They didn't speak. Sharina realized that the only words she'd heard from them were the first rider's commands to his mount.

A bronze boat was sailing toward them over the plowed fields. It was large enough to hold more than the dozen men already aboard it. The one in the bow had a face like a monkey's. He wore a sky-blue robe and peaked hat, and he was beating the air with a copper athame. Some of the others were People like the hunters who'd captured Sharina, uniformly still and pale-skinned, but half the boat's passengers were ordinary men like the wizard in the bow.

The boat settled, sinking into the soft earth. The wizard lowered his athame. Though he tried to seem relaxed, he was breathing hard from the effort of his wizardry.

Sharina didn't recall having seen any of the boat's passengers before, but the tall, black-bearded man with a grim frown looked so much like Lord Waldron that she'd be willing to bet he was Bolor bor-Warriman. He turned to the wizard, and said without affection, "This is Sharina, the usurper's sister, Hani. How did she get here?"

"She must have the ring," said the wizard. "That means there was trouble in Valles, but there'll be time enough to learn the details later. Two of you lift her aboard, and we'll go back to the lake."

A pair of ordinary men climbed out of the boat. They were dressed in velvet and gold, but both looked more like street thugs than noblemen. The short one's nostrils had been slit, and his taller companion was missing three fingers on his left hand.

As they lifted Sharina, dizzy with renewed pain, into their vessel, she saw the man who hadn't crowded to the railing to look at her the way the rest had. His face was that of the oversized bronze sculpture of Valence the Second Stronghand that she'd just seen in front of the mausoleum of the bor-Torials. She was looking at Valgard.

Ilna backed a step as the parasite walked toward her. Swam toward her, really: it looked like a dollop of slime floating on top of a pond. It wasn't moving very fast, but she couldn't go any farther back unless she wanted to slip into the pool of the worm's wastes below.

If that happened, the creatures living there would probably object before she could convince them that she hadn't arrived to steal their filth. It wasn't only human beings who jumped to the worst possible conclusions without giving the other fellow a chance to explain. . . .

Ilna walked to the right and started forward. The parasite stopped. The tiny legs around three-quarters of its flat body wriggled furiously, turning the creature like a wheel; then—in its fashion—it charged Ilna again.

By advancing she'd come close to a second parasite, this one slightly larger than the first and wearing a different pattern of black smudges on its brown back. It pulled its beak from the worm, just as the first one had, and started toward her also.

Ilna smiled in a combination of amusement and triumph. That was what she'd expected would happen. Patterns weren't merely something that appeared on the backs of monstrous bugs. She retreated a step quickly. The two parasites drove together and began fencing with their long beaks, trying to force each other out of the space they both were claiming.

Ilna walked around the back of the first parasite at the pace the surface held her to. Her feet set up slow waves in the worm's flesh, undulating the length of the creature. If she took her usual rapid strides, the ripples would trip her.

It was like walking on a huge fresh intestine. And at that, she didn't suppose there was much difference between a worm and a sheep's gut. All either one did was turn food into waste in the course of its trip from one end to the other.

The parasites were scarcely more intelligent than the worm. They couldn't think, so they reacted. So long as they were reacting against each other, Ilna had nothing to fear from them. It only meant that to walk from the worm's tail to its head, she had to zigzag instead of going in a straight line.

The next creature up the worm's back pulled its beak out with a slurping sound. As soon as it was ready to move, Ilna started around it to the right. It and the parasite nearest lunged together with the same mindless determination as the first pair. When they were firmly locked together, she went on to the next.

On firm ground Ilna might've been able simply to run the gauntlet of the parasites instead of tricking them into fighting for territories, but she didn't trust this jellied sponginess. Besides, she'd never been interested in running. If it was something good, it'd wait till she got there. If it was bad . . . Well, if it was bad, she wasn't going to run away from it.

She guessed life'd be easier for her if she treated obstructive people the way she did these flat bugs: trick them into fighting one other so that they left her alone. Instead she met them head-on and smashed them into a proper awareness of their mistakes. Human patterns weren't any harder to grasp than those of bugs were. Because they were fellow human beings, however, Ilna felt a need to correct them instead of leaving them in their errors.

She smiled as she negotiated the parasites. In her heart of hearts, Ilna'd never been able to believe that she really *was* a human being. Perhaps her assumption of duty to her fellows was merely self-deception.

The worm was nervous, moving its rear portion side to side in what for it must be major exertion. That was probably Ilna's fault. The parasites she'd passed continued to struggle, in pairs and occasionally four at a time, locking their beaks against one another and shoving sideways. This must be the first time in a great while that the worm had been free of their attentions.

Change was always distressing, even change for the better. Ilna knew that as well as anybody did. The puckered wounds where the parasites withdrew must itch terribly. Besides, the interval of peace wouldn't last. The parasites would settle their differences and stab into the worm's soft flesh again. That was the way of the world. Ilna's world, anyway.

There were only two parasites still ahead of her: one a double pace to the left, the other farther by a similar distance and offset to the right. She'd finally come far enough to understand the rhythm of the worm's movements. Instead of pausing, she stepped quickly and delicately to a point between the parasites. The wave pulsing through the mass of white flesh lifted her with gentle power and launched her the rest of the way onto the worm's horny head. She was past before either parasite reacted.

Ilna hadn't paid any attention to the jewel while the problem of reaching it remained. Now, standing within arm's length, she considered it for the first time. She'd seen many things in her life and been impressed by few. This jewel, nonetheless, took her breath away.

It was egg-shaped and bigger, even crossways, than Ilna could circle with both hands. From the way it scattered highlights over the inside of the cocoon, she'd assumed the surface was faceted, but instead it was as smooth and slick as an eyeball: the dance of light came from inside. She couldn't understand how, since the crystal seemed as clear as a water droplet.

Ilna touched the surface, finding it warm to her fingertips. It resisted slightly when she pulled, as if it were glued to the worm's head. When it came away, though, the underside had the same glassy feel as the rest of it.

The jewel was much lighter than she'd expected. If she'd closed her eyes, she could've imagined that she held only a soap bubble. Light it might be, but it had a power, a presence. Ilna understood at last why Arrea demanded it as the price of her cooperation.

She didn't know what Arrea intended to do with the jewel, though she presumed it would be something evil: that was what people like Arrea did if they had the opportunity. First things first, though, and Ilna's first concern was for Merota. If Davus said Arrea's agreement was necessary for them to enter the place where they'd have the best chance of finding Merota, then they would pay Arrea's price.

And they would deal with whatever happened next. Because of what she'd seen in Arrea's eyes, Ilna would find as much pleasure as she took in anything to deal with Arrea as an enemy.

The parasites had sorted out their hierarchy and returned to pretty much the locations in which they'd started. A few of those at the worm's far end were beginning to settle back into their routine, probing for the spot where they'd stab down again.

Ilna was frequently angry but almost never felt pity. When she thought of this worm, though . . . What could a worm have done to deserve the torture it was receiving?

She'd expected to dance back through the parasites the same way that she'd come from the tail to the head. To her surprise, the ugly creatures now edged away like cats from a sudden blaze, leaving an alley down the middle of the worm's back. They stood quivering on the edges with their beaks raised.

Ilna suspected it was a trick and darted quick glances over her shoulder as she went on. The parasites she'd passed remained where they were until she was several times her own length beyond them. When they did move, it was simply to resume feeding on the worm's white flesh.

It was good, of course, that the parasites avoided her . . . but she'd gotten through them once and had no doubt that she'd have made her way back safely as well. The difference this time was, *must* be, the jewel she carried. Ilna didn't know what that meant, but both instinct and judgment caused her to distrust the thing if only because Arrea wanted it. Well, she'd be shut of it soon.

Ilna'd reached the worm's slowly writhing tail. She could jump to the wall of the cocoon easily enough and climb down, the reverse of the way she'd gotten here; but that meant having her hands free.

She smiled grimly, then pulled the neck of her tunic out and squeezed the jewel down the front of the garment to where the tie around her waist held it. The stone's warmth against the skin of her belly was vaguely unpleasant, like the heat rising from freshly turned compost.

She jumped to the cocoon, catching double handfuls of silk. After hanging for a moment to kick footholds, she slanted crosswise and down toward the path to the cliff. There must be a similar tube floating out to sea, siphoning in fresh, cool air to expel what the worm had breathed.

Ilna started up the tube with the wind at her back. Its soughing and the splash of the creatures swimming in the worm's wastes were the only sounds behind her. She'd rarely been more willing to leave a place.

She smiled. If it came to that, there weren't a lot of places she'd wanted to remain, either. She was going toward Chalcus and perhaps Merota if—luck, fate; perhaps another word that her mind shied away from. Toward Merota too, if the universe was willing that they find her.

Ilna went upward at the same quick pace by which she'd gone down into the cocoon. She wondered why Chalcus and Davus hadn't been able to see the silk and wondered why she could. She didn't often think about her mother. Her father, Kenset, had left Barca's Hamlet for adventure. He came back with two infants and no ambition but to drink himself to death. No one else had seen her mother, and Kenset never talked about her.

Ilna's unknown mother wasn't an answer, only a longer series of questions. It was empty nonsense to think about things that nobody could answer!

She saw daylight and walked out into it. Her heart lifted to a degree that surprised her, certain though she'd been as she climbed that she'd be glad to be out of the cocoon forever.

The tube ended high enough above the water that the worm wouldn't be drowned when storms lashed the pale violet sea. Ilna continued surefootedly up the sheet of silk that would shortly split into bundles, then individual cords. She was tempted to take the jewel out of her tunic so that she'd have an excuse to walk up the final line instead of using her hands to crawl, but that would mean putting her dignity ahead of Chalcus' concern for her safety. She wouldn't do that.

Chalcus shouted and waved. Davus was waving also. Ilna raised her hand to wave back, a little puzzled that her companions were so demonstrative.

Davus wasn't waving: He was launching a large stone from the sash in his right hand.

Ilna looked over her shoulder in sudden realization. The giant bird, larger than a warship, was sailing toward her on rigid, silent wings. Its toothed beak was open, and its eyes glittered like the sun on polished coal.

The right eye *splashed* and went dull. The left wing convulsed, and the huge bird tilted sideways, then plunged toward the sea without making a sound. It was so close that its death throes flapped a storm wind that almost lifted Ilna off the cord.

She walked the rest of the way to the cliff's edge as steadily as she'd begun, but she was breathing quickly through her open mouth. As she neared the rock and her friends, she heard the shrill voice of Arrea calling, "The jewel! Bring me the jewel!"

"I stood the regiment to when that black monster appeared in the sky, your highness!" Lord Rosen said as Garric and the Blood Eagles came to a clattering halt at the main gate of the palace. He leaned closer to Garric, and added, "Truth to tell, I figured the men'd be steadier shoulder to shoulder with their mates than they would sitting around and wondering about what all this wizard nonsense meant."

The Blaise armsmen were drawn up in four ranks, the whole regiment together in front of the building. That meant there were no squads in the Audience Hall and other important rooms the way Garric had directed when he left for the temple that morning.

Rosen had been right to change the troop dispositions. Garric had scattered squads throughout the palace to remind Wildulf's intimates that they were part of the kingdom. Now that open rebellion had flared, splitting the royal forces was asking for them to be massacred in detail.

Liane was talking to one of her clerks, a mousy little man of indeterminate age. He nodded and went into the palace. He was unlikely to arouse attention even though he was walking quickly.

"Right," said Garric. The ammonite in the sky had dissipated while he and his troops jogged back through streets deserted owing to terror of the omen. It'd been another illusion, an empty threat, but a threat nonetheless.

"Hold them here in readiness. I'm taking Attaper's men into the palace to arrest Balila's wizard and at least discuss matters with Balila herself. I don't know how Wildulf's going to react to that."

"It's going to happen no matter how he reacts," Lord Attaper said in a bleak voice.

Garric looked at his guard commander sharply. "Yes it is, milord," he said. "But I trust you and your men haven't forgotten that we're in Erdin *not* to start a war. If you have, I'll take Lord Rosen and a section of his men in with me."

"Honored to accompany you, your highness!" Rosen said, stiffening to attention. The Blaise nobleman looked pudgy, but there was real muscle under the layer of fat and a quicker intelligence than Garric was used to finding among soldiers.

"Don't get above yourself, Rosen," Attaper said. There was a chuckle rather than a snap in his voice, the tone you'd use to reprove a puppy who wanted to play at an inappropriate time. "Your highness, we kept the lid on at the temple an hour ago. We'll do the same here till you give us different orders. Let's go talk with Dipsas, shall we?"

Several of Wildulf's mercenaries guarded the palace entrance, but there wasn't the full squad that'd usually been on duty. Garric wondered if others had run away when the image appeared in the sky. In any event, those present got out of the way as he and his escort of Blood Eagles trotted through the archway and into the central plaza.

One of the Sandrakkan courtiers stood there alone, hugging himself with his eyes turned to the ground. Garric remembered him from the levee following the coronation.

"Lord Ason," Liane said—trust her to remember a name she'd only heard once. "Where are the earl and countess?"

The courtier twitched and continued staring at the stone pavers. "Wildulf's in his Audience Hall right there," he said. "I don't know where she is."

He looked up at last. With a flare of anger he added, "But if she and that wizard of hers are behind the things that're happening, I hope they're in Hell! I don't care how much Wildulf thinks of her, I hope they're in Hell!"

"Can't say I disagree with him," said Carus, who'd stayed watchfully quiet in Garric's mind since the fighting ended. The ancient king was a constant presence and resource, but he knew better than to be distracting when Garric had to concentrate.

Nor do I, Garric agreed silently, as he and his escort double-timed across the courtyard. The Blood Eagles' boots made a sparkling cacophony on the stone. *And it may be we'll be sending them there very shortly.*

Somebody'd started to shutter the colonnade between the courtyard and Audience Hall. Only a few of the hinged partitions had been closed, though. They formed a fourth wall during severe weather, but under normal circumstances the open plaza was additional space for the public to hear the earl's pronouncements.

The threat hadn't been weather this time, but the thing in the sky. Earl Wildulf sat slumped on his throne, leaning on his left elbow. A score of courtiers and servants remained in the big room, but others must've fled.

The pair of servants who'd started to shutter the room were sobbing by a half-closed partition. They'd worked blindly until a pin had stuck in its track. Terror hadn't left them enough courage or intelligence to overcome even a trivial setback; instead they'd broken down completely.

The priestess, Lady Lelor, stood by the throne. She turned on Garric, and shouted, "You don't know what it's like! You've only seen them a few times. If you'd had to live with those things in the sky for a month, you'd understand why we're, why we're . . ."

She couldn't finish the sentence. She didn't need to, of course.

"Earl Wildulf," Garric said without ceremony. "Where's your wife, and particularly where's the wizard Dipsas?"

"She hadn't anything to do with it," Wildulf said, straightening. Anger replaced his previous despair and he regained some of his manhood. "They were both here when it started. They weren't responsible!"

"Dipsas may not be behind the apparitions," Garric said, "but she was in league with Tawnser. I'm not going to give her another chance to bring the kingdom down. You say she was here? Where's she gone, milord?"

"You can't talk like that in my court!" Wildulf said. His belt and sword hung over the back of the throne; it wasn't practical to wear the long blade while seated in an armchair. A pair of Blood Eagles stepped behind him and removed the weapon.

"She and the countess went off together," Lady Lelor said in a harsh voice. "Toward the countess's apartments. They left as soon as the *thing* appeared in the sky."

She turned to Earl Wildulf, and said, "Milord, I've pretended there was nothing happening for as long as I could. That Dipsas is a demon from the Underworld, and she's tricked your wife into helping her!"

"They couldn't have done this!" Wildulf shouted. "They were here in the chamber when it started!"

"They may not be behind the things in the sky," Lelor said, "but they *roused* whatever it is that's doing it. Doing that and worse things. I'm as sure of that as I am of anything in the world."

She shook her head, and added miserably, "I don't know what else there is I can be sure of now. Not even the sunrise, the way those things cover more of the sky each time they appear. And they last longer besides."

Garric glanced toward Liane. She was at an inner doorway, talking to the clerk she'd sent as messenger and to a younger man in the sash and tunic of a palace servant. The servant was protesting volubly.

The spy, Garric realized. *The spy who marked the route for us to follow through the tunnels beneath the palace.*

Aloud to Lady Lelor, he said, "Were the countess and her wizard alone?"

"They had her boy with them, that was all," Wildulf himself said. "The boy and her bird."

In a tired voice, Wildulf added, "She brings the boy to bed with us. It's not natural, and I know it, but I can't say no to her."

"Your highness?" Liane said. "Master Estin knows the direct route to where Dipsas has probably gone. I suggest that we go with no more than a squad of soldiers"—she didn't bother to say "you send" because she knew full well that Garric wasn't going to leave the task for others—"to arrest her, because a larger force will be dangerously cramped in some of the passages."

"Right," said Garric. He turned to his guard commander, and continued, "Lord Attaper, pick an officer and ten men who aren't bothered by tight places"—he grimaced—"and wizardry to accompany me. We'll go immediately."

"I'm the officer," Attaper said, as Garric knew he would. "Ensign Attarus, a squad from your section."

"Yes sir!" said a boy who wasn't having much luck growing a beard yet. "Squad Three, form behind me!"

"I didn't say—" Attaper started angrily.

Garric put a hand on Attaper's wrist. "It's all right, milord," he said, "your son can come with his men."

If Attarus was man enough to command a doomed rear guard, then he can have what he and all his fellows consider a place of honor now.

"You lied to me!" Estin said bitterly. "You've unmasked me before the whole court. What's my life worth now, do you suppose?"

"It's worth less than the kingdom's safety," Garric said. He was repeatedly amazed at the way people saw themselves at the center of the universe. "As is my life. Take us to Dipsas, and I'll make you a palace gardener in Valles if you're looking for safety."

"Go," Liane said crisply. "We may not have much time."

The spy led them into the north wing of the palace at a trot. Servants with frightened expressions squeezed into wall niches or stared at the running soldiers through doors that were barely ajar.

"Her suite's to the left of the corridor," Estin said. He appeared to have gotten over his anger at being identified in public; that, or it'd been put on to begin with. "The earl's suite's across from it. There, the one covered in blue leather."

The door was set in an ornamental frame like the entrance to a miniature temple. No soldiers were guarding it, but it'd been barred from the inside.

Garric stepped back to kick the panel. Attaper touched his shoulder, and said, "A job for boots, your highness. Attarus, on three. One, two—"

Father and son raised their hobnailed right feet together.

"Three!" and they smashed the door open in splinters and torn leather facings. Estin slipped through behind the Blood Eagles, with Garric and Liane following closely. The remainder of the squad brought up the rear.

A few of the Blood Eagles carried javelins. Garric and the others had drawn their swords.

The ground level was a reception area and servant's quarters; Balila's bedroom and intimate chambers would be up the stairs. A maid in silk tunics knelt over a chair seat with her face in her arms, weeping in terror.

"Through to the back," the spy said. "The entrance is in Dipsas' quarters, and you can bet nobody but her and her mistress go *there*."

He slid open a black velvet curtain. Attaper reached past left-handed and tore the hanging off its rod, then flung it to the side. There was a second curtain just inside the first. Estin wasn't able to tear it free, but again Attaper did.

The windows of Dipsas' room were shuttered. The only light was from a lamp of scented oil. Rugs piled in the center of the room must serve as a bed. The only other furnishing was a tall cabinet standing in a corner.

"The entrance is through that!" Estin said, pointing. Garric jerked it open. The cabinet had hidden brick steps leading downward.

"Wait!" said Liane, who'd pulled a pair of rushlights from her case. She held one in the lamp till the waxed pith ignited into pale yellow flame. She stepped to Garric's side and smiled, saying, "Now we can go."

They started down the stairs. Garric was a step ahead with his sword forward, but Liane stayed close to give him the benefit of her fluttering light. Estin, from immediately behind, said, "We go right in the passage at the bottom."

"Your highness—" said Attaper.

"I've been here before," Garric said. "Just not by the short route. I belong in front."

"With all respect, you do *not* belong in front," Attaper said in a tired voice. "But I won't knock you over the head and drag you out of here, so I've got to live with your bad decision. Your highness."

"He's right." Carus chuckled. *"But so are you, lad. These aren't times for a king who thinks about ways he could hang back. If there ever was that kind of time."*

They reached the passage, an interior hallway that survived from the building that'd been there a thousand years before. There were niches for decorative objects, but all had been removed except an alabaster urn that lay broken on the floor. There must have been people in every age prowling these tunnels, for loot or simply curiosity.

"Dipsas might've been told about the chamber below," Garric murmured. "Instead of searching it out herself."

"I wonder if we can block this up?" Liane said. Then, regretfully, she added, "I don't suppose so. There's just too much of it."

"Left at the end," Estin said. "And watch it, it's steep."

At the bottom of a natural cleft, Liane lighted her second rushlight some moments before the first crumbled to orange embers. They went on, more quickly now because Garric recognized the route. In the darkness to the left was the way he and Liane had taken from their bedroom the previous night.

"I hear something," Attaper said quietly. "Voices, or . . ."

"Yes," said Garric. "I hear it too."

He couldn't make out the words, but there were two voices. One was the deep rumble that he'd heard when they entered the caverns before, the sound that hadn't come from anybody present in the vault. The other was high-pitched and scarcely human. It shrieked words in counterpoint to the thunder of the deep voice.

"By the Lady!" said a soldier farther back in the column. "By the Lady!"

Occasionally Balila's pet screamed. The bird didn't like this business any better than Garric did. . . .

Violet light quivered through the vault's egg-shaped opening. Garric had seen hints of it before, but he'd told himself that it'd been his eyes tricking him in the near darkness.

He glanced over his shoulder. "Master Estin," he said, "you can go back now if you like. I'll see to it that you're compensated for the dangers to which we've subjected you."

"I'll see it through," the spy said. He didn't have a weapon. "I'll make sure you get back so you can take care of that compensation."

Garric shrugged. He crouched at the opening and looked through. Attaper moved Liane back with his arm and knelt beside Garric. He swore softly.

A lamp burned from a niche in the sidewall, but a violet shimmer filled the air itself. It trembled as the bass voice thundered words of power.

The great bird paced back and forth at the rear of the chamber, opening and closing its hooked beak. The horny edges clopped together, but the bird had ceased to scream. Its eyes flashed with rage.

Balila and Dipsas stood on opposite sides of a circle chalked on the vault's basalt floor. In the center, hanging by his blond hair from a tripod made of wooden poles, was Balila's cherub. He still wore his gilt wings. When the bass voice ceased its thunder, the boy's lips began to shriek a response in a high treble. As he spoke, his dangling body rotated slowly.

"They're demons," Liane whispered. "They're not human to do that to a child!"

"We'll end it now," Garric said, forcing the words out past the thick anger in his throat. He stepped through the opening, his sword before him. Dipsas had information that would be of value to the kingdom, but in his heart Garric knew that nothing the wizard could say would please him as much as the knowledge he'd rid the world of her.

The boy continued to swing and chant, but both women turned to face Garric. The air was alive with swirling phantoms, coalescing in the edges of his vision but never directly where he looked.

"That's enough!" Garric said, raising his sword.

Dipsas pointed her athame at his chest, and shouted, "*Temenos!*"

Garric tried to take one further step to bring the wizard's throat within reach of his steel. He couldn't move. The word bound him in violet light.

"*Sanbetha rayabuoa!*" the bass voice and the cherub chorused together. Dipsas broke into cackling triumph.

The vault's basalt floor cracked across the middle. The halves tilted upward, knocking over the tripod and making the women stumble backward. Things as pale as the mushrooms growing on corpses began to crawl up through the cracks.

The wizard's laughter changed to a scream as one of the things grabbed her ankle.

Chapter Sixteen

Garric was deaf and frozen in a world of purple light. He couldn't swing his sword or blink, and his heart had stopped beating. He was fully aware of what was happening in the vault. Not happy about it, but aware.

The creatures crawling through the crack in the rock looked as though a child had tried to mold men out of clay. They were hideous, maggot-pale travesties. As many had three limbs or six as had four. Some were headless, their eyes and mouth gaping from their chests; one hopped on a single leg and held an edged stone paddle in its single hand. Yet clearly, and most horrible of all, they'd been meant to be human.

The countess backed toward the opposite wall of the vault, wearing a stupefied expression. Even though Balila wasn't a wizard herself, she'd been enough involved in the spell that it'd numbed her to events in the waking world. She seemed only partially aware of her surroundings.

A troupe of not-men rose from the crack the way spring sap bubbles from a cut in a maple tree's bark. They shambled toward Balila. Their weapons were mostly of stone or bronze, but one carried what looked like the tusk of a monster in each of its four hands.

Garric thought of the passage Liane had showed him just that morning: a thousand years ago the wizard Dromillac had trapped invaders under Erdin. Like the People who attacked Valles, the race that the chronicler called pirates hadn't been quite human.

After a thousand years in darkness, their descendents were very much less human than the originals had been.

The thing that gripped Dipsas' ankle had one arm and no neck. Instead of legs it crawled on a nest of squirming tentacles. It grinned at the wizard, ignoring her wild struggles. She was probably part of the reason the monsters had broken free of the Underworld, but she obviously hadn't known everything that her incantations were doing.

Because Garric couldn't hear, he could only guess that when Dipsas pointed her athame at the creature holding her she was screaming a spell. If so, it failed on the not-man.

A creature with the head and torso of a handsome man minced toward Dipsas on the legs of a deformed goat. It held a copper trident with a short staff.

Six not-men advanced on the countess. Her bird opened its great beak; its tongue trilled a cry that Garric couldn't hear. It raised its crest, flapped its stubby wings, and lashed out with its right foot.

The bird's three claws were blunt, meant for running instead of gripping prey the way a hawk does, but its leg was immensely strong. The blow disemboweled a not-man and flung its two-headed corpse across the chamber.

The remaining five creatures converged, swinging their weapons. The bird grabbed a not-man in its hooked beak and shook violently, tearing an arm off before dropping the body and seizing another.

A blow from the bird's wings had batted a not-man to the floor, but it gripped the bird's legs with bonelessly flexible arms. The bird stamped twice, ripping the creature open with its dewclaws, but other not-men struck from left and right with stone clubs. The bird's skull was large to give the beak muscles leverage, but the bones were still bird bones, lighter than a mammal's of similar size. The clubs smashed it like an egg.

The bird leaped into the air, bouncing off the high stone ceiling. It fell on its back, flailing its four limbs, but somehow got its legs under it again and ran across the chamber. The bird's wild career knocked down several not-men before it slammed into the wall not far from Garric. Its wings and legs gave one more spastic twitch; then the corpse fell, limp and bloodless.

Garric didn't know whether the spell that paralyzed him had also affected his companions. His body blocked the opening to the vault. Attaper hadn't or couldn't move him out of the way—otherwise, he would've.

Three not-men advanced toward Garric, but for the moment no more rose up through the crack. The right half of the vault's floor lurched, then dropped out of sight, carrying with it the cherub shrieking on his frame of poles. A horde of white monsters, no longer constrained by the narrow passage, filled the darkness beneath. They began climbing.

The pair of not-men who'd killed the bird now closed on the countess herself. Her eyes were unfocused, but her lips moved in prayer.

Both not-men struck Balila in the face. She fell forward, leaving a smear of blood on the rock behind her. A greater pool flooded out to soak her bloody hair.

Dipsas used her athame to stab the creature holding her. Its broad mouth continued to giggle. The goat-legged not-man jabbed its trident into the wizard's throat and twisted. She thrashed in a gout of blood, then went limp. Her corpse continued to dangle from the trident's barbed points.

Garric could move again.

He stepped into the trio of not-men, finishing the stroke he'd started a lifetime ago by beheading the creature on his right. The blade carried on to bury itself in the lower spine of the not-man in the center. The creatures' bodies were as solid as those of humans. Garric had struck with the rage that'd bubbled while he was helpless.

He stepped back and to his right, pulling hard to drag his steel from the not-man's bone. Attaper lunged past, thrusting through the mouth of the third creature before its copper mace hit Garric. The weapon flew from its fingers and rang musically from the wall.

"Back to the surface!" Garric said. "We can't hold them long, there's too many tunnels. Back to the surface, and we'll bring the army over from Volita!"

Two Blood Eagles shoved through the opening. One had a javelin, and both had shields.

"Retreat!" Garric said. He backed out of the vault as the next wave of white not-men met the soldiers. Several monsters went down in the first flurry, but a stone club dented one man's helmet. "Back to the surface!"

Garric wasn't worried about staying there to prove his courage. Somebody had to take command against the danger, and he was the only one who really understood what was happening.

The remainder of the vault's floor fell inward, exposing a pit that seethed with monsters the way maggots squirm in rotting liver. They climbed upward, holding weapons in their hands; those that had hands.

In the midst of them, sitting on a litter made of human bones, was a gray, wizened figure. Though it was nude, Garric couldn't guess at its sex. It was chanting words of power and beating time with a tourmaline athame: the wizard who'd led the invasion a thousand years before had been trapped in the earth with his creations. He was returning with their descendents.

"To the surface!" Garric bellowed. Liane's hand was on his shoulder, tugging him back. "To the surface fast!"

Or may the Lady save us, for we'll never be able to save ourselves in this warren of darkness.

Davus reached down with his right hand. Ilna took it and let him swing her onto the cliff's edge. He was, as she'd expected, extremely strong.

"Bring me the jewel!" Arrea cried. "The jewel is mine as the whole world will be mine!"

"Master Chalcus," Davus said, "she's returned safely. You can turn now while I watch our front—"

Chalcus turned and caught Ilna in his arms. His face was set in lines as hard as a sea-washed crag.

"—if you choose," Davus concluded, laughing.

"I never doubted you'd succeed," Chalcus said. His hands were locked on her waist. He wasn't squeezing her, but Ilna doubted she could've pried his fingers apart if she'd tried. "Never in my life did I doubt that, dear one. But I'm glad you're back."

"Yes," said Ilna. "So am I."

Though when I looked over my shoulder at the bird, she added silently, *I certainly doubted.*

Perhaps thinking the same thing, Chalcus leaned over the edge of the cliff. Ilna looked down also, aware of the sailor's grip. She was less likely to fall than if she'd been tied to a tree with an anchor cable.

The great bird floated upside down in the sea; its belly was a sulfurous yellow. Fish were nosing into the corpse. Some of them had worked through the feathers, because blood was beginning to cloud the pastel sea.

"The jewel!" Arrea shrieked. "The jewel!"

Chalcus turned with a fey smile. Davus had looped the sash back about his waist. The men's eyes met as Ilna glanced between them.

"That was a fine shot you made this day," Chalcus said. "And never a better time to have made it, I think. Call on me if you've a wish, and you'll have it if it's in my power to grant."

"And a considerable power that is," said Davus with a nod. "But first things first, and your Lady Merota is first. Mistress, if you'll give me the jewel?"

Ilna lifted the gleaming stone from her tunic. It was bubble-light in her hands, but when Davus took it from her she felt a great weight pass from her soul.

"The jewel!" Arrea said. Her eyes glinted brighter than sunlight filtered into the shadowed alcove could account. She began to chant under her breath, mouthing a spell.

Davus walked toward the half-blocked entrance, holding the jewel out in his left hand. "The jewel in exchange for our passage, Arrea," he said in a hard, distant voice. "That is the bargain I offer you. Come out and take the jewel."

"Give me the jewel now!" Arrea said. "I'll blast the flesh from your bones, I'll fill your marrow with liquid fire!"

"You may do all those things," said Davus, halting a double pace from the low wall and the woman behind it. Ilna and Chalcus were to his right and left.

The sailor's hands were open, emphasizing that he wasn't holding his weapons; Ilna's fingers knotted cords within her cupped palms. Davus knew what he was doing, so he was in charge, but they'd act if the situation started to spin out of control. If it wasn't already out of control . . .

"You may do all those things," Davus repeated, "but you must come out from your cave and give us passage. Do you think to command me while I hold *this,* Arrea?"

He tossed the shimmering jewel in the air and caught it one-handed. He was grinning.

Arrea said nothing, but her whole form quivered. Ilna waited, her face perfectly blank. She had no idea of what was about to happen, but something—

Davus tossed the jewel up again. Arrea crashed through the masonry wall, scattering the blocks. Her human head and torso were joined to the body of a serpent so large that it filled the tunnel beyond.

No wonder Davus said that beheading Arrea wouldn't gain them a way into the Citadel. That mass of flesh rotting would be as complete a barrier as the rock itself.

"Come out, Arrea, come out," Davus said cheerfully, tossing the jewel and catching it. "When you've opened us the passage, I'll give you the price you claim. As I swore."

As Davus spoke he stepped back and toward Ilna. She scrambled away, hoping she wouldn't manage to stumble over the cliff while her attention was on the monster.

"What is that thing, Master Davus?" said Chalcus. "What in the name of all Gods is she?"

More loops of Arrea's massive body curled out of the cave. Her scales broke sunlight into a rainbow haze; each was as broad as a spread hand.

"Arrea was a snake, no more than the scaly friend who keeps your hut free of rats," said Davus, continuing to sidle to his left as he tossed and caught the jewel. "But she found her place here beneath the Citadel and held it against her fellows, soaking in the power that trickled down through the passage. And in time she was not a snake but an echidna, a snake that hates humans because she wishes she were human. Yet she will give us passage."

The creature was following him. Ilna remembered winding a wire worm out of a sore, taking it up slowly on a straw until she'd removed the worm's full length and could swab the festering wound with spirits.

"Give me . . ." Arrea said, her voice an inhuman buzz like someone trying to form words with a bone rattle. Her tail squirmed clear of the tunnel mouth. She was as long as a trireme, but even so, the serpent body seemed heavy. The ground shuddered as her weight slid over it. ". . . the jewel."

Davus had brought them circling around to the entrance. The echidna's body lay in a great loop along the cliff edge, virtually penning Ilna and her companions against the face of the Citadel.

"You've kept your bargain," Davus said approvingly. "And I will keep mine."

He tossed the jewel to Arrea. She caught it with hands that seemed absurdly tiny now that the full body was visible.

Davus gestured toward the tunnel mouth. "The two of you can start up, now," he said. "I'll stay here—"

"I've given you passage," Arrea cried. She set the jewel on her human-looking head; it clung there, much as it had to the larva that Ilna took it from. "I gave you passage, and now I'll kill you!"

Chalcus started forward, light trembling on his sword blade. Davus touched his arm and Ilna's both, saying, "No. Wait."

"*Aleo*," Arrea chanted. "*Sambethor basultha. . . .*"

She pointed her right hand toward the humans.

"*Erchonsi!*" she shouted, and began to laugh.

The jewel flashed brighter than the sun. It shivered and shrank without losing brilliance. Arrea's triumphant laughter turned to a high-pitched scream.

"In truth, it's an object of great power, just as Arrea thought," Davus said. He sounded calm, but Ilna could feel his fingertips trembling on her forearm. "But it's an egg, not dead crystal. The king wears such a jewel that's been properly prepared; it gives him power like no other in this land. But using the egg for wizardry without preparing it first—"

The jewel had shrunk to a wire-fine glitter extending from Arrea's forehead. It vanished down the hole it'd bored into the echidna's skull.

"—causes it to hatch."

The serpent body gave a convulsive twitch. A loop rolled over the edge of the cliff, its weight pulling more loops after it. The whole echidna slid over with a rolling crackle and a cloud of broken rock.

"In time," Davus said, lowering his arms, "the hatchling will grow into a creature like the one in the Citadel now. A creature like the new king."

The echidna struck the water loop by loop, sending a long column of spray to dance above the crumbled cliff. For a long moment, Ilna could hear nothing but the waves.

"Let's go," Chalcus said quietly. He started to sheathe his sword, then paused and closed his eyes. Only when he'd opened them again did he slide the blade home. He whispered, "I hate snakes."

"Only the two of you," Davus said calmly. "I'll stay here at the tunnel mouth or another snake will take up residence. The power calls them, you see. It calls them to a treasure beyond the dreams of their scaly minds."

"But . . . ?" Chalcus said.

"Go," Davus said. "Merota is your friend. And I must be here if we're to succeed."

"All right," said Ilna. She'd picked her yarn out and replaced it in her sleeve. With her back straight and her head high, she entered the tunnel.

She didn't know what was waiting at the top. Now that she knew what the new king had grown from, though, nothing but her sense of duty would have sent her to face it.

Ilna smiled wryly. If she'd believed in the Great Gods, she'd have thanked them for that sense of duty.

Sharina lay like a rolled carpet in the bottom of the boat, slowly getting her breath back. All she could see was the sky, the vessel's curved bronze sides, and the men aboard with her.

Her head was toward the bow. Though she heard Hani chanting words of power, she couldn't see him without twisting around uncomfortably. There was nothing about the wizard that would've justified her strain.

The hull hummed like a taut line in a breeze. Sharina might not have noticed it through her thick sandals if she'd been standing, but lying down, the vibration was more uncomfortable than the aftereffects of hitting the tree.

The People paid her no attention. They looked out over the landscape, rarely moving even their heads and not speaking that she heard.

The two humans who'd lifted her aboard were another matter. "Pretty little blond thing, isn't she?" said the man with the slit nose. He giggled. "I like blondes."

"You like anything, Wilfus," said the taller man who was missing fingers. "I've seen you, remember?"

"Yeah?" said Wilfus, flashing suddenly hot. "Well, at least I stick to living ones, don't I? Which is more than some people can say!"

"Ah, shut up," muttered the tall man. "I was drunk, that's all."

Wilfus sniggered again, making his nostrils quiver oddly. "Well," he said, bending to fondle Sharina. "This one's alive, anyhow."

Sharina thrashed at him as best she could with her ankles tied to her wrists. Wilfus' face settled into a hideous snarl. He stepped back and kicked her thigh in response. He was wearing velvet slippers, but Sharina would've preferred hobnails to the touch of Wilfus' fingers.

Bolor was in the stern with two somewhat older men, more likely colleagues than retainers. Sharina saw him grimace. She shouted, "Is this how the bor-Warrimans treat noblewomen, then?"

Bolor flushed. "That's enough, Wilfus!" he said.

The taller thug turned, and snarled, "You can't give us orders, Bolor! We're as good as you!"

Bolor stepped forward. The thug tried to dodge but bumped into Wilfus. Bolor hit him in the face with his clenched fist, knocking him down. Sharina twitched her legs up so that he didn't land on her.

Bolor smiled grimly, rubbing his knuckles with his left hand. One of his companions had drawn his sword. "Hani may need you, Mogon," Bolor said. "I don't. Next time you can try breathing through the top of your neck."

The older man who hadn't drawn his sword hooked his thumb toward Wilfus. "You two trade places with us," he said in a gravelly voice. "Now!"

The thugs shuffled sternward along the starboard side of the hull while Bolor and his companions moved up to port. The man with his sword in his hand watched Wilfus and Mogon closely, but Bolor and the other noble who'd spoken knelt on either side of Sharina to lift her into a sitting position.

"I can't—" she said, but Bolor already had his dagger out. He cut the cord linking her wrists and ankles, then, after a moment's hesitation, freed her ankles as well. She stood up, careful because she was so stiff.

The People appeared to take no interest. The wizard in the bow said nothing either. He might not even have noticed; the effort of keeping them airborne must take most of his energy.

Sharina looked forward. The boat was traveling as fast as a horse could trot. Just ahead was the long, low building she'd seen as she sailed down onto the island. This side was a blank stone wall instead of a colonnade like that opening onto the lake.

She turned to Bolor again. "Thank you for that," she said, with a curt nod to the thugs glowering in the stern. Mogon was dabbing at his bleeding lips.

"Those two served the queen," said the man with his sword still out. "There's more of them that've joined us. Too many, I'd say."

"Why did you come here, milady?" Bolor said. He looked angry and embarrassed. Sharina noticed that though he didn't say, "Your highness," he nonetheless gave her the honorific due a fellow noble.

"I accompanied your uncle, Lord Waldron," she said. "He's hoping to talk sense into you and avoid bloodshed."

Valgard had been as silent as the People. Now he turned his head and examined Sharina expressionlessly. He still didn't speak.

"There won't be bloodshed," Bolor said harshly. "The people are rising to support the true King of the Isles, Valgard son of Valence. There won't be a fight because there won't be anybody standing with the usurper Garric!"

Sharina shrugged. Bolor's very vehemence proved he knew better than that. "People like your friend Wilfus support Valgard, you mean?" she said.

"Others as well, milady," said the man who'd ordered the thugs to the stern. His voice was calm and perhaps a little tired. "Ornifal isn't to be ruled by a usurper when there's a true prince of the royal line present."

Bolor glanced at him and grimaced. He looked embarrassed again. Obviously he didn't know how to treat a prisoner for whom he felt more respect than he did his allies. After a moment's further hesitation he said, "Calran bor-Ranciman. And his cousin Lattus thinks it's worthwhile to watch the dirt in the stern."

Lattus turned, sheathing his sword with a *clack* of crossguard against the lip of the scabbard. "They could still bite, you know," he grumbled to Bolor.

Sharina was frightened, and her whole left side throbbed. Standing and keeping her balance was even more painful than lying in the bottom of the boat, though she knew moving was the best way to get her strength and coordination back. Similarly, she knew she was better off acting like a princess before these rebel noblemen than she would be letting them know she was hurt and afraid. So—

"And does Valgard speak?" she said, glaring at the claimant.

"When there's need for speech, I speak," Valgard said. He had a deep voice, well in keeping with his powerful frame, but it lacked fire. His words were a flat statement without the sneer that would've made them a gibe at Sharina's frightened talkiness. . . .

The boat curved around the end of the building; the plaza in front extended into the lake. The keel was over the water for a moment. Sharina looked down as a fish jumped, but the ripples of their passage kept her from seeing what had driven it into the air.

Hani lowered his arms; the boat settled with a bell note louder than she'd expected from the keel's gentle contact with the pavement of stone blocks. The wizard turned, fatigue in every line but his eyes madly bright.

Sharina suddenly wondered just how old Hani was. Middle-aged she'd thought when he looked down at her from the bow of the boat, but there was a hint of something as ageless as black diamonds in those glinting eyes.

"Bring her out," Hani said. "I think she'll be useful later."

He giggled, and added, "Or at least her bones will, eh?"

Mogon and Wilfus didn't move, but a pair of People stepped close to lift Sharina by the elbows. She backed as much as she could, and said to the wizard, "Cut my hands loose, and I'll get down by myself. Or are you afraid I'll wring your neck if my hands are free?"

"You don't give orders here, girl," Hani said in a tone of tired disgust. "Set her down, I said."

Bolor drew his dagger and sawed the cord binding Sharina's wrists. "I'll take responsibility for her," he said to Hani, with a touch of challenge in his voice. "She can't run far with bruises like that."

"Thank you, milord," Sharina said. "For acting like a gentleman."

Though I might surprise you if I saw anyplace to run to, she thought as she swung over the side of the boat, gripping the thin bronze gunwale for support. The effort made her body flash white with pain, but she didn't let herself fall, only stumbled a little when her left foot came down. She caught herself and smiled brightly at her captors.

"Faugh!" Hani said. Though Sharina didn't hear him give an order, the People who'd started to grip her lifted him out of the vessel instead. The rest of the passengers disembarked also. The thugs climbed over the stern, keeping well away from Bolor and his companions.

Though narrow, the building stretched a quarter mile in either direction from the central archway. The columns along the front were white marble but so simple they might've been turned out of wood by a journeyman cabinetmaker. They were neither fluted nor adorned with either bases or capitals.

Sharina glanced from the colonnade to the People escorting Hani. The stone pillars bore the same relation to what she'd have seen on an ordinary public building in Valles as the People did to the soldiers who might've been guarding that building.

She kept close to Bolor and the cousins, who seemed pleased enough by her presence. The Ornifal noblemen weren't the sort to consort with brutal criminals like Wilfus and Mogon under normal circumstances, and they'd have been unusual if they'd liked being around wizards either.

Sharina pumped her arms back and forth, hoping to work the stiffness out of them. The movement hurt as though she were splashing herself with boiling water. She was dizzy for a moment, but she *had* to make herself ready to run or fight when she got an opportunity.

Hani led them into the building. Though the whole front was open for the sake of light, the interior was several steps from the surface. A central staircase dropped to lower levels. Sharina glanced over the railing; the stairs went down farther than she could see.

The building was filled with waist-high tanks filled with cloudy fluid. Hani raised his athame and intoned, *"Maradha cerpho!"* in a harsh voice. A flash of blue wizardlight flooded the tank nearest Sharina, illuminating what the thick liquid had concealed. It wasn't a man, but it was what a man might be if his flesh were being deposited from the inside out on an armature that crudely resembled a human skeleton.

The light faded, returning the tank to white opacity. Hani swayed; one of the People reached out to support him.

"What do you think of King Valgard's army, princess?" the wizard cackled. "He'll take Ornifal easily. By the time he's done that, there'll be an even greater force to carry his authority over all the Isles, do you see?"

He started down the line of tanks, glancing into each one. After a few paces his body straightened, working out the fatigue induced by wizardry. The People walked with him; Bolor gestured Sharina forward and fell into step with her. Calran and Lattus were immediately behind, a barrier ahead of the two thugs.

"You tried that in the past, wizard," Sharina said, feeling her stomach drop into a pit. There'd been tens of thousands of People when they attacked before; there'd be more this time, probably many more, or Hani wouldn't be so confident. "You failed. You'll fail again!"

"The army that invaded in Stronghand's day had no leader, milady," Lattus said. He spoke as before, with the calm certainty of a priest reciting the ritual. His cousin Calran's expression was furious, though, and Bolor too looked as troubled as Sharina felt inside. "These men follow King Valgard. And follow us, the king's military advisors."

"We have five thousand, maybe more, northern troops," said Calran more forcefully. "As good troops as there are in your brother's army. And the men with your brother, they'll come over to our side when they realize there's a proper king!"

"Waldron bor-Warriman didn't foreswear his oath, Lord Calran," Sharina said. "Do you think other of your neighbors are more apt to become traitors than he is?"

"It's not treason!" said Bolor. "Valgard's the *true* king."

"And there're the troops *we* command!" Wilfus called from the rear of the entourage. "Nobody'll dare stand against us, and if they do, they'll get treated like they deserve!"

"Troops!" Calran muttered.

"Valgard's *their* proper king, maybe," said Sharina. "Not king for a decent man like you, Bolor."

Valgard, walking beside Hani, turned and smiled at Sharina. "I'm Bolor's king and your king too, mistress," he said mildly. "As my loyal subjects will prove."

He was big enough to have been Stronghand's son, and he could've passed for a portrait bust of the former king; but there was no heat in him. It was like looking at an image of fire cut from red silk.

As they walked down the line of tanks, Sharina saw that the fluid within became less cloudy, and the figures within were increasingly well formed. Those near the end looked like men sleeping in a vat of clear water; their chests rose and fell slowly, as though they were breathing. There was a clear similarity from one figure to the next, but they weren't identical any more than Lattus and Calran were.

Sharina stopped abruptly; Lattus bumped her and recoiled with a half-swallowed curse. She pointed to the tank, and said, "I've seen him. He's real, he's not one of your monsters, Hani."

The wizard tittered. "He's indeed mine, princess," he said. The look in his gloating, glinting eyes was as filthy as Wilfus' touch had been. "And who knows? Perhaps not too long from now, one who looks exactly like you will be mine and will do my bidding."

The figure in the tank was Memet, the soldier who'd brought Sharina word of Cashel's disappearance. He was tanned, stocky, and had curly black hair—as distinct from the People as Sharina herself was.

"We don't war on women, Hani," Bolor said harshly.

"We war on anybody who stands in the way of our rightful king!" Mogon said sanctimoniously. "Anything less is treason to King Valgard. Isn't that right, *Lord* Bolor?"

Lattus turned his head, touching his sword hilt again. "Don't push your luck, dog," he said.

His quiet menace made Sharina think of Cashel when he was very angry. She felt a surge of desperate longing, but even the memory of Cashel's strength and steadiness calmed her. She smiled, surprising the men around her.

When folk like Cashel or-Kenset supported the Good, what chance did Evil have? And others, including Sharina herself, would do what they could as well.

"No matter," said the wizard. "No matter at all. It's time we finish the business on Ornifal and prepare the next stage."

They'd reached the wall at the end of the building. A silver ring ten feet, two double paces, in diameter, was set in the smooth white stone. Cast into the ring's surface were same words in the curving Old Script that Sharina had read on the ring that had snatched her to this island.

A susurrus of shuffling feet had grown louder as Sharina and her companions walked along the line of tanks. She looked behind her. A solid line of men in armor—People, man *things* in armor—stretched back to the stairway in the center of the building. As the People paced slowly forward, more of their sort climbed the stairs from unguessed depths and joined the end of the line.

"Lord Bolor's army has marched toward Valles down the north road," Valgard said. "Your friend Lord Waldron is facing them just outside the city with the garrison and the troops he brought with him."

"I don't want a battle with my uncle," Bolor said. "Besides . . . he's a stubborn old fool, but with him putting backbone in the royal army, it won't be an easy fight. That is, the usurper Garric's troops."

"Especially with half our forces made up of cutthroats and gallows birds," Lattus said with a sour look at Wilfus and Mogon.

Hani, holding the ring he'd retrieved from Sharina, began to chant words of power in an undertone; his copper athame beat time. The ring on the wall began to rotate, at first slowly, then with increasing speed. The wall behind it blurred into a violet haze that grew steadily fainter.

"Not half my forces, not a tenth," said Valgard. His voice was still soulless, but it grew louder with every syllable. "And the bulk of my army will arrive *behind* Waldron."

The wall within the great silver ring had vanished. Sharina looked through the shimmer into the basement of the temple from which she'd been snatched to this island. The bodies and vats had been removed, but Tenoctris stood with her fingers tented, facing Sharina. As the image sharpened, Tenoctris smiled as though she was aware of what was happening.

The wizard-made People began marching through the opening, into Sharina's world. Tenoctris sat unmoved.

"We'd best go across ourselves," Hani said, panting hard. Now that the portal was set, it continued to spin without his chanting. "To control the dispositions, Lord Bolor. So that we don't have another failure."

"I hope Waldron has better sense than to fight," Bolor said. "But it *has* to be. The kingdom and its rightful ruler leave us no choice, even if my uncle's too pigheaded to see reason."

"And we'll kill them all!" Wilfus chortled. "Everyone who stands in our way. Everyone!"

The shaft halted. The doors drew open onto Ronn's rooftop plaza with the same magical smoothness as they'd closed to take Cashel and others down to the lightless, haunted cellars of the city. The Heroes stepped out, and when they had exited, Cashel followed at Mab's side.

The many, many people gathered on the plaza gave a swelling cry. Not even Garric or Sharina could've counted so many people. The ones standing nearest the shaft saw who'd arrived, and their excitement spread around the vast space like a ripple across a pond.

Mab raised her arms. She'd entered the shaft as an aged crone, but when Cashel glanced at her now he staggered as though a mule had kicked him unexpectedly: she looked exactly like Ilna. She had the slight, trim build; the black hair cut short; and the firm, disapproving set of the jaw. Only Mab's fingernails, dazzling with their own light in the bloody glow of sunset, were different from those of Cashel's sister.

"Citizens of Ronn!" Mab said. From the way the crowd reacted, everybody on the plaza heard her just as they'd heard those speaking in the

Assembly Hall. With different emphasis Mab went on, "*Men* of Ronn. Your Heroes have come to lead you. Will you follow them?"

The crowd breathed deeply, like a team of oxen facing an oncoming storm. One voice spoke across the plaza for all: "Lady, the Made Men are here. They're filling the plain, and soon they'll climb our walls."

The sun was so low that only the upper rim showed where the hills to the west curved to meet the sea. There were no clouds, but the sky didn't have the crystal transparency Cashel remembered from the previous night there. The fairy lights that drifted over the crowd were scarcely bright enough to see.

"That's why you needed leaders," Virdin said. His voice rumbled through the twilight like distant thunder. "That's why you sent for us."

He and the other Heroes walked deliberately toward the knee-high parapet on the north side of the plaza. The spectators parted like water from the prow of a royal barge. Mab nodded agreement at Cashel's glance. Together they followed the Heroes at a respectful double pace, close enough that the citizens returning to where they'd stood before didn't crowd them.

The Heroes reached the parapet and stared down on the darkening plain. "It's the worst I've seen them," Hrandis said. "Worse even than the last time. My last time before now."

"There's six of us," said one of the twins. "That's different as well."

Dasborn touched Valeri's shoulder, moving him away, then nodded Cashel forward into the space he'd opened. "Go on, Cashel," Mab said. "You're here, so take a look."

Cashel looked down. The sun had fully set, and the sky was darker than it should've been at that hour. It was too shadowed for there to be shapes, but he could see, could *feel,* the movement on the plain below.

"There'd never be a bad time to finish this," Valeri said. "It shouldn't have waited a thousand years. It won't wait any longer."

"Tonight will finish it one way or the other," said Dasborn. "I don't suppose it really matters which, in the greater scheme of things."

"I didn't come here to lose," Cashel said. He held his staff upright in his right hand; his thumb gently rubbed the smooth wood. He looked over his shoulder and saw Mab smiling. "Mab didn't bring me here to lose. Ma'am, what do we do next?"

"We attack them," said Virdin. He stepped onto the parapet and turned so that he could be seen as well as heard across the vast assemblage. "We attack and finish them once and for all, just as Valeri said."

He raised not his arm but his long, straight sword. A flicker of blue wizardlight ran up the blade.

"Men of Ronn!" he said, silencing the whispers running like surf across the plaza. "Tonight we take back our city and gain our freedom forever! Go to your homes and arm yourself with the weapons your grandfathers' grandfathers left for you. In an hour, my companions and I will lead you onto the plain to sweep from the earth the monsters that claim the name of men."

The crowd quivered but didn't move. Its collective will spoke in the voice of a young man, probably someone much like the Sons who Cashel'd led down to be changed into what the times required: "It's night. We should wait for dawn!"

"If you wait," boomed Hrandis, "there'll never be another dawn for you and yours. The race of men will be extinguished from Ronn, and the king's minions will walk the city's halls forever!"

There was a murmur of wordless despair. They wanted a softer choice, but all the Heroes offered them was to do or to die.

"It isn't fair!" the voice of the crowd cried.

Cashel sighed. He felt sorry for the citizens, but they were trying to quarrel with the universe. A shepherd learns early that wishing there wasn't a blizzard won't save your sheep if you don't get them to cover in time.

Mab gestured before her and murmured softly. Her hands spread light across the sky. The glow was no brighter than a crescent moon, but by displacing the darkness it lifted people's spirits like a brilliant sunrise.

"Men of Ronn!" Mab said. "Arm yourselves and follow your leaders to freedom!"

"Freedom!" echoed the crowd's voice. This time the people were moving, dissolving down the stairs and shafts that would take the men to their weapons and the women to their homes.

The Heroes watched with varied expressions—Virdin approving; Valeri with an angry sneer; Dasborn smiling at the wry joke in his mind. Menon and Minon looked cheerful, and squat Hrandis checked the edges of his axes. They were six different people, not one man with six faces; but they were each of them the man for this work.

As was Cashel or-Kenset. He flexed his shoulders, waiting for the crowd to thin a little more so that he could give his quarterstaff a trial spin.

He looked over the parapet. The plain still moved, but now that Mab's power had lighted it Cashel no longer thought of waves on the Inner Sea. This white mass seethed like maggots in rotting meat.

Chapter Seventeen

Wildulf's left the palace, your highness!" Lord Rosen said, as Garric followed Liane out of Dipsas' dark cubby and into the windowed portion of the countess's suite. "I think he's gone to his army west of the city!"

"I knew we couldn't trust him!" said Attaper, behind Garric and thus forming the rear guard. "The attack this morning was probably his doing!"

"We don't know that," said Garric in exasperation. "Anyway, it doesn't matter now. We've got to get out of this palace and set up a cordon around it, which'll take all the troops we can gather. If Wildulf brings his own forces in, so much the better!"

Garric didn't imagine Wildulf *did* have anything to do with the mob's attack. The frozen, frightened earl they'd found in the Audience Hall wasn't a man who'd been weaving cunning plots—and Wildulf's hatred of Dipsas, who certainly *was* involved in the plot, hadn't been feigned.

Attaper assumed the worst about the people around him. Garric supposed that was part of commanding the royal bodyguard, but it still made the man difficult to be around at times.

They reached the hallway. Servants stood against the walls, whispering in shock and horror to their fellows.

"Go on, get out!" Garric shouted to them. "The building isn't safe!"

When he'd come up from the tunnels he'd had a momentary urge to rip the screens of patterned fabric off the windows and let the sunlight blaze in, but it was more important to simply get out while they could. The ground beneath was a warren, and the things squirming through its passages were far worse than rats. There was no safety within walls that might at any instant spew murderous creatures as white as fungus sprouting from a corpse.

"Your highness, I suggest we tell the City Prefect to get all civilians out of the city as quickly as possible," said Liane. She held up a wax tablet with a few lines of writing and the impression of Prince Garric's seal—which she carried.

She must've composed the document in the moments since they'd reached the surface. That was amazing enough; it was beyond imagination that even Liane should've written the order while they were scrambling through the dark.

"Why in the Lady's name would we do that?" Attaper said, speaking more harshly than he normally would've. "Once we're out in the open, those slugs on legs won't have a chance!"

Attaper liked and respected Liane, which was enough to bridle his tongue in any circumstances short of the present chaos. In addition to his ordinary courtesy—well, Attaper wasn't a toady, but a sense of self-preservation should've kept him from snarling at someone so dear to Garric, especially when Garric was stressed also.

But the kingdom came first. That was true not only for Garric, but also for the ancient king watching through Garric's eyes. Carus was remembering for both of them the many times in his own reign he'd *failed* to put the kingdom first.

"Send the order," Garric said. Liane was already giving the tablet to a waiting courier. "Lord Attaper, when these creatures appeared before, they took Erdin and held it for a year till a wizard drove them underground. I'm hoping we can do better than that, but we *don't* need civilians getting in our way. Besides, we owe it to give them a warning about what may happen."

"Which most of them will ignore," noted Carus. *"But that's on their own heads, not ours."*

"Lord Lerdain?" Garric said, suddenly aware of his young aide. He'd refused to take Lerdain into the tunnels, so the boy'd been waiting with a pained, put-upon, expression when Garric returned to the surface. "Get to the harbor and cross to Volita. Order Admiral Zettin in my name to bring the whole army across as fast as he can. I want each ship to come as soon as it's loaded. He's not to wait till the whole force is ready."

"*Yes,* Prince Garric!" Lerdain said, heading for the palace entrance before he had the words out. He hadn't even taken time to re-form his expression from its sour pout.

Lerdain had been sulking to indicate his hurt at being denied a chance to do something dangerous under circumstances where his presence wouldn't benefit anybody. "Honor" might be an empty word, but it drove some men as surely as a love of money drove others.

"Aye, and honor drives the best men," Carus agreed with a smile. *"For all that I'll agree that personal honor shouldn't be the first thing on a king's mind, as it was on mine."*

Garric and the Blood Eagles had just reached the other side of the courtyard. They were entering the passage to the front entrance of the palace when the sky darkened. Scores of terrified people screamed from the rooms around the courtyard, servants and courtiers who hadn't heard the order to evacuate or had chosen to disregard it.

The cloud frightened them, Garric thought.

In the artificial shadow, monstrous white creatures with stone and bronze weapons poured out of the Audience Hall and the front of the palace. Their gabbling was as meaningless as the croaking of frogs.

"Get out of the palace!" Garric shouted, as his escort locked shields. "Don't fight them here! We'll cut our way clear!"

The sword he'd sheathed when he left the tunnels was in his hand again. Carus' instant reflex had drawn it before Garric's conscious mind was aware of the need.

There isn't time to think about your actions in the middle of a battle. You act reflexively, doing what you're trained to do with no more consciousness than a heliotrope facing toward the sun.

Carus/Garric's trained reflex was to hit harder and faster than anybody believed could happen. He didn't have a shield, so he drew his long dagger in his left hand. The monsters in the entrance passage were the business of the forty-odd Blood Eagles ahead; *he* strode into those swarming from the Audience Hall.

An arm and the curved axe it held sailing off to the side, Garric's blade continuing through the creature's throat. Monster blood was as red and spouted as high as that from a human. Dagger catching a club, sword thrusting quick as an eyeblink; more blood, much more blood. Pivoting, striking right, backhand left, striking right; twisting the dagger and jerking it free of the single eye socket in the center of dwarf's sloping forehead.

And back, because the Blood Eagles had cleared a way through the entrance passage, and the creatures that had attacked from the side weren't a threat anymore, were a wrack of distorted body parts; and blood, so much blood, sloshed over the stones.

But they weren't human, weren't human, weren't men.

And if they *had* been men, it would've had to be the same for the kingdom's sake. . . .

"Your highness, in the Lady's name!" Lord Attaper shouted, putting himself between Garric and more corpse-skinned creatures surging from the side of the courtyard. "Out of the palace! Out of the palace!"

Garric ran into the passage; Attaper and the rearmost squad of bodyguards fell in behind him. A Blood Eagle'd fallen; over his corpse lay the six monsters who'd halted to hack at the victim while other humans slaughtered them in turn. Garric leaped the pile of corpses. Liane waited at the arched doorway, safe for the moment but unwilling to go farther without him.

"Abandon the palace!" somebody shouted from outside through what must be a speaking trumpet. "Abandon the palace!"

But when Garric ran out of the passage and under the soot-black sky, he could hear human screams coming from the building behind him. Many, many human screams.

The gate wasn't like the other parts of Ronn that Cashel had seen, even down in the fungus-blighted lower levels. It was tall and broad enough for six people to walk through together, but it had no decoration unless you wanted to say the heads of the rivets holding the iron cross braces onto the iron leaves. The metal showed a dusting of rust, and it didn't look like anybody'd been here in a long time.

At the hair-fine join of the gate leaves stood the woman who'd spoken for the Council of the Wise since the older man collapsed. She looked hopeless but resigned to it, like a ewe who knows she's going to be slaughtered and doesn't have the spirit to fight.

That happened a lot of the time—with sheep. Cashel knew it happened with people too, but not with people he thought there was any profit in knowing.

"Nobody's walked through this gate in a hundred and fifty years," Mab said, glancing at Cashel without expression. "In the days just after Valeri's last great victory, citizens came down the stairs outside the walls and played in the gardens for the day; but not for many years, and even then they didn't go out through the gate. It reminded them of things they thought were better forgotten."

Cashel didn't much like the look of the gate or the bare, sheer-walled passage that led to it. Unlike most of Ronn except the roof terraces, this was open to the sky. The walls were living rock for half the way up, and above that, as crystal gray as the winter sea. You could tell where the one stopped and the other began by the sheen of their surface, but the color was all the same.

Virdin was leading the citizens massed behind this central gate; he glanced at Mab. "They'd have done better to have remembered and to have finished the job," he said, speaking with no more emotion than a shopkeeper counting out change. "Of course that was true in my day too. I led the people out three times; but never all the way to the end, as if nine steps were enough when safety was ten steps away."

Waiting behind Cashel, Mab, and Virdin were as many men as you could fit into the passage without squeezing to the point they couldn't breathe. They weren't talking in real conversations, but the mutters and prayers and the clink of armor touching armor were as loud as the rattle of leaves when a storm sweeps through woodland.

"You were at fault," Mab said calmly. "And those who followed you were at fault as well; and most of all, the queen was at fault. The fault will end this day; in victory I hope, but end regardless."

Women and children looked down from the parapet. Those on the highest terrace were so far away that Cashel couldn't see figures, just the shimmer of movement as hands waved scarves. They were trying to be encouraging, he knew, supporting the grown males of the city who had the muscles to swing the swords and bear the armor; but it was also desperate prayer.

Virdin laughed, deep in his throat. He looked at Cashel. "What do you figure to do, kid?" he said.

"I'll stay with Mab," Cashel said. "I'll keep her clear of trouble the best I can."

He'd heard the challenge in the Hero's tone, but he didn't let it bother him. Virdin was pushing a little because pretty quick other things were going to push a lot harder. You needed to know how the people beside you would behave before the trouble started, not after.

"I guess you will at that," Virdin said. He quirked a smile at Cashel.

Maybe he'd have clasped arms if it weren't for the weapons. Virdin held his shield and bare sword, and Cashel had the quarterstaff in both hands. To Mab, he added, "Are the others ready?"

"Your fellows are," Mab said, smiling in much the same way as the Heroes smiled at one another. "Whether anybody else is besides them and ourselves, that I won't swear to."

"We'll learn soon enough," Virdin said. Then in a loud voice he called, "Open the gates!"

A trumpeter in the crowd, the mob—not the army, nothing like what Cashel knew an army looked like—blew two notes, descending and rising. A trumpet answered from the distant roof of Ronn; then, very faintly, came the notes of another, a second, and finally a handful of trumpets.

The Councillor raised her wand and mumbled words of power. Her tongue caught in the middle of the incantation, bringing her to a stumbling halt. Mab frowned, her eyes glinting like the sun on frozen lakes, but the Councillor recovered enough to finish with forceful strokes of her wand.

Ruby light crackled up the joint in the middle of the door; the valves creaked inward. For an instant the Councillor stood in the opening, still beating the wand though her tongue was silent. Beyond her, covering the plain like white scale on a leper's hands, were the Made Men. In their midst, on a litter of human bones, hunched the king himself.

The Councillor squealed and pressed herself against the side of the passage where the folded-back door leaves provided a little concealment. The king swung his bone athame forward, and the creatures he commanded began to advance as a mass of purulent flesh.

"We mustn't be late to the party," muttered Virdin. He lifted his sword at a slant, and shouted, *"Charge!"* as he strode through the gateway.

Cashel glanced over his shoulder as he and Mab followed. The mass of citizens in the passage behind were lurching forward too. The ones in the lead looked frightened, and the words they were shouting weren't always the sorts of things Cashel liked to hear from the folks fighting on the same side as him—"Mama!" was one of them, and some of the crowd kept saying, "God help us! God save us!" Still, they were coming, and that was more of a relief than Cashel'd have figured before the feeling rushed over him.

Mab looked calm and businesslike. As she walked, her fingernails traced brilliant patterns in the air. Cashel didn't know what she was doing until a dazzling blue thunderbolt shot toward them from the king's athame. It vanished with an earthquake *crack!* midway between the armies.

Mab rocked back like she'd walked into a tree while she was thinking about other things. Cashel put out a hand to steady her, but she'd already got her balance and was walking on.

The king flopped onto his back in the litter, flailing the air with his athame. He looked like an overturned beetle kicking. Cashel grinned. He was just there to help, but it felt good to be proud of the lady he was helping.

Men with swords and shiny armor were coming out of Ronn's other gates to left and right. Cashel could only see the ones closest to where he was, but he guessed each of the Heroes was leading the men of a district, just as they'd planned.

Cashel had seen flocks of sheep keep better step and look more soldierly, but the citizens of Ronn were trying. From the roof and the terraces lower down, silks and shining metal gauze were waving, and the men were down here on the plain—scared half to death and like enough to die in all truth. They were doing all they could; and Cashel was proud to stand with them, too.

The Made Men called out in a burbling gabble as they shambled along. The sound less resembled words than they did gulps of liquid leaking from a week-dead corpse.

Cashel stepped to the side for a little room and spun his quarterstaff overhead. Duzi, those white monsters weren't in any better formation than the citizens were, and besides that they didn't have shields or armor. If the people of Ronn kept their faces to the enemy, this might turn out all right after all!

The ground stepped downward from the city in a series of wide terraces. They'd been decorated with hedges and terra-cotta tubs, though by now everything was pretty well overgrown. Farther to the north the land started rising again into the black hills and gorges from which still more Made Men poured.

Virdin strode down the slope to the second terrace, carrying the boldest of the citizens with him. Mab halted well short of the break and drew in the air with her hands. Cashel took one pace forward and crossed his staff before him, putting himself a little to Mab's left. He wanted to keep her in the corner of his eye. With two mobs like these mixing, there was no telling what direction trouble'd come in.

A Made Man, slight-bodied but with spider-thin limbs so long that he was much taller than Cashel, charged Virdin, gobbling. The creature swung a curved bronze sword far out to the side, then brought it around to strike the back of the Hero's skull.

Virdin lopped the Made Man's arm off at the elbow. The forearm and blade together spun away like an elm seed. The Hero punched the boss of his shield into the creature's chest, crushing ribs and flinging the body back into the faces of other oncoming creatures.

The straggling front of armored citizens hit the straggling front of Made Men, both sides hacking furiously. Cashel waited, his legs spread into a good stance. His instinct when he saw a fight was to get into it. Not that he liked to fight, exactly, but the emotions that seeing a fight roused in him made him want to do *something* instead of just stand there.

But standing there was the right thing just then, so Cashel did it. He was used to doing hard things, even when that meant doing nothing till the right time came.

The lines of men and Made Men fighting didn't move much after the first contact midway down the second terrace. Neither side was any good at what it was doing. If the citizens'd been chopping trees, they'd have turned them all to wood chips instead of timber. For their part, the Made Men moved in great leaps and slashes like they were dancing for an audience instead of closing with enemies.

The difference was in the shields and armor the humans wore. The Made Men didn't have the skill to pick apart armored men the way Cashel'd seen Garric and Chalcus do when they faced better-equipped enemies. The citizens couldn't have landed two blows on the same spot if their lives'd depended on it—but one blow was enough every time, shearing through white skin and pale flesh. The sprays of blood were as red as what ran in the veins of real men.

Rows of Made Men went down. More citizens joined the line, taking the place of men whose arms were already weary with unfamiliar exercise, or whose stomachs were churning to see how the inside of a body looks when the heart's still beating and the guts spill out in writhing coils.

Ronn was a city. City folk don't know the things that every peasant child sees in the fall when the flock's thinned so that there's fodder enough to take the survivors through to new growth in spring.

But the citizens went on and fought—or anyway hacked at their enemies. Some of the strokes were so wild that Cashel suspected the fellows were swinging their swords with their eyes shut, but they weren't running away.

They weren't advancing much either. By then enough of them had come out of the gates, this one and the ones to either side, that there was a solid line of citizens chopping at the king's cavorting monsters. More humans came from the city, but many more Made Men swarmed out of the distant hills. Cashel thought of soldiers facing the sea with their swords—and the tide sweeping on regardless, as the tide always will. . . .

Three lances of red wizardlight stabbed from the king toward Mab, as quickly as heartbeats. Two exploded midway, a blast and a blast, pushing the fighters away from each other for a moment. Cashel rode the shocks the way he'd have ridden gusts of wind at the start of a storm.

Instead of exploding, the third bolt vanished a hand's breadth from Mab's forehead, then lashed back at the king. A fireball lighted the walls of Ronn and the slopes of the barren hills. The bone litter flew apart. The creatures carrying it flattened, and the king dropped out of sight behind the wall of his minions.

For a moment Cashel thought Mab had killed her city's enemy, but nearby Made Men threw down their weapons and lifted the king again on their bare shoulders. He'd been scotched but not finished. Well, that'd been a lot to hope; and anyway, the sky seemed brighter than it'd been before the exchange of bolts.

Because Cashel stood two double paces above the battle, he had a good view. The whole width of Ronn was lined with men in polished armor, with the Heroes each advanced slightly beyond the ordinary citizens.

Virdin had laid an arc of bodies before him and was building it into a wall with every further stroke or jab with his shield. Cashel was impressed by his skill, all the more remarkable for the clumsy butchery going on to his right and left. Virdin worked like an expert shearer stripping the wool from a sheep without wasting a motion.

Mab's face was raised. Her hands wove patterns, and her lips moved, but Cashel couldn't hear what she was saying. The shouts and crash of battle were deafeningly loud, but Cashel had the feeling that she wasn't really talking with her mouth.

The sky grew steadily brighter. The Made Men were giving way, not quickly but being pushed back nonetheless. Men were down—many men were down, when you looked both ways along the line of battle—but the king's creatures had fallen the way wheat does before the scythe.

Darkness swelled together in the sky like fog beading on cold glass, then dived at Mab on black wings. Cashel moved without thinking, bringing his quarterstaff up and around. His ferrule smashed into the attacker where its neck met the wings.

The blue flash more than the impact flung the creature up and back; it vanished as suddenly as it'd appeared. It'd been a crow the size of an ox, literally a thing of night whose destruction made the sky lighter.

Another image formed and sprang, a cat this time, with its claws spread and its fanged mouth open wide enough to swallow Mab's head and shoulders. Cashel shifted, stepping across Mab's front to meet the attack with the other butt of his staff. Iron crunched beneath the cat's eye socket. Blue wizardlight flashed across the whole huge form, lighting the sky and devouring the cat as though it'd never existed.

Cashel's hands were numb. He flexed them on his staff, knowing he might need them again shortly.

The sky continued to brighten. A spot appeared in the high sky, a white blur like the sun showing through overcast. Darkness ripped back like fabric tearing, turning the whole sky bright. It wasn't daytime any more than the shadow the king cast was true night; *this* was the opposite of black.

The Made Men seemed to shrivel individually as they broke and tried to run. They'd come in like the tide and now like the tide they were washing back. They left behind only blood-soaked ground and a wrack of bodies.

The citizens of Ronn surged after them. The men who'd fought in the front line stumbled, too exhausted to follow their routed enemies for more than a few steps. Other men poured through their lines, though—and women as well, come down from the parapet and balconies, wielding kitchen implements and hurling stones wrenched from the ornamental walkways meandering across the terraces.

The king squatted in a dome of ruby light, hunched like the pale, wizened pupa of a grasshopper that the plowshare turns up into daylight. He was mouthing words of power as he beat the air with his athame. His minions had fled or died, but the citizens of Ronn avoided him the way they'd have gone around a glowing oven.

Cashel glanced at Mab, expecting to see her looking triumphant. Mab's hands were the only part of her moving. Her body was as rigid as a statue's, and her face was twisted into a grimace of agony.

This is the real fight. Not the bumbling slaughter of men and not-men finishing in an equally bumbling race.

Cashel shrugged to loosen his tunic again, then strode down the slope onto the second terrace. There'd been a fountain there; fed by pipes coming out of Ronn, he supposed, but that must've ended when the king's influence oozed back into the rock-cut levels of the city. All that remained was a coping whose tiled roof had filled the basin when the four stone maidens supporting it fell.

Cashel felt a twinge of sadness for the statues. They'd never been alive, of course, but it still bothered him that pretty things meant to make people happy lay broken and covered by corpses. Well, maybe they'd be raised and repaired rather than replaced. It wasn't their fault what'd happened to them, after all.

At the place where the two lines had stood and fought the longest, there were enough bodies to make Cashel choose his footing with care. The Made Men's corpses squished underfoot and turned like bladders full of wet mud. Cashel tried not to step on real men, but sometimes he had to. He figured they didn't care anymore, or anyway that they understood that there are things that happen even when you'd rather they didn't.

Cashel approached from the side of the king in his shimmering dome. He didn't know what'd happen if he put himself between Mab and the king, but the best result of that was nothing. The worst . . . well, Cashel had seen enough of wizards that being blasted to bits wasn't at the bottom of what he thought *might* happen.

The king watched with tiny eyes as Cashel approached, but his athame kept stroking the air toward Mab on the higher terrace. Cashel thought he felt hatred through the protective red glow, but he guessed the king was one of those people who hated whatever it was he saw. It didn't make Cashel special, and it *sure* wasn't just wizards who acted that way.

Citizens were watching Cashel too. An overweight fellow who must have been sixty knelt on the ground in front of his helmet. Sweat gleamed on his bald scalp. He looked so tired that he couldn't move, even to sit down properly, but there was blood on the blade of the sword he still held. His eyes tracked Cashel.

So did those of the woman cross-legged on the ground not far away. She was probably as old as the exhausted man, but she was tall and slender and looked every inch a queen. Her robes were white, but whites of several different shades that swirled together into a pattern that Cashel knew would've impressed his sister.

Blood stained the garments and continued to drip from the open mouth of the young man whose head she cradled in her lap. Cashel guessed the fellow must've bitten his tongue in half when a Made Man thrust his barbed bronze sword through the human's visor. The wound itself wasn't bleeding. The woman looked like she'd cry when she'd had time for what'd happened to sink in. Mothers did that, even mothers who looked like queens.

There were more dead and many more wounded. There'd been too many of both, that day and in the years before. It was time to end the business.

Cashel stepped toward the king, keeping the length of his staff from the dome of wizardlight. The hairs on Cashel's arms and the back of his neck prickled the way they always did when he was around wizardry. He began to spin his quarterstaff sunwise in front of him, building speed.

The king glared at Cashel. He was a tiny little thing, shrunk with age till he was barely a child in size. Cashel didn't recall ever seeing hate quite that bright in anybody's eyes before.

The quarterstaff was spinning faster; the ferrules trailed sparks of blue fire. Cashel could feel power shivering through his limbs. It wasn't something in him or of him, it was a thing that wore his flesh the way he wore a tunic. It was almost time—

The king pointed his athame toward Cashel's face. His mouth was open to shout words of power.

The dome protecting the king collapsed inward, leaving nothing but a blue spark where he'd squatted. There was a thunderclap and a jet of azure light spiking through the pale heavens.

The shock wave threw Cashel onto his back, stunned and deafened. Above him shone the stars of a normal night, as brilliant as powdered jewels.

Valgard and the wizard Hani walked through the whirling ring together. Sharina hesitated.

"Go on, milady," Bolor said, gesturing her toward the portal. In the temple cellar, Tenoctris reacted to the men's arrival with no more than a smile of greeting. Valgard put one heavy hand on her shoulder. Sharina stepped through the ring, wincing as her left foot came down on the cellar's stone flooring.

Bolor and his two henchmen arrived a moment later. From this side Sharina saw only empty air until the men appeared. It was as if they'd walked from shadow into bright light. Their striding legs, their arms swinging forward—and then they were as solid as they'd been on the island a moment before.

"Let her go!" Sharina snapped at Valgard. "She's an old woman. She can't do you any harm!"

Valgard glanced at her without emotion. He continued to hold Tenoctris by the shoulder till Hani said, "Yes, you can let her go. I thought she was a threat because she was a wizard—but she's not much of a wizard, that's clear to me now."

"I'm not very powerful, if that's what you mean," Tenoctris said easily. "I sometimes see things that others have missed, but I'm afraid I'm rarely strong enough to act on what I see."

She smiled warmly at Sharina. "Hello, dear," she said. "I was worried about you. I should never have asked you to look at the ring until I'd examined it more closely myself. I didn't realize it was self-actuating."

"You didn't know what a great wizard I am, eh?" Hani said with a cackle of delight. "So great that my tools give ordinary dogs the power to work wizardry!"

Wilfus and Mogon entered the cellar. The room was beginning to fill up, since so much space was taken up by the stone table. The pair of thugs sidled to the left, putting that table between them and the three Ornifal nobles.

The People resumed their march out of the air in double columns and continued up the stairs to the sanctum of the temple. By now they must be spilling onto the street.

"Hani?" said Bolor. He'd been frowning more sternly with each passing moment. "I ought to be with the army now. Uncle Waldron isn't the sort of man to dither about. He might decide to attack at once if I'm not there to suggest a parley."

Hani grunted in irritation. "You think what I do is easy?" he said. "That wizardry is all waving a wand around with no labor?"

"I think if I'm not with the army shortly," Bolor snapped, "I might better never have been born! If this conspiracy turns to disaster for my family and friends because you weren't able to do what you claimed, then be assured, Master Hani, that I'll take your head off before I fall on my sword."

Calran and Lattus faced the lines of marching People with their hands on their sword hilts, their backs to Bolor and the wizard. They couldn't stand for more than a moment if the People turned against them, but a moment was as long as it'd take Bolor to accomplish his threat.

"Don't be a fool," Hani muttered. "You'll be there in plenty of time. All we need to do is chip the plaster off the wall. Come, we'll go upstairs now."

People stopped appearing for a moment, opening a gap in the line. Hani and Valgard started up the steps. Tenoctris started forward also, gladly taking the arm Sharina offered for support.

Hani looked over his shoulder. "I'll show you something you didn't know about this temple, hedge wizard!" he said to Tenoctris.

Tenoctris smiled. "I don't have much experience with hedges," she said, "but I take your point. And I'm always pleased to learn new things."

Hani didn't realize Tenoctris was mocking him, but Sharina did. That and the old woman's general composure proved that the situation was going as planned—as Tenoctris had planned, that is. Sharina couldn't imagine what that plan was, but she didn't have to know, or else Tenoctris would've found a way to tell her.

"I created the island from a chip I took from the wall of this temple," Hani said. Valgard steadied him as they climbed the stairs together. "Grew the island and grew men on it. Has there ever been so great a wizard as I?"

"As if that was something a decent man'd brag about!" growled Bolor, following the women along with his cousins.

"And where'd you be without him?" Mogon said in a shrill voice. "Lord Hani's the one who found and freed our gracious Prince Valgard from the dungeon where his brother Valence imprisoned him!"

Sharina glanced over her shoulder at Bolor. "Is that the story, Lord Bolor?" she said. "Do you really believe that?"

"Valence isn't right in the head," Bolor said, but he didn't meet her eyes. "It's proper—necessary, in fact—that his brother succeed him."

Valgard laughed like an iron bell tolling. "Don't you believe I'm Stronghand's son, lady?" he said in his heavy voice. "Who else could I be with this face and form, eh?"

They entered the sanctum. The doors were open; scores of People who'd gone up the stairs ahead of them were forming in plain sight in the street below the temple. Hani—or more likely Bolor—was showing his forces in order to sow panic in the city garrison.

The cult statue had been removed from its base and leaned against the sanctum's front wall, under a tarpaulin for protection. The plaster had been chipped off the back wall, leaving the underlying stone clear. Set into the wall of rough-cut limestone was a six-foot-square panel of polished granite ashlars, like a painting in its frame.

The broken plaster had been swept to the sides. On the floor someone—Tenoctris, almost certainly—had drawn a star with four points; words of power were written in a circle around the figure.

Tenoctris' satchel lay open nearby. Three scrolls, a codex, and a stoppered bottle of wine sat to the right of the figure, while on the left was a bundle of the disposable bamboo splits that Tenoctris used in place of an athame.

Hani took two steps into the sanctum and turned with a look of mingled fury and amazement. "What?" he shouted at Tenoctris. "You knew about the Mirror?"

Sharina moved to put the older woman slightly behind her, in case Hani lashed out. He was certainly that angry.

"I told you that I see things," Tenoctris said calmly. "I saw how power was focused here, so I asked Captain Rowning's soldiers to clear the wall before they left the city. But—"

She gestured to her scattered paraphernalia.

"—as you see, I haven't the strength to open the portal even though I could identify it. No doubt you *are* strong enough, Master Hani."

"No doubt I am!" Hani snarled. "As you'll see soon enough. Mogon and Wilfus, hold them—both the women. I can't risk them interrupting me during the incantation."

Wilfus stepped toward Sharina; she held out her right hand for him to take. He reached for her waist instead. She slapped him hard.

"You—" Wilfus said, cocking his fist to repay the blow. Lord Lattus shoved him away with his sword hand.

"Get back, scum!" Lattus said. "That's not needed."

"No, let him hold my wrist," Sharina said. "But just that. I won't pretend to approve of this horror, milord, so I can't accept your parole."

Lattus glared at her, then shrugged and turned. "All right, hold her," he muttered. Then he added, "There's more than you as don't approve of this, milady. But we don't have any choice."

All the true humans who'd come with Hani were in the sanctum now. The lines of People in polished armor resumed their march up the stairs and into the street. Sharina had an image of liquid bronze leaking into Valles, eventually to fill the city.

Hani seated himself on the floor, a simple mosaic of white-and-greenish tesserae in waving lines. He started to wipe away the figure Tenoctris had drawn in red lead, then paused instead to check the words written around the circle.

"Come on!" Calran muttered, showing his nervousness by letting his anger out. "You can stare at the dirt anytime!"

Hani looked up at Tenoctris in puzzled irritation. "This is all correct," he said. "You *did* know about the Mirror."

"Yes," said Tenoctris equably. She didn't seem aware of Mogon's grip on her right arm. Even the thug seemed a little embarrassed. "I didn't have the power to open it, though. Besides, it wouldn't have done me much good, since only the members of your party have amulets made of the same stone to link with the Mirror here, not so?"

"You think you're smart!" Hani said, a growl but with a hint of underlying fear. What Hani meant was that *he'd* begun to realize how smart Tenoctris was.

He bent over the figure, tapped his athame, and began chanting, *"Ereschigal aktiophi . . ."*

Calran muttered, "By the Sister!" He raised his sword as if to hack at the wall. Lattus touched his arm; Calran shivered and lowered the sword. The cousins stood close together with their backs to the wizardry, pretending to look at the army of People forming below the temple. Lord Bolor forced himself to watch Hani, but the fury and loathing in his expression were unmistakable.

"Berbiti baui io," said Hani. The four-pointed figure quivered. Sharina thought it was beginning to rotate, but it could be the red wizardlight was blurring the lines Tenoctris had drawn in cinnabar. *"Ereschigal aktiophi . . ."*

Sharina hadn't understood what the two wizards meant by "the Mirror," but as the incantation continued she saw the granite blocks shimmer brighter than their polish and the chips of mica in their fabric explained.

She stared, trying to make out the figures hinted within the stone.

"*Berbiti baui . . .*"

"Sister take me if I like this!" Wilfus muttered. His grip tightened on Sharina's wrist, but that was a sign of the man's fear rather than bullying.

"It's like it was back when we worked for the queen," said Mogon. "We had any woman we wanted, anything we wanted to eat and drink. Those were good days. . . ."

Wilfus cursed under his breath. Tenoctris moved slightly, brushing the wine bottle with the hem of her green silk robe. The contact wasn't quite enough to knock the bottle over, but it rocked on its base with a clicking sound.

"*Io!*" Hani shouted. He'd have fallen back onto the floor if Valgard hadn't caught him by the shoulders.

The star and writing were smeared into a blush of red lead over the cool curves of the mosaic. In place of the inset granite was a window onto a hillside filled with armed men and their horses. Goldenrod bloomed among the grasses, and on the upper slopes of the hill sweetgums and cedars were beginning to replace the lesser growth.

The sound of the bottle caught Wilfus' attention. "What's that?" he demanded. "Is it wine?"

A soldier on the hillside stared pop-eyed at Bolor and the others with him. He tugged furiously on the sleeve of the officer in gold-chased armor who was bending over marks he'd cut in the sod with his dagger. The officer gestured to half a dozen other men who had their own opinions on the subject under discussion.

"The keeper of Stronghand's vineyard gave it to us," Tenoctris said, giving Wilfus a cheerful smile. "I had it in my bag"—she nodded to the satchel in which she carried the books and instruments of her art—"and took it out a moment ago."

The officer on the hillside looked up with an angry expression, then saw why he'd been interrupted; his curly beard was jet-black except where it'd grown in white over the scar that continued up his left cheek. He clutched the amulet dangling in front of his breastplate. Jumping to his feet, he cried, "Bolor! It *is* you. We were afraid . . ."

"I'm here, Luxtus," Bolor said. "And the army Master Hani promised, that's here too. My uncle will know better than to fight."

Bolor hadn't spoken as if he believed what he'd said—and from what

Sharina knew of Lord Waldron, Bolor would've been a fool if he *had* believed it. Still, though Waldron would fight despite being trapped between a force of his friends and relatives on one side and a huge army of People on the other, Sharina didn't see how he could win.

"Look, you're done with your chanting, aren't you, Hani?" Wilfus said peevishly. "There's not going to be more of that?"

The wizard grimaced at him but didn't speak; couldn't speak, very likely. He was regaining his color, but the effort of the spell he'd just completed was obviously at the edge of his ability.

Wilfus picked up the wine bottle. He kept hold of Sharina's wrist until he'd straightened again, but he had to let her go to twist off the wax-sealed ceramic stopper. "Hey, give me some!" said Mogon, still holding Tenoctris by the arm.

"You wanted to join your army," Hani said. "Go on through, then. All you need to do is step through the Mirror."

The granite had vanished, but a quiver of crimson wizardlight framed the square where it'd been. Bolor and the cousins eyed the portal dubiously. The soldiers on the hillside backed slightly, all but the bearded man who'd spoken. Word had spread through the army, and faces were turning toward the tableau for as far as Sharina could see through the opening in space.

"Just jump!" Hani snapped. He'd recovered enough to sound waspish. He put a hand on the floor to push himself up, smudging the film of cinnabar; Valgard silently lifted the wizard fully onto his feet. "You wanted to join your fellows—join them!"

Bolor ducked, then stepped over what amounted to a sill of limestone with a sizzling, shimmering rim. The men waiting on the hillside gave a shout of wonder as Bolor crossed to their side of the square opening.

"Come on," he muttered, gesturing to the cousins still in the temple.

"What about Princess Sharina?" Lattus said, looking from Bolor to Hani as he spoke. "She can come—"

"She stays with me," Hani said. He giggled. "I have use for her bones. Perhaps I have use for the rest of her first."

The stopper popped as Wilfus finally pulled it from the neck. "Bloody well time!" he said. Then as purple fluid began to bubble from the wine bottle, "Hey!"

It wasn't fluid: it was oily smoke, thick and opaque. It wasn't purple either, or rather it was *also* purple, the way mother-of-pearl has no single hue depending on the direction from which you see it.

"What's this?" Wilfus shouted. "What's *this*?"

Calran cried out in horror. He raised his sword, apparently planning to slash at the smoke, then shouted again and leaped headfirst through the opening. He hit the ground beside Bolor and rolled, still shouting. His cousin hesitated a moment, then jumped after him.

Valgard stood unmoving, his face as calm as a death mask. Hani wrenched free of his grip. He pointed the athame, started to speak, and choked on his terror.

The cloud had boiled to the trusses of the sanctum's high roof. "The Sister and all Her demons!" Wilfus said. He flung the bottle against the floor, shattering it. He took a step backward.

Sharina snatched Wilfus' dagger out of its belt sheath. Wilfus turned, reaching for her throat with both hands. He shouted, "I'll kill you, you—"

Sharina stabbed the thug at the base of the neck. He fell backward, with blood spraying from his mouth and nostrils.

"Sharina, get through the Mirror!" Tenoctris called. Mogon struck the old woman in the face with his clenched fist. Sharina drove the bloody dagger under Mogon's raised arm and across the width of his chest. He spasmed backward, pulling the dagger out of her hand.

Sharina caught Tenoctris as the older woman crumpled, then carried her through the portal. Sharina's leap was as graceful as a deer's, but she overbalanced on the other side and sprawled full length. By landing on her elbows she kept from battering Tenoctris again. The sod felt cool and soft.

The men around Sharina were shouting, but none of them paid any attention to her. She looked back at the interior of the temple through the square-edged window in the air. The roiling smoke sucked down with a rush, forming a shape that could've been Valgard modeled from purple shadow.

The dark image reached out and gripped both Hani and Valgard by the throat. Valgard stood quiescent for a moment. There was an audible snap, and his head lolled on its neck. Pink, wholesome flesh slumped off the way sand washes from a clamshell. What remained were the bones and rotting muscles of a long-dead corpse. Its features were still recognizably those of the bor-Torials.

"I have use for her bones . . . ," Hani had said about Sharina. He'd already used the bones of Valence Stronghand to form a counterfeit heir for the dead king.

The wraith of Stronghand smiled as it continued to squeeze the throat of the wizard who'd stolen its body. Hani's tongue stuck out; his face flushed almost as dark as the thing of smoke that was strangling him. His right eye popped out to hang from the nerve; then the spine cracked. The portal in the air broke into shards like those of the shattered bottle, then vanished.

Sharina lay on a hillside, cradling Tenoctris in her arms. Across a valley to the south she saw Lord Waldron's army flying the standards of Ornifal and the bor-Warrimans. In the distance beyond them were the walls of Valles, and from the nearest gate the People were advancing in close order.

"Go up," Davus said as he bent over the fireset he'd laid just in front of the passage upward into the Citadel. "Your friend Merota's there, Ilna, if she's anywhere; and there's no one better than you to find her."

He struck a chip of quartz against the golden pyrite crystal in his other hand, showering sparks into the tinder. When he blew softly, flames licked up to wrap the kindling he'd bruised into loose fibers between a pair of large stones.

"Why do you need a fire, Master Davus?" Ilna said. Chalcus was already within the tunnel, just in sight as he waited for her. She thought/felt that she should understand what their guide and companion was doing, though, before they left him behind.

Davus smiled gently as he rose, holding the branches that he'd feed in when the fire had grown to the point it could sustain more fuel. "The passage draws serpents, mistress," he said. "Now that Arrea isn't here to bar them, many will come. Trying to replace her, you see."

"I hate snakes," Chalcus said softly. "I hate them all."

"They're like people, Chalcus," Davus said. He squatted and held the ragged end of a branch into the flames though without yet letting it sit on the kindling. "Some good, some bad but—"

He smiled at Ilna. He seemed a different man since he'd lured the echidna to destruction.

"—some would be very bad to have crawling up behind Mistress Ilna while she's otherwise busy. And I thought I should be the one to bar them here before they enter the passage. Not that I think you're afraid of them."

"I *am* afraid," Chalcus said. "It wouldn't keep me from acting, but . . . you're a clever fellow to have noticed that, Davus; and a friend."

A snake came out of the underbrush. It was black with a faint chain pattern on its scales; heavy-bodied for being no longer than Ilna's arm. It was quite harmless, the sort of lodger a housewife likes to have in her thatch to keep the mice down.

But some people fear snakes as others fear spiders. Far better that Davus spread hot coals across the tunnel entrance than that Chalcus have to deal with things he feared and hated—though Ilna had no doubt that he could do that, just as he said.

Ilna feared and hated stone.

She walked around Davus and entered the stone tunnel that should take her to a creature whose glance would turn *her* to stone. "Very well," she said. "Master Chalcus, will you lead or shall I?"

"And am I not leading already, dear heart?" the sailor said as he started up the passage. He'd drawn his sword and dagger. He held the shorter blade forward like the cane a blind man uses to tap his way through darkness, but the long, curved sword was back to thrust at the first hint of danger.

The tunnel was a rising coil, moderately steep but not dangerously so. Ilna'd expected the interior to be pitch-black, but the entrance behind her lighted the lower portion. As they climbed higher the air remained faintly gray—not bright, but at least bright enough to distinguish space from stone.

But stone—dense, black basalt—was on all sides. *This is very unpleasant,* Ilna thought; and grinned. If she'd spoken those words to strangers, they'd have been taken as a mild complaint, no more than another person saying, "I've drunk better ale than this."

In fact, the comment was as damning as Ilna could make. She didn't choose to raise her voice when she was complaining, that was all. And of course she *hadn't* spoken the words aloud.

Chalcus didn't speak either as they went up. That was natural caution since they were entering the lair of a creature that would kill them or worse if it caught them, but it wasn't just the stone that made Ilna draw into herself as she did in times of stress.

Davus had said that the tunnel was a natural formation that been improved over the years. Now that she was in it, she wondered whether the improvements had anything to do with human beings. The coil was perfectly regular, the sort of pattern a worm might've made gnawing through the rock.

A worm, or something less familiar than a worm. Perhaps the sort of thing that grew in the living corpse of an echidna after eating its host's brain.

Ilna smiled. Arrea'd gotten what she'd demanded, and the world was better for that happening. Ilna was getting what she'd demanded also, passage into the Citadel of a monster greater by far than the echidna. If things went badly, there'd be no lack of people who'd say that too made the world a better place.

The not-darkness ahead of them was becoming actual light. There were even hints of color, the trembling hues of a rainbow. Chalcus hesitated for a few heartbeats as a silent warning to Ilna, then continued.

She followed, still smiling faintly. Generally when Ilna went into a dangerous situation her hands would knot patterns in twine, less for use than to settle her mind. Now Chalcus' hands were full, so if anybody was to snatch Merota and run off, it had to be Ilna herself. It wasn't likely she'd get the opportunity, but that slight chance was the only reason she and Chalcus had come there.

Ilna was becoming more sure with every step up the curving slope that Davus had different reasons for guiding them, though. She was beginning to understand the pattern of events, though it wouldn't make any difference in how she acted.

Chalcus stopped. Beyond his poised figure was brilliant light, colors split and rejoined by the facets of the Citadel's crystal crown. The only sounds were the deep whisper of air breathing up the tunnel behind them and the rapid beat of Ilna's heart. Chalcus stepped into the structure, and she followed.

She halted to take in her surroundings. The crown was beautiful, a word she'd never thought she'd use to describe stone. She didn't *like* it, but Ilna gave everything its due; anything less would be a lie.

Chalcus frowned, disoriented by the highlights and distortions of the crystal walls. The crown was a series of coiled tubes, laid within and above one another. There were openings within the walls from tube to tube, but the whole was knotted in a system as complex as Ilna's finest work. She followed the pattern in her mind, untroubled by the confusion that the scattering light made for her eyes.

Chalcus started forward, feeling his way with the toes of his boots. Ilna could've taken the lead, but she didn't see any reason to. They didn't have a destination, just a purpose, and the sailor's cautious progress was as likely to bring them to that purpose as Ilna could by striding quickly through these crystal tunnels.

She *hated* stone. The beauty of the structure around her didn't make her like it any better.

"There's a new sound, dear one," Chalcus said, his voice barely a whisper. He waited, standing on the balls of his feet with his blades out to either side. His head darted quickly from side to side, covering all directions but unable really to see in any of them.

Ilna listened also. Because of Chalcus' warning, she noticed the sound—a rapid ticking like pebbles washing down a stone millrace. She couldn't judge distance or even direction with certainty, though it seemed—

"I think it's above us," she whispered. *Could the king hear the way humans did?* "This crystal is many tunnels, all connected."

Chalcus flashed her a smile. It was false, and the beads of sweat on his forehead were real. He resumed his tense, shuffling advance.

The ticking diminished and perhaps vanished, though Ilna's mind continued to tell her that it remained just beneath the threshold of hearing. *Had the creature passed through the tunnel above and continued on in a sloping path that would bring it face-to-face with them?* The material from which the tunnels were made was as clear as sunlit air, but its angles and surfaces sliced images into so many pieces that not even Ilna's mind could re-create them from a passing glance.

Well, they'd learn soon enough.

There was something ahead, a darkness that the scattering light distorted but couldn't hide. Chalcus stepped more quickly, almost running. Ilna followed, her mind as blank and clear as a sheet of ice.

Chalcus reached it, the statue of a girl in black basalt. The stone was too coarse to have recognizable features in this rainbow light, but there was no doubt in Ilna's mind that they'd found Merota: found her the way they'd known from the first they'd find her, a victim of the new king like so many others in this land.

Chalcus sheathed his dagger. He ran his fingertips over the girl's stone cheek and gave a terrible cry.

The ticking was growing louder, very rapidly. Ilna let the structure's pattern fill her mind. There was an opening, a doorway, between the tube they were in and the next one to the left. The crystal's shimmers and reflections concealed it from sight, but Ilna stretched out her hand and confirmed its presence.

"Chalcus!" she said. "Follow me! We have to get out of this tunnel quickly!"

"Fight a *man* for a change, monster!" Chalcus shouted. He leaped forward, sword and dagger gleaming with the all-colored light of the crystal. For an instant he was around the curve of the tunnel from Ilna.

A flash filled the crown and Ilna's world. Where Chalcus had stood was a smear of blackness in the mirrored perfection.

Ilna stepped into the adjacent passage and moved quickly along it. She knew why Davus had brought her to this place now. She would accomplish the task that he and the universe had set her.

And for all the rest of her life, however long that was, she'd wish that she'd never been born.

Chapter Eighteen

There was a lull in the battle beneath the cloud's false twilight. Garric drew a deep breath and went down on one knee. A Blood Eagle lay beside him, dead from a blow to the face by the spike of a bronze axe. Garric gripped the sleeve of the man's tunic and jerked it off at the seam.

The dead man was named Soutilas, a common trooper. He'd saved Garric's life twice before losing his own; if he'd survived he'd have been promoted to file closer.

But Soutilas didn't survive, and Garric needed to get the blood and bone chips off his blade. He wiped the cloth along the patterned steel, careful not to slice the web of his hand as he did so. It was easy to make a mistake when you were tired, and making a mistake with weapons was a very good way to get hurt.

Attaper stood with his hand braced on a trooper's shoulder while Liane bandaged the cut in his forearm. The wound wasn't deep, but it was bleeding badly enough to be dangerous in the longer run if it weren't closed. They had to plan for the longer run, because Garric couldn't see any quick way to end this eruption of Hell-creatures into the waking world.

In all truth, Garric couldn't see any way at all to end it unless the Underworld ran out of monsters before he and those standing with him all died. Eventually he'd learn which was the case . . . but if the wizard behind this attack had been building his forces for a thousand years, the odds weren't on the side of humanity.

Several hundred infantrymen were double-timing up the street from the docks. Garric saw three separate standards, but there were probably more units than those represented.

Admiral Zettin was carrying out his orders to get troops across as quickly as possible. That meant they were appearing in half-organized or disorganized lumps, but they wouldn't need to make complicated maneuvers today. All the soldiers had to do—all they could do—was to form a cordon around the earl's palace and slaughter monsters till they themselves were slaughtered in turn.

"The Sister and Her demons, here they come again," a soldier said. He didn't sound angry, and he certainly wasn't frightened, just resigned.

Over a hundred slug-white monsters ran and hopped and slithered from the palace entrance. In the course of the afternoon they'd come in seemingly random sequence from every door and window of the building, never less than a score at a time. Once nearly a thousand had spilled from the east wing. Garric had seen the attack, but it was beyond the ability of the troops around him to support those on whom it fell.

Besides, he didn't dare strip any point in the cordon to reinforce another. A further onslaught might spurt toward the newly emptied portion at any instant.

Garric straightened, lifting the shield he'd taken from a man who no longer needed it. In his mind his ancient ancestor waited, judging the situation with the eyes of long experience. This attack wouldn't break through, though no individual in the line could be sure *he* would survive.

Attaper flexed his arm to make sure the bandage held, then drew his sword again. A soldier threw his javelin. It wobbled because the tip had twisted when he pulled the missile from its previous target, but the creatures were tightly grouped. The cast might have missed its intended victim, but it thudded into the chest of a monster with three heads and a cleaver in either hand, knocking it backward. Then the monsters squelched into the thin line of humans.

A creature with a spear charged Garric. The weapon was all bronze, head and shaft cast together. Garric caught the point on his shield boss and thrust into the monster's single eye. He put his boot on the chest of the thrashing creature and kicked as he jerked hard on his sword hilt, withdrawing the blade from the bone gripping both edges. He slashed right, then left, more by instinct than plan. Two more creatures dropped, one twitching till Attaper broke its neck with his shield

The attack was over. Garric gulped air, tired and nauseous. The creatures' blood was red like that of humans, but its sulfurous undertone made the stench of this slaughter even worse than that of a normal battlefield. The long rows of monsters smelled like mules dead three days in the hot sun.

Another soldier was down and a second was swaying. He'd have fallen if he hadn't thrust his sword into the ground like a cane.

The fresh troops arrived. Three captains, none of them men Garric recognized, pushed to the front. "Your highness—" they shouted, more or less in chorus.

"Around the palace to the left," Garric said, aware as he spoke of how weak his voice was. He could only hope they understood him over the noise of fighting in the near distance and the sounds wounded men made. "Report to Lord Rosen and go where he puts you."

The Shepherd knew the line here in front had been thin to begin with and was half that strength now. If the creatures' attempts to break through were equal on all sides, as they seemed to be, the cordon must be weaker still in the rear. The front of the palace was closest to the harbor, so reinforcements arrived there first.

For as long as there were reinforcements available. Perhaps that would be long enough. "Your highness!" Liane said loudly. "Earl Wildulf's returning at the head of his army!"

She pointed to the left, reaching past Garric's face to make sure he noticed. Horsemen in four and five ranks abreast, as many as the pavement and the riders' skill would allow, were riding up the street from the west gate. That was where the Sandrakkan feudal levies had camped. Wildulf and several courtiers were in the lead.

"Bloody Hell!" Lord Attaper muttered. "Your highness, you shouldn't be here. Look, head back for the docks and stay there till—"

"Enough, milord!" Garric snapped. "This is exactly where I belong."

The sound of weapons and screaming rose into a dull crescendo from the east or northeast of the rambling building. A fire had broken out in that direction: smoke rose in swelling, rapid puffs. Garric couldn't tell whether the flames came from the palace or if the latest assault by the monsters of the pit had broken the cordon and the city proper was beginning to burn.

Lord Renold rode around the southeast corner. He'd lost his helmet, and there were collops cut from the rim of his slung shield. "Your highness!" he shouted. "We need support! You've ignored my couriers, so I've come myself! The hellspawn's going to break through if you don't send reinforcements!"

"Renold, I'll send you the next troops that arrive from the docks!" Garric said. "I haven't sent you any sooner because I don't have any to send."

He looked over his shoulder, hoping to see another battalion clashing its way up the brick street. There weren't any soldiers in sight, but plumes of smoke showed there were fires that way too. Was it accident, or had the creatures managed to circumvent the cordon through tunnels that reached beyond the palace?

Earl Wildulf and his cavalry arrived in a clash and rattle of horseshoes on brick pavers. Garric couldn't speak through the noise; he could barely think over it.

The earl himself and Lord Renold's professional cavalry were experienced in riding on pavement, but most of these horsemen were rural nobles with their retainers. As the squadron drew up, several horses slipped and hurled their armored riders to the bricks, adding to the cacophony. Wildulf bellowed a curse over his shoulder, then bent to glare at Garric.

"Your lordship!" Garric said, getting the first word in. "You're just in time to hold these monsters back before the rest of my troops from Volita arrive. If you'll take your force to where Lord Renold directs you, we can prevent a breakout. The ground under the palace is a nest of them for the Shepherd knows how far down!"

"Right, there's no time to lose!" said Renold. He tried to pull his horse around; it obeyed the reins sluggishly. "It may be too late already!"

"Hold them back be damned!" Wildulf said. "You, *boy*—where's my wife? Where is she?"

"Your lordship . . ." said Garric. He'd regained his voice but he was too tired to react, even mentally, to the Earl's discourtesy. "I'm sorry but the creatures her wizard called up"—Dipsas certainly *hadn't* called up the monsters and their ancient creator, but this wasn't the time to split hairs—"killed the countess in the tunnels before we could rescue her. The patrol I sent down—"

Again shading the truth, but Wildulf hadn't been rational about his wife even before the present cataclysm. Garric wasn't about to admit that he'd watched Balila die.

"—was barely able to get up alive to bring a warning."

"Wildulf, by the Lady, don't dally!" Marshal Renold said. He was the earl's retainer but a noble in his own right, and he had a very good grasp of how desperate the situation was. "They were coming out of the servants' quarters when I left!"

"Cowards!" Wildulf shouted. "You're all cowards!"

He drew his sword. Attaper tried to step between Garric and the horsemen; Garric shouldered him back. The greater danger was that Wildulf would cut at Lord Renold—and the greatest danger of all would be for Garric to be seen to back down before a raving lunatic.

A fresh wave of white monsters spilled from the palace entrance like corpse fat bubbling from a cook pot. They mouthed syllables even more inhuman than they themselves were.

Earl Wildulf wheeled his horse toward them. "Sandrakkan with me!" he shouted. "The countess is in danger!"

He and first the leaders, then the whole of his troop, crashed into the pallid swarm. This was a major outbreak, hundreds at least of the creatures, but the weight of the horses and armored riders rode them down with relative ease. For a moment the battle continued at the gate and gutted windows to either side; then Wildulf dismounted and, with his men, hacked his way into the palace itself. His voice drifted back, calling, "Sandrakkan with me! For the countess!"

Marshal Renold watched the troops pouring into the building with a look of amazement and horror. He hadn't seen Balila being clubbed to death, but he knew that the tunnels under the palace were a certain trap for anyone fool enough to enter them.

"Attaper, give the marshal ten men," Garric said tiredly. He wanted to vomit at what was about to happen, but Prince Garric had the survival of every human in the kingdom to ensure right now. The earl and his followers were throwing themselves away, but Garric could give their deaths *some* purpose. "Those poor devils will take the pressure off here for a time. Renold, hold till I can get you reinforcements. There's some coming now."

Wildulf had left the Sandrakkan infantry behind when he hurried to the palace with the horsemen. Best send a courier to make sure they were actually on their way . . .

The last of the Sandrakkan troop had entered the building. They hadn't left horseholders; their mounts milled and stamped in the forecourt, excited and frightened by the stench of blood and eviscerated monsters.

The ground quivered. "Bloody Hell, what's this—" Attaper said.

The palace and nearby structures shook like a dog come in out of the wet. Garric and everybody in sight lost their footing. A long crack ripped down the middle of the street, lifting bricks to either side; then the three-story buildings to the east of the palace crashed down in spurts of pale dust that hung against the black sky like giant puffballs.

The palace shivered inward a moment before the ground beneath it collapsed, swallowing the site whole. The ruin shuddered and fell a second stage, taking with it the surrounding plaza the way an undercut riverbank slips into the current.

"Get back!" Garric shouted, scrambling on all fours until he could get to his feet again. He'd lost his shield but still gripped his sword. "Back! on your lives!"

The ground continued to quake. *Duzi, how long would the shocks continue? Would the whole city fall into the bowels of the earth?*

Liane was safe, most of Garric's troops were safe. The crater'd gulped down the corpses, those of men as well as the windrows of monsters they'd slain. At least one wounded soldier had dropped into the pit with a despairing cry.

That man was dead, and others were dead, and maybe they'd *all* be dead soon, but for the moment, Garric was alive. He'd fight for the Isles and his friends as long as he could.

Gouts of night like black fire spewed from the pit, darkening the sky still further. In the cauldron beneath, Garric saw the ancient, shrivelled wizard gesturing with his tourmaline athame.

Around him, crawling toward the surface with their weapons and hatred of humanity, were thousands of white monsters. More of the same sort pushed upward behind them.

Garric gripped his sword, leaning forward a little to make it easier to breathe. He waited, to fight and very likely to die.

But until he died, to fight.

Ilna heard the new king pass on in the adjacent corridor, clicking and sizzling like a rain-soaked tree a moment after lightning struck it. The creature didn't cross from the outer track to the inner one where Ilna waited. Its motion shifted the light in the crystal fabric, turning a shimmer of green-blue-indigo momentarily into yellow-orange-red, but Ilna couldn't guess as to its shape or even size through the wall separating them.

She had her cords out; her fingers were plaiting a calm pattern. The creature's movements were as easy to predict as the next swing of a pendulum.

This new king did certain complex things, but it did them by rote and, therefore, predictably. It had power through the jewel and enough cunning to supplant its human predecessor, but it was no more intelligent than the great black-and-yellow spiders whose dew-drenched webs dazzle those who see them on autumn mornings.

The new king had passed. It would return, but not until a fixed future time, a time far enough in the future for Ilna to complete her preparations.

She stepped into the other corridor and looked at the two basalt statues. She touched the back of Merota's hard stone hand, then walked a few paces on and ran her fingertips down the curve of Chalcus' throat. He'd had a lovely voice. It was the first thing she'd noticed about Chalcus, back in that bygone time when there'd seemed a reason for living.

No matter. Ilna strode through the corridors of the Citadel, letting the cords in her hands direct her to a place she'd never been. She had a purpose, had work to attend to.

To Ilna's surprise, there were other stone victims within the crystal halls. Three were men, but one was a child not much older than Merota had been. There was a dog as well, a mongrel with a sharp nose and a back as sharp as a sawhorse. How had they come to be in this place where living things found only death?

The dog was just down the corridor from what Ilna was looking for, the spine of a sunburst that ended in a point sticking out of the crystal crown. She went as far into the tapering spike as she could go without hunching, then sat and began to work.

Ilna'd been picking yarn from the skirt of her tunic even as she walked. She'd clipped the hem with her bone-cased paring knife, but after that start she'd worked the threads loose by hand with the same quick skill as she'd used to weave the fabric. The lengths of yarn she carried in her sleeve for normal situations weren't adequate for this.

She wouldn't be certain that anything was adequate until afterward, of course. She was tempted to say that it wouldn't matter if she failed, but that wasn't true. To Ilna os-Kenset, failure was never an acceptable choice.

She sniffed. The world would be a better place if more people lived by the same standards as she did, but that wasn't going to happen in her lifetime. And besides, what other people did was none of her business.

When Ilna had enough yarn, she began knotting it into the new pattern. She could've worked with greater subtlety if she'd had something to hold the knotwork, but there was nothing to make a frame; the Citadel's inner surfaces were as slick as ice on a roof slate. She'd have to stretch the pattern between her raised hands. The result would be crude, but there was no one to critique the work except the new king and Ilna herself.

She heard the clicking/ticking again. Perhaps it'd been getting louder for some time, but she'd ignored it, lost in her work and the pattern she was creating.

The pattern was rather interesting after all, she found. It shrank into itself, level repeating level repeating level, each multiplying the pattern's effect . . .

Yes, the sound *was* coming closer, and rapidly. Ilna tied a final knot and stood, holding the edges of the pattern together for the moment. The close, glittering walls pressed in on her unpleasantly, but she wouldn't have been able to do what was necessary in any other setting. She was used to discomfort; a little more wouldn't matter.

The structure trembled at the creature's approach. Patches of color wriggled and shivered as the crystal flexed, twisting the light that passed through it. Ilna hadn't noticed such vibration the first time the new king passed close to her. It must be that now she was standing in a narrow passage with only a thin, taut layer between her bare feet and the ground furlongs below.

She spread her arms, looking out through the pattern she held. It was a skeleton of fine wool, no denser than the interplay of elm twigs against a winter moon. A spider uses only a tracery to catch its prey. Ilna didn't even need to catch something, only—

The new king rolled into sight, moving like a drunk who staggers but never loses his balance. The creature was of sparkling black glass, all points and angles; more like a sea urchin than like anything else of flesh and blood, but not especially like an urchin either.

It moved by toppling forward, putting down points and shifting the rest of its edges and spikes over the new supports. The creature's total size with all the limbs and nodes added together might have been as much as a bellwether or even a young bull; Ilna couldn't be sure. It was like trying to guess how small a space would hold a dandelion's fluff if it was squeezed together.

On top of the black spears and sheets, advancing but never dipping or rising from the perfect level it maintained, was a diamond-bright jewel like the egg Ilna had snatched from the cocoon under the sea. The Citadel's walls threw light of every color across it, but the jewel gleamed clear as a dewdrop.

The creature halted. It saw or sensed Ilna's presence, though it had no eyes on its shimmering black surface. Ilna's belly tightened, but she smiled at the thing that had killed the two people closest to her. She would join them now, or she would avenge them.

The creature extended a limb toward Ilna in a series of jagged motions. It paused; then three bolts of wizardlight—blue, scarlet, and blue again—ripped from the point like lightning slashing off a high crag into the clouds.

Ilna's filigree of yarn absorbed the blasts and flung them back reversed, red and blue and red. The shock stunned her. For a moment she swayed, blinded by the flaring light. Her skin prickled as if she'd been boiled in seawater, and her pulse was thunder in her ears.

Her vision cleared. She was trembling, so she lowered her arms slowly. The yarn pattern remained rigid: the wool had been changed to basalt.

Ilna shouted in disgust and flicked the pattern into the crystal wall, breaking it into a shower of pebbles. She regretted doing that almost immediately: because she'd lost control, but also because she'd smashed the fabric that'd saved her life. It deserved better of her, but what's done is done.

The new king had been a smooth, shimmering thing of liquid obsidian, vibrant even when it was at rest. The corpse was still black, but it had become the dull black of basalt; silent and dead and opaque. The spell flung at Ilna had rebounded, killing the creature who'd killed so many in the past.

Ilna sank to her knees. She wanted to cry, but she couldn't, and tears wouldn't have brought Chalcus and Merota back anyway.

The jewel on top of the stone corpse winked. Her eyes blurred, and she found that she could cry after all.

She heard whistling, the clear notes of the ballad she'd heard in Barca's Hamlet as "The House Carpenter" but which Chalcus sang under a different name: *Well met, well met, my own true love . . .*

Ilna wiped her eyes with the back of her hand, then dried them properly with the shoulder of her tunic. Rising, she stepped around the frozen creature and looked down the corridor. Davus was sauntering toward her, his lips pursed as he whistled "The Demon Lover." When he saw Ilna, he smiled.

"Well met indeed, Mistress Ilna," he said. "And a deservedly ill meeting for the creature that thought to rule men, I'm glad to see."

Ilna's face contorted. "Aren't you afraid that snakes will make this place their home, Master Davus?" she said, her voice echoing the sneer on her lips. "Now that you've left your post?"

Davus chuckled. "There'll be no danger from snakes, Ilna," he said as he stepped past her. He lifted the gleaming jewel from the head of its last victim, careful not to prick himself on the hedge of black stone points. "The king is back, you see."

Smiling, Davus placed the jewel on his head. It hovered, denting his brown hair without quite touching his scalp.

"A wizard named Dromillac drew me to the world where you found me," he said calmly. "He forced me to set a troll on the enemies besetting that place."

He laughed again. "Those enemies were no friends of mine nor of any man," he continued, "so I wasn't sorry to scotch them. Only when I'd done that and before Dromillac loosed the geas by which he'd bound me to his will, the creature whose egg I'd stolen for my tool"—Davus touched the jewel with the tips of his right forefinger and middle fingers, still smiling—"caught me unawares and snatched my talisman. With which it turned me to stone and took my place."

Ilna nodded coldly. "I thought as much," she said. "After I began to understand the situation, of course."

She thought for a moment, then continued, "Master Davus, you said that you'd allowed that creature"—she nodded toward the angled basalt corpse, unwilling to touch the thing even now that it was dead—"to live because you'd taken its offspring and were unwilling to wrong it further. That's what you meant, at any rate. Is it not?"

"Yes," said Davus, setting his feet slightly apart. "That's what I did. I suppose you're going to tell me I'd best change if I'm to resume the rule of the land, not so?"

"Not so," Ilna said, as cold and formal as Davus—as the king—had become when he thought she was challenging his judgment. "*Don't* change. The land, as you call it, survived a thousand years of rule by a creature that didn't care about humans. I don't believe it would've survived a ruler like you if he didn't sometimes let mercy soften what reason told him was the sensible course. A ruler like you, or like me."

Davus didn't speak or move for a moment, though fire pulsed in the heart of the great jewel above him. He chuckled again, and said, "Well, no matter, girl. I'll go on the way I've been going because I'm too old to change."

He bent over the statue of the mongrel dog. "What were you doing here, I wonder?" he said, stroking it behind the basalt ears.

Light flooded the corridor, burning bone deep through Davus and Ilna both. The dog gave a startled yelp. It turned, snapped at Davus' fingers— he jerked his hand back in time—and went running up the corridor trailing a terrified *yi-yi-yi!* behind it.

Davus straightened and grinned at Ilna. "Shall we find Merota and our friend Chalcus, now, Ilna?" he said. "I've a thousand years of misrule to correct, but first things first."

Ilna swayed, more stunned than she had been by the bolts the creature had flung at her. Then, blind with tears of joy, she began stumbling toward the statues of her family.

Tenoctris lifted herself from Sharina's lap. Mogon's blow hadn't hurt the old woman seriously, though the balas-ruby he wore in a gaudy ring had left a welt along her cheek.

"Graveyards focus even more power than temples do," she said with a smile of gentle pride. "Hani knew it, of course, but I don't think he understood that when he raised Stronghand's body he was also calling back Stronghand's spirit. When wine bottled from grapes grown on Stronghand's tomb was uncorked at a portal that Hani'd used his great power to open . . . well, I'd hoped something helpful would occur, but the result was beyond my expectations."

Horns called among Lord Waldron's regiments. In the rebel army there were shouts but no proper signals because the commanders were arguing. Bolor and the cousins who'd been with him on the island were talking with Lord Luxtus and his officers. Sharina noticed the courier who'd brought warning of the rebellion to Lord Waldron on Volita.

Sharina touched her scalp. Her hair had begun to grow back, but it'd be years before the present soft fuzz became the blond banner she'd had a few weeks ago. The courier's vessel had made a good passage to return to Ornifal so quickly without the aid of nymphs . . .

"Here, help me up," Tenoctris said, but she'd rolled onto all fours before Sharina could react. They rose together, the old woman smiling brightly—and Sharina smiling also, a little to her surprise.

This was a bad situation and might well become a fatal one, but Sharina was back among human beings. Bolor and his confederates were rebels and her enemies, but compared to a monster like Valgard—well, there were worse things than death.

Three horsemen under a white flag rode out from the royal lines. Sharina's lips pursed when she realized that Waldron himself was one of the envoys. They'd presumably intended to meet a party from the rebels midway between the armies, but Bolor's return—and what had come with it—had thrown the parley awry.

A lance with a white napkin tied to it for a flag was butted into the ground near the rebel nobles, but they were too lost in their own discussion to take notice. Calran seemed to have forgotten he still held his sword in his right hand; his excited gestures would've looked like threats to anyone at a distance.

The rebels had forgotten other things as well. It was time for Princess Sharina to remind them. A mace dangled from the pommel of the nearest of the drop-reined horses. Sharina lifted the loop of the weapon free, then rapped the butt against the boss of a shield leaning against a lance. The din cut through the argument and jerked around the heads of all the rebel commanders.

"Well, milords," she said, holding the mace head and patting the butt into her left palm. "Are you going to fight for mankind against monsters today, or do you intend to leave all that for Lord Waldron? I'd say—"

She pointed the reversed mace toward the lines of People marching from the city gate in perfect order. Their bronze armor was unadorned, but every piece shone like a curved mirror. In the sunlight their ranks were a brilliant golden dazzle.

"—that there're enough wizard-made monsters to give *every* human somebody to fight, but if you lot prefer to watch instead of playing the man, I'm sure Lord Waldron will take care of the matter himself. Or die trying, of course. *He's* a credit to the bor-Warrimans!"

Bolor scowled in red-faced embarrassment. "Milady, we don't recognize your brother as the rightful King of the Isles!" he said. "He's, well—"

"Whom do you recognize, then?" Sharina said, speaking loudly but pitching her voice deeper than normal so that she didn't sound shrill. The men around her would take that as a sign of fright, which neither she nor the kingdom could afford. "A moment ago you bowed to the glamour a wizard hung on a corpse! Now the wizard's dead and the corpse is dead again—and there's an army of monsters preparing to swarm over Ornifal and the Isles beyond. Which side are you on, man or monsters?"

Lord Waldron, with an official from the City Provost's office whom Sharina didn't know by name and another officer carrying the truce flag, had waited between the armies for several minutes. Now they rode slowly toward the rebel army.

"Look, your highness . . . ," Lord Lattus said awkwardly. "We've taken arms against Prince . . . , well, against your brother. And marched on Valles. We have no choice now but to go through with it. Or hang, that's all."

"What do you mean, 'No choice'?" Sharina objected, sweeping her gaze around the circle of eyes watching her all up and down the hillside. Most of the army couldn't hear the discussion, but they could see her imperious posture and the deference the rebel nobles gave her. "You have the choice of following Princess Sharina of Haft against monsters like those your grandfathers routed forty-nine years ago. There's that choice, or there's sitting on your hands while real men save the Isles! Which will it be for you?"

"Sister take it!" said Lord Luxtus. "We came here to fight. And I for one won't be sorry if I'm not fighting my own sister's son, as I see carrying Waldron's banner!"

Bolor nodded, and muttered, "Yes, all right." He turned to face the commander of the royal army, now close enough to touch with a lance.

"Uncle Waldron!" he said in a deep, carrying voice. "Princess Sharina summoned us to come to your support. May I request that you place me on the right flank against the People?"

Lord Waldron, as lean and hard-featured as a hawk, glared down from his saddle at Bolor. Just as Sharina opened her mouth to speak, Waldron said, "You can request anything you please, nephew, but I'll not be giving up the place of honor in an army I command, to you or to anybody else. Apart from that, though, I'm glad of your loyal support. The kingdom"—his eyes flicked to Sharina; he nodded, as close as he could come to making a full bow from horseback—"has always been able to depend on the bor-Warrimans."

A trumpet signalled from the royal army. The ranks of People had begun to advance like a long bronze wave.

"And now is the time we prove it," said Bolor. "Gentlemen, tell your regimental guides that we'll be marching obliquely to the left, putting our right on the left of my uncle's forces—which I trust will shortly be facing around."

Sharina dropped the mace and took the reins of the horse. A former rebel opened his mouth to object, then subsided without speaking.

"Tenoctris," Sharina said, "I'm going to mount, then pull you up behind me. We'll be rejoining Lord Waldron for the battle."

And not coincidentally rejoining Undercaptain Ascor and his squad of Blood Eagles. They were the only troops in this army who considered it of the first importance to keep Tenoctris alive. The past few hours had convinced Sharina once again that if anything happened to the old wizard, the kingdom wouldn't long survive her.

Trumpets had started sounding from the battlements as soon as the citizens of Ronn had returned from a field piled with the bodies of the Made Men. Their brassy tunes skirled over city and plain alike, joyously triumphant. Cashel could hear them faintly even there in the stone-cut cellars of the city.

The sun had been rising over the eastern mountains when Cashel, Mab, and the Heroes entered the shaft that dropped them to the city's lowest level. Mab said that this time they didn't need to walk the last half of the way down. All danger to Ronn ended when the king let down his defenses to deal with Cashel, allowing Mab to blast him as though he never was.

Mostly Cashel liked to hear music, but right now he'd sooner that the trumpeters would just stop. It wasn't right to be happy when so many fellows were freshly dead or were missing limbs. Sure, it was good that Ronn was safe and the king wouldn't trouble its citizens anymore—but that didn't bring the dead back to life.

Light wicking from the city's roof and walls brightened the depths also, now that black algae no longer curtained the crystal windows in the ceilings. The slimy growths covering everything when Cashel first came there had dried to fine powder that swirled away through the ventilation system. When Cashel stirred up a pinch of dust that'd hidden in some cranny, it had a pleasant sharpness that made him sneeze the way he did when Ilna grated ginger into a stew.

"In a few days the streams here will be running clear again," Mab said. "The plantings will take longer to regrow, but not much longer. And very shortly people will return to these levels."

She grinned at Cashel. Since the battle Mab had gone back to looking like she had when Cashel first met her on the hillside where he followed the ewe: a woman in her thirties, good-looking but too queenly to be called pretty. She added, "Not everybody likes to have only clear crystal between them and the outside, you know."

Cashel shrugged though he didn't speak. He knew what Mab said was true, but he didn't understand how it could be. He'd sooner sleep on an open hillside than in a thatched hut, and these rock caverns made him uncomfortable just to visit—let alone live there. But there was no accounting for taste, in sheep or people, either one.

The Heroes hadn't spoken since they entered the shaft with Mab and Cashel. Now the surviving twin, holding the left arm of his dead brother over his shoulders, said, "I thought the first time I made this trip would be my last."

"It would've been," said Dasborn, supporting the corpse's right arm, "if you'd finished the job you started. And if you'd done that, I wouldn't have failed in turn and raised Valeri to fail."

He laughed. It was hard to tell with Dasborn if he really thought all the things he laughed at were funny, but Cashel guessed he probably did. That was true of a lot of soldiers, it seemed. Garric had gotten that way since he left Barca's Hamlet and started wearing a sword.

The doors of the temple were open. It looked different by daylight than it had when Cashel was here first, fighting his way through a fog of evil that was cruel and determined and angry at its own existence. Now the doors' surfaces were bright. Their carvings showed all manner of people living happily, city folk on the right valve and on the left countrymen. One big fellow watching sheep on a hillside could've been meant for Cashel himself.

"Well, we're done with it now," Valeri said harshly. "And not before-time!"

He and Virdin carried Hrandis' body on a stretcher made from two spears and a blanket. A sword stroke had torn off Valeri's helmet; blood soaked the left side of the bandage around his head. Virdin limped from the wound in his right thigh, and the blow that'd dented his breastplate must've bruised ribs if it hadn't broken them.

Cashel had offered to replace either of them on the stretcher—or carry the corpse alone; Hrandis was a heavy weight, but the task wasn't beyond Cashel's strength. "You're a stout lad," Valeri had replied, his tone just short of sneering. "But this isn't for you."

Mab stopped at the temple entrance. Cashel placed himself at her side, holding the staff upright and close in to his body. He figured his job now was to keep out of the way. He'd figured that when he offered to carry the dead Hero, too, but he'd offered help anyway because courtesy required him to. It wasn't the first time he'd gotten snapped at for being polite.

Virdin paused before entering. He said in a soft voice, "I wonder what it's going to be like to rest? Others have done it, so I suppose I can learn; but . . ."

"You've earned it, Virdin!" Mab said harshly. "Never has anyone earned his rest more than you have!"

Virdin looked at her. He had the features of a young man, though Mab said he'd been old when he came down to the temple the first time. The look in his eyes was older even than that: it was older than the rock of this mountain.

"It hasn't anything to do with what's earned or not earned, mistress," he said, his tone that of a mother to her sleeping infant. "It's granted or it isn't granted. And if there's any justice in the decision, then it isn't justice as men see it. As you know well."

"Yes," said Mab. She smiled, an expression that took Cashel's breath away for its mixture of love and sadness and cold, bright certainty. "But sometimes there's man's justice also, if only by chance. You have your rest now, Heroes; and the thanks of one who used you hard in the past."

"Come on, Menon," Dasborn said to the living twin paired with him. "The lady has much to do; and unlike us, she'll have no more rest than she's had the past thousand years. Not so, milady?"

Mab's smile became a mere twitch at the corners of her mouth. "Not for a time," she agreed. "Ronn uses her servants hard. But perhaps even for me, one day."

The Heroes walked into the temple, three and then three. The living men set their dead comrades against the sidewall, then began stripping off their own equipment. Dasborn's right arm dangled from a broken collarbone. Cashel hadn't noticed the injury while the sardonic Hero wore his armor.

"Well, Cashel," Mab said as they waited. "You've done as much to save Ronn as anyone has, myself included. What would you like as your reward?"

"Reward?" Cashel said, genuinely surprised. The word took his mind out of here-and-now immediacy to a world where people made plans and agreements. "Oh, ma'am, I have everything I need and more. Just take me back to my friends and, and, Sharina."

Mab gave him a funny expression. It was a smile, he supposed, but there was more to it than that.

"Ah, ma'am?" he added. "You said when you brought me here that my mother needed help. Was that really true, or were you just saying that to get me to come along? I guess that wouldn't be a lie the way most people look at lies."

"Wouldn't it be?" Mab said tartly. "*I'd* call it a lie."

She smiled, and in a gentler voice, went on, "Your mother was in the worst sort of danger, but when you saved Ronn you saved her as well."

She looked like she might say something else, but in the end she didn't. Cashel waited a moment longer, then said, "Ma'am, it'd have been all right. I guess Ronn has better folks and worse ones, same as anyplace does; but the things the king made weren't . . . ma'am, they shouldn't've *been*. The king had the power to make them, and he made them, but they hadn't any more reason than that. I'm sorry so many folks got hurt wiping the earth of them—"

He glanced at the Heroes returning their gear to the racks it'd come from. The temple's interior had a soft glow of its own, not sunlight brought down to the cellars through crystals.

"—but it had to be done; and I'm glad for anything I did to help."

Mab nodded, but she was frowning at thoughts a long distance from the present. She looked sharply at Cashel, and said, "Cashel, how well did you know your father Kenset?"

He shrugged, frowning in turn. "Ma'am, not real well," he said. He let his eyes drift off because the talk embarrassed him, but he went on, "He was around, but he didn't have much to do with me and Ilna. Sometimes he got a little money ahead and gave something to our grandmother, but more likely he came by to cadge the price of ale from her—and got sent away with a flea in his ear."

Cashel cleared his throat. "We weren't ashamed of him," he went on. "Only he made it clear he didn't want to be around us, and we didn't have any call to be around him."

Mab didn't speak for a moment. Her face had the stillness of a statue's, a poised but emotionless expression. "Yes," she said. "I can see that. Though it was his own choice!"

Suddenly fiery, she looked at Cashel. "What did Kenset say about where he'd been?" she said. "Where he'd been, and who your mother was!"

"Nothing, ma'am," Cashel said. "Not to Grandmama, not to me and my sister. Not to anybody."

"What's happened to us?" said Herron—not Virdin but Herron, who'd just set Virdin's sword on the rack from which he'd taken it a day or a lifetime before.

He and his friends walked out of the temple uncertainly. "What's— Orly, the queen's back!"

"Yes," said Mab. "You brought me back. You and your fellows"—she turned her head back toward Cashel—"and Cashel here. Now it's time to return to the Assembly Hall, fellow citizens, and give thanks for the city's survival."

"But . . . ," Herron said, his face white. He was limping worse than Virdin had when the Hero wore Herron's flesh, and he leaned sideways to favor the bruises on his chest.

"Manza's dead," said Enfero, looking back at his friend's corpse, laid out in front of the twin Minon's gaudy armor and equipment. "Manza's *dead*. And Stasslin!"

"Yes," said Mab, "and many others as well. But Ronn and her people are safe, today and in the future, because of their sacrifice and of yours."

"It's not worth it!" Orly said. He was clutching his right arm to his chest with his left to keep it from swinging and making the pain of his broken collarbone worse. "I thought it was when we were playing at heroes, but it isn't!"

Mab shrugged. "I don't know whether it's worth it or not," she said. "It's done, for now and forever."

She nodded to the bodies on the temple floor. "It's fitting for them to remain in the shrine," she said. "They earned the right."

She made a glittering azure gesture with her right hand; the temple doors swung closed with the smooth assurance of a wave climbing the shore.

"If I'd known . . ." Orly said, his body turning but his face cast down to the pavement of living rock.

"It was worth it for men," said Cashel. He stepped over to Herron and offered the wounded man his arm. "It was worth it for you and your friends. You proved you were men when you came down here. Your city's lucky to have you in it."

"Thanks, but I can make it," said Herron, forcing himself to straighten. He touched Cashel's shoulder but then released it to shuffle along on his own.

They walked toward the shaft that would carry them to the surface again. The stone plaza had an inviting bright emptiness as sure as it'd threatened before. The Sons stood taller than they had when they came through the darkness; they were no longer boys.

"In addition to sending you back, Cashel," Mab said, "I'll come along for a time. Though you may not need anything yourself, I believe you'll find that your friends do."

She laughed, a sound more cheerful than any that can have echoed in this place for long ages since. "And your world is lucky to have you as well," she added with the same merry lilt.

"Glad to see you again, your highness," said Undercaptain Ascor, holding the horse's reins while two of his men lifted Tenoctris down from the pillion. "I wasn't sure how I was going to explain to Commander Attaper how it was I'd managed to lose you."

Ascor sounded aggrieved. Bodyguards felt the folk they guarded shouldn't just disappear on them. Sharina more or less agreed, but she had more important things on her mind than trying to explain to the soldier a situation that she didn't fully understand herself.

She swung herself out of the saddle once Tenoctris was clear. "Lord Bolor's troops are reinforcing the royal forces," she said, remembering that none of the troops gathered under Waldron's banners realized that the rebels of a few moments before were now valued allies. "It's very important that Tenoctris reaches the temple where all this started. Lord Waldron's sending me a company of the troops he brought from Volita with him, but *I'll* be in command. My orders to you"—she nodded to Ascor but then swept her gaze around his six troopers—"are to keep Lady Tenoctris from being injured. If anything happens to her, I fear that the kingdom is doomed."

"You heard the princess," Ascor said. "She and Lady Tenoctris both get through this, or we don't. Not"—he glanced sideways at Sharina and gave her a hard grin—"that I think you boys needed to be told that."

Sharina smiled back. It was a rebuke of sorts, but she wasn't going to apologize for making the situation explicit. With Hani dead, nobody but Tenoctris *could* end the flow of People into Valles until the supply ran out, and the cellars in the wizard's lair had gone very far down.

The People were arrayed eight deep. They had no flags or standards, though ordinary men rode behind the lines and shouted orders. The humans were easy to spot simply because their equipment wasn't identical the way that of the People was. They were probably thugs like the late Mogon and Wilfus: survivors of the queen's servants, criminals to begin with or corrupted by the service of Evil.

The royal army was in eight ranks also, though Waldron had faced half his men around when the People began to stream out of the Northeast Gate behind him. This region outside Valles was a mixture of truck farms and small villas, more open than the city proper but not terrain that lent itself to cavalry sweeps and iron control by individual generals.

Ascor, thinking along the same lines, said, "Looks like a soldier's battle this time, lads. And I don't see any soldiers on the other side—just rows of dummies in armor."

"Princess, ma'am?" Trooper Lires said, bringing out a silk-wrapped bundle that he'd been carrying in the hollow of his shield. "You didn't have this with you when you went away, but I kinda thought you might like it now."

He handed her the bundle: her Pewle knife, with its belt and sealskin sheath. The single-edged blade was heavy and the length of her forearm. It was the tool a Pewle Island seal hunter used for all his tasks, from chopping driftwood for a fire to letting out a man's life. The knife and her memories were Sharina's legacy from the friend who'd died to save her.

"Thank you, trooper," Sharina said, feeling a sudden rush of warmth and peace. She fastened the belt around her. The buckle, carved from a pair of whale teeth, was shaped like dragons coupling. "Thank you more than I can say."

She wasn't likely to need a weapon: she had the Blood Eagles themselves, after all. But the Pewle knife was much more than a weapon to her.

A troop of a hundred or so horsemen approached. Captain Rowning was in charge, the man who'd commanded the escort when Sharina and Tenoctris visited Stronghand's tomb. Based on the way he and his men had reacted that day, Sharina was glad to have them with her again.

"Captain Rowning?" she said, shouting to be heard over the thuds and ringing as the troop reined up. "We'll be entering Valles by the Jezreal Gate to the east of here. From there we'l make our way to the temple where we had the trouble the other day. That's where the People are coming from."

"You want my troop to attack the enemy from the rear, your highness?" Rowning said. There was nothing beyond quiet curiosity in his tone, but his eyes flashed instinctively toward the lines of bronze-clad People advancing on the royal forces. The contrast between those thousands of armored figures—at least ten thousand by now—and his hundred-odd was too marked for even a brave man to accept without qualms.

"No, we're just going to capture the temple so that Lady Tenoctris can cut off their reinforcements," Sharina said. "And I'm not sending you; Tenoctris and I are going along. There'll be fighting but not—well, suicide."

"Right, your highness!" Rowning said, noticeably brighter. "Though you understand, we're willing to do whatever the kingdom requires."

"Of course," Sharina said. She gripped the pommel of the horse she'd appropriated and swung back into the saddle. She reached down to help Tenoctris mount, but Lires was already lifting the older woman by the waist to where she could get her legs onto the pillion. "Ascor, you'll stick close to us."

She knew that Rowning wasn't speaking empty words when he said his men would've attacked a hundred times their number if she'd ordered them to. It didn't make any sense in a logical fashion, but it was true for the sort of people a kingdom needs to survive. Pray to the Shepherd that the Isles had enough of them, soldiers and old women like Tenoctris . . . and girls like she herself had been, Sharina os-Reise.

The Blood Eagles had mounted also. Rowning's men were horsemen from childhood. Some of the Blood Eagles came from cavalry regiments, but for the most part they were former infantry and often no more comfortable on a horse than Sharina herself. They'd learned to ride, but they were soldiers on horseback rather than cavalry.

Rowning led his troop in a wide circuit to the left around the back of the royal forces. Either he or one of the men with him in the lead knew the area, because when they cut across a field there was always a gate or a stile on the other side.

The rear ranks of the royal forces were generally in sight; when Sharina's troop neared the left flank, Bolor's men were still falling in. The battle must've already opened on the right: the clash of weapons was unmistakable, and the shouts were shriller and more urgent than those of men trying to find their proper places in the line.

Soldiers turned to watch with doubtful expressions as Sharina and her escort rode past. "Hope they don't think we're running away," one of the Blood Eagles muttered.

"Don't matter what they think, Onder," Lires said. "We're guarding the princess. That's all we got to worry about."

That wasn't true, of course. These guards—these men—would've accompanied her even if she'd really been running away from the battle, but they wouldn't have been happy about it. The sort of men who joined the Blood Eagles—who were *allowed* to join the Blood Eagles—were those to whom it was important not only to be brave but to be seen to be brave.

The Jezreal road got traffic only from the large villas and the market towns in the hills east of Valles. It was graveled, not paved with flagstones, and only indifferently leveled at that. Sharina's group struck it less than a furlong from the city walls, though, so the ruts didn't matter.

Normally there'd have been a squad of soldiers on duty at the narrow gate, but Waldron had withdrawn them. A pair of City Watchmen with knobbed batons stood there, along with scores of civilians made nervous by trouble whose cause was a complete mystery to them.

Rowning rode through, barely slackening enough to let the frightened townsfolk get out of the way. One cried, "What's happening? Are the rebels attacking?"

The soldiers didn't reply. Sharina called, "There's no rebels. We're going to arrest a wizard, that's all!"

It was something the civilians could understand in a few words. The whole truth would've taken much longer to tell, without being in any real sense more informative.

Tenoctris leaned back and gripped the cantle of the saddle instead of clinging to Sharina's waist as Sharina would've done had their places been reversed. Tenoctris was a noblewoman who'd been taught the skills of her station from earliest youth. Age was the only reason she needed to ride pillion.

Smiling at the incongruity, Sharina wondered if the old wizard could sing courtly romances, accompanying herself on a lyre. Very possibly she could.

"Tenoctris?" she said. "Who's leading the People now that Hani's dead? He is dead, isn't he?"

They crossed the boulevard running inside the walls. Though choked with barrows of merchandise and poultry, it'd have been the simplest route toward the temple. Rowning's guide was taking them by back streets so they'd approach their goal from the rear instead of charging straight into the line of creatures marching to join the battle.

"Certainly dead," Tenoctris said, bending forward to put her lips close to Sharina's right ear. "When we have leisure, I intend to dispose of his body beyond risk of anyone's raising him again, but I don't think there's much risk of that happening regardless. As for their leader—"

They rode down a narrow alley, scattering children and driving adults back from their stoops. Washing hung on poles from second-story windows on both sides of the street. The spears of the leading horsemen hooked the clothing, setting off shouts and curses from both the owners and the tangled soldiers. The troop rode on. There'd be time to pay for damages later, if there was time for anything at all.

"—I don't believe they have a leader, dear," Tenoctris continued, bending to pluck a child's tunic from the right stirrup and toss it back toward where it'd been hanging. "They have a purpose, is all. They intend to capture Valles, then conquer Ornifal and, finally, all the Isles. Not for any reason, but because that was what they were directed to do. In that sense they're rather like a flung stone, but far, far more dangerous."

The troop rode into a plaza with four unequal sides and a well curb in the center. Civilians, mostly women, shouted frightened questions from doorways. The standard-bearer at Rowning's side held his pole crosswise over his head.

"Hold up!" Ascor translated in a shout. More quietly he explained, "They didn't use the horn like usual because we're trying to surprise them. Your highness."

The Blood Eagles led Sharina to Captain Rowning's side. The plaza was too small to hold the whole troop on horseback, but it provided enough space for the leading section to form without being trampled by the men behind them.

"We'll round that corner . . ." Rowning said, pointing down one of the five streets joined in the plaza, "and be right on top of them. I want you to keep well back, your highness, until we've got the temple cleared."

"No," said Sharina before Tenoctris could speak. "The temple can't be cleared until Lady Tenoctris is there to block the portal. She and I will go in immediately with our escort"—she nodded to Ascor—"and set to work. You and your men will keep the creatures who've already reached Valles from attacking from outside."

Rowning and Ascor looked at one another. Both grimaced.

"No help for it, then," Rowning muttered. To his cornicene, he said, "Sound Charge, Sessir. They'll know we're coming in a heartbeat no matter what."

The cornicene's horn was curled around his body. He put his lips to the bone mouthpiece and blew a quick tune. The trained horses lurched into motion at the first touch of their riders' heels—Sharina's included, and much more suddenly than she was expecting. The signaller repeated his call as the troop charged down the cobblestone street and around the elbow that put the east side of the temple directly ahead of them.

A line of People marched two abreast from the entrance of the small temple toward where the Northeast Road left Valles. The column was several blocks long, moving at a measured pace. Neither the sounds of battle beyond the city wall nor the residents openly gaping from roofs, windows, and even the street itself seemed to affect them. The invaders' first priority was to destroy organized military resistance; that they were about to do.

Captain Rowning and half a dozen of his troopers were ahead of Sharina; the Blood Eagles hedged her to either side. They burst out of the narrow street and into the broader one that the temple faced. For a moment the People ignored them: then all the smooth bronze helmets turned at once. Their shields came up, and their right hands drew the swords that they hadn't bothered to unsheathe before.

The mounted troopers rode through the straggling line, knocking down the invaders before they could form a shield wall. Horses won't charge home against a hedge of points, but trained cavalry mounts had no hesitation in using their weight and shoulders against individual men the way they'd have ridden through brush. Rowning reined his horse around to return to the temple, but many of his troopers continued their charge up the twisting street and out of sight.

The Blood Eagles dismounted at the temple steps and ran upward, hacking to death pairs of People as they met them. Sharina was a hair slower because she needed to hand Tenoctris to the ground. When she jumped down herself, the older woman was already climbing the steps, avoiding the sprawled, manlike bodies pouring their blood onto the worn marble.

Sharina curved her left arm around Tenoctris but didn't actually touch her. The support was there if the older woman stumbled, but at the moment, Tenoctris appeared to be as vibrantly alert as Sharina herself. The Blood Eagles bunched briefly at the entrance, four of them trading strokes shield to shield with an equal number of People.

A Blood Eagle dropped dazed to his knees, his helmet falling to the temple porch, but then the People were thrashing in their death throes and the Blood Eagles were through into the sanctum. Sharina and Tenoctris followed. Behind them the sixth guard was wobbling forward again also, though he'd forgotten to retrieve his helmet.

The interior was just as Sharina'd left it when she'd leaped to safety with Bolor and his fellow rebels. Stronghand's body, half-preserved by decades in a sealed coffin, sprawled hideously in Valgard's armor; Hani had decayed to a scattering of dust in his tunic and sandals. *How old had the wizard really been before he roused the ghost of a vengeful warrior against him?* she wondered.

Wilfus and Mogon lay on their backs, their eyes open and their faces distorted; both dead by Sharina's hand. The world was better off without them . . . but she'd pray to the Lady on their behalf if she survived this day, as she prayed for others already.

Two more People strode through the portal, swinging their swords at the Blood Eagles waiting for them. Both went down, but one had split Lires' shield from the rim to the boss. Lires stepped back, giving his place to a fellow, and traded his broken shield for the bronze buckler of a dead invader.

More movement through the portal. Swords and armor clashed, People went down. Eventually, though, the humans' blunted swords and tired arms would take their toll.

Tenoctris sat cross-legged and scooped the fallen ring from the dust of Hani's finger. She held it bezel upward between her left thumb and forefinger while she rummaged in her satchel, still open beside the figure she'd drawn before Hani returned Sharina from the island.

Sharina drew the Pewle knife, as much for comfort as because she might need to use it. She glanced out into the street. Rowning's men had dismounted and formed an arc in front of the temple. They stood shield to shield, their horsehair-crested helmets a gay contrast to the People's smooth bronze.

A few humans were down, but for the moment the troop didn't seem seriously pressed by the People who'd turned to recapture the temple. The fact that the cavalry mounts were wandering loose, excited by the blood and clangor, showed how bad the situation really was, though: Rowning didn't think he could spare every fourth man as a horseholder.

Tenoctris began chanting. The figure she'd drawn in cinnabar on the floor had spun into a red smear when Hani opened the portal. It was spinning again, but this time sunwise. Wizardlight made spiteful blue crackles around the edges of the opening, but People continued to stride through and slash at the Blood Eagles before being cut down. The pile of leaking corpses grew, driving Sharina's guards back as invaders climbed over the tops of their dead fellows.

Ascor's foot slipped. He shouted a curse and went down. One of the People vaulted from the bulwark of corpses and stabbed him through the lower body. Lires hacked the invader from behind, knocking his helmet off but not felling him.

Two more People appeared at the top of the pile. The wounded one raised his sword to cut at Tenoctris, seated at his feet.

Sharina swung, judging the stroke as she'd have split kindling. The Pewle knife sheared through the invader's wrist. Hand and sword flew sideways. Lires finished the job by decapitating the creature with an angry curse.

Tenoctris hadn't flinched as the sword rose to strike her; Sharina wasn't sure she'd even noticed. She continued chanting, her eyes on the vellum codex on the floor beside her. A strip of lead held the pages open. The ring in Tenoctris' left hand snapped sparks of wizardlight toward the portal as she gestured with the split of bamboo.

Two People started through the portal. Ascor and two of his men were down, and another of the Blood Eagles wavered. He hadn't dropped his sword, but it hung at arm's length, pointing to the floor.

The portal flashed vividly azure like a sun-struck tile. The invaders in it vanished, flung backward by the same forces that'd been bringing them from Hani's island to Valles.

The portal were still shimmering wizardlight instead of the wall of polished granite it'd been before Hani started his incantation. The light sizzled, and the ring continued to spit blue sparks toward it.

"Sharina," Tenoctris said. Her voice was hoarse, but there was an unfamiliar febrile brightness in her eyes. Normally a major spell left the old wizard drained almost to the point of being comatose.

"Yes, Tenoctris?" Sharina said, squatting to put their heads on a level. She hoped she was hiding the concern she felt.

Lires turned and looked at them. Toward them, rather, because his eyes were staring a thousand miles away. His helmet had taken several hard blows, and the shield he'd snatched to replace his own was hacked and battered into scrap.

"I said Hani's portal wouldn't take me anyplace I wanted to go, dear," Tenoctris said, forcing the human syllables through lips that'd twisted around words of power. "I was wrong. It'll send a person to Volita. I don't know why Hani created that passage, but I doubt it was something we'd approve of. I think your brother's in danger."

"What can we do?" Sharina said. *"What?"*

"I think the portal still focuses enough power to take us through," Tenoctris said, nodding toward but not looking at the quivering blue field. "If you'll carry me, I'll try—"

"Yes," said Sharina, wiping the Pewle knife clean on the tunic of the invader she'd dismembered with it. She sheathed the blade, then put her arms around the wizard's back and thighs. It was like lifting a bird, frail and much lighter than she unconsciously expected.

"Lires!" she said, speaking loudly to cut through the soldier's black reverie. "Pull some of these bodies out of our way!"

Lires dropped the ruined shield but he didn't let go of his sword. He gripped the topmost invader by an ankle and jerked him off the pile. He did the same with two more People, using a wrist and a throat for handles.

The other Blood Eagles were either wounded or helping their wounded fellows. They looked at what was happening, but they didn't have energy enough to speak.

Sharina mounted the bottom layer of twitching corpses. Behind her she heard human cheers and the brassy triumph of a dozen horns and trumpets: Lord Waldron's forces had broken the line of People and fought their way into the city, coming to the rescue of the survivors of Captain Rowning's troop.

"*Ereschigal aktiophi berbiti* . . ." Tenoctris said in a husky whisper. A fat spark spat from Hani's ring. The wall of blue fire went blank.

Sharina had no thought but that she would do what she could, for Garric and for the Isles. She stepped into the emptiness as Tenoctris in her arms spoke the remaining syllables of the spell.

Chapter Nineteen

Mab stood facing Cashel in the center of Ronn's great rooftop plaza. Around them, none quite close enough for Cashel to touch with his staff, stood the assembled citizens. They filled the open area, all but the immediate circle.

Mab spread her hands, palms down. All sounds stilled, not naturally but with the suddenness of a vault door closing between Cashel and the crowd. For a moment Mab's fingernails blazed, spots of color brighter than the noon sun; then they went black, and her body became a figure of wizardlight, flaring red and blue alternately in a rapidly increasing cycle.

She raised her hands, her mouth working. Cashel couldn't hear the syllables Mab spoke, but the scene beyond the two of them pulsed in his vision as she spoke.

The world flip-flopped. Cashel still faced Mab, but instead of being on the sun-drenched roof of Ronn, they were in a city amid the ruins of buildings thrown down by earth shocks. The sky above was black and the air choking with sulfur. A few double paces away hunched men in armor, facing the distorted monsters who climbed and crawled from an acres-broad crater.

A wind, cold as the Ice Capes, howled across the land. Humans were screaming also.

Mab turned to face the crater and the thin line of soldiers standing against the creatures it spawned, then stepped into what'd been an arched entranceway. To either side was a square column base; the rest of the building had collapsed. Fluted columns lay on top of roof tiles, marble sheathing, and the brick core of the walls. Dust still rose from the wreckage.

"Very well," she said crisply. "Cashel, protect me as you did before. It may be harder this time."

"All right," said Cashel. He moved in front of Mab, planted his feet, and began to spin the quarterstaff sunwise.

Cashel didn't mind things being hard. This was one of those times when a man needed to stand up for what was right, no matter what it cost.

Mab raised her hands, gesturing in a pattern that thrilled Cashel when he glanced over his shoulder. He didn't understand what the wizard was doing, but he could see and feel the art of it. It was so pretty to watch that he had to remind himself that his business was looking out for Mab, not gawping like he had the first time he saw a city.

He guessed this was Erdin; he'd been here a year ago. *Duzi! but it was in a bad way, though.*

A whole herd of creatures bubbled from the crater and came on down the street toward the waiting soldiers. They were white like the Made Men, and their weapons were pretty much the ones the Made Men carried, but none of *these* things could pass for human. Some were even legless, with flipper hands sticking out below their snarling faces. They used the whole length of their slimy bodies to swing their weapons.

Bolts of red and blue ripped from between Mab's weaving hands to strike the overcast. They slashed it like swords through dirty burlap.

Thunder slammed twice. Bright, clean sunlight flooded from the uncovered sky. Where it fell across the white creatures, they writhed like slugs on a griddle.

The monsters must be making the high keening Cashel heard. The human defenders who'd been falling back steadied and hacked their squirming opponents to death.

The black sky closed again over the sunlight. More of the white monsters lifted from the crater, moving toward the line of soldiers. Two humans had gone down in the attack just finished. Soldiers lay on the pavement in ones and twos, all the way back to the edge of the pit.

The barrier was growing thinner. Cashel could see companies of monsters setting off in all directions, not just toward the men directly in front of him. A few human reinforcements were moving up the road from the harbor, but only a very few.

The man on the far end of the line knelt, bowing his head. The smaller figure beside him, a slim spearman, who wasn't wearing armor, lifted the first man's helmet to let the cold breeze cool his scalp.

Mab's hands moved together with the whirling precision of hawks mating in midair. Wizardlight blasted from between them, throwing back the darkness to either side the way skin gapes away from a deep cut. The sun blazed down. Creatures of the false darkness shrivelled.

The spearman was Liane. She lowered the helmet back onto Garric's head. He rose and braced himself for the new assault, because despite the sunlight, the monsters still came on with the fury of the damned.

Blackness burped from the crater. Instead of streaking upward to heal the wound in the overcast, it coalesced into the shape of a two-legged reptilian nightmare. The thing strode heavily down the cracked pavement toward Mab.

It wasn't an illusion. The corpses of white monsters burst like foul grapes as the three-clawed feet crushed down on them. The lifting foot kicked a dead soldier; he hurtled several double paces through the air before falling again to the bloody pavement.

Cashel had his staff spinning at a moderate rate, alternating sunwise circles and widdershins to loosen all his muscles against the time he needed their full strength. He guessed that time was at hand.

The thing of darkness marched on. The only light on the sooty form was the eyes, searing orange-red blotches on either side of the narrow skull. The creature bore down on Mab—and standing in front of Mab, Cashel.

"Get out of the way!" Cashel shouted as he spun the staff faster—sunwise now, certain of every next move; certain of everything but the outcome. His voice was thick with rage. "Garric, get your men out of the way! This one's mine!"

Cashel couldn't tell if the soldiers heard him or not. The two in the center of the line edged a little toward either side. They raised their shields and cocked their swords back to strike if the lizard-thing bit down at them, but they didn't run.

The creature strode through the living ranks of white not-men, crushing and slashing them aside with the same disregard it'd displayed for the windrows of their corpses. Dying things, already stunned by the torrent of sunlight, mewled in horror; the stench of their gutted bodies was worse than a tanyard in hot summer.

"Move aside!" Cashel said.

The lizard reached the line of soldiers, breaking paving stones every time its feet smashed down. The two nearest men weren't cowards, *couldn't* be cowards to stand where they were; but they didn't throw themselves in the path of something they knew they could no more stop than they could stop an avalanche walking on two legs. The lizard-thing passed between the soldiers, heading for Mab with the unswerving assurance of an arrow. Cashel stepped forward to meet it.

His staff was spinning, scattering coils of blue wizardlight. He could see every bit of the pattern—the way the creature would move, the way he'd move; the perfect arc of his quarterstaff and the point his leading butt cap would meet the creature's long jaw.

Cashel could see everything but what happened *then*: whether the creature went down or it snapped him up on its way to Mab. That depended on how strong he was and how strong the creature was. There was no way of telling that except by trying, just as in any other fight.

That didn't bother Cashel. He didn't start fights himself, but his size drew fellows who needed to prove they were better than him. Thus far they'd all been wrong; and if this lizard was right, well, Cashel had won too often to complain about losing once.

The creature seemed to slow down, but that was what always happened at times like this. Cashel was seeing everything with the eyes of experience, all the little pieces that were really happening at the same time.

The lizard was the same dull color all over, no shades or highlights. It was like a shadow wrapped around something that could've been a crocodile on two legs. The bright sunlight didn't make any difference. Cashel saw the teeth only when the open jaws were canted to silhouette them against something on the other side. The maw, the throat, the pits of the nostrils—all were the same black that was really no color.

The lizard's left foreleg reached for Cashel, but he stepped inside it as he brought the staff around. It was all the way he'd seen it in his mind, the movements working together just the way the gears of his grandfather's mill in Barca's Hamlet turned and made the grindstones spin. Everything was perfect.

His sunwise-spinning butt cap struck midway on the creature's long jaw.

Cashel expected a shock and a blue flash. Instead, time stopped. Cashel's heart didn't beat, and the stench of death and sulfur was only a memory in his nostrils. He saw Garric and Liane from beyond the creature's outthrust leg. Garric's mouth was open to shout, but Cashel heard nothing in this slice of forever.

Crackling blue wizardlight licked across the monster the way a downpour covers a statue. The living darkness flew apart as suddenly as chaff lifts in a windstorm.

Cashel fell backward, deafened and numb. The shattered dust of the lizard swept across him, bearing him down and smothering him. As he toppled, he felt the ground lift with a shock far greater than any that had struck the city before.

Sharina stepped from the sanctum of the temple, brightly lighted through the open doors, onto the foreshore of Volita. The sky was covered by a black cloud almost as opaque as the block of stone on which she stood. She stumbled, more from surprise than because she'd just passed from one place to a distant other place in a single step.

"Ah!" said Tenoctris. "Set me—"

Sharina was already bending to put Tenoctris' feet on the ground. She lifted the wizard upright, then cautiously released her. Tenoctris' spirit was indomitable, but her friends had learned techniques to cope with the weakness of an elderly body. For Sharina and Cashel in particular, these were by now second nature.

The water was only twenty feet away. Sharina stepped off the stone. It was a thin, square slab with sides an arm's length across. It didn't seem to have come from the ruined mansions just above the tide line.

"Bolor's courier must've placed it here," Tenoctris said, glancing at the slab approvingly. "It's sheltered by these pilings, so when someone appears here, he looks like he's just stepped into view normally."

A trireme stood fifty feet out in the strait, broadside to the shore. Only the uppermost bank of oars was manned. Fully equipped soldiers were boarding by a pair of rope ladders. The warship rocked violently on its narrow keel, but the fact it didn't capsize indicated that its officers had men standing on the opposite outrigger to balance the weight of those climbing.

A few other vessels were beached nearby, but most of the royal fleet had crossed to the mainland. The trireme's sailing master stood in the stern, bellowing through a speaking trumpet, "Two more only! Any more and we'll bloody sink in the chop!"

Soldiers, many of them with signs of injury, stood on the sand in twos and threes to watch the loading. Civilians, apparently refugees from Erdin, formed in larger groups apart from the troops.

Sharina stepped out of cover. "Where's Prince Garric?" she demanded loudly. "Is he still here on Volita?"

Some people turned to look at her, though others continued staring in numb amazement at the devastation across the strait. No one spoke.

"Where's Prince Garric?" Sharina shouted, pointing her finger at a soldier. He wore his cuirass but no helmet because of the bandage on his head.

Instead of the soldier, a barefoot woman in expensive robes answered, "He's at the palace, fighting the demons from below. He's there if he's still alive."

"Hurry!" Tenoctris said. "We've got to get aboard the ship."

There was no help for it, then. Sharina was tired, physically as well as mentally, but without hesitation she picked the wizard up again. She ran into the water shouting, "I'm Princess Sharina! Help me! I've got to reach my brother in Erdin!"

Those aboard the trireme probably couldn't hear her, but the soldiers waist deep in the strait waiting their turn to climb the ladders did. Three of them bellowed in unison, "Hold up for the princess coming aboard!"

The warship rode as close inshore as it could without grounding, but the sea would still be up to Sharina's chest. The troops at the back of the line saw the women's problem. One grabbed Sharina's arm and handed her forward. The next man did the same, not carrying her and Tenoctris but shoving from one man to the next so that Sharina didn't have the problem of trying to walk in deep water.

"You've got no business there, your highness!" the sailing master replied through his trumpet. If the captain—a nobleman who wouldn't be expected to know about ships—had an opinion, he kept it to himself. The sailing master turned, and ordered, "Crew, prepare to set off!"

Soldiers continued to pull and push the women toward the vessel. Aboard the trireme, a soldier handed his javelin to the soldier beside him, then drew his sword. He laid the point of it against the sailing master's throat. The sailor flung his speaking trumpet into the air in shock. He probably would've jumped himself if the soldier hadn't been gripping his shoulder.

"Come on, your princessship!" shouted the soldier holding the javelins. His unaided lungs gave up nothing to the sailor's orders through the speaking trumpet. "We'll wait for you!"

Sharina finished the journey to the ship with her face in the water half the time. She hoped Tenoctris was all right; the wizard's occasional sneezes were reassuring. When they reached the tarred black hull, a pair of men lifted them out of the water together and two more—the soldiers who'd convinced the sailing master of his duty—jerked them over the railing with about as much consideration as you'd give sacks of grain.

They'd gotten the job done. Delicate men wouldn't have. Sharina felt a rush of gratitude to them.

"Now you can get moving, sailor boy," said the first soldier as he retrieved his javelin from his buddy. "And don't waste a lot of time, hear?"

If the sailing master had an opinion, he swallowed it and merely shouted orders to the crew. The flutist seated under the sternpost began blowing time, and the oars took up their beat. The trireme groaned forward and swung slowly toward the mainland.

"Don't guess you'd remember me and Pont, your princessship," said the soldier who'd been speaking. "We met back in the ice a time ago, but there was a lot going on then."

Sharina looked at the men. They were noncommissioned officers in a line regiment, and at least the age of her father. There were several hundred men like them in the royal army. But—

"I do recognize you!" she said. "File closers Pont and Prester! You saved my brother's life, and he gave you estates! What are you doing here?"

The trireme laboriously gained speed. It rode deep in the water, just as the sailing master had warned. Sharina hoped the lowest range of oar ports had been blocked when the warship was converted into a transport, but worse come to worst she could swim to the far shore even if she had to pull Tenoctris along with her.

"Oh, ma'am, what do we know about farming?" Prester said. "Anyway, your brother saved my ass and Pont's both a time or two, as I remember it. With a little seasoning he'd make a real soldier, he would."

"But it's good of her to remember us, Prester," said his partner. "A lady like that, a *princess,* and she remembers us."

"Pont and me signed back on," Prester said. "Camp marshals, that makes us warrant officers. That's why we were still on Volita. Somebody had to chivy stragglers over."

"Are we going to be in trouble because we didn't, you know, wait for the last ship out, Prester?" Pont said. "Looks like there's another coming after all."

He pointed. A stubby patrol vessel, packed with troops and only one of its two oarbanks manned, was wallowing away from Volita in the trireme's wake.

"No," Sharina said with a decisive nod. "You're not going to be in trouble."

"Anyway, we may've screwed the pooch this time anyhow," said Prester, in a surprisingly cheerful tone given what he was saying. "Nothing like fighting in a city to get yourself killed."

"But there's loot, Prester," said his partner. "Remember those temple dishes we got in Durance?"

"I remember the hangover they bought me," Prester said. "*That* I'm never going to forget."

Wizardlight slashed out of the city, ripping a long gash in the overcast. The sun poured down, more than doubling the light that'd been seeping in around the perimeter of the artificial shadow.

Prester looked at the flashes and the sky of roiling blackness, then looked out to sea past Sharina. "Well, we seen wizards before," he muttered. "It's no big thing that we're seeing 'em again, I guess."

"Anyhow," said Pont cheerfully, "it's nice to have sunlight."

He looked at Sharina in sudden concern. "But it's all right if we don't, your princessship," he added. "I mean, whatever you want, ma'am. You can count in me 'n Prester to cope."

"Thank you, Marshal Pont," Sharina said formally. *Did they really think she controlled the wizards battling in Erdin?* "I have no doubt at all that you will cope, as you've done before. As we've all done before."

The trireme's mast was stepped, though the spar and sail had been left onshore. The lookout at the masthead shouted down, "Master Darrin! All the slips are full, and there's ships tied to the ones already moored. We'll have to go upriver!"

The sailing master stepped onto the pivot of the steering oar, gripping the railing with his left hand. "Hanging on like that looks very dangerous," Tenoctris said in a tone of mild disapproval. "Though I suppose he knows what he's doing."

Sharina opened her mouth to reply. The ridiculousness of the statement—here, from Tenoctris to her—struck her. She giggled. Tenoctris looked at her in surprise, then started to chuckle also.

Sharina's giggle became laughter that was barely on the right side of hysteria. She leaned over the railing to take the pressure off her chest.

"No, we'll berth alongside the *Sword of Ornifal* here in the harbor," the sailing master decided aloud. He didn't seem to be speaking to anybody in particular, but he spoke loudly enough that everybody on deck from the mast sternward could hear. "The passengers can cross the other ships to the quay. If we go up the river, the Shepherd knows what we'll find."

Turning to the helmsman, he added, "Two points to starboard, Henga. Master Estin, prepare to back water."

Pont cocked an eye at the sailing master. "That all right with you and your friend, princess?" he asked.

"I won't be able to carry Tenoctris from ship to ship by myself," Sharina said. "But he's probably right—the river will be choked. Warships are too long to turn in the channel, and . . ."

"Oh, that's no problem, princess," Prester said. He turned to survey the soldiers nearest to him on deck. "Mallus and Jodea, you're carrying the old lady here, got it? Unter and Borcas, you two take their spears and be ready to grab if something goes wrong. You got that?"

A soldier blinked. His fluffy blond moustache flared into sideburns and disappeared under his helmet. "How far do we carry her, Marshal?" he asked doubtfully.

"Until I bloody tell you to bloody put her down, you bloody fool!" Prester replied like a thunderclap.

"Back 'em, back 'em!" the sailing master shouted, still clinging to the oar block. "Four, three, two, one—*ship oars*! Ship oars, or you'll pay for the broken shafts, I swear it!"

The trireme wobbled as it slowed, pummeled by the wake of its forward passage and the stroke of its reversed oars rebounding from the vessel it slid toward. That one, the outermost of three triremes already moored, held several score civilians but none of the regular crew. A few refugees seemed to be trying to get the vessel under way, but the others were simply huddling on deck. This was as far as they'd been able to run from the destruction occurring in their city.

The ships scrunched together, rocking violently. The passengers hindered the deck crew, but there were hawsers across to the inner vessel before they drifted apart again. Soldiers had started leaping over before the ships were lashed together firmly.

"Make way for the princess and the old lady!" Prester bellowed. He glared at the men he'd detailed to carry Tenoctris, and added in a scarcely quieter voice, "Mallus and Jodea, hop to it!"

The troops crashed and slid their way across the ships till they'd reached the stone quay. A couple of them managed to fall into the water, but they were able to rescue themselves because cut rigging already hung from the vessels' sides. Troops must've fallen previously, and soldiers had no compunction about destroying a ship—or most anything else—to save a buddy's life.

The men holding Tenoctris negotiated the route without difficulty; they must've been either sailors or mountaineers at an earlier point in their lives. It struck Sharina that Prester and Pont might be simple men in many respects, but their knowledge of troops and the things required to keep troops alive was of a very sophisticated order.

The trireme had carried at least two hundred soldiers besides the oarsmen. No wonder it'd ridden low in the water! The men first across to the quay were starting up the boulevard that led to the harbor.

"Halt and form ranks of twelve, you miserable disgraces!" Pont cried, moving in a rolling trot to the front of his men. "Are you the prince's royal army, or are you a herd of bloody *cats,* eh?"

Men crunched and clattered into place. Though they must be a mixture of several or many different units, they fell into formation as easily as grain fills a sack. The only problem seemed to be the length of the front rank, and Pont quickly trimmed that back to the twelve he'd demanded.

"Do we fall in, Marshal?" one of the soldiers carrying Tenoctris asked plaintively.

"You bloody well do *not*," Prester snarled, his eye restraining as well the pair of soldiers holding the bearers' javelins. "You stay back with me and the princess, you got it?"

All four men nodded. Prester's tone was so commanding that Sharina, half-numbed by all that had happened, almost nodded also.

"Forward . . . ," Pont called from the left front of the formation. "March! Hup! Hup! Hup!"

Hobnails on stone, the studded aprons of the soldiers and pieces of their equipment jouncing together combined deafeningly. It sounded like wagons full of scrap metal driving over the edge of a quarry.

"Double . . . ," Pont called. *"Time!"*

Prester glanced at Sharina as they kept pace with the rear of the formation—him trotting, her in what was more a leggy walk than running. "This all right with you, princess?" he asked.

"Yes, of course," said Sharina. "But can troopers Mallus and Jodea keep up?"

"They can if they know what's good for them," Prester said with baleful significance. "We don't have packs, you see. And it's just up to the palace the messenger said where we meet his princeship."

The air was chilly. Fires were burning at half a dozen places in the city, adding their smoke to the unnatural overcast, but in addition the atmosphere had the cutting, choking stench of sulfur.

The ground continued to jump the way a dead frog does, a spastic trembling unlike the two real earthquakes Sharina had experienced. Many buildings had collapsed. Sometimes the lower stories of brick and stone remained, but the lath-and-plaster construction above them had shaken into the street. A few corpses lay on the pavement, but the people who could flee were already gone.

Wizardlight continued to tear the overcast. The bolts were searingly bright, but they didn't leave afterimages on Sharina's eyeballs the way direct sunlight would've done.

The boulevard bent to the right between a pair of government office buildings, still standing while lesser structures had fallen. Men were fighting monsters at the head of the street, but the earl's palace had vanished into a cauldron of black vapors and grubs trying to be men.

Garric and Liane were at the left end of the line, where a street leading toward the river joined. Fallen buildings half choked the cross street, but troops were using the rubble as artificial hills to defend against the creatures attacking.

The battle was ending as Sharina and the reinforcements double-timed up. The monsters didn't retreat: they died, throwing themselves forward like rabid dogs and sometimes drawing blood before they were butchered.

"Detachment . . . ," Pont said, as his troops neared the present defenders. He paused for three more crashing double paces, then cried, "Halt!"

"Bring Tenoctris!" Sharina said as she ran to her brother.

Garric turned slowly but didn't seem to recognize her. He was breathing through his mouth, and his eyes were focused in another time. His sword was so bloody that only in streaks and patches could Sharina see that the blade was patterned in gray waves.

Liane began moving down the line of soldiers, offering them drinks from a helmet filled with water. She lifted the improvised bucket to each man's lips; for the most part they were too exhausted to raise it themselves.

"Garric, you're in danger!" Sharina said. His arms hung at his sides, weighed down by his equipment. His shield'd been hacked to half its original dimensions. What was left of its leather facing held together the wooden core.

"I'd noticed," Garric said. He started to laugh, but the flash of humor turned into a cough. He went down on one knee.

"A wizard on Ornifal planned something against you," Sharina said. Mallus and Jodea set Tenoctris beside her, then stood beaming as they waited for further orders. The stench of inhuman corpses was nauseating, even beyond the other reeks.

Tenoctris seated herself in the littered roadway and opened the satchel she'd carried in her lap from Valles. "Now that I'm here, I hope I can learn just what the danger is. I'm afraid I couldn't tell when I was in Valles," she said. She started drawing a figure by pouring powdered sulfur from a flask.

"Whatever it is," Garric said wearily, "it'll have to wait its turn."

He looked at the reinforcements and suddenly smiled. He lurched upright again. "Pont, you're a warrant officer, now?" he said.

"Yes, prince," Prester said. "Me and Pont are camp marshals. Ah—this is pretty much the tailings from Volita, I'm afraid. Where do you want us?"

Garric looked over his shoulder. A mass of white creatures with weapons as distorted as their bodies rose from the cauldron. Garric's face lost the moment's happiness Sharina had seen there.

"It's like the surf hitting a cliff," Garric whispered. "Not all at once, but again and again. Until it stops, or the cliff goes down, and I don't guess this surf is going to stop."

"There's troops coming up from the river too, your princeship," Pont said. "Dunno how many, but some."

As Pont spoke, he nodded toward the handful of soldiers coming up the street from the left. All were line infantry. Lord Attaper was on the other side of this boulevard and a few more guards remained in the line, but the pavement back to the cauldron had many more bodies in black armor.

"Marshal Pont," Garric said, drawing himself straight. "Leave ten men here with me. Take the rest widdershins around the perimeter, leaving detachments where in your judgment they're most needed."

He drew a shuddering breath, no longer Sharina's brother but a tortured soul whose determination burned through the wasted flesh. "Which is everywhere, as I well know, but do your best. Do your best, all of you."

"Aye aye, *sir*," Pont said, clashing down his right foot and turning on his heel. He tapped the man who'd been next to him with his spear butt, and said, "Rastin, you're sticking with me. Rest of you beggars in the front rank, you stay here with the prince."

Prester eyed the men falling out of the detachment. He said, "And *don't* let me hear you embarrassed me, or I'll come back and piss on your worthless corpses, you hear?"

"From the left by ranks . . ." said Pont, who'd looked at the debris-choked street they'd be following as they went off to the right. "Form column of fours! Detachment, *march!*"

Liane jogged toward the courtyard of a mews just down the street, carrying the helmet that was now empty. She wasn't fleeing: Sharina could see a well curb in the courtyard of the mews.

The creatures from the cauldron were within twenty double paces of the human line. They didn't approach any faster than a man could walk, but they gave the impression of disgusting unity. They resembled less a formation of soldiers than the blotches on a slug's slimy body.

"You want these boys, princess?" Prester asked in a low tone, as the detachment marched off under Pont. He nodded to the four men who'd accompanied Tenoctris, still standing close by. "They're not half-bad, if I do say myself who trained 'em."

Sharina shivered. Garric was spreading the reinforcements along the thin existing line. Yes, she did want Mallus and the others by her very much, but it wasn't her decision to make.

"No," she said. "Thank you for your help, Marshal Prester, but you have your duties to carry out. And may the Lady guard you!"

Prester and the four troopers followed their fellows at a thudding run. Sharina grimaced, then glanced down at Tenoctris. The wizard was chanting words of power softly over the six-pointed star she'd drawn in yellow sulfur. *She's too close to the fighting here!*

Sharina drew the Pewle knife Lires had handed her on Ornifal. They could use Lires and his fellow guards here. They could use all Waldron's five regiments, as a matter of fact, though it probably wouldn't make any difference in the long run. . . .

The battle of wizards, bolts of light against jets of blackness, continued. The sky was becoming more open, but though sunlight seemed to hurt the white creatures, it didn't keep them from coming on.

There was a windrow of bodies where the most recent fighting had occurred, most of them monsters, but with a leavening of men. Garric had pulled his remaining troops slightly back to keep his enemies from leaping straight down on them from the pile. This next wave crawled up the corpses of their fellows, then slithered toward the humans with the mindless determination of leeches scenting blood.

A blue thread lifted from the center of Tenoctris' pattern. She continued to chant. The line of light rose arm's length from the ground, then twisted to the left and continued to grow longer.

The creatures met the line of soldiers. Garric stabbed, then struck overhand. His blows were quick as a snake's tongue; it was hard to believe that moments ago he'd seemed so weary.

A thing with a bronze mace swung at Garric from the side. He caught the blow on his shield but went down on one knee. A soldier coming from the river threw his javelin, skewering the fat, multilegged body of the creature with the mace. It curled in on itself like a broiled spider; Garric regained his feet.

Most of the reinforcements from the river joined the fighting as the monsters forced the line of defenders back. One of them strode stolidly toward Garric. He didn't have a javelin, but he'd drawn his sword. The thread of wizardlight from Tenoctris' hexagram extended till it touched the center of the soldier's breastplate and followed his progress.

Sharina looked sharply. The man was Memet, who'd brought her news of Cashel's disappearance. Or at least he wore Memet's face, as the creature forming in Hani's tank on the island had done.

"Garric!" she shouted. "Watch—"

A pair of monsters with three legs and three heads between them closed with Garric. He knocked one back with his shield as his blade blocked the other's axe. Memet raised his sword.

Sharina grabbed Memet's wrist with her left hand and stabbed the Pewle knife into the pit of the man's stomach. The keen steel point belled on the bronze cuirass, punching through to the depth of a hand's breadth.

Memet struck. Sharina's weight on his sword wrist couldn't prevent the blow, but she slowed it. Garric was dodging back after slashing through one throat of the creature attacking from his right. Memet's sword hilt rang on his helmet instead of the blade cutting his spine as it was intended to do.

The false soldier shook Sharina loose and raised his sword for another stroke. She fell back, dragging her knife from the wound. A gout of black decay squirted through the cuirass as the blade came free. The semblance of life washed from Memet's face, leaving behind a skull half-covered with rotten flesh. Memet had said his father'd died on Ornifal a few years previous. . . .

Sharina got back to her feet. The latest attack was over, though new regiments of monsters were rising from the cauldron.

She looked around. Tenoctris swayed, apparently bewildered by the fact her spell had ended unexpectedly.

Sharina squatted and hugged the old woman, careful not to touch her with the Pewle knife. "It's all right, Tenoctris," she said. "You've ended the danger."

The earth shook violently. Dust lifted from the ground, and showers of roof tiles rattled down from apartment blocks that were still standing.

Sharina looked seaward. Something terrible was happening across the strait on Volita.

Davus stood on a wisp of crystal that stuck out from the Citadel's crown. His right foot was in front of his left because the slender beam wasn't wide enough for them side by side. The wind's whimsy snapped his tunic to and fro.

Ilna, on the crown also but well back from the edge, watched without emotion. Davus had known what he was doing throughout their past acquaintance, so she supposed he still did now that he was king again. And if Davus fell, well, he was an adult. She had enough difficulty living her own life not to want to get into the business of deciding what other people should so.

"Ilna, what if he falls?" Merota said. She didn't whine, but she was holding Ilna's right hand and Chalcus' left tight as oysters grip the rocks.

Chalcus chuckled with his usual cheerful ease. "Well, then, my dear girl," he said, "the three of us will have to find our own way back to our friends. Which no doubt we'll do, though I'll admit at the moment I haven't decided how."

He glanced at Ilna over the child's head. "Eh, love of my life?" he added.

Ilna sniffed. "I doubt most things, as you well know," she said. She felt her tight, disapproving lips loosen into a smile. "But I don't doubt that the three of us would *try* to find passage home, until we succeeded or we . . . couldn't try anymore."

Davus turned with a laugh of pure joy. He walked toward the three outlanders, as sprightly as a dancer at the Harvest Fest. "Oh, my friends," he said, "I can't tell you how good it feels to be back in my land at last."

"You've been back, I'd have judged," Chalcus said, "for the week and more that it's taken us to walk from there"—he pointed to the south, where the cliffs of their arrival were a purple-brown line on the horizon— "to here." His foot tapped the crystal, a sheet as smooth and broad as an iced-over pond. "Not so?"

"Indeed, not so," said Davus. His smile was good-natured but as hard and certain as Ilna's own when she told people truths that didn't fit their understandings. "I was in this land, but it wasn't mine until Mistress Ilna made it mine. A deed I couldn't have accomplished myself, and one that puts me in her debt for so long as I live. A good long while, I would expect that to be."

He threw his head back and laughed again, a man satisfied with the world and his place in it. The jewel hovered just above his scalp, softly scintillant despite the rainbow blaze from the mass of crystal on which he stood.

"Sir?" said Merota. "I'd really like to go home now."

"Yes," said Ilna, more tersely than she'd really intended. She understood Davus being pleased to recover the throne he'd been ousted from a thousand years before, but they too had been gone from their world longer than she cared to be. "I don't consider you to be in my debt, Master Davus; but as a matter of courtesy, I'd appreciate you sending us home as you said you would."

"Aye," said Davus. "You'll be in time, I promise you. But we can go now, if you like."

"In time for what, my friend?" said Chalcus, his fingers playing almost forgetfully with the hilt of his sword.

"In time to watch, is all, my friend," Davus said. "But I'll try to give you a proper show. It's my second trip to your world, you'll recall, and the first was memorable right up to the end."

Instead of continuing, Davus paused to rub his bare feet on the ground in obvious pleasure. Ilna turned her head, looking out over the land she hoped she was about to leave. It was much the same in all directions; some portions greener than others, some hilly. She could see the far shore of the body of water lapping the east of the Citadel, but it continued northward out of sight even from this high vantage.

There was nothing improper in what Davus was doing, but Ilna wasn't comfortable watching somebody else so wrapped in emotion. Ilna smiled faintly. She supposed being uncomfortable with emotion was a flaw in her, but she had enough other flaws that she didn't expect to have time to fix that one no matter how long a life remained to her.

"I'd never have built this myself," Davus mused, his mind returning to the same world as his three companions. "The crown, I mean. It's a marvelous thing, a lens to focus the powers that the jewel controls over a much wider range. Perhaps if it were finished, it'd control the whole cosmos. Well, we'll never know that for sure."

Chalcus detached his hand from Merota's, patted her on the head, and absently reached for the dagger in his sash. He was probably going to juggle it to settle him the way the cords Ilna plaited did her; but his conscious mind caught him.

He opened his hands, grinning wryly. "What did your pet do with his pretty palace, then?" he asked. "Not simply turn young ladies into statues, I suppose?"

"Not even that," said Davus. "The jewel alone suffices for such matters. From what the stone's memory tells me—"

He grinned, pausing a moment to allow his audience to protest at the notion stone could remember. Ilna grinned back, her finger stroking the hem of her tunic. She returned in that touch to the meadow south of Barca's Hamlet where the sheep had been pastured.

"—the poor beast did nothing whatever with his creation, just prowled about it and built it higher. The creature had purpose, you see; but not a mind as we humans talk of minds."

"It has less than that now," said Chalcus, "for which I'm thankful. I'm not a vindictive man—"

He too paused, smiling. All of them, even Merota, understood that in the sailor's mind the righting of wrongs wasn't vengeance but rather a necessity of life; and they all agreed with him.

"—but if I were to stay here longer, I'd take a maul to what our Ilna turned the thing into. I wouldn't risk that on some black day it returned to life, the way I did and Lady Merota."

"But I *don't* want to stay," Merota said, hugging herself with one arm and holding Ilna even tighter with the other. "Please."

Davus sobered. "Yes, milady," he said. "You've been ill-treated because of my errors. I'll do my best to make that up to you—"

Ilna listened with her face stiff. There was no mockery in the king's tone; which was a good thing for all concerned.

"—and to your world. Chalcus, Ilna—friends. Join hands in a circle with me and Lady Merota, if you will."

Davus extended his arms, palms up. Ilna's left hand was free. She took his right without hesitation. Chalcus took his left so quickly and smoothly that only someone who knew him as well as Ilna did would've recognized that he *did* hesitate. He grinned in wry apology to her over Merota's head.

Davus had the grip of a plowman—firm, with enormously strong muscles beneath the callused skin. "I'd expected this would require a degree more of ceremony," he said calmly, "but thanks to the lens my predecessor built it'll be very simple. I hope you're properly thankful to him, as I'm sure I am."

Chalcus laughed, and said, "So long as I don't have to—"

They were standing on a high rock, not the Citadel's crystal crown, though they were about as high as they'd been before. There'd been no feeling of change: they just *were*.

Far below the sea washed the shores of an island. A city was burning on the mainland across a narrow strait; the sky was a pattern of soot and streaks of bright sunlight like claw tears in a dirty blanket.

"We're on the Demon!" Merota said. "We're back on Volita! Oh, thank you, Master Davus!"

Ilna quirked a smile. She didn't have much interest in geography—she divided the world into places she could weave and places she couldn't—but even granting Ilna's own inadequacies, it was obvious that Merota had a very good eye for her surroundings. She didn't doubt that Garric would find a use for the child's talents once she was a little older. He and the kingdom through him used weavers and reformed pirates, after all . . .

"I need to be down there," Chalcus said. His voice was controlled but very tense. "There's people fighting. I don't know who they are, but what they're fighting *isn't* people as best I can tell."

"You'd only be in the way," said Davus calmly. "They call this the Demon, you say, milady? In that they're wrong, for it's no demon. It's the"—he bent and laid his hand flat on the weathered stone surface—"troll that I brought here when Dromillac summoned me."

Pure crimson light danced, cascading down through the rock in brilliant majesty. Ilna's hair stood on end. Merota cried out, but only once; standing then as a lady should. Chalcus said nothing. His sword and dagger were out and his eyes were trying to look in every direction at once.

As the wizardlight descended, brush and coarse grasses sloughed off the granite. With a crackling roar, the hunching troll began to straighten. Waves danced away from Volita's shores in expanding ripples as though the island itself had just dropped into the sea.

Davus squatted, keeping his spread hand against the stone. Though he continued to smile, Ilna saw a hint of tight concentration in the lines of his face. The jewel hovering over him pulsed brighter, dimmed, and grew brighter still.

The troll stepped forward, crushing the ruins of shoreside buildings thrown down by time or whatever it was that'd happened a thousand years ago. The movement was jerky but slow. Ilna's first instinct was to fall flat on what she supposed was the troll's scalp, but dignity made her stand since she *could* stand. She held out her hand to Merota, who gratefully took it.

The odd thing was that the troll remained stone, a granite outcrop with only the roughest suggestion of a creature that walked on two legs. Yet it *did* walk, swinging its arms alternately. Their motion balanced the movements of the legs; never far from the torso but shifting in a different rhythm from the larger mass.

The troll didn't speak, but the rock of its body squealed so loudly that the splash as it stepped into the sea was lost in the greater sound. Spray shot as high as the creature's armpits, spattering a few salt droplets onto Ilna. Chalcus wiped his sword quickly dry on his sleeve.

The troll took another step, throwing the sea into fiercer motion. At rest the water would come only to where the troll's knees should've been, though its legs bent in arcs rather than angles.

Paired, dazzlingly intense bolts of wizardlight ripped the black sky: crimson followed in a heartbeat by azure. More daylight flooded down, lighting a crater in the heart of the city. Foul white parodies of men crawled from the basin, spilling to every side like froth from an overheated kettle. A ring of human soldiers stood against them, but already some of the creatures were penetrating into the wider city through gaps worn in the defenders' line.

Ilna leaned slightly as the troll took its third step. They'd reached the midpoint of the channel now, and still the water didn't come to the troll's waist. Davus murmured gentle encouragement in the tone Cashel used when his oxen were starting a heavy haul.

Davus' real communication with the troll was through the touch of his hand. His fingers shifted with greater or lesser pressure, much as a lute player's did on the neck of his instrument.

A wizened figure in black stood on a platform in the middle of the crater. Ilna might not have noticed him except for the haze of wizardlight about him like a ball of red gauze. He pointed his athame. Black smoke/soot/vapor shot from it and filled a rip in the overcast. An instant later another pair of bolts tore the blackness open even wider to the light.

The troll stepped forward again. It moved with jerky deliberation: every stride was a separate thing instead of all being part of the motion of walking. The harborfront was crowded with ships. Some had already been swamped by waves the troll threw up, but people—from the look of them, civilians rather than proper sailors—were trying to launch one of those remaining. They suddenly broke and fled like lice from a corpse in either direction down Harbor Street.

A female wizard stood between a pair of fallen pillars as she tore the black sky open; her back was to the sea. She was younger than Tenoctris, but that was as much as Ilna could see from behind.

The broad, *solid* man who stood between the wizard and the pit could be no one but Cashel. His quarterstaff moved in circles as lazy and powerful as those of a whale herding fish before gulping them.

The wizard in the crater began to move, but not under his own power. His creatures raised him on an open litter and carried him toward the back edge, away from the river and the oncoming troll.

Soldiers in the boulevard from the harbor turned from the next wave of pallid monsters. Their heads rose as they stared at the troll. One man started to run, then caught himself or was caught by the unheard command of an officer. They faced the crater again, waiting to meet the onrush of creatures they might stop and ignoring the thing they could not.

Ilna didn't like soldiers or what soldiers did: a life spent killing other people wasn't a fit life for a human being, in her view. But she'd always done her duty, and she respected people who did theirs. Not even Ilna os-Kenset had anything to teach *these* men about duty.

"Get out of the way, Prince Garric!" Davus shouted.

"Get out of the way, Prince Garric-c-c!" the troll said, his voice the thunder of an avalanche shouting.

"Let me by to end this for good and all/ *Let me by to end this for good and all-l-l!"* Davus and his minion shouted.

The female wizard lowered her arms and touched Cashel's right shoulder. He slowed the quarterstaff and brought it upright on his left side, glancing back at the woman, then letting his gaze rise to the oncoming troll.

The boulevard was wide enough that even something the size of the troll could pass down it without hitting buildings. Cashel didn't run; he shifted slightly to put himself between the woman and the mountain walking toward them.

Ilna looked at him and smiled, then glanced at Davus with her face growing still again. "Easy," he murmured as his fingers caressed the stone. "Easy, easy . . . Now!"

The troll's leg came up with a sucking sound and a bloom of silt lifted from the bottom. The strait's current drew the mud westward, away from the creature's step. The troll didn't have feet; the ends of its legs spread slightly when its weight eased onto them. Its hands were fingerless paddles with outcrops to the side that worked as thumbs.

The troll lowered its right leg toward the mainland of Sandrakkan, shaking the ground. The tremor lifted an expanding ring of dust from the city. His foot touched a pair of warships; they flew to splinters, though Ilna on the troll's head hadn't noticed the contact.

"Gently," Davus said to his charge. "Gently, give them a little time. Time doesn't matter to us. . . ."

The soldiers defending the broad street were moving aside: grudgingly, haltingly; several of them helped by their comrades. They'd been standing in the path of the monsters from the pit; but barely standing, too battered and exhausted to have run even if their courage had finally failed them.

The white creatures stumbled/crawled/slithered toward the gap. Sunlight scoured them unmercifully. Ilna heard a moan of inhuman agony even over the crackling thunder of the troll's body, but still they came on.

The creatures had carried their leader, the wizard on the litter, over the rim of the crater. He'd continued to work spells, but his gouts of darkness could no longer blot out the sun even though his female rival watched arms akimbo instead of clawing further rents in the overcast.

"Now, my mighty one," Davus said, his voice rising. He was fixed to the troll like a hummingbird on a high twig. "Now, my bold fellow, three strides and we'll have them!"

The troll stepped forward, its left leg coming out of the sea. The limb heaved through the air with the inevitability of a swelling thundercloud drizzling seawater and lowered to the street.

The contact seemed delicate, but a shock wave rippled through the city, and the pavement buckled. A row of four-story tenements several furlongs away swayed and fell into a geyser of smoke and shattered plaster.

The troll's right leg lifted. The soldiers were battling the edges of the column of monsters that filled the entire street and spilled beyond it, scrabbling over the ruins of fallen buildings. The troll's leg came down, crushing masses of the white creatures with a squelching sound. Black blood sprayed to every side. It was like seeing a horse step on a gorged tick, only on a much, much greater scale.

The street was of flagstones over concrete set on a gravel base thicker than Ilna was tall. It shattered. Men and monsters fell, then rose to continue their battle.

Davus crooned to the troll, then glanced aside to his human companions. He blinked as though surprised to see them, then smiled, and said, a little awkwardly, "I get so caught up I could forget to breathe. It's time that we part, my friends. Ilna and Chalcus, it's been an honor and a pleasure. Lady Merota—"

The troll halted in the wreckage between the edge of the pit and the humans who stood as a barrier against the creatures swarming from that pit. Below, the battle continued. Farther into the city, the streets were choked with civilians fleeing earth shocks and rumors of a disaster whose reality they couldn't have imagined in their worst nightmares.

"—again, I regret that you were caught in trouble from which your innocence should've protected you. You comported yourself with the grace I would expect from one who associates with Ilna and Chalcus."

As Davus spoke, the troll's left arm rose in a series of tiny increments like sand sliding down a slope. The paddlelike palm spread. A seam of mica in the granite caught the sunlight and shimmered.

Chalcus sheathed his dagger and bent forward on one knee. Davus touched/gripped the troll with his right palm, so Chalcus extended his left arm for the king to clasp.

"I've had a few good comrades over the years," Chalcus said. "I've never had a better one."

Davus laughed. "Aye," he said. "Hard times, but they had to do. Now, join your friends while I pay my debt to Mistress Ilna for freeing me and mine."

The troll's palm, a granite shelf with dips and hillocks, touched the gray stone scalp beside them. It was flat only in the sense that Ilna could hold her own hand flat.

Ilna laughed also. "It was a pleasure," she said, marvelling at life and at herself. "As much pleasure as I find in life."

She stepped onto the stone hand. Merota darted across beside her, and Chalcus followed an instant later.

What Ilna'd said was true: striking down the new king had given her a rush of fierce joy. Ilna hadn't believed that the past could be retrieved, but the thought *Never again!* had warmed the soul that her loss of her friends had turned to ice.

The troll bent at the waist, lowering them toward the ground. Ilna examined the stone creature as she dropped past it. It didn't look human or even alive. Its head was a lump on its clifflike torso; its right arm hung at its side and seemed a part of the greater mass. Eyes, nose, and mouth were smudges in the rock, no more facial features than the whimsies a child invents while watching summer clouds.

But the troll lived and moved. There was no doubt about that.

Davus waved his free hand to them. The way the troll was bending put him head down, but he showed no sign of strain or discomfort. He seemed a part of the stone, a flesh-colored statue carved from the underlying granite.

The troll's hand stopped. The silence as the stone arm halted its grinding progress was more noticeable than the fact they'd stopped moving down. They were in what had been a courtyard before the surrounding building had collapsed.

Sulfur and windblown grit made Ilna sneeze; her eyes filled with tears.

The troll's hand was so thick that she'd expected to climb down rather than jump and risk a broken leg, but the rubble to every side was much the same height as the stone palm. The gap was arm's length or less, no more of a strain than hopping a mud puddle.

"Quickly!" Ilna said, because Davus had sent them away for a purpose. Merota stayed with her; Chalcus already stood on the piled masonry, watching out for his female companions and checking for their closest enemies.

The troll straightened again in the same nonliving motion. Ilna withdrew the hank of cords from her sleeve, but a swatch of wizard-made cloud plunged her into shadow for the length of a long, slow breath. She put the cords away and uncoiled the silken rope from her waist. Her art wouldn't work on anyone who couldn't see her patterns clearly, but a noose around an enemy's neck was almost invariably useful.

"Ilna," Merota said, trying very hard to be a stern-faced lady and not a frightened child. "What shall we—"

A pair of creatures with human heads and torsos climbed the rubble pile. One had two legs and the other six. Chalcus' incurved blade made a single diagonal stroke, through the rib cage of the first and the neck of the second.

He danced aside. The six-legged thing turned and sprang like a grasshopper back in the direction from which it'd come, but the almost manlike monster strode forward despite its lungs spilling out. It turned toward Ilna, holding a broad-bladed axe overhead in both hands. Before she could toss her noose, Chalcus cut the creature's spine from behind. It collapsed in its tracks, its head toppling forward. Chalcus had slashed the tendons as well as the nerves.

Ilna saw soldiers fighting in the ruins closer to the crater, but the solid wall of defenders had been breached even before Garric withdrew his troops to give the troll passage. The creatures boiling from the pit would spread throughout the city and the Isles unless something stopped them—as men could not.

The troll bent toward the crater. White creatures continued to spill out, unaffected or even unaware of the mass of granite lowering over them. Their wizard stood beyond the lip of the pit, his arm pointing. Crimson bolts—bright, brighter, and finally hotter than the sun—spat from his athame. They vanished into the troll's broad chest.

Davus laughed through the stone lips, a sound as joyfully terrible as the howl of a tornado. The troll thrust its hands into the ground to either side of the crater. Its thumbs gripped the inner edge of the cavity, crushing some of the white creatures. Others continued to crawl away, squirming into the city over whatever obstacle stood in their way.

For a moment, nothing moved except that the earth trembled. The troll gave a deep, booming roar. It raised its right leg with the slow inevitability of a glacier, then slammed it down at the edge of the crater like a man kicking the jamb of a sticking door.

Buildings danced on the horizon. Ilna fell to her knees, holding Merota, and even Chalcus danced for a moment as he might've done on a storm-tossed spar.

Dust lifted in an expanding cloud, chokingly thick. Ilna slitted her eyes, then covered her nose and the child's with a fold of her sleeve.

The troll straightened; slowly, as it did all things. Dirt and rock cascaded from its hands. Only when it started to turn and the fall of debris slowed did Ilna realize that the troll hadn't gouged out handfuls of earth: it'd wrenched the crater's lining out of the ground.

The pit that remained was simply a hole filled with flying grit. Its walls fell inward, covering the bottom with lifeless rubble.

The troll raised the lining, a cauldron of shimmering purple light a furlong across, to the height of its towering shoulders. The wizard's pale monsters still climbed over the rim, but they burst bloodily like falling spleens when they hit the ground.

Davus and the troll he was part of laughed in one thunderous voice. The troll flung the cauldron seaward, spinning the great purple bowl through the air. The whole business seemed slow, but Ilna realized that the troll's size made its movements deceptive to eyes used to judging things on human scale.

Monsters continued to spill out, flailing until they hit. On land, they splashed; over the sea, it was water that splashed. The white bodies sank out of sight in the churning froth.

The cauldron landed in open water beyond Volita and exploded like all a storm's thunderbolts released together. Steam rose higher than the eye could follow.

Ilna, knowing what was coming, clapped her hands over Merota's ears and opened her own mouth. She couldn't cover her ears and the child's as well, so the choice was clear.

The blast lifted them and everyone in the city into the air like children tossed in blankets. They dropped back where they'd been in stunned amazement.

The sea drew out, baring the bottom of the strait: for a moment Ilna on her rubble heap saw fish flopping in the mud. When the water rushed back, it curled up the shore and deep into the ruins of Erdin. Spouting and foaming from cellars, it undercut the remaining walls as it withdrew.

The troll's laughter was so loud that Ilna felt it through her flesh though her ears were utterly deaf. The troll turned and leaned forward. Davus, a tiny figure on the granite head, waved.

The troll dived into the cavity it'd torn the cauldron from, striking with another cataclysmic shock. There was a white flash. When Ilna opened her eyes again, she saw that what'd been a hole in the middle of Erdin was now a mass of lifeless granite.

Garric got to his feet cautiously. He wasn't sure whether the ground was still trembling or if the shudders he felt were just his body reacting to all that'd gone before.

He squinted against the dust. Liane handed him a swatch of cloth she'd ripped from her tunic and dampened from the helmet she was using as a water bucket. Garric let his shield hang from the strap buckled behind his right shoulder and gratefully covered his nose and mouth to breathe.

Many creatures had gotten out of the cauldron before the troll tore it from the earth. Instead of attacking as their fellows had done earlier, they ran for hiding places like startled rats. The troops who'd been fighting all day let the pallid survivors slip through gaps in the line.

The battle was over. The men who'd fought it had their bellies full of slaughter; and besides, the rats still had their weapons. Let them crawl into cellars, if that was all they wanted to do. . . .

Garric started forward. He swayed for the first few steps, but he was all right when he got moving properly. Erdin had been nearly flat. Now a mass of granite like the citadel of Carcosa rose in the middle of the city. He wouldn't climb it—he didn't think he could in his present condition, living on his nerves with no margin of physical or mental strength—but he could go around.

He *had* to go around. The wizard responsible for this had escaped northward just before the troll hurled the cauldron into the sea. The soldiers there would see no more reason to stop their fleeing enemies than the men nearby did.

The wizard had survived a millennium underground to rebuild his inhuman army. He'd do so again if he got the chance. Garric wasn't going to give him that chance.

He jogged near three pale monsters. They were hunching toward an alley half-closed by the jumbled barrels of a fallen column. The nearest of the trio turned and faced Garric, moaning softly and raising the axes in two of its hands. When Garric went by, it dropped forward to lope after its fellows, brachiating on its lower pair of arms. It'd behaved like a frightened dog, willing to bite if necessary but desperate to get away.

The wizard's foul overcast had dissipated, allowing sunlight to bathe the granite plug. The stone was gray with streaks of white and pink, seemingly normal in every way save the manner it'd come here.

It was warm, though. Garric felt the heat pulsing as he passed close to the rock on his way around.

The breeze teased a valley in the swirling dust. Garric saw a clump of white creatures—perhaps four of them, perhaps many—carrying something toward the Temple of the Shepherd Who Overwhelms. The massive temple would have deep foundations.

Garric didn't try to run faster. He knew that if he lost his pace, he'd almost certainly stumble. He'd reach them in time. The mismatched creatures moved like a broken-backed centipede, each interfering with the others.

The ground *had* stopped shaking, so the dust was settling gradually. The layer at Garric's mid-chest was thick, almost opaque, but above that, only motes danced. They twinkled like droplets of spray over a breeze-whipped ocean. Four thick-bodied, thick-legged monsters carried a litter that'd been pegged together from human bones. On it rode the wizard Garric had briefly glimpsed in the underworld, a hump under a black robe.

The wizard turned. Its face was that of a corpse that'd half decayed before being mummified. It pointed its athame.

"Die!" Garric cried, his sword lifting as he strode the last two paces to his enemy.

There was a red flash. Garric's muscles froze. His skin prickled, and the sword flew out of his hand. He skidded forward on his chest.

A javelin arced out of the sky, skewering both the creatures supporting the back of the litter. They bawled and collapsed, spilling the wizard to the pavement. The athame's point caught in a crack between two cobblestones; the tourmaline blade splintered.

Garric could move again. He squirmed forward and grasped the wizard's throat. He neither knew nor cared what the other two litter-bearers were doing. He squeezed, feeling bones and muscles as dry as dead bone crunching. Then there was nothing in his hands, and nothing but stinking dust spilling from the black robe.

Garric looked around. Prester and Pont trotted toward him, wearing satisfied expressions and drawing their swords. Behind the two marshals came a squad of soldiers who appeared worn beyond human endurance.

Lord Attaper had finished three of the bearers whom the javelins had put down. He stared in a mixture of amazement and disgust at the fourth creature, a pin-headed monster whose forearms were the size of a strong man's thighs.

Liane knelt on the back of the fourth bearer. She'd cut its throat but seemed determined to continue thrusting her little dagger between its ribs as long as it was still twitching in death.

Chapter Twenty

Garric had taken off his armor. By the end of the fighting his helmet had looked like scrap that a tinker had snipped repeatedly to make patches for cookware. He'd wiped blood off his sword with a piece of bedding that'd been blowing in the street. Now that the patterned gray steel was clean, he was sharpening it with the small stone he kept in a pouch on his sword belt.

The sky was clear, and the wind off the sea had cleared Erdin of the smell of sulfur. A number of fires had started when buildings collapsed onto lighted braziers, but they weren't out of control.

The bodies remained. Even the stench of the monsters' gutted corpses seemed less nauseating in bright sunlight.

"Lord Tadai is here, your highness," Liane said primly.

Garric looked up in amazement. He was seated at a conference table pulled from the wreckage of a house that the troll had bumped on its way to . . . to saving the Isles, Garric supposed. Certainly on the way to saving Garric or-Reise and the people dearest to his heart and soul.

Soldiers had placed the table—and straight chairs from a nearby ruin—in a small plaza not far from where the palace had stood. Ensign Attarus commanded the detachment of Blood Eagles guarding the prince, but Garric had sent Lord Attaper to take stock of the army as a whole.

Garric remembered giving that order and a series of similar ones, to prevent looting and to reorganize the army in case something *else* happened suddenly. That had been—he looked up at the sun—over an hour ago. He didn't remember anything from that point till now.

King Carus smiled a little sadly from Garric's mind. *"There are different ways to cope,"* he said. *"Cleaning your weapons is a good one. But any way that gets you through to the next dawn is a good one."*

"Lord Tadai," Garric said, nodding to the plump nobleman. He'd have gotten up for courtesy's sake—he was the prince, of course, but Tadai was very powerful, very skilled; and (along with his rival Royhas) as much a real friend as Garric had at the highest levels of his government.

He *would* have gotten up, but he was just too tired.

Tadai's robe of peach-colored silk was spotless and perfectly arranged. He'd probably donned a fresh one in the past few minutes, before he set off for an audience with Garric. He'd lost part of the nail of his right index finger, and the layer of tinted rice powder on his cheeks couldn't conceal the scratch from his left ear to the point of his chin.

"I'm glad to see you looking so well, your highness," Tadai said. He bowed but a stitch in one muscle or another made him stiffen in blank-faced pain; he didn't sweep as low as he'd normally have done.

"I was afraid you . . . ," Garric said. He stopped, because there wasn't any honest way to continue.

In all truth, he hadn't thought about Tadai and the rest of the ministerial delegation to Erdin since the trouble broke out in the temple library in the morning, a lifetime ago. Apparently they, or at least Tadai, had gotten out of the palace before the creatures of the pit slaughtered everyone they found. Garric was glad of that, but he'd had more pressing problems until this very moment.

He grinned. Including the problem of cleaning and sharpening his sword.

Tadai cleared his throat. "I've set up an interim city administration," he said. "The earl hasn't been seen in some time—"

"He won't be," Liane said. Her voice was musical, but there was a hard finality to it. "Ever."

"Ah," Tadai said. He cleared his throat again. "Well, that may be for the best. I've made contact with many of the watch committees and used them to organize bucket brigades. Erdin doesn't have a paid fire watch. Ah—"

"Milord!" Garric said, sounding harsh even in his own numb ears. "I have every confidence in your ability to deal with this . . . to deal with this—"

His hands were trembling. He laid the sword flat on the table and laced his fingers. Liane, who'd been studiously formal to that point, pressed her hand on top of his.

Garric rose cautiously. It was a good idea to work the muscles a little, though it'd be—

An honest grin spread across his face.

—a long time before he was up to digging ditches.

"Tadai, I don't have enough mind right at the moment to guess which direction the sun'll rise in the morning," Garric said gently. "I'm glad you do, I'm lucky, and Erdin is more than lucky that you're able to take charge in this crisis. But you don't need to give me progress reports. You have my backing until I tell you otherwise."

"I understand, your highness," Tadai said. He turned his face away while he gathered his courage to blurt what he'd really come to say. Just before Garric snarled something gruffly to prod the man, Tadai went on, "Your highness, it's the soldiers. They're hunting the, the *things* that got out into the city before . . ."

He pointed a hand vaguely toward where the palace had been. Garric wasn't sure how he'd have described the way the crisis ended either. Rather than let Tadai choke for lack of a word, he said, "I understand. Some of the creatures got through the cordon before the wizard who'd raised them was defeated. The troops are carrying out my orders to kill them all."

"Yes, of course, *kill* them," Tadai said. "But they're making a game of it! They're making bets about who can throw a spear through each creature from the farthest distance. The officers are encouraging them to behave like that. A game, your highness, a *game*!"

Garric looked at Lord Tadai: a brave man who was both decent and self-sacrificing by the standards of his class. By any standards, really; there were few enough peasants in Barca's Hamlet who'd have willingly undergone the dangers and discomfort Tadai had that day and many days in the past.

Still, Tadai was a cultured gentleman who ate pork but had never seen a pig clamped by the snout to be butchered.

"Milord," Garric said gently, "my officers have had the wit to turn a dirty, dangerous, *necessary* job into a training exercise. Maybe there's no way the creatures could fester and breed in the caverns below Erdin now that their wizard's dead, but I don't know that for sure. I'm not going to let this"—he swept his right arm in an arc, encompassing the devastated center of the city—"happen again a thousand years from now to people who don't deserve it any more than the poor devils you're organizing into bucket brigades do. Milord—*Tadai,* my friend Lord Tadai—these are the men who saved as much of Erdin as could be saved! Not because they care about Sandrakkan *or* the Isles or much of anything else. They stood because it was their job and because their fellow soldiers were standing. And if now they're going to have fun finishing the job instead of treating it as a distasteful duty, more power to them. Don't expect me to get in their way."

Garric crooked a smile at Tadai, a man he genuinely liked as well as respected. "And don't get in their way yourself, please; because the kingdom needs you. Just as it needs them."

Tadai bent his head slightly, rubbing his brows in a fashion that hid his eyes for the moment. "I was frightened," he said, so softly that only Garric and Liane could hear the words. "I've been pretending that things are normal, just a little disrupted. But they never were normal."

Tadai lowered his hands and met Garric's eyes. He smiled wryly. "Not the way I pretended in my well-appointed office, where servants brought me sherbet cooled with last winter's snow when I was thirsty. When I shouted at my chamberlain if the sheets weren't turned down at precisely the correct angle when I was ready to go to bed."

Tadai looked around, then nodded with an expression of cool resolution. "I'd best get back to my duties," he said. "Quite a number of people need temporary shelter and, of course, food till normal services are restored. I have assistants making quick inventories of the warehouses along the river, looking for wine and bulk grain. It'll be a fiscal mare's nest to sort out afterward, but we can't let people starve, can we?"

Garric smiled, then embraced the plump nobleman. "No, Lord Tadai," he said as he stepped away. "The kingdom doesn't let its citizens starve."

He'd smudged the clean robe, but Tadai was beaming as he bustled off with a retinue of aides. The kingdom was indeed lucky to have him.

"And lucky to have the officers who turned the cleaning-up operation into javelin practice instead of cut and thrust that'd cost more lives," Carus noted with a smile of his own. *"My guess it wasn't any hereditary nobleman who came up with the notion, eh?"*

Garric grinned back at the ancestor in his mind. Veterans like Pont and Prester had gotten to be old soldiers by learning how not to get themselves needlessly killed. Having them around to pass on their knowledge meant that a lot of younger men would live to be old soldiers.

He let his eyes drift over the scene around him. Tenoctris lay under a shop awning, sound asleep on a salvaged mattress; drained by the hard work of wizardry, Garric assumed. Tenoctris had a wonderful ability to keep going as long as her skill was needed, but the effort still had to be paid for.

Sharina sat on the pavement beside her, holding the Pewle knife on her lap unsheathed. Garric frowned at his sister's disturbingly empty expression. Something had happened to her, but he didn't have any idea what. Maybe it was just the overwhelming disaster. . . .

Cashel squatted with Sharina, facing the other way down the street. His left elbow touched her right, that was all. Because he was Cashel, he provided more support than a whole regiment of Blood Eagles could; but he did it without saying a word or even seeming to be aware of what he was doing. Cashel had been the best shepherd in living memory in the borough, but his talents were far too great to spend on sheep.

Garric smiled again. "Spend on sheep," not "waste on sheep," because sheep had value also. Garric or-Reise had been a pretty decent shepherd himself.

Garric walked toward Cashel and Sharina, leaving his sword on the table behind him. It was part of his present life, a tool on which the safety of the kingdom might depend; but there'd been a previous life when things were simpler. They hadn't seemed simple at the time, but they certainly did now that he looked back at them.

Garric wished there were sheep around him, grazing on a sunny hillside. There weren't, but he had his friends from that time, which was even better.

Cashel murmured something to Sharina. She brightened and slid the knife back in its sheath. They stood up together, graceful despite having gone through pretty much what Garric had, he suspected.

Chalcus came through the brick archway from the interior of the adjacent mews, one of many surviving buildings that'd become temporary hospitals. His lips smiled as his eyes darted in all directions. Ilna and Merota walked slightly behind him, safe if there'd been some unlikely danger waiting in the plaza.

Their clothing—the child's as well—was dusty and blood-splotched; they'd been helping with the injured, bandaging wounds and bringing water to men crying for it. There was nothing incongruous about Chalcus working to save lives: like any longtime fighting man, he must've had plenty of occasion to treat those injured by violence.

Their faces and hands were freshly scrubbed. Trust Ilna to see to that.

Garric gripped arms with Cashel, then embraced his sister and stepped away. He looked at his friend, and said, "Cashel, you brought a wizard with you. Was she . . ."

"Was she killed?" was what he meant, but he didn't need to say that.

"Is she all right, that is?" Garric substituted.

"Her name's Mab," Cashel said shyly. "And I guess she's fine, but she had to go back and take care of things back home. She's a queen, you see."

He smiled to greet his sister, continuing, "And Ilna? Mab said to tell you that we're both credits to our parents. Do you know, part of the time she looked like the spittin' image of you?"

"Did she say anything else about your parentage, Cashel?" Tenoctris asked. She'd risen to a sitting position, looking rumpled but as bright as if she'd spent the day reading on a couch. Sharina helped her up.

"No, ma'am," Cashel said. "Not really."

Ilna looked up from the pattern she'd just knotted with yarn from her sleeve. She met Tenoctris' calm gaze. The older woman nodded; Ilna shrugged in response, then began picking out her knots again.

"Did you say she was a wizard, Cashel?" Ilna said as she put her yarn away.

"She sure was!" Cashel said. "A really powerful one but, you know, good, like Tenoctris."

"If Queen Mab is who I think she is . . . ," Tenoctris said, speaking with the careful neutrality of somebody trying not to say the wrong thing,

". . . she's something very different from a wizard. As you and Ilna are, Cashel. Mab is your mother."

Her expression loosened into her usual cheerful calm. She added, "But you're right about her powers. I wouldn't care to speculate on the limits of them."

"Mother?" Cashel said. He looked at Ilna, who nodded. "Oh. That explains, well, things."

Garric looked over his shoulder at the ruins of Erdin. The despair that he'd avoided by refusing to think about the future suddenly crashed down on him.

"We won the battle," he said in a bleak voice, "but a disaster like this is the end of the kingdom. *Look* at what we've done to the second greatest city in the Isles!"

"Yes, look," said Liane as clearly as a trumpet. "A few buildings destroyed, but not a fraction of the city."

"You're forgetting the dead!" Garric said, furious because the only thing he felt at the moment was despair, and Liane was taking that away too.

"I'm not forgetting them," she said, not angry but not in the least afraid of the man she faced. "A thousand civilians died, I know that. But not a *hundred* thousand civilians as died when the city fell a thousand years ago. And the reason most people here survived is because the royal army, the army of all the Isles and not just this island, stood between monsters and men!"

Liane stamped her foot. "*This* Erdin grew back from total destruction a thousand years ago," she said. "Think of what can grow from the majority that survived today! Garric, if ever there was proof we need a united kingdom, you gave it today. Sandrakkan couldn't save itself, but the Kingdom of the Isles saved it. And the story will spread till all the Isles hear it."

Garric felt his tight jaw muscles relax. For a moment he glimpsed a future in which the kingdom was united, not by force as King Carus had held it, but by every citizen's knowledge that unless men stood together, Evil would crush them all individually under its heel. Not a certain future, nothing was certain, but—

Chalcus whipped out his sword and pointed it skyward. "Garric and the Isles!" he called.

Soldiers and civilians turned, in the plaza and in the buildings fronting it. "Garric and the Isles!" a woman shouted.

The plaza filled with echoing shouts that spread beyond those who heard the first cry: "*Garric and the Isles!*"